Praise for t
by *New York Tim*
Marie Force

The Fatal Series
by *New York Times* bestselling author
Marie Force

Suggested reading order

And look for the next sizzling book
in the Fatal Series

Fatal Reckoning

MARIE FORCE

Fatal
INVASION

HQN™

ISBN-13: 978-1-335-00043-9

Fatal Invasion

Recycling programs
for this product may
not exist in your area.

This edition published by arrangement with Harlequin Books S.A.

For questions and comments about the quality of this book, please contact us at CustomerService@Harlequin.com.

® and TM are trademarks of Harlequin Enterprises Limited or its corporate affiliates. Trademarks indicated with ® are registered in the United States Patent and Trademark Office, the Canadian Intellectual Property Office and in other countries.

www.HQNBooks.com

Printed in U.S.A.

Dedicated to the memory of
K-9 officer Sgt. Sean Gannon,
Yarmouth, MA, police department.
Killed in the line of duty
April 12, 2018.
May he rest in peace.

Fatal
INVASION

CHAPTER ONE

"THIS IS A classic case of be careful what you wish for." Nick placed a stack of folded dress shirts in a suitcase that already held socks, underwear, workout clothes and several pairs of jeans. Only Nick would start packing seven days before his scheduled departure for Europe next Sunday, the day after Freddie and Elin's wedding. "That's the lesson learned here."

"Only anal-retentive freakazoids pack a week before a trip." Sam sat at the foot of the bed and watched him pack with a growing sense of dread. "*Three freaking weeks.* The last time you were gone that long, I nearly lost my mind, and I don't have much of a mind left to lose."

"Come with me," he said for the hundredth time since the president asked him to make the diplomatic trip, representing the administration on a visit with some of the country's closest allies. Since President Nelson was still recovering—in more ways than one—from his son's criminal activities, several of the allies had requested he send his popular vice president in his stead.

Sam flopped on the bed. "I *can't*. I have work and Scotty, and Freddie is going on his honeymoon for *two* weeks and... I can't." No Nick at home to entertain her. No Freddie at work to entertain her. The next few weeks were going to totally suck monkey balls.

"Actually, you *can*." Nick hovered above her, propped

on arms ripped with muscles, his splendid chest on full display. "You have more vacation time saved up than you can use in a lifetime, *and* you have the right to actually use it. Scotty will be fine with Shelby, your dad and Celia, your sisters and the Secret Service here to entertain him. We could even ask Mrs. Littlefield to come up for the weekends."

Their son's former guardian would love the chance to spend time with him, but Sam didn't feel right about leaving him for so long. However, the thought of being without Nick for three endless weeks made her sick. His trip to Iran earlier in the year had been pure torture, especially since it kept getting extended.

"Why'd you have to tell Nelson you wanted to be more than a figurehead vice president?" She play-punched his chest. "Everything was fine when he was ignoring you."

He kissed her lips and then her neck. "You're so, *so* cute when you pout."

"Badass cops do *not* pout."

"Mine does when she doesn't get her own way, and it's truly adorable."

She scowled at him. "Badass cops are not adorable."

"Mine is." Leaving a trail of hot kisses on her neck, he said, "Come with me, Samantha. London, Paris, Rome, the Vatican, Amsterdam, Brussels, The Hague. Come see the world with me."

Sam had never been to Europe and had always wanted to go, so she was sorely tempted to say to hell with her responsibilities.

"Come on." He rolled her earlobe between his teeth and pressed against her suggestively. "Three whole *weeks* together away from the madness of DC. You know you want to go. Gonzo could cover for you at work, and things have been slow anyway."

There hadn't been a homicide in more than a week, which meant they were due, and that was another reason to stay home. "Don't say that and put a jinx on us."

"Come away with me. Scotty will be fine. We'll Face-Time with him every day and bring him presents. He'll be well cared for by everyone else who loves him." He kissed her neck as he unbuttoned her shirt and pushed it aside. "You'd get to meet the Queen of England."

Sam moaned. She *loved* the queen—speaking of a badass female.

"And the Pope. Plus, you'll need some clothes—and shoes. *Lots* of shoes."

"Stop it." She turned her face to avoid his kiss. "You're fighting dirty."

"Because I want my wife to come with me on the trip of a lifetime? I *need* you Samantha."

As he well knew, she could deny him nothing when he said he needed her. "Fine, I'll go! But only if it's okay with Scotty and if I can swing it at work."

"*Yes*," her husband said on a long exhale. "We'll have so much fun."

"Will we actually get to see anything?"

He pushed himself up to continue packing. "I'll make sure of it."

"Um, excuse me."

"What's up?"

"My temperature after your attempts at persuasion."

A slow, lazy smile spread across his face, making him the sexiest man in this universe—and the next. "Is my baby feeling a little needy?"

She pulled her T-shirt over her head and released the front clasp on her bra. "More than a little."

"We can't have that." Stepping to the foot of the bed, he grasped the legs of her yoga pants and yanked them off.

"Lock the door."

"Scotty's asleep."

"*Lock the door*, or this isn't happening." With Secret Service agents all over their house, Sam couldn't relax if the door wasn't locked.

"This is definitely happening, but if it'll make you happy, I'll lock the door."

"It'll make me happy, which will, in turn, make *you* happy." She splayed her legs wide-open to give him a show as he returned from locking the door, and was rewarded with gorgeous hazel eyes that heated with desire when he saw her waiting for him.

"You little vixen," he muttered.

"I don't know *what* you're talking about."

"Sure, you don't," he said, laughing as he came down on top of her and set out to give her a preview of what three weeks away together might be like.

THEY BROKE THE news to Scotty the next morning at breakfast. "So," Nick said tentatively, "what would you think if Mom came with me to Europe?"

Thirteen-year-old Scotty, never at his best first thing in the morning, shrugged. "It's fine."

"Really?" Sam said. "You wouldn't mind? Shelby, Tracy and Angela would be around to hang with you, and Gramps and Celia too. We thought maybe Mrs. Littlefield could come up for a weekend or two if she's free."

"Sure, that sounds good."

Sam glanced at Nick, who seemed equally perplexed by his lack of reaction. They'd expected him to ask to come with them, at the very least.

"Is everything okay?" Sam asked her son.

"Uh-huh." He finished his cereal and got up to put the bowl in the sink. "I'm going to finish getting ready for school."

"Okay, bud," Nick said.

"Something's up," Sam said as soon as Scotty left the room.

"I agree. He didn't even ask if he could miss school to come with us."

"I thought the same thing."

"We'll have to see if we can get him to talk to us before we go—and not in the morning," Nick said.

"I'll ask Shelby to make spaghetti for dinner. That always puts him in a good mood." Sam's phone rang, and when she saw the number for Dispatch, she groaned. "Damn it. You jinxed me!" So much for getting out of Dodge without having to worry about work. She took the call. "Holland."

"Lieutenant, there was a fire overnight in Chevy Chase." The dispatcher referred to the exclusive Northwest neighborhood that was home to a former U.S. president, ambassadors and other wealthy residents. "We have two DOA at the scene," the dispatcher said, reciting the address. "The fire marshal has requested Homicide detectives."

"Did he say why?"

"No, ma'am."

"Okay, I'm on my way." Thankfully, she'd showered and gotten dressed before she woke Scotty. "Please call

Sergeant Gonzales and Detective Cruz and ask them to meet me there."

"Yes, ma'am."

Sam flipped her phone closed with a satisfying smack. That smacking sound was one of many reasons she'd never upgrade to a smart phone.

"You'll still be able to come with me, right?" Nick asked, looking adorably uncertain.

Sam went over to where he sat at the table and kissed him. "I'll talk to Malone today and see if I can make it happen."

"Keep me posted."

A RINGING PHONE woke Christina Billings from a sound sleep. Two-year-old Alex had been up during the night with a fever and cold that was making him miserable and her sleep deprived. Her fiancé, Tommy, had slept through that and apparently couldn't hear his phone ringing either. He was due at work in an hour and was usually up by now.

"Tommy." She nudged him, but he didn't stir. "*Tommy.* Your phone."

He came to slowly, blinking rapidly.

"The phone, Tommy. Answer it before it wakes Alex." He needed more sleep and so did she, or this was going to be a very long day.

Tommy grabbed the phone from the bedside table.

Christina saw the word *Dispatch* on the screen.

"Gonzales."

She couldn't hear the dispatcher's side of the conversation, but she heard Tommy's grunt of acknowledgment before he ended the call, closing his eyes even as he continued to clutch the phone.

Christina wondered if he was going back to sleep after being called into work. She was about to say something when he got out of bed and headed for the shower.

Nine months ago today, his partner, A. J. Arnold, had been gunned down right in front of Tommy as they approached a suspect. After a long downward spiral following Arnold's murder, Tommy had seemed to rebound somewhat during the summer. But the rebound hadn't lasted into the fall.

In the last month, since his new partner, Cameron Green, had joined the squad, Christina had watched him regress into his grief. He'd said and done all the right things when it came to welcoming Cameron, but he was obviously spiraling again, and she had no idea what to do to help him or how to reach him. Even when lying next to her in bed, he seemed so far away from her.

Sometimes, when she had a rare moment alone, she allowed her thoughts to wander to life without Tommy and Alex at the center of it. She loved them both—desperately—but she wasn't sure how much more she could take of the distant, closed-off version of the man she loved. They were supposed to have been married by now. Like everything else, that plan had been shoved aside to make room for Tommy's overwhelming grief. It'd been months since they'd discussed getting married. In the meantime, she took care of Alex and everything else while Tommy worked and came home to sleep before starting the cycle all over again.

They didn't talk about anything other than Alex. They never went anywhere together or as a family. They hadn't had sex in so long she'd forgotten when it had last happened. She was as unhappy as she'd ever been. Something had to give—and soon, or she would be forced to decide whether their relationship was still healthy for her. She did *not* want to have to make that decision.

Only the thought of leaving Tommy at his lowest moment, not to mention leaving Alex, had kept her from making a move before now. She loved that little boy with her whole heart and soul. She'd stepped away from her own career as Nick's chief of staff to stay home with him and had hoped to add to their family by now. When she thought about the early days of her relationship with Tommy, when they'd been so madly in love, she couldn't have imagined feeling as insignificant to him as a piece of furniture that was always there when he finally decided to come home.

Christina hadn't told anyone about the trouble brewing between them. In her heart of hearts, she hoped they could still work it out somehow, and the last thing she needed was her friends and family holding a grudge against him forever—and they would if they had any idea just how bad things had gotten. Her parents had questioned the wisdom of her giving up a high-profile job to stay home to care for her boyfriend's child, especially when she'd made more money than him. But she'd been ready for a break from the political rat race when Alex came along, and she had no regrets about her decision. Or she hadn't until Tommy checked out of their relationship.

This weekend they'd be expected to celebrate at Freddie and Elin's wedding, and she'd have to pretend that everything was fine in her relationship when it was anything but. She wasn't sure how she would pull off another convincing performance for their friends. Tommy was one of Freddie's groomsmen, so she'd get to spend most of that day on her own while he attended to his friend.

Dangling at the end of her rope in this situation, more

than once she'd thought about taking Alex and leaving, even though she had no legal right to take him. Another thing they'd never gotten around to—her adoption of him after his mother was killed. What would Tommy do if she left with his son? Call the police on her? That made her laugh bitterly. She'd be surprised if he noticed they were gone.

Tommy came out of the bathroom and went to the closet where he had clean clothes to choose from thanks to her. Did he ever wonder how that happened? He put on jeans and a black T-shirt and then went to unlock the bedside drawer where he kept his badge, weapon and cuffs.

She watched him slide the weapon into the holster he wore on his hip and jam the cuffs and badge into the back pockets of his jeans, the same way he did every day. Holding her breath, she waited to see if he would say anything to her or come around the bed to kiss her goodbye the way he used to before disaster struck, but like he did so often these days, he simply turned and left the room.

A minute later, she heard the front door close behind him.

For a long time after he left, she lay in bed staring up at the ceiling with tears running down her cheeks. She couldn't take much more of this.

CHAPTER TWO

SAM WAS THE first of her team to arrive on the scene of the smoldering fire that had demolished half a mansion in one of the District's most exclusive neighborhoods.

"What've we got?" Sam asked the fire marshal when he met her at the tape line.

"Two bodies found on the first floor of the house, both bound with zip ties at the hands and feet."

And that, right there, made their deaths her problem. "Do we know who they are?"

He consulted his notes. "The ME will need to make positive IDs, but the house is owned by Jameson and Cleo Beauclair. I haven't had time to dig any deeper on who they are."

"Are we certain they were the only people in the house?" Sam asked.

"Not yet. When we arrived just after four a.m., the west side of the house, where the bodies were found, was fully engulfed. That was our immediate focus. We've got firefighters searching the rest of what was once a ten-thousand-square-foot home."

"Any sign of accelerants?"

"Nothing so far, but we're an hour into the investigation stage. Early days."

"Has the ME been here?"

"Not yet."

"Could I take a look inside?"

"It's still hot in there, but I can show you the highlights—or the lowlights, such as they are."

Sam followed him up the sidewalk to what had once been the front door. Inside the smoldering ruins of the house, she could make out the basic structure from the burned-out husk that remained. The putrid scents of smoke and death hung heavily in the air.

"That's them there," the fire marshal said, pointing to a space on the floor by a blackened stone fireplace where two charred bodies lay next to one another.

Sam swallowed the bile that surged to her throat. Nothing was worse, at least not in her line of work, than fire victims. Though it was the last thing she wanted to do, she moved in for a closer look, took photos of the bodies and the scene around them, then turned to face the fire marshal. "Anything else you think I ought to see?"

"Not yet."

"Keep me posted."

"Will do."

He walked away to continue his investigation while Sam went outside, carrying the horrifying images with her as she took greedy breaths of fresh air. As she reached the curb, the medical examiner's truck arrived. She waited for a word with Dr. Lindsey McNamara.

The tall, pretty medical examiner gathered her long red hair into a ponytail as she walked over to Sam.

"Fire victims," Sam said, shuddering.

"Good morning to you too."

"Hands and feet bound with zip ties."

"Here we go again," Lindsey said with a sigh. "Looks like it was quite a house."

"Ten thousand square feet, according to the fire marshal."

"I'll get you an ID and report as soon as I can."

"Appreciate it." Sam opened her phone and placed a call to Captain Malone. "I'm at the scene of the fire in Chevy Chase."

"What've you got?"

"Two DOA, bound at the hands and feet, leading me to believe this was a home invasion gone bad. I need Crime Scene here ASAP."

"I'll call Haggerty and get them over there."

"I want them to comb through anything and everything that wasn't touched by the fire, and they need to do it soon before the scene is further compromised. We've got firefighters all over the place."

"Got it. What's your plan?"

"I'm going to talk to the neighbors and find out what I can about the people who lived here while I wait for Lindsey to confirm their identity."

"Keep me posted."

Sam slapped the phone closed and headed for her car to begin the task of figuring out who Jameson and Cleo Beauclair had been and who might've bound them before setting their house on fire. If the bodies were even those of the Beauclairs. Cases like this were often confounding from the start, but they would operate on the info they had available and go from there.

Her partner, Detective Freddie Cruz, arrived as Sam reached her car, which she had parked a block from the scene.

"I guess it was too much to hope our homicide-free streak would last until after the wedding," he said.

"Too much indeed. We've got two deceased on the

first floor of the west side of the home, hands and feet bound."

"Do we know who they are?"

"We know who owns the house, but we're not a hundred percent sure the owners are our victims," she said, passing along the names the fire marshal had given her. "Let's knock on some doors and then go back to HQ to see what Lindsey can tell us."

"I'm with you, LT."

"Any word from Gonzo?"

"Not that I've heard yet."

"He can catch up."

PAIN WAS LIKE WATER. It flooded every available space until there was only pain and nothing else. It became all consuming, and someone in that kind of agony would literally do anything to make it stop, even meet a known criminal to buy the one thing that could offer relief that only lasted a few hours. The pain always won. Always.

The transaction happened so quickly and seamlessly it was over before it started. To a casual observer, it would look like two men who hadn't seen each other in a while meeting on the street and exchanging an affectionate greeting that included the clasping of hands.

Gonzo walked away with what he needed to get through another couple of days. He got in his car, immediately took a pill and chased it with coffee left from yesterday. Then he zipped the rest of the pills into the inside pocket of his jacket. Resting his head back against the seat, he waited and gritted his teeth against the unrelenting torture that made it impossible to do anything but hurt.

In the last few weeks, he'd started to notice it was taking longer for the pills to work. He needed something stronger. The doctor he'd gone to when he twisted his back taking down a suspect at the beginning of the summer had cut him off after the third refill, so he'd resorted to back channels to fulfill his needs.

His phone buzzed with a text from Cruz.

Leaving the scene and heading back to HQ. Two DOA in Chevy Chase fire, hands and feet bound.

Ugh, fire victims were the worst. If he waited a little longer, he wouldn't have to view the charred bodies in the morgue. They'd need dental records to ID them anyway, so there wouldn't be any info for a while. He had time to close his eyes for a few minutes, and then he'd be good to go.

AFTER GETTING NOWHERE with neighbors, who didn't answer their doors, Sam and Freddie returned to HQ, entering through the morgue entrance. Before they stepped into Lindsey's lab, Sam stopped him with a hand to his arm. "This is gonna be bad. Take a minute if you need it."

"I'm as ready as I ever am to go in there."

"Step back if it's too much for you. No judgment."

With his face set into a grim expression, he nodded and took a deep breath to calm himself.

No matter how many years one spent on the job, some things never got easier, and viewing dead bodies, especially those from a fire, was right at the top of the nightmarish list of things that could never be forgotten.

Her stomach turned at the thought of it, but someone had to do it. The moment the two people in the morgue had been killed in her city, they'd become hers, and she would do her very best for them. With justice in mind, Sam took a step forward, triggering the automatic doors that led to the morgue where Dr. Lindsey McNamara had the bodies on side-by-side tables.

Sam tried not to look too closely. "What've you got, Doc?" Lindsey's brows knitted with concentration as she stood over the deceased. They were in good hands with her on the job.

"Nothing yet. If you could find their dentist, that would help."

"We'll get on that." Sam glanced at Freddie and gestured for him to go get started on tracking down the dental records. They had an email they could send that would alert every dentist in the capital area that they were seeking records. Hopefully, one of them would recognize the Beauclairs' names and get back to them quickly. A positive identification was the first step in a case like this.

Freddie bolted from the cold, antiseptic-smelling room to send the message.

"They were bound with zip ties that melted into their skin." Lindsey pointed to the waxy remains of the zip ties while Sam choked back a gag. "Both were wearing wedding rings. One is male, the other female."

Sam didn't ask how she could tell that. "Anything else I should know?"

"Nothing yet, but I'm just getting started."

"Okay. Check in with me when you're done."

"You know I will." She looked up at Sam. "So the guys will be gone for *three weeks*, huh?" Her fiancé, Terry O'Connor, was Nick's chief of staff.

"Yeah."

"I can't bear the thought of three weeks without him," Lindsey said with a moan. In any other profession, it might've been odd to engage in girl talk over the charred remains of two people who'd been alive twenty-four hours ago. In their profession, it was just another day. "What kind of simpering female does that make me?"

"The kind who loves her guy."

"I really do love him," she said with a sigh. "He hasn't even left yet, and I already miss him. Maybe we can do a girls' night out or something to break up the time."

"I, um, sort of agreed to go on the trip last night, if I can get the time off."

"No way! Ugh, I'm so jealous. I'd love to go."

"Why don't you?"

"I'm saving my vacation for the wedding and honeymoon. We set a date finally."

"Oh, that's big news. When?"

"Next August at his parents' farm in Leesburg."

"That'll be amazing."

"I can't wait. I asked Shelby to help me plan it. I hope that's okay."

"Of course it is." Sam and Nick's assistant, Shelby Faircloth, had been one of the District's most sought-after wedding planners before she took the job with them after planning their wedding. She still owned her wedding business but had stepped out of the day-to-day management. "She's the best of the best."

"That's why I wanted her. Your wedding was the nicest I've ever attended."

"It was rather awesome, wasn't it?" Hard to believe it had already been a year and a half since then. "I'd better get to it. I'll be looking for your report."

"I'm on it."

Sam exited the morgue and took the winding hallway that led to the Homicide detectives' pit where Detectives Cruz, Green and McBride were discussing the fire, the victims and next steps in the investigation. "Where's Gonzo?"

"Not here yet," Cruz said, meeting her gaze, his concern apparent.

"Give him a call."

"Already did. No answer."

What the fuck? It wasn't like her sergeant to fail to show up at a crime scene or to check in with them if he was going to be late. She went into her office, closed the door and called Christina.

"Hi, Sam," Christina said, her tone lifeless. "What's up?"

"I'm looking for Gonzo. Did he get the call about the homicide this morning?"

"He left an hour ago," she said, sounding concerned now. "He's not there yet?"

"No sign of him."

"Where could he be? He got the call from Dispatch and left a few minutes later."

"I have no idea, but we'll see if we can track him down. I'll let you know if we hear from him if you wouldn't mind doing the same."

"Of course. Sam. I… Tommy, he's…"

Sam waited impatiently for her to finish the sentence.

"Never mind. I'll talk to you later."

Before Sam could respond, the line went dead. Now what the hell was that about? She hated when people left statements half-finished. Nothing was more aggravating. Well, receptionists who tried to keep her from seeing people she needed to talk to during investigations were more aggravating. They might very well be the most annoying people in existence.

Her mind kept going back to the despair she'd heard in Christina's voice and the fact that Gonzo wasn't where he was supposed to be this morning, not to mention how distracted and "off" he'd seemed in recent weeks. She released the clip that held her long hair out of her way when she was working and ran her fingers through it while trying to figure out what to do about Gonzo.

Reaching for the extension on her desk, she buzzed Detective Cameron Green and asked him to come into the office.

When he knocked on the door and poked his head into her office, she waved him in. "Close the door."

"What's up, LT?"

She liked the clean-cut blond man who'd joined their team right after Labor Day. He'd done an admirable job of filling the spot left vacant by their murdered colleague. Though the rest of them dressed casually in jeans, Cameron came to work every day in a shirt and tie. He was squared away in more ways than one. "I have a delicate question to ask." She gestured to her visitor chair.

Sitting, he said, "Okay."

"How does Gonzo seem to you lately?"

"Um, fine. I guess."

"I know I'm putting you in a bad spot asking about your partner and your sergeant, but he's late today and hasn't checked in, which isn't like him, and well… I'm worried about him. Again."

"I didn't know him before, so I'm not sure what's normal for him."

Losing a team member in the line of duty firmly split life into *before* and *after*. "Fair enough," she said, sighing.

"But lately, he's seemed a little…distracted, I guess you could say." Cameron chose his words carefully because it wasn't the best career move to speak to the big boss about your partner, who was also your sergeant.

"How so?"

After a long pause, Cameron said, "I'd like to leave it at distracted, if that's all right with you."

"Of course."

"I hope you understand. It's been a bit of a delicate proposition to take his late partner's place and…"

"Say no more. I get it." Partners had each other's backs on the street and in the house. Asking one of them to talk to a superior officer about the other was a dicey thing at best. "Thanks for coming in."

"If I could say one more thing."

"Please. Whatever's on your mind."

"I told you that I worked for my family's funeral home business when I was younger."

She nodded. His connections to the Greenlawn Funeral Homes had come in handy during a recent investigation.

"One of my jobs was to set up for the grief groups that used to meet in our function room. I was in charge of keeping them in coffee and cookies, so occasionally I would hear some of what was said. I remember this one guy, who'd lost his young son in an accident, said how everyone kept watching him for signs that he was getting better when the pain was actually getting worse with every day that went by."

Sam absorbed this information, feeling a sense of shock and dread that her close friend and colleague could be getting *worse* rather than better, and she hadn't noticed.

"Cruz mentioned this morning that it's nine months

today since Arnold died. Perhaps that might have something to do with what's going on with Gonzo?"

Sam swallowed the lump that suddenly formed in her throat. It'd been *nine months* since Arnold died, and the new guy had to remind her of it? "Could be," she managed to say. "I really appreciate your insight."

"I'll keep an eye on him. Try not to worry."

"Thank you." Though he told her not to worry, Sam wondered how she would do anything but. And now she had reason to wonder if Gonzo could handle being in charge of the squad for three weeks if she took the trip with Nick.

Opening her phone, she placed a call to Gonzo that went right through to voice mail.

Now she was officially worried.

A LOUD NOISE woke Gonzo from a sound sleep. He opened his eyes to realize he was in his car, parked on a side street and a uniformed member of the Metro PD Patrol division was looking in the driver's side window.

Gonzo reached into his pocket for his badge and found himself on the business end of the other officer's service weapon. He put up his hands.

The door swung open. "Keep your hands up and get out of the vehicle."

"I'm on the job. I was reaching for my badge." With a department of more than four thousand officers, it wasn't possible to recognize everyone, but most officers recognized him as the guy who'd let his partner get killed a foot from him.

"Let me see it," the young Patrolman said, still holding the gun on Gonzo.

Gonzo pulled the leather billfold from his back pocket

and flipped it open to reveal the gold shield he'd worked so damned hard to get, for all he cared about it now.

The Patrolman holstered his weapon. "My apologies, Sergeant, but when you reached for something, I had to assume it was a weapon."

"I understand."

"Are you all right?"

"I'm battling the flu and was taking a minute to regroup. I'd appreciate if you didn't report this to anyone."

"I won't if you won't." Pulling a weapon on a superior officer wasn't the best career move, even if it had been warranted.

"You got it."

"Hope you feel better."

"Me too." *Anytime now.* Gonzo got back in the car and glanced at the time on the dashboard. "Holy shit," he whispered, realizing he'd been asleep for two hours. He checked his phone, which was full of missed calls from Cruz, Christina and Sam. *"Fuck."* Shifting the car into Drive, he pressed the accelerator and promptly crashed into a passing vehicle.

Slamming the palm of his hand hard against the steering wheel, he let out a string of curses, and then, ignoring the pain radiating up his arm, he got out of the car to see how bad it was.

CHAPTER THREE

"CRIME SCENE IS on the way to Chevy Chase," Captain Malone said as he stepped into Sam's office. "What else do you need?"

She corralled her hair into a ponytail, twisted and clipped it to get it out of her way while she reported the little she knew so far to the captain. "Cruz," she shouted.

He came to the door. "You bellowed?"

"Where are we with the dentists?"

"I've heard back from about seventy-five percent of them. Nothing yet."

"What've we got on the victims?" Malone asked.

"Still assuming the victims are the people who lived in the house, not much of anything," Cruz said. "They have almost no online presence, which is odd these days."

"There has to be something," Sam said.

"We're digging, but we aren't finding anything."

"Let's go try again with the neighbors."

"Sounds good."

"Give me five," Sam said.

After Cruz walked away, Sam returned her attention to the captain. "I was going to request some time off, but now I'm not sure I should with a new case."

"If you're thinking we can't function without you, Lieutenant, I assure you that's not the case."

"You won't function *as well* without me, so don't try to deny it."

"I would never be so foolish as to deny the truth. What kind of time are we talking?"

"Nick wants me to go on the Europe trip with him." Under her breath, she added, "Three weeks."

Malone's gray eyes went wide. *"Three weeks?"*

"I have the time." She'd rarely taken so much as a day off before she married Nick, so the time had stacked up.

"I'm well aware that you have more time on the books than just about anyone in the department."

"So, it shouldn't be a problem if I take some of it, right?"

"You'd be back before Stahl's trial?" he asked.

The reminder that she'd soon have to testify against her former lieutenant made her feel sweaty and sick, so she didn't allow her mind to go there. "Well before." The trial was firmly stuffed into a compartment in the back of her mind that wouldn't be accessed until it absolutely had to be. Not one second before.

"Let me run the request up the flagpole and get back to you. I assume you'd leave Sergeant Gonzales in charge of Homicide?"

Sam hesitated but only for a second. Whatever was going on with Gonzo, she'd get to the bottom of it before she left. Looking up at Malone, she said, "That's the plan."

Cruz came back to the office door. "Gonzo has been in an MVA. He's fine, his car is fine, but the car he hit is pretty messed up. He's dealing with that now and will be in shortly."

"All right." Sam wondered if there was more to the

story. "Text him to meet us in Chevy Chase and tell Green and McBride to come too."

"Will do."

Sam gathered her handheld radio and car keys. "Was there anything else, Captain?"

He looked like he might want to say something else, probably about her punching out of work for three weeks, but he shook his head.

"Catch you later, then."

THE BEAUCLAIRS' BEAUTIFUL neighborhood was marred only by the blackened frame of the house that had burned. In most neighborhoods, emergency action of any kind drew a crowd. Chevy Chase wasn't most neighborhoods. A lone woman with a dog on a leash stood outside the yellow crime scene tape wiping tears. She wore her blond hair in a ponytail and was dressed in workout clothing.

"Excuse me," Sam said as she approached the woman while Freddie conferred with the firefighters.

The woman glanced at Sam and then did a double take when she recognized her. That happened far too often for Sam's liking since Nick became vice president and raised their already-high profile even higher. Sam hated the added attention, but she'd gotten used to it. Sort of.

"You're…"

Ignoring the reference to her second lady status, Sam said, "Did you know the family who lived here?"

She nodded. "Are they all gone?"

"All being who?"

"Jameson, Cleo, Alden and Aubrey. Jameson has an older son, Elijah, who's away at college."

Sam pulled her notebook from her back pocket and

wrote down the names. "How old are Alden and Aubrey?"

"They're five-year-old twins."

Sam waved Green over and spoke so only he could hear her. "Let the fire marshal know we're looking for five-year-old twins in the house."

Green winced and nodded before seeing to her order.

"What's your name?" Sam asked the woman.

"Lauren Morton. I live one block over. My kids play with Alden and Aubrey."

"How well do you know the parents?"

"I don't know Jameson well at all. He works a lot. But I know Cleo through the kids." Lauren looked at Sam, her eyes watering with new tears. "Are they…"

"We have two adult victims, but we haven't found the kids."

Lauren nodded and wiped her tears. "Was it an accident?"

"We don't know yet." Sam couldn't and wouldn't divulge details that could compromise the investigation. "Do you know what they did for a living?"

"He was in some sort of international business. Cleo said he worked all the time, and I know he traveled a lot, because she was alone with the kids. She doesn't work, but she volunteers at the kids' school."

"What school is that?"

"Northwest Academy on Connecticut."

Sam made a note. "Do you know where his older son goes to school?"

"Princeton, I think."

They needed to track down Jameson's son so they could undertake the dreadful task of notifying him of his family members' deaths after they got positive identifications. "Could you please give me your full name, address and phone number?" Sam asked, handing her the notebook and pen.

"How come?"

"In case I have follow-up questions."

"I've told you what I know."

"I like to be thorough, so if you wouldn't mind…"

Lauren stared at the notebook for a second before she reluctantly took it and wrote down the info Sam had requested. "My husband doesn't like when I get involved with neighborhood drama."

"This hardly counts as drama. I'd categorize it under neighborhood tragedy. Did Mrs. Beauclair have other friends in the neighborhood?"

"A few."

"Write down their names, addresses and phone numbers, if you would."

Lauren used her cell phone to look up the numbers and wrote down three names with the accompanying information. "You don't need to tell them you got their names from me, do you?"

"No."

"Oh good. I'd rather not be involved."

Honestly, Sam wanted to say. *People are dead, and you're worried about getting involved?*

"Why are you investigating the fire?" Lauren asked after she handed over the notebook. "I thought you were a Homicide detective."

"I am."

"Oh, so, does that mean…"

"It means we're conducting a full investigation."

"I see."

No, you don't. "Is there anything else you can tell me about the family that might assist in our investigation?"

"I heard she fired her housekeeper yesterday," Lauren said. "Cleo suspected her of stealing from them. The housekeeper had worked for them for years and was very hurt by the accusation, according to my housekeeper."

"Do you know her name?"

"Her first name was Milagros. I never heard her last name."

Sam made a note. It was the closest thing to a motive she'd heard yet and the timing lined up. "What did you know about Cleo's background?"

"Not much. Just that she's from out West originally. She never did say where. She didn't talk about her life before DC."

"And you never wondered why?"

Lauren shrugged. "People are private. I'm private. I don't pry into areas that are clearly off-limits with my friends."

"Did she ever express concern for her safety or that of her family?"

"No, nothing like that. Not to me anyway."

Sam handed her a card. "If you think of anything that might be relevant, call me. My cell number is on there."

"I will."

"Thanks for your time." Sam went to confer with Freddie, who was talking to another neighbor. "Anything?" she asked when the man had walked away.

"Nah, he didn't know them. Just curious about the people who died."

It constantly amazed Sam that tragedy drew spectators the same way sporting events did. "I'll never understand the attraction to watching someone else's life fall apart."

"Makes them feel better about their own lives, I suppose."

"I guess. I've got the names of some neighbors who knew the family. Let's go see if they're home."

They walked a block and a half to the address Lauren had given her for Janice McMillian.

"I'm trying to imagine being able to afford to live in one of these houses," Freddie said. "We're in the wrong business."

"You're just now figuring that out?"

He laughed. "We're in the wrong business for many reasons, not the least of which is that we'll never be able to afford this neighborhood."

"That may be true, but not one of these people could do what we do every day—and trust me, they're damned glad we're out here doing it."

"That's for sure." He rang the doorbell, which chimed like church bells. "Aren't you going to tell me that rich people have better doorbells than the rest of us? You always say that."

"I don't *always* like to be predictable."

Freddie peered into the window at the side of the door and then rang the bell again. "God forbid you should be predictable."

A uniformed woman came to the door. "May I help you?"

Sam held up her badge. "Lieutenant Holland and Detective Cruz to see Mrs. McMillian. Is she at home?"

The woman stared at Sam, seeming stunned to see the second lady on her employer's doorstep.

"Hello?" Sam said, waving her hand in front of the lady's face. "Mrs. McMillian. Is she home?"

"Just a moment." She closed the door and walked away.

"I can't believe she didn't invite us in for tea and cookies while we wait," Sam said.

"People around here aren't used to cops showing up at their front doors."

"Hard to believe this neighborhood is in the same city as some of the other places we frequent."

A trim blonde woman came to the door, also dressed in workout attire. Was that the new dress code for upper-class women? "I'm Janice McMillian. You wanted to see me?"

Sam and Freddie showed their badges again as Sam introduced them.

"May we come in for a minute?" Sam asked.

"Sure," she said, the word dripping with reluctance.

Here was another neighbor who probably didn't want to get involved in the tragedy unfolding down the street.

"What can I do for you?" she asked after showing them into one of those fancy rooms wealthy people kept pristine for guests.

"You're acquainted with the Beauclair family?"

"I am. My children are close in age to the twins. They play together. I was heartbroken to hear about the fire. It's such an awful tragedy."

"Yes, it is," Sam said.

"Are they all…"

"We found two adult victims but haven't yet positively identified them. We're still looking for the children."

Janice's blue eyes filled with tears.

"How well did you know the Beauclairs?"

"I only knew him socially. He traveled a lot for his business. I knew Cleo quite well. We're both stay-at-home moms and met at the park about two years ago. Since our kids are around the same ages, we hit it off right away."

"What do you know about her personally?" Sam asked.

"Just that she was very devoted to her kids and her family."

"Where is she from originally?"

"I… I don't know. We never discussed that. We mostly talked about our kids and coordinating rides to activities and things like that."

"Did you ever get a sense of the Beauclairs' marriage? Were they happy together?"

"Oh yes. She worshipped the ground Jameson walked on. They were very much in love, or at least they seemed that way to me the few times I saw them together."

Sam made a note of that.

"Her only complaint was that his business took him away from home too much. She missed him when he was gone. She lit up around him. After a neighborhood Christmas party last year, my husband commented that they're like newlyweds because they held hands the entire night."

"Did you know her housekeeper?" Sam consulted her notes. "A woman named Milagros?"

"I've met her, yes. I heard they let her go yesterday."

"Do you know Milagros's last name or where we might find her?"

"I don't but let me ask my housekeeper."

"If you wouldn't mind," Sam said, "bring her in here when you ask her."

"Why?" Janice asked, seeming perplexed.

"Because I asked you to."

She clearly wasn't used to anyone speaking to her that way, and her displeasure was obvious in the tight set of her lips. "Just a moment."

"She didn't like that," Freddie muttered.

"Too bad. I want to see the housekeeper's reaction when we ask about Milagros."

"I know that, and you know that, but she's pissed that you're telling her how to manage her own staff."

"Whatever."

Janice returned with her housekeeper.

"Your name, ma'am?" Sam asked.

She glanced at Janice, who nodded. "Luisa Sanchez."

"Do you know the Beauclairs' housekeeper, Milagros?" Sam asked.

Luisa, who had dark hair and pretty brown eyes, nodded. "I know her. They fired her."

"One of the other neighbors told us that. Do you know where we can find her?"

Luisa looked to Janice again.

"If you know where she is, I need you to tell me," Sam said.

"Tell her," Janice said harshly. "Right now."

"I—I don't want to get her in trouble. She's undocumented."

"I'm not interested in her immigration status. We need to talk to her about what happened to the Beauclairs."

"She wouldn't hurt them. She loved them. They hurt *her*."

"That's enough, Luisa," Janice snapped.

"I need her address," Sam said.

"I have it in my purse in the laundry room."

"Hurry up and get it," Janice said.

Luisa scurried off while Sam, Freddie and Janice co-existed in awkward silence until Janice cleared her throat.

"We don't want any trouble."

"I'm sure the Beauclairs didn't either." Sam had zero compassion for this privileged, pampered woman who was only worried about herself when her friend and her friend's husband were most likely dead and their children missing.

Luisa returned with a slip of paper on which she'd written Milagros's address.

"Thank you," Sam said. "Please don't tell her you spoke with us."

"She won't," Janice said. "Is there anything else we can do?"

"Not at this time." Sam handed her a business card. "If you think of anything else that might be relevant, let me know."

Janice started to speak but stopped herself.

"Whatever you know," Sam said, "it's better for you to tell us now than have us find out later that you held out on us. That can lead to charges."

Janice swallowed hard. "I'm not sure if it's relevant."

"Every detail is relevant at this point in an investigation."

"I liked Cleo a lot," she said hesitantly. "She was a lovely person, but I remember telling my husband months after we'd met that I felt like I didn't really know her at all. She didn't give much away, if you know what I mean. We never made it past the surface."

"That's interesting." Sam wrote down the information to stew over later. "Did she have other friends that you knew of?"

"A few of the other neighborhood moms." She listed names that Sam had already gotten from Lauren. "She also volunteered at the kids' school."

"Did she ever mention being afraid of anything or anyone?"

"Not that I ever heard, but I doubt she would've confided in me. She wasn't like that."

"Did she have friends she would've confided in, that you know of?"

"I can't think of anyone she was extra close to."

"Thank you for sharing that. We appreciate your time."

"I hope it's okay to say that my husband and I admire you and your husband very much."

"That's nice of you," Sam said, surprised by the change in tone. Perhaps the thought of criminal charges had softened her. "Thank you."

"We were sort of hoping Nelson would resign."

"We're sort of glad it didn't come to that," Sam said, deadpan.

Janice laughed. "I'm sure you are. I don't get why anyone would want that job. It's somewhat thankless."

"Yes, it is."

"You don't have Secret Service protection?"

Sam shook her head and rested a hand on her service weapon. "I can take care of myself." At the front door, she turned back to face the other woman. "Thank you again for your help."

"They were a sweet family. I'm heartbroken that this has happened to them."

"Call me if you think of anything else."

"I will."

Outside, Sam turned to Freddie. "Impressions?"

"We might be spinning our wheels talking to the friends if she kept her relationships at a surface level."

"Agreed. What I'd like to know is *why* she did that? In my experience, women overshare more than they undershare."

"Is *undershare* a word?" Freddie asked. "It rhymes with underwear."

"Stop," she said, cracking up. "I'm actually being serious here. Women talk about *everything*. It's weird that she didn't."

"Just to play devil's advocate… *You* aren't like that."

"I'm talking about *regular* women, not badass cop women."

"I see, and I stand corrected. As always, I bow to your wisdom, Lieutenant."

"Quit your sucking up. Despite your limited experience with women, you know exactly what I'm talking about."

Freddie rolled his eyes, as she'd known he would. She loved to razz him about marrying the first woman he'd slept with. He said he preferred *quality* to quantity. Elin made him happy, which was good enough for Sam.

"What's next?" he asked as they got in her car.

"A stop at the kids' school on Connecticut Ave."

"While we're in that area, can I pick up my tux?"

"No personal errands on city time," she said sternly, directing the car toward Connecticut Avenue.

"It's *so* close." He rubbed his always-empty belly. "And it is almost lunchtime."

"Fine. If you must."

"It's the only thing Elin told me to do this week."

"You guys get off *so* easily when it comes to weddings. You show up in a monkey suit at the appointed time and get married."

"You're tossing around a lot of stereotypes today, Lieutenant. I'll have you know I was heavily involved in the planning of my wedding."

"You were *not*."

"Yes, I was! I helped decide on everything."

"From choices she had pared down from thousands of options."

"You don't know that."

Sam gave him a withering look. "About to get married and still so much to learn about women, my young grass-hopper. *She* has been planning this day in her mind since she was old enough to know what a wedding was. *You* did *not* help to plan the wedding. You validated choices she'd already made."

Scowling, he said, "I'm getting married this week. You could take the week off from being mean to me, es-pecially since you're my best man-woman."

"How am I being *mean*?"

"You just are. I helped whenever she asked me to."

"I'm teasing you. Don't be oversensitive. It takes the fun out of it."

"For who?"

"Me, of course."

"And it's *all* about you, even the week of *my* wedding."

"Duh."

He huffed out a laugh. "At least you're consistent."

"I pride myself on my consistency and my predict-ability—most of the time."

"I still can't believe Nick made such an insanely cool place available to us to use for our wedding. Elin and I want to pinch ourselves that we get to be married at the Naval Observatory," he said of the traditional home of the vice president.

"He is rather awesome, and he's not using it, so it's all yours." When he became vice president, they had stayed in their own home, primarily to remain in close proximity to Sam's paralyzed father, who lived three doors down the street from them.

"It was so nice of him to offer it," Freddie said.

"He was thrilled to do it. It's a beautiful spot for a wedding."

"It certainly is. We couldn't be happier about it. I feel like Saturday is never going to get here."

"It'll be here before you know it."

CHAPTER FOUR

SAM TOOK A left into the driveway of the school, where they were forced to stop at a monitored gatehouse. "Whoa. Check this out. What's up with the gate guard?"

"The president's grandchildren and other VIP kids go here."

"How do you know that?"

"I read the paper. Do you?"

"Not as much as I did before my husband was the daily headline." At the gatehouse, Sam showed her badge. "Lieutenant Holland, Detective Cruz, MPD."

"What can we do for you, ma'am?" the guard asked, his eyes bugging at the sight of her.

"We'd like to speak to the administrator, please."

"May I ask what this is in reference to?"

"You can certainly ask, but I won't tell you. Please let us in."

"One moment, please." He went back into his hut and picked up the phone.

"Add security guards to the list of people who annoy me."

"Above or below receptionists?"

"Below. Way below. Receptionists are in a category all their own."

Freddie pretended to make a note. "Got it."

Sam adored him and the way he rolled with her. He

certainly made work a lot more entertaining than it had been before he'd been her partner. "Let me ask you something."

"What?" He'd learned to be wary where she was concerned, and she liked him that way.

"Gonzo."

"What about him?"

"Is he up for keeping things together if I take a few weeks off?"

"Why wouldn't he be?"

Sam chose her words carefully. Since she wasn't sure she had anything to be worried about, she didn't want to alarm him needlessly, especially this week. "No reason. Just wondering."

"He seems okay to me. He's different than he was before, but that's to be expected, I suppose."

"Yeah." Sam looked over to find the guard still on the phone. She leaned on the horn.

He scowled at her.

She hit the horn again. Out the window, she said, "You're wasting my time, and people who waste my time irritate me."

"You don't want to irritate her," Freddie said.

"I'm about to drive through this gate."

"Ohh, do it," Freddie said gleefully. "I dare you!"

Sam eyed the gate, trying to decide if it was worth potentially damaging the BMW Nick had tricked out for her. Just as she was about to hit the gas, the gate went up. "Bummer."

Freddie busted up laughing.

Sam navigated the driveway that led to a large stone structure with ivy on the walls. "This is a *preschool*?"

"It's a *rich people* preschool."

"Ahh, that explains it." She parked in the fire lane outside the main entrance and got out.

"Ma'am, you can't park there," the same security guard from the hut said, huffing from the effort it took to chase after her.

"Already did." Sam took the stairs two at a time and encountered another roadblock—a locked door and an intercom. Flashing her badge at the security camera above the door, she pushed the button three times. "Lieutenant Holland, MPD. Let me in right now, or I'll arrest everyone in the building."

"I'm not doing that paperwork," Freddie said.

She buzzed three more times, and the door clicked open. "For fuck's sake," she said as they went inside, where they landed in the main office, staffed by women who stared at them as if they were aliens.

"Who's in charge here?" Sam asked.

All eyes turned to an older, stern-looking woman, who looked like she'd been sucking on a particularly sour kosher dill for the last five years. "What do you want?" she asked in a tone dripping with disdain.

Sam went to her. "I need to discuss a fatal fire at the home of the Beauclair family. I understand their children are students here."

At that, her pickle puss eased ever so slightly. "The children…"

Sam lowered her voice so the others wouldn't overhear. "Have not yet been located. We believe the parents are deceased. May we speak in private?"

"Yes, of course. Right this way."

Dead people had a way of opening doors. Sam and Freddie followed her down a hallway into an elegant room that looked more like a Victorian parlor than an office. "May I offer you some coffee or tea?"

"No, thank you," Sam said before Freddie could accept. This wasn't a fucking social call. "What's your name?"

"Beatrice Reeve."

"And you are?"

"The school director."

"And you're acquainted with the Beauclair family?"

"Oh yes. Cleo and the children have become a big part of our community. This is their first year here, and we've so enjoyed having them. They're very well behaved and just a joy to be around. They aren't… The children…"

"We don't know yet. What can you tell us about Cleo Beauclair?"

"She's a lovely person, a dedicated mother. She's given so much of her time to the school this year. Most of the mothers drop their children and leave, but she spends the day here helping out until it's time for the kids to go home."

"And that's unusual?"

"Oh yes. Highly unusual. Don't get me wrong—many of our parents are exceptional volunteers but few give as much time as Cleo does. Or did. Is she really gone?"

"We don't know that for sure yet. Did you know Mr. Beauclair?"

"I met him once when they came to tour the school before enrolling the children."

"Going back to what you said about Mrs. Beauclair volunteering," Freddie said. "Did she stay every day that the kids were here or just some of the days?"

"Every day. We were so thankful for her help. There's always something that needs to be done."

"And how many days a week did the children attend school?" Freddie asked.

"Five days. They were in our kindergarten program, which runs from eight until one every day."

Freddie wrote the info in his notebook.

"If there's anything at all we can do to assist you, I hope you'll let me know." She gave each of them her business card.

"Thank you," Sam said, handing over hers. "I appreciate that. I'd also appreciate being waved right through if I have to come back for any reason."

"Why would you need to come back?"

"Hard telling. But you should instruct your tin soldier at the gate to let me or any member of my team through without a hassle. We're just doing our jobs. We appreciate people who make our jobs easier."

"I understand."

"I hope so." To Freddie, she said, "Let's go."

When they were in the car and on the way back to HQ, she said, "What do you think?"

"I don't have kids, but do you find it odd that Cleo stayed at the school *every day* that her kids were there?"

"Very odd. It tells me she was afraid of something happening to them when she couldn't be there to keep them safe. What was she afraid of? That's what I want to know."

"I'd like to know that too. Don't forget we need to stop at the tux place."

"Yeah, yeah."

Freddie's phone rang, and he glanced at the caller ID. "Speaking of the future Mrs. Cruz," he said, grinning like a loon. "Gotta take this. Hey, babe." He paused. "Elin? Elin! What the hell?"

"What's wrong?" Sam asked.

"She said my name, and then the phone went dead."

"Call her back."

He put through the call.

Sam kept one eye on the road and one on him.

"It went right to voice mail."

"Where is she today?"

"Home. She took the week off."

Sam checked her side-view mirror and then made a U-turn toward the Woodley Park neighborhood where Freddie and Elin lived. She flipped on emergency lights and pressed the gas pedal to the floor.

"You don't think…"

"Overabundance of caution."

"Yes, that's good," he said, clearly trying to stay calm. "She's fine. Of course, she is."

"Track her phone."

His fingers moved over the screen of his phone while Sam steered the car through an intersection, bracing for an impact that didn't happen. After being hit broadside a few weeks ago, now she expected it every time she ran a red light in the line of duty.

"It's off." The two words conveyed a world of panic. *"Sam."*

"Breathe. Just breathe. We'll be there in two minutes."

They both knew a lot could happen in two minutes. "Call it in."

"What am I calling in?"

"Get us some backup at your place. Just in case we need it."

He seemed frozen as he pondered the implications of needing backup.

"Freddie! Call it in!"

He made the call, and she heard fear in every word as he asked for backup at the home he shared with Elin.

They darted around traffic, ran red lights and made fast time getting to Woodley Park.

"Go left here," Freddie said. "It's shorter."

Sam followed his directions, tires squealing as she took the turn, tightening her hold on the wheel so she wouldn't lose control of the car. The ten minutes it took to get there felt like an eternity to her. She couldn't begin to imagine how Freddie must feel. She slammed on the brakes outside his building and was out of the car before it even stopped moving.

Freddie was ahead of her, his hands shaking as he used his key to gain access to the vestibule. It took two tries, and Sam was about to take the keys from him when the door swung open. The first thing she saw was blood on the floor and stairs, as well as a cell phone lying on the bottom step. She propped the door open so other officers could get in.

"That's her phone!"

"Don't touch it!" She gave him a push up the stairs, which he took three at a time.

Noting the trail of blood on the stairs, Sam scrambled to keep up with him as they made their way to the third floor, where they found his apartment door wide-open. She grabbed his arm to stop him from going in and reached for her weapon.

"Freddie," Sam whispered, pointing to the other side of the doorway. She watched him marshal the fortitude to follow procedure, to not barge into a possible crime in progress without proper preparation. She could see it took everything he had to stop himself, to think like a cop and not like the man in love with the woman who lived there with him.

"Go," she said softly, letting him take the lead while she covered him. She hoped their backup would be right behind them.

They walked into a bloody nightmare, blood on the floor, the sofa, the kitchen counter and a knife on the floor also covered in blood.

Freddie's knees buckled.

Sam grabbed him, which was the only thing that kept him standing.

"Elin," he said on a whimper.

"Sit." She pushed him into a chair while she went to check the bedroom, which was clear. Sam returned to the living room and holstered her weapon.

"What the hell?" The sheer terror in his expression fueled Sam's panic. Where the fuck was she?

"Remember not to touch anything." Sam made a second, more urgent request for backup and then called Malone to fill him in.

"There's blood everywhere and no sign of her?" Malone asked.

"Right, and a bloody knife on the kitchen floor. She called Freddie and said his name before the phone went dead. We found the phone in the vestibule but didn't touch it."

"I'll be right there."

Sam closed her phone and tried to remain calm for Freddie.

"What do I do?" he asked, standing. "I have to do something."

"We'll find her. Just keep breathing. There might be a perfectly reasonable explanation."

"You don't believe that any more than I do, so don't blow smoke up my ass." He bent at the waist, hands on knees. Then he straightened. "I'm going down to see where the blood leads."

While he did that, Sam knocked on the neighbors' doors. No one was home in the first three she tried. The fourth was answered by an older woman who let out a scream of surprise at seeing Sam on her doorstep. In the background, the TV was set to blare.

"You're the second lady! Oh my God! I am such a *huge* fan of your husband's!" In a low, sultry tone, she added, "He's *so* handsome and sexy."

Sam showed her badge, which shut the woman up as she'd hoped it would. "Did you hear anything in the hallway in the last hour or so? My partner lives three doors down and came home to blood all over the place."

"Oh no! I didn't hear a thing, but my TV is loud, so I can hear it. He's such a sweet young guy, and the two of them are so in love. They're adorable. Is she…"

"We don't know anything yet. If you're sure you didn't hear anything, I'll let you get back to your day."

Before the woman could continue talking, Sam walked away, placing a call to Gonzo as she went. He answered on the second ring.

"Hey, sorry about this morning. What a clusterfuck—"

"Gonzo!"

"What's wrong?"

"You need to get over to Cruz's place right away. Elin is gone, and there's blood everywhere."

"*What?* What happened?"

"We have no idea. She called him, said his name in a frantic tone, and then the phone went dead. We found the phone in the vestibule along with a lot of blood."

"I'm on my way."

"Bring the cavalry, Gonzo. We have to find her."

"Got it. We're coming."

Sam walked to the stairway as Freddie came back up, dodging the blood on the stairs as he went. "What'd you find?"

"The blood ends at the curb. She got into a vehicle."

Sam thought about that for a second. "Do you know her phone code?"

"Yes."

"Go get it. Bag it, bring it up and let's charge it. We can check her activity."

He moved quickly down the stairs and was back within seconds. Careful to not touch or disturb anything in the apartment, Freddie plugged the phone into a charger, while keeping it in the evidence bag. "I've been telling her she needs to get a new phone. This one doesn't hold a charge. But she's been so busy with the wedding and everything."

His voice caught on the last word, and he hung his head.

Sam put her hand on his back, wishing she could find a way to comfort him. "Try not to go to worst-case. Not yet."

He eyed the bloody knife on the floor and the blood all over the counter and floor. Then he brought his tortured gaze to meet hers. "You mean to tell me you wouldn't be freaking out if you came home to this?"

"I would be, and I understand why you are, but she's smart and resourceful and—"

"And she's bleeding. Profusely."

The two of them stood over the phone, willing it to charge.

A few minutes later, the pound of footsteps on the stairs had her running for the door to greet Gonzo, Green, Jeannie McBride and Malone, noting that they too hadn't touched the blood smeared onto the stairs. The four of them looked as undone as Sam felt.

"Holy shit," Gonzo whispered, taking in the blood all over the apartment.

Sam's brain finally began working again as the shock wore off. These things were so different, from a police standpoint, when the person involved was a close friend or loved one. "Assuming the blood is hers, Cruz was able to determine she got into a vehicle at the curb. I want you guys checking every hospital in the city to see if she's there. And someone call emergency dispatch to see if there was a call made from her phone. Freddie! What's her number?"

He rattled it off while Jeannie wrote it down.

"We're on it," Jeannie said. "We'll find her, Freddie."

Freddie nodded in acknowledgment. "Thanks."

Gonzo went to him, put a hand on his shoulder and spoke softly to his friend. Whatever he said brought tears to Freddie's eyes. Gonzo hugged him. "We're going to find her."

Freddie nodded again and wiped his tears. Through the bag, he pushed the button to turn on the phone, but nothing happened. "Come on!"

"Give it a few more minutes," Sam said, knowing as he did that every second counted and minutes were like hours at a time like this.

While Freddie continued to stare at the phone, willing it to charge, Sam went to speak to Malone.

Hands on hips, he took a good look around the stylishly furnished apartment. Sam was ashamed of the fact

that she'd never been there. When they got together outside of work, they usually did so at her house where it
was easier for Nick. After the wedding, she'd make sure
they came to Freddie's place for once.

"What the hell is this, Sam?"

"I don't know. I wish I did."

Jeannie, who'd been in the hallway working the phones
with the others, poked her head in. "No 9-1-1 call from
her number."

"Okay," Sam said, her heart sinking. She'd hoped that
Elin had called for help and had been picked up by an
ambulance or Patrol officer who might've taken the call.
"Speaking of Patrol, where the fuck are they? We called
for backup twenty minutes ago."

"They're dealing with a huge accident over by Penn
Quarter," Malone said. "Ten cars involved."

"What if we'd encountered an active shooter here or
a crime in progress?"

"Thankfully, you didn't."

They passed a tense fifteen minutes with detectives
working the phones while Sam tried to keep Freddie
calm.

A shout went out from the hallway.

Green came to the door. "GW E.R. has her! She has
a severe cut to the hand that was bleeding so hard she
didn't wait around for help. She flagged down a cab."

Freddie covered his face with his hands as his shoulders shook. "Thank you, Jesus."

Sam went to him, wrapped her arms around him and
held on tight until he got himself together. "Let's go. I'll
take you to her."

"I thought…"

"I know, but she's fine. She's *fine*. Or she will be after some stitches from the sound of it. Come on. Let's go."

Keeping her hand on his back, Sam led him to the door.

"Thanks, you guys," he said to his colleagues. "I appreciate it so much."

"No problem," Jeannie said for all of them. "We're glad she's okay."

"Can you…" Sam tipped her head toward the apartment.

"Yes, of course," Jeannie said. "We'll clean up."

"Thank you." To Malone, Sam said, "We talked to the administrator at the Beauclair kids' school. The mom never left them there alone. Worked as a volunteer every day that they were in attendance, which was five days a week."

"That's something," Malone said.

"I also have the address of the Beauclairs' recently fired maid." She handed him the page from her notebook. "Send Green and McBride to talk to her."

"Got it. We'll pick it up. You stay with Cruz for as long as he needs you."

"See you back at the house." She escorted Freddie downstairs, noting he still stepped around the blood on the stairs like the trained professional he was. "The others will clean up."

"They don't have to. I'll do it when we get home."

"They want to help."

"How long do you think it'll be before my heart beats normally again?"

"It's apt to be a while."

"I was thinking of every perp I've ever arrested, every

altercation I've ever had on the job. The list of people who'd have reason to get even with me is long."

"Not as long as mine."

"Long enough that it wouldn't take much to ruin my life." They got into her car. "We're moving to a building with better security. If we'd had a doorman, this whole thing never would've happened."

"True, but can you afford that?"

"No, but I can less afford to lose her. I had forty-five minutes to ponder life without her, and I'll pay whatever it costs to ensure her safety."

"Can't say I blame you. That was pretty fucking scary."

"Yeah."

That he didn't comment on her language told her just how scared he'd been. It would take a while for the fear and shock to work their way out of his system—and hers.

CHAPTER FIVE

FREDDIE'S HANDS WERE still shaking when they arrived at the George Washington University Hospital fifteen torturous minutes later.

Sam drove up to the E.R. entrance. "Go. I'll park."

"Thank you."

He jumped out of the car and rushed inside to the main desk, where the nurse recognized him. "She's not here. We haven't seen her in a while." It took a second for him to realize she meant Sam, who was a frequent flier. "My fiancée was brought in earlier with a cut hand. Elin Svendsen?"

"Oh right. I didn't realize she was your fiancée. Right this way."

Freddie wanted to correct her. Elin wasn't just his fiancée. She was his whole world, and when he'd thought he might've lost her… The rest of his life had stretched before him like a barren wasteland.

He followed the nurse down a hallway and heard Elin crying and asking for him. The nurse pointed to a door, and Freddie rushed past her, into the room where he found Elin in a bed, her face so pale she blended in with the linens. Though tears had made her eyes puffy and red, she had never looked more beautiful to him.

"Freddie!" While a doctor tended to her left hand, she held out her right hand to him.

He took her hand and bent over the rail to kiss her.

"You have to hold still," the doctor said.

She whimpered. "Hurts."

Freddie couldn't speak or move or do anything other than breathe her in. He wanted to know what'd happened, but he couldn't find the words to ask. His only thought or emotion was pure relief.

"Freddie."

"I'm here, baby."

She cried out in pain.

"Sorry," the doctor said. "We're going to numb it and stitch you up. The numbing will be the worst of it, but after that, you won't feel anything sharp or painful. Ready?"

Elin looked up at Freddie, her pale blue eyes big with fear and shock.

"Stay focused on me," Freddie said. "Just look at me."

Tears exploded from her eyes as the first shot was administered.

He wished he could take the pain for her. Holding her head against his chest, he ran his fingers through her white-blond hair, feeling her tense with each subsequent shot to the palm of her hand.

"That was the last one," the doctor said.

Elin relaxed ever so slightly. "I can't believe this happened! Why this week?"

"What exactly happened?"

"I was using the knife to get a price tag off one of the candles and it slipped, slicing my palm wide-open. I tried to call you, but my phone went dead. I dropped it at some point. What a disaster!"

"You have no idea."

"What does that mean?"

"After you called, Sam and I went home to check on you and found blood *everywhere*—the vestibule, the stairs, the apartment. Your phone was on the floor inside the vestibule, and our apartment door was open. You can't begin to know the scenarios that ran through my head, especially after I saw a bloody knife on the kitchen floor."

"I'm so sorry, Freddie," she said, breaking down again. "You told me to get a new phone, but I've been so busy. And the blood was just pumping out of my hand. I almost passed out. I ran for the street and got a cab. The guy yelled at me for bleeding all over his car, but I didn't know what else to do."

"You did the right thing getting yourself to the hospital quickly."

"Indeed," the doctor said as he sewed the wound. "You lost a lot of blood."

"We're getting married on Saturday," Elin said. "Can you make it so I don't have a huge ugly bandage?"

"We'll set you up. Don't worry."

Elin breathed a sigh of relief.

"You're not allowed to ever scare me like this again, you hear me?" Freddie asked, filled with gratitude as he stared at her gorgeous face. "You took ten years off my life."

"And mine," Sam said when she joined them. "How's the patient?"

"She's going to be just fine," Freddie said, kissing Elin's forehead.

"Thank God for that," Sam said.

"Yes," Freddie said. "Thank God for that."

AFTER THEY FINISHED cleaning up the bloody disaster in Cruz's apartment, Cameron Green drove Jeannie Mc-

Bride to the District's southeastern quadrant to interview the Beauclairs' former maid.

"That was insane back there," he said after a long silence.

"Totally. Imagine what he had to be thinking coming home to that."

"I can't imagine. The poor guy. Thank goodness she's okay."

"What a thing to have happen the week of their wedding," Jeannie said with a sigh.

"Thankfully all's well that ends well." He glanced over at her. "Could I ask you something?"

"Of course."

"The LT called me in to talk about Gonzo this morning. She acknowledged the tough spot she was putting me in, but she wanted to know if he's seemed off to me."

"What'd you say?"

"A little, maybe? I'm not sure I know him well enough yet to say, which is why I wanted to ask what you think."

"He's way off and has been since Arnold was killed. If you knew him before, you'd know what I mean. He's like a totally different person now, although I can't really blame him." After a long pause, Jeannie said, "What happened to Arnold was so awful, and there was nothing he could do but watch his partner die. And this was after Arnold saved Gonzo's life when a bullet grazed his neck. Gonzo would've bled out without Arnold's quick thinking."

"Oh damn. I've seen the scar on his neck, but I didn't know how he got it."

"Part of me was surprised when he came back to work after Arnold was killed. He was so traumatized that I wondered if he would quit, but he told Cruz he had to come back because he has a family to support. Walking away isn't an option for him like it was for Will."

"Didn't Will end up with a cool security job?"

"Yep."

"Maybe that would be better for Gonzo after everything he's been through."

"Possibly, but I'd sure hate to lose him on the squad. We're like family to each other. Losing A.J. and then Will. It's been a tough year."

"You ever wonder how long the LT can hang on to the job in light of her husband's career?"

"She says she's not going anywhere. Nick certainly knows what the job means to her."

Cameron's phone directed them to the address Sam had given them. "That's it there," he said, pointing to an apartment building that had seen better days. He pulled into a no-parking zone.

He and Jeannie walked up a flight of stairs outside the building to the second floor.

"Was this a motel at one time?" he asked.

"I think it might've been."

Outside apartment 2F, they stood on either side while he pounded on the door and said, "Metro PD." He held his badge up to the peephole while listening for signs of life inside. At first, he didn't hear anything.

"What do you want?" a fearful-sounding female voice asked.

"We need to speak to you about the Beauclair family."

"I didn't steal from them! I love them! I would never steal from them."

"This isn't about that. Would you mind opening the door please?"

A series of locks disengaged, and the door opened

to reveal a pretty young woman with a tearstained face. "I didn't do what she said. I swear to God." Though her speech had a heavy Spanish accent, her English was perfect. She broke down into sobs. "A-are you going to arrest me?"

"Could we come in to speak in private?" Cameron asked.

"Show me your badges again."

They held up their gold shields for her inspection. After a close look at their badges, she took a step back to admit them to the clean, well-decorated room that included a bed, kitchen, sitting area and television. She had made herself a nice home in the run-down building.

"Ms. Cortez, I'm sorry to have to tell you, but there was a fire at the Beauclairs' home last night."

She gasped. "The babies! My Aubrey and Alden! Please tell me…"

"They're currently unaccounted for. We did find two adult victims, however. We haven't yet positively identified them."

She broke down into what could only be called heartbroken sobs. "Oh no, no, *no*. Not my family." Wrapping her arms around herself, she rocked as she sobbed.

"We're so sorry for your loss," Jeannie said.

"They were good people," Milagros said. "I was hoping they would find out who stole the jewelry, so I could go back to work there. I loved them and their sweet babies. Oh, Elijah! Mr. Beauclair has an older son. Did someone tell him?"

"We're taking care of notifying him," Cameron said.

Milagros sagged into the sofa. "I can't believe this has happened."

"Ms. Cortez," Cameron said, "if I may ask, when were you let go from your job?"

"Yesterday afternoon." She wiped away new tears. "Cleo… She said jewelry was missing from the box on her dresser, and since I was the only one who had access, it had to be me. I tried to tell her it wasn't me, but she wouldn't hear it. She said I was to take my things and get out immediately. I couldn't believe it. One minute we were chatting like we did every day, and the next she was so cold and heartless."

Cameron glanced at Jeannie, wondering if she found that as strange as he did. "And it wasn't like her to be that way with you?"

"Oh *no*. We were *friends*, or so I thought. Every day, when she and the kids came home from school, we'd have hot chocolate and cookies together, and the kids would tell us what they learned." She jumped up and went to her refrigerator, returning with handfuls of colorful drawings that she thrust at them, as if needing them to see how close she'd been to the family. "The children made these for me. I have their school pictures." She gestured to framed photos prominently displayed next to her television. "They are my *family*." Her eyes filled with new tears that slid down her cheeks.

"Ms. Cortez," Cameron said, deciding to level with her, "it's quite possible that Mrs. Beauclair saved your life by firing you."

She gasped. *"What?"*

"Did someone enter the house before you were let go?"

She thought about that for a moment, and then her eyes widened. "I went to the bathroom that's off the laundry room. I heard the doorbell, and the missus said she would get it." Her hands began to shake. "When she came back, she… Oh my God. There was someone else in the house, and she wanted me to go!" She broke down again. "She didn't fire me because I stole from her. That wasn't why."

"No, ma'am," Cameron said softly.

"What time did the doorbell ring?" Jeannie asked.

"It had to be around four thirty. The kids had gone upstairs to play."

"What time did Mr. Beauclair usually get home?"

"Seven or after, but he was due home early that night because it was their anniversary. They'd planned to go out to dinner, which is why I was doubly surprised when she accused me of stealing and told me to get out. I was supposed to stay with the kids while they went to dinner."

"Do you know where they had reservations?"

She mentioned a five-star restaurant in Georgetown that Cameron had heard of. He made a note of it, intending to call to see if they'd let the restaurant know they weren't coming.

"One other thing," he said. "Can you tell me if they had a security system in the house?"

"They did, and it was always on when they were asleep."

"And was it monitored off-site?"

"I don't know anything about it."

We need to figure that out, Cameron thought, making a note to follow up. To Jeannie, he said, "I'm going to call this in." He stood and went outside where he called the restaurant, asked to speak to the manager and confirmed that the Beauclairs had missed their reservation the night before and hadn't called to cancel.

"Were they regulars?" Cameron asked.

"At least twice a month," Martin, the manager, said.

"It was unusual for them to not call to cancel?"

"Very much so. They were always very courteous. Has something happened?"

"There was a fire at their home last night."

"Oh no! Are they all right?"

"I really can't say anything more at this time."

"We'll pray for them and their family."

"Thank you for your help."

"I wish it could've been more."

Cameron ended that call and placed one to Malone to update him on what the maid and restaurant manager had told him.

"This gives us a timeline to work with on when the invasion began," Malone said. "You don't like the fired maid for this?"

"Not one iota. She loved them and was heartbroken to be let go. When I told her Mrs. Beauclair probably saved her life by getting her out of there, she bawled her head off."

"Good work, Detective. Thanks for the update."

"It's the lieutenant's good work, and Detective Cruz's. They tracked down the maid. We just did the follow-up. Any word on Cruz's fiancée?"

"Sam called to say she's getting stitches but doing well."

"Glad to hear it. We'll be back soon. We need to figure out who monitored their home security."

"See you when you get here."

CHAPTER SIX

THE CLOCK HAD inched closer to three by the time Sam returned to HQ. She'd driven Freddie and Elin home and had promised to check on them later. Another day, another crisis. Such was her life. This one had thoroughly rattled her, especially coming days before their wedding. She'd tried to stay strong for Freddie, but her mind had gone in some rather disturbing directions in the time it took to track down Elin.

In the course of their work, they encountered all sorts of people who'd love to exact revenge on cops by going after their families. Thankfully, the Secret Service protected Nick and Scotty, but Freddie, Gonzo and the others had no such security trailing their loved ones. The thought of something happening to one of them because of the job was too unbearable to consider.

She had two minutes alone in her office to collect herself before Captain Malone appeared in the doorway.

"Knock, knock," he said.

"Hey."

"How is she?"

"Going to be fine, thank God."

"Hell of a thing to have happen the week of the wedding."

"I was just thinking the same thing," Sam said. "We were both so afraid someone had grabbed her."

"I was too."

"There're no shortage of scumbags who'd like to see us suffer."

"No, there aren't." He sat in her visitor chair and brought her up to speed on what Green and McBride had gotten from the maid and the restaurant manager.

"Cleo got her out of there, knowing there was going to be trouble. Whoever it was must've pulled a gun on her and had it on her while she was getting rid of the maid."

"No doubt, or she would've told the maid to send help. Green said the next step is figuring out what company monitored their home security."

"With the kind of money the Beauclairs obviously had there had to be top-notch security."

FBI Special Agent in Charge Avery Hill knocked on her open door. "Sorry for the interruption," he said in a honeyed South Carolinian accent.

"I wish I could say it's nice to see you, Agent Hill."

Avery smiled. He did that a lot lately. Since he and Shelby had worked out their differences and committed to each other, it was obvious to everyone who knew him that he seemed lighter and less burdened. "Always a pleasure, Lieutenant. But about the Beauclairs… They're ours."

"Excuse me?"

"They're under federal protection. Or they were. Have we confirmed the identities of the people found in the house?"

Surprised to hear about the Feds' involvement, Sam glanced at Malone, who shook his head. "Not yet," he said. "We're having trouble locating dental records."

Avery held up an envelope. "I have them."

Sam stared at him for a long moment. "Are you willing to share?"

"If you're willing to work together on this one. We need each other."

Sam didn't want his help, but she *did* want those dental records. "Define 'work together.'"

Avery gave her a withering look. "We undertake a cooperative partnership aimed at solving a case that involves us both."

"What does that mean?"

"I'm afraid I can't divulge that information—or hand over the dental records you need—until I'm certain we've entered into said cooperative partnership."

Sam sat in her chair and rolled her eyes to the ceiling. "This, right here, is why I hate Feds."

"And I thought we were *such* good friends," Avery said with the spark of humor that only added to his appeal.

And, yes, she found him attractive despite everything he'd put her through by being attracted *to her*. In another lifetime, she might've been interested. In this lifetime, she was happily married and interested in only one man. Thankfully, Avery seemed to have gotten his crush—or whatever you wanted to call it—under control for his sake, her sake and Shelby's. Calling him a good friend might be taking it too far. She'd learned to tolerate him, at best.

"Enough," Malone said. "We'll play nice with each other and figure out who killed these people. Hand over the dental records, and we'll tell you how they died. Then you can tell us why they were under federal protection and how you guys managed to let them get killed on your watch."

Avery winced. "Ouch." He handed the envelope to Sam. She picked up her phone and dialed Lindsey's extension. "I have dental records," she said when the ME answered. "Come and get 'em."

"On my way," Lindsey said.

"Conference room," Sam said to Hill. "You can tell us all at the same time."

Avery turned and left the office.

"Do I really gotta play nice with him, *again*?" Sam asked Malone.

"You really gotta."

"You're no fun."

"I know. That's my job. Someday, you'll be the captain, and it'll be your turn to be a gigantic bore."

"Really? You think I'll be the captain?"

"Only a matter of time, Lieutenant. Of course, I'll have to retire and get out of your way."

"Don't even think about it. I like everything exactly the way it is and have no desire to be the captain. At this time. Sir."

He snorted with laughter. "Don't worry. I'm not going anywhere for a while yet. For some sick reason, I'm still having fun here."

"Don't you dare leave me to fend for myself. I need constant adult supervision, as you know better than anyone."

"*That* is a fact."

Lindsey appeared in the doorway. "What's a fact?"

"That the lieutenant needs constant adult supervision."

Lindsey's lips quirked with the effort not to laugh.

"It's okay," Sam said. "You can laugh. I said it about myself."

Lindsey laughed—hard.

"You don't need to have fits over it," Sam muttered,

amused by her friend's reaction as she handed her the envelope with the dental records.

"Where'd this come from?"

"A little gift from our friends at the Federal Bureau of Investigation," Sam said.

"We have friends at the Federal Bureau of Investigation?" Lindsey asked, brows raised in surprise.

"Agent Hill brought them over along with the info that they were under federal protection."

"Uh-oh," Lindsey said.

"Exactly, and now I have to play nice with him and 'work together.' Ever since elementary school I've gotten marked down in the 'plays well with others' category."

"A problem that has dogged you well into adulthood," Malone said.

"What can I say?" Sam asked with a cheeky grin. "I'm apparently known for my consistency." To Lindsey, she said, "Let me know when we have positive IDs."

"Will do." Lindsey left to continue her examination of the bodies.

"Let's get this over with," Sam said, following Malone from her office to the conference room where Gonzo, Green and McBride waited with Hill.

"Close the door if you would, Lieutenant," Hill said.

Sam closed the door and leaned against it, sending him the signal that the floor was his. She took in the photos of the victims, alive and dead, that someone had posted to the murder board they would add to as the investigation unfolded.

Hill went to the computer station, plugged in a flash drive, clicked around on the keys and the screen lit up with what looked like a PowerPoint presentation.

Huh, Sam thought. *Didn't know we could do that.*

"What I'm about to tell you is extremely sensitive information and needs to be treated with the highest degree of discretion. None of this is for public dissemination." He clicked a handheld device that moved the presentation forward to a photo of a handsome man in his mid- to late-thirties.

"Jameson Beauclair, née Jameson Armstrong, chief executive officer of APG Group, a now-defunct technology company headquartered in Silicon Valley. They made software that was widely used in the warehousing, shipping and distribution sectors." Hill flipped through photos that showed the software program's packaging, as well as Armstrong with a group of others celebrating the company's initial public offering.

"Their IPO four years ago was a big hit, with more than five billion in revenue in the first six months. Armstrong and APG were on top of the world." The slides showed press coverage of the aftermath of the IPO when the company was widely referred to as Silicon Valley's newest darling.

Sam watched and listened and waited for the other shoe to fall.

"A year after the IPO, Armstrong began to suspect that Duke Piedmont, the P in APG, had committed insider trading offenses ahead of the IPO, sharing information with potential investors that drove up the price of the shares. Armstrong found himself in a tight spot. Going public with the information might destroy the company and the reputations of the partners. Remaining silent could lead to charges for all of them down the road if the truth came out. Look at this series of photos taken of Armstrong over a six-month period."

As Hill clicked through the photos, Sam watched

Armstrong age before her eyes. His dark hair turned gray. He went from all smiles to pinched, strained expressions, and his eyes…

"Stop there for a second." She moved closer to the screen for a better look at eyes that told the story of a tortured man. "Wow. The change in him is remarkable."

Hill clicked on the next slide. "This is Duke Piedmont," he said of the strapping blond man with a winning smile who'd stood next to Armstrong in the IPO celebration photo. "The two men were roommates at Stanford and founded the business together almost fifteen years ago. By all accounts, Armstrong was the technical genius and Piedmont the business guru. Dave Gorton, the third partner, comes from a solid background in warehouse science, inventory and distribution. For a while, theirs was a typical American dream story. They found a need, figured out a way to address it and made billions. And then one of them decided that wasn't enough." He flipped through a series of slides showing Piedmont in a variety of social settings, always at the center of a group wearing a big, jovial smile.

"We first began to look at Piedmont four years ago after a series of personal stock trades set off alarms within the SEC. Their investigators, working in concert with ours, convinced Armstrong to flip on his partner three years ago, which is when Piedmont took off."

"Any idea where Piedmont went?" Green asked.

Hill shook his head. "He's considered a fugitive. During the time Armstrong went from this," Hill said, clicking on the happy, smiling photo of Armstrong, "to this." He clicked on the gray-haired version of the same man. "He conducted a complete internal investigation that yielded far more than insider trading concerns. Piedmont had gotten involved with organized crime, was up to his eyeballs in a number of different rackets and was suspected of at least two murders, both people who'd gotten in the way of his schemes. When Piedmont learned that Armstrong had turned on him, he sent an email to Jameson from an untraceable account that put him on notice that he'd get even if it was the last thing he ever did. And that Jameson—and his family—should be very, very afraid. That's when it was decided that the Armstrong family had to go into some sort of protective custody far away from Silicon Valley."

"I'll never understand how someone makes billions of dollars and isn't satisfied," Jeannie said.

"I was just thinking the same thing," Green said. "What does it take to be happy?"

"Armstrong handed Piedmont to us on the proverbial silver platter," Hill continued. "He spent months sifting and digging through company records and servers, working twelve, fourteen, sometimes sixteen hours a day until he had what he felt was the complete picture of Piedmont's activities in the years since APG was founded. It was one hell of a dossier."

"Could we see it?" Sam asked.

"I'm telling you everything I can."

"I thought this was a *collaborative partnership*?" Sam asked. "I see how this is gonna go."

"I got you the dental records you needed, didn't I?"

"Is this all you're going give us? The rest is on us?"

"I'm giving you the deep background on why Armstrong was under protection. That's info you didn't have an hour ago."

"When you say he was under protection," Jeannie said, "does that mean witness protection?"

"Not technically," Hill said. "That would've been our preference, but Armstrong refused to give up everything he'd worked so hard for because his partner had turned into a lying, cheating scumbag. In cooperation with the SEC and the FBI, Armstrong and Gorton dissolved the corporation and sold off the stock at bargain basement prices. Their investors took a loss, but that's the risk you take when you play the game with the market. The only one we were after on criminal charges was Piedmont.

"Armstrong's personal assets weren't impacted by the investigation, so he was able to afford to live under an assumed name in a five-million-dollar house in Chevy Chase, send his kids to an elite private school and keep his life and the lives of his wife and children very similar to what they were in California."

"Did people from his life there know where they were?" Green asked.

Sam noticed that Gonzo was studying the screen but didn't seem engaged in the conversation.

"We believe their family members did," Hill said, "but no one else. They quietly left town after APG shut down operations."

"That would explain why the Beauclairs have no social media presence," Jeannie said.

"Right," Hill replied. "They were instructed on the importance of keeping a low profile until we're able to apprehend Piedmont."

"Where does that part of the investigation stand?" Malone asked.

"I wish I could say we're close, but we're not. He literally disappeared into thin air, which leads us to suspect he either had help or he'd been planning to make a run for some time. He has the resources to stay deep underground for the rest of his life."

"What kind of security did the Beauclairs have after they were under your protection?" Green asked.

"They had a fairly sophisticated home security system that included panic buttons they both wore around their necks. We believe that the perpetrator recognized the medallions as panic buttons and removed them from their persons. I checked with the monitoring company and learned that the system had been deactivated yesterday morning, per usual, and was never reactivated last night. The couple had declined active surveillance within their home, and because the system wasn't activated during the day yesterday, there's no footage from the time period in question."

"Is there any chance at all that the murders and the fire aren't related to Piedmont and what happened to the company?" Cam asked.

"Highly doubtful," Hill said.

"So the FBI's theory is that Piedmont took them out?" Malone asked.

Hill nodded. "Or he got someone to do it for him, so Armstrong won't be able to testify against him in the trial that was going forward without the defendant."

"Wouldn't that put the other partner, Gorton, at risk too?" Sam asked.

"We have him in protective custody as of this morning, but he wasn't the linchpin in our case against Piedmont. Armstrong was. Without him, our insider trading case isn't as strong, but we still have enough to go after him on other charges."

"The thing I don't get is why go to the trouble to relocate your family and change your name if you're not

going to take it all the way to full witness protection?"
Jeannie asked.

"After speaking with agents involved in Armstrong's
case, I learned that his wife resisted full witness protection. She couldn't handle being permanently separated
from her parents and sisters."

"Even if it meant staying alive?" Sam asked.

"Apparently."

"How would Piedmont or anyone know where to find
them?" Gonzo asked. "He had a new name, new city, new
address. I assume they were given new Social Security
numbers, passports, licenses, etc. It's not like their family members would tell the guy who caused this where
to find them. So how would he find them?"

"We believe Piedmont would've been able to track
Armstrong through his business contacts," Hill said.
"Armstrong continued to be involved with the software
he'd founded while living here as Jameson Beauclair."

Sam's phone rang, and she took the call from the fire
marshal. "Holland."

"We found the Beauclair kids," he said. "Alive."

CHAPTER SEVEN

SAM CALLED Special Victims Detective Erica Lucas and asked her to assist with the Beauclair children and to take the DNA sample from them that the Crime Scene investigators would need for the process of eliminating family member DNA from the crime scene. Lindsey could also use the children's DNA to help complete the identification of their parents.

"I'll meet you at the hospital," Erica said.

The fire marshal had told Sam that the children, who'd been found together asleep behind clothing in an upstairs closet, appeared to be in good condition, but would be transported to the hospital to be checked before they were released to social services. Apparently, they'd been found on a second sweep of the house.

"What's being done about notifying the older son, Elijah, who's in college at Princeton?" Sam asked Hill.

"We haven't gotten that far yet."

"That needs to be done."

"Let me check with our people on how best to handle that."

"What do we do about the kids?" Sam consulted her notes. "Alden and Aubrey. Do they have family who will want to take them in?"

"Let me track down the older son and find out the deal with the extended family."

"Be quick about it. These kids will be traumatized, and they'll need their family—if they even remember their extended family."

"I'm on it."

"Keep us in the loop on anything else regarding this case."

"You do the same, Lieutenant."

Sam turned away from him and walked into the pit. "Gonzo, you're with me. McBride and Green, get me everything you can find on APG, Jameson Armstrong, the Armstrong family, Piedmont, Gorton, the IPO, all of it."

"On it," McBride said. "Lieutenant, would it be okay to notify the maid, Milagros, that the children were found? She seemed very genuine in her affection for them."

"Yes, please go ahead and do that." Sam led the way to the morgue exit, glancing over her shoulder to make sure Gonzo was with her. He had his hands jammed into the pockets of his jeans and his head down as he walked behind her.

"First things first," she said, ducking into the morgue to check in with Lindsey. "What've you got for me, Doc?"

"I'm not sure yet. Still working, but the dental records on the male victim aren't a slam dunk. He has some teeth missing."

Sam winced at the thought of the guy losing teeth during the attack. "Can you tell if that was a recent development?"

"I'm working on it."

"All right. We'll get out of your hair. Call me when you have more."

Lindsey never looked up from her examination of the victims. "You'll be the first to know."

"Ugh," Gonzo said, taking deep breaths of fresh air when they were outside. "Fire victims are the worst."

"Yep. That was my third visit with them."

"Sorry I was late earlier. Won't happen again."

"What happened, exactly?" she asked when they were in her car and heading for GW.

"Didn't Cruz tell you I was in an accident? I pulled out of a parking space and sideswiped a car that was in my blind spot. Took Patrol forever to respond."

"They never showed up when we called them to Cruz's place."

"That's fucked-up. Good thing it wasn't a bigger deal."

"Agreed. I mentioned it to Malone." She glanced over at him. "Everything all right with you?"

"Why do you ask?"

"You seem a little…off…lately."

"Because I was late once I'm *off*?"

"It's not just today, and I talked to Christina—"

"When did you talk to her?"

"When I called to find out where you were this morning."

"What'd she say?"

"Nothing, but I got the sense that she thinks something is up too."

"She needs to mind her own business and stay the fuck out of my job."

Stunned, Sam glanced at him and quickly brought her gaze back to the road. If they'd been anywhere but in the car, she would've been tempted to stare at him. Was this the same Tommy Gonzales who'd fallen so hard and so fast for Nick's colleague almost two years ago? After he learned he had a son he hadn't known about, she'd stood by him—when their relationship was still brand-new.

She'd left her job to help care for his son and had again stood by them both when the baby's mother was murdered, when Gonzo had been briefly considered a suspect in that murder and when his partner was gunned down.

Christina hadn't always been Sam's favorite person, but she certainly deserved better than him thinking she needed to mind her own business and stay out of his job. Sam made a mental note to get a copy of Gonzo's accident report.

"It's nine months today," Sam said.

"What is?"

"Since Arnold."

Sam felt as much as saw Gonzo's entire body go rigid, as if he'd been struck, proof that the topic was still a raw wound for him. Of course, it was. If, God forbid, the same thing happened to her, she'd never get over losing Cruz the way he'd lost Arnold. She couldn't even bear to consider the possibility. She'd probably have to leave the job and find something else to do while she wallowed in her grief.

"I know it's hard," she said softly.

"You don't know dick."

"Excuse me?" she said, biting back the angry retort in which she would remind him who she was to him, not that he should need reminding.

"You heard me. Don't give me platitudes, Sam. They don't help. And don't pretend to know what it's like, because you can't possibly know."

Wow. This was a whole new side to someone she thought she knew as well as anyone. She'd wanted to talk to him about covering for her while she was away, but now she wondered if she should go at all. At the hospital, she pulled into a parking space and got out of the car. When she heard the passenger door close, she clicked the lock button on her key fob.

"Sam."

"What?"

"I'm sorry. I shouldn't have said that."

"No, you shouldn't have."

"I said I was sorry."

Sam stopped walking and turned to face off with him. "What's going on with you?"

"What do you mean?"

"You're not yourself. People are noticing. You're late for work—"

"*Once!* I was late *once in twelve years*! Are you really going to make an issue of that?"

"Yeah, I am, because it's not like you to fail to show up when you're called to a homicide. That's not who you are."

"And you're an expert on who I am?"

Again, Sam stared at him in disbelief. "I'm your friend, Gonzo. I know you. And this *hostility*... It's not you."

"Maybe it's the new me. Did you ever stop to consider that?"

"If it is, I don't like the new you, and from the brief interaction I had with your fiancée this morning, she doesn't like him either."

His eyes narrowed with fury he didn't try to hide. "You have no right to stick your nose into my relationship. You're my boss, not my mother."

"Maybe you ought to go home until you can get your head out of your ass or wherever it currently is."

"Pulling rank on me now, *friend*?"

"Yeah, I am. I've got two traumatized kids on my

hands who might've seen their parents murdered. I don't need this shit on top of that. Go home, Sergeant. Come back when you're in a better state of mind and ready to work."

"Fuck this shit," he said as he turned and walked away from her.

What. The. Fuck. Stunned that things with him had come to such an ugly head, Sam watched him go. Her phone rang, and she took the call from Nick.

"Hey," she said, walking toward the emergency entrance.

"Hey, babe. How's it going?"

She paused for a second, closing her eyes and wallowing in the comforting sound of his voice. "I've had better days." She told him what'd happened to Elin. "And I just had a big fight with Gonzo."

"Really? Over what? And is Elin okay?"

"Yeah, she's fine, but it might be a year or two before Freddie's nerves return to normal. And Gonzo. I don't know what's up with him, but it's nothing good. I just sent him home."

"Yikes, that must've been some fight."

"He said some things... I don't know."

"Sometimes it's not easy being the boss when your subordinates are your friends."

"Yeah. That."

"Are you going to be home late?"

"I've got one thing to do, and then I'll be home." She'd had enough of this day.

"Shelby made spaghetti. We'll wait for you."

"Don't wait if you guys are starving."

"We'll wait."

"Did you talk to Scotty about what was up earlier?"

"A little. I got the feeling that school is overwhelming him at the moment, so we're going over everything he's got to do before dinner."

"I hope that's all it is."

"I'm on it. See you soon. Love you."

"Love you too." She loved him so damned much and knowing he was waiting for her at home with their son made what she had to do next bearable.

GONZO KEPT HIS head down as he walked away from Sam, fuming over the altercation with someone who ought to understand far better than she did. Arnold had been one of *hers*. One of *theirs*. You didn't just move on from something like that as if it had never happened. That's how it seemed to him—that everyone had forgotten and moved on. Even Arnold's cubicle was occupied by someone else now, as if he'd never been there.

Green was a good enough guy, a great detective and a decent partner. His only "crime," if you wanted to call it that, was taking Arnold's place when Arnold was irreplaceable. That someone else could occupy the space in Gonzo's life that had belonged to his young, earnest, funny, often-irritating partner, defied comprehension.

And Sam, *of all people*, ought to get that. But she was just like everyone else who thought they got it when they didn't. They didn't get it at all. His colleagues didn't get it, Christina didn't get it. No one did.

Unzipping the inner pocket of his jacket, Gonzo fished out another pill and popped it into his mouth, swallowing it without water, and then jolting when it got stuck in his throat. He swallowed frantically, until it finally dislodged and dropped into his stomach, but the disgusting medicinal taste in his mouth remained.

He walked aimlessly, heading eventually for the closest Metro stop, intending to go home to his son, the one person who didn't want anything he didn't have to give lately. On the way, he popped into a convenience store to buy a bottle of water and drank the whole thing. Then he found a bench to sit on while he waited for the pill to kick in.

His phone rang, and he fished it out of his pocket to glance at the caller ID. Christina. Gonzo declined the call. He didn't want to talk to her. He didn't want to talk to anyone. What good did talking do? Trulo, the department shrink, had put him through hours of pointless *talking* after Arnold was killed, forcing him to attend regular sessions for months to keep his job.

He'd gone through the motions, given them what they wanted, simply because he needed the money, not because he gave a flying fuck.

The phone rang with another call from Christina. What the fuck? Didn't she know he was working? But then he thought of Alex and took the call.

"Tommy." She sounded frantic.

"What?"

"Alex has a hundred-and-four-degree fever! I'm taking him to the E.R."

His chest contracted with fear. "Where?"

"GW."

"I'm near there. I'll meet you."

"Tommy…"

She wanted him to reassure her that everything would be fine, but he couldn't do that. He'd learned that wasn't true. Sometimes it wasn't fine. But his little boy… He had to be fine. "I'll meet you there," he said again, because that was all he had.

"Okay," she said, her voice wavering before the line went dead.

Legs pumping, lungs working overtime, he ran as fast as he could.

He hoped he wouldn't run into Sam in the hospital. He didn't want to see her. Not now. She was probably pissed anyway, and with good reason. But what did he care? Let her be pissed. What was she going to do? Fire him? Right. She needed him. Everyone needed him, wanted a piece of him, expected things from him when his well was empty. He had nothing to give them. Couldn't they see that? What the fuck did they want with someone who had nothing to give?

Even his parents and sisters had been relentless lately, calling him all the time, asking how he was. How did they *think* he was? They asked if he was feeling better. Was he supposed to feel *better*? What did feeling better entail? Not thinking about Arnold every minute of every day? Not hearing the desperate, horrifying gurgling sound of him choking on his own blood as the life seeped out of him? That sound was on a never-ending loop in Gonzo's brain, torturing him with the reminder of how fast it had happened. The poor guy hadn't stood a chance. He was nearly dead before he hit the ground.

And it *should've* been *him*. Any other time, it would've been *him*. He always took the lead. *Always*. Arnold was just a kid, still learning the ropes. He wasn't ready to take the lead. Gonzo relived those last hours they'd spent together every day—sitting in the freezing cold car, waiting for their guy, Arnold bitching nonstop about the cold, the late hour, his empty stomach. Until Gonzo had made him a deal—shut the fuck up and I'll let you take the lead when he comes.

Arnold's eyes had lit up with the kind of glee you might expect from a kid being given a surprise trip to their favorite theme park. They'd walked through the steps, practiced it until he was ready—or as ready as anyone ever was to confront a suspect who'd already shown his disregard for the law.

And then it had all gone so horribly, horribly wrong.

Gonzo's chest began to hurt, badly enough that he stopped running and sucked in greedy deep breaths. Tears rolled down his cheeks, and he angrily used the sleeve of his jacket to wipe them away. Fucking tears. They sneaked up on him at the worst times, like in the middle of a shift with his colleagues all around him. Like when he walked into the pit and had to once again absorb the blow of Cameron Green sitting where Arnold should be, where he *would* be if only Gonzo hadn't been so easily annoyed and so desperate to *shut him up* that he'd let his partner walk into an ambush.

He'd certainly gotten what he'd wanted. He'd succeeded in shutting him up. Forever. A sob choked him, and tears blinded him. He fell to his knees in the grass of a park he'd never noticed before. He had no idea where he was, but what did it even matter? "Goddamn you, Arnold. How could you do this to me?" In a soft whisper, he said, "How could you leave me like this? What am I supposed to do now?"

All he could see when he closed his eyes was Arnold's big goofy smile and his childlike wonder at getting to do the only job he'd ever wanted. From the time he was the littlest kid, his mother had told Gonzo, A.J. had wanted to catch the bad guys.

Overwhelmed by grief, Gonzo dropped his head and

prayed for the sweet relief that should be coming any minute now. If he stayed perfectly still, the relief could find him that much faster.

CHAPTER EIGHT

CHRISTINA WAITED WITH Alex in a room full of sick people that only further shredded her already-frayed nerves. She had signed the consent form and listed herself as the child's mother. Let anyone try to question her. She'd probably rip their heads off.

Where the hell was Tommy, and why was he not answering his phone? Christina called Sam, who answered on the second ring.

"Hey, what's up?"

"I'm so sorry to bother you, but is Tommy with you?"

"No, he is definitely *not* with me."

"I'm not sure what that means."

"You're right—something is up with him, and if he doesn't get his shit together—and soon—I may not be able to protect him at work."

"Wh-what happened?"

"We had *words*."

Christina reeled at the thought of him getting mouthy with his superior officer, even if she was his good friend. "What did he say?"

"It doesn't matter. It's part of an ongoing issue that's going to have to be addressed—and soon."

Christina experienced another jolt of panic at the thought of him losing the job he had once loved almost as much as he had once loved her. That couldn't happen.

What would happen to him? To them? "Alex is in the E.R. with a high fever. He said he was nearby and coming but that was a while ago."

"Damn it," Sam said. "I'll have Patrol find him and get him there."

"Thank you." She paused, took a deep breath and said, "When you get a minute, I think we're long overdue for a conversation about what to do."

"I agree. I can't do it right now, but soon. I'm at the hospital too. I'll check on you guys before I leave."

"Thank you, Sam."

"No problem."

Christina ended the call and then checked to see if she had any new texts from Tommy. Nothing.

"Mama," Alex said.

"I'm here, baby." She held him close as heat radiated from his little body. One thing was becoming increasingly clear to her—if she left Tommy, she would take Alex with her. She again wondered if he'd even notice they were gone.

SAM MADE THE call to Patrol to get them looking for Sergeant Gonzales in the neighborhoods surrounding GW and then greeted Detective Erica Lucas. "Thanks for coming," Sam said, shaking her hand.

"Anything for you, Lieutenant. What've we got?"

"A fire in Chevy Chase. Two adult DOA found burned with their hands and feet bound. We're awaiting positive ID that they're the kids' parents. The fire marshal tells me the kids were found together in an upstairs closet. Not sure if they saw or heard anything, but we need to find out."

"Ugh, sometimes I hate this job," Erica said bluntly.

"Right there with you."

"What do they know about the parents?"

"I assume nothing yet, and we say nothing until we know for sure."

"Got it. While I was waiting for you, I cleared the way with the triage nurse. Let's get this over with." Erica nodded to the nurse, who gestured for them to follow her.

"We need the DNA sample right away," Sam said.

"I'm on it."

People in the waiting room recognized Sam and began to buzz as she walked through with Erica. Sam avoided eye contact, not in the mood to be waylaid by people wanting selfies or autographs or other things that would interfere with the job she was there to do. At times like this, having a Secret Service detail would come in handy, but it was the rest of the time, when she didn't need their help, that kept her from agreeing to it. The thought of being tailed through her days on the job made her twitchy.

"Big wedding for you guys this week, huh?" Erica asked.

"Yep."

"And you're his best man?"

"Best man-woman. Get it right."

Erica laughed. "My apologies. He's adorable. I'm so happy for him."

"Yes, he is, and so am I. Don't ever tell him I said he's adorable. That'll make him even more unmanageable than he already is."

"I won't breathe a word."

The nurse stopped outside a cubicle where two little blond heads huddled together under a blanket.

Sam couldn't look away. They were so tiny and alone and frightened. She wanted to scoop them up, take them out of there and make sure they were never afraid or hurt again. She'd never experienced anything quite like the immediate reaction she had to seeing their faces for the first time.

"Please wait here for the doctor caring for the children," the nurse said, as Sam continued to stare at them. "He'll be right with you."

"Thank you." Erica leaned against the wall and glanced at Sam. "You still have a spot to fill in Homicide?" Sam had offered the spot vacated by Will Tyrone to Erica, but she'd chosen to remain in Special Victims.

"Yep." Sam finally tore her gaze away from the kids and blinked to focus on Erica. "Are you reconsidering my offer?"

"I might be. Things in SVU have been stressful lately."

"How so?"

"One word—Ramsey."

Sam cringed. She hated the son of a bitch SVU sergeant who'd said she'd gotten what she deserved when Lieutenant Stahl took her hostage and tortured her. "What about him?"

"Ever since the U.S. Attorney decided not to charge you for assaulting him, he's been even more out of control than he was before. If I had to vote someone most likely to start shooting up the workplace, Ramsey would win. Hands down."

Sam straightened out of the slouch she'd been in as she too leaned against the wall. "Why do you say that?"

"He's so angry. *All the time.* Ranting about you and the unfairness of you getting away with assaulting him and how you sucked your way to the top and how women have no place in the department and—"

"*He actually said that? Out loud?*"

"Yep."

"Who else heard it?"

"Our entire squad, except for Davidson," she said, referring to their lieutenant, "was there for the latest diatribe on Friday."

"You need to report that, Erica."

"I know," she said, sighing. "I've been thinking about it all weekend. It's just so exhausting dealing with jackasses on the job."

"Believe me, I know."

"I'll talk to Malone in the morning."

"You didn't ask for my advice, but I'd call him tonight. Sooner is better for something like this."

Erica nodded. "I hear you, and I'll do it tonight."

Dr. Anderson, the E.R. doctor Sam knew far too well, approached them. "Lieutenant, I'd say it's good to see you, but…" He glanced at the children with sympathy.

"How are they?" Sam asked.

Lowering his voice, he said, "Physically unharmed, but very quiet. We conducted physical examinations on both, and neither said a word, even in response to questions. The hospital's social worker has been called in."

"We need DNA samples," Sam said. "Can you help us with that?"

"Yes, no problem."

"What's been lined up for them until we figure out the family situation?" Erica asked.

"Nothing yet," Anderson said. "We were waiting for you to arrive with plans to go from there."

"I'll take them," Sam said without hesitation.

The other two looked at her as if she'd lost her mind. Maybe she had.

"Nick and I jumped through the foster parent hoops when we first had Scotty. We're licensed."

"Sam," Erica said. "You don't have to do that."

"I know I don't have to, but they need a place to sleep tonight. I can give them that with the best security in the world around them." The more she thought about it, the more it made sense. To her anyway. She'd worry about what the Secret Service had to say about it when she got home. What were they going to do? Toss two kids who'd most likely been orphaned out on the street? They wouldn't do that. Would they?

"If you're certain, I can bring in our staff social worker and go from there," Anderson said.

"I'm certain," Sam said, even as a little voice inside her said she probably ought to at least check with Nick before she agreed to such a thing. But it was one night. She knew him well enough to be sure he wouldn't object to hosting two kids in need for one night.

"Before we go in," Sam said, "I need to notify their school that they were found alive. Give me one second."

"Come in when you're ready," Anderson said. "I'll take care of the DNA."

Sam withdrew the business card Mrs. Reeve had given her and put through the call. "This is Lieutenant Holland, MPD."

"Yes, hello. How can I help you?"

"I wanted to let you know that Alden and Aubrey Beauclair were found alive in their home."

"Oh thank goodness. That's such good news."

"They're understandably traumatized."

"Of course. If there's anything we can do, you need only to ask."

"Will do. Thanks again." Sam closed the phone and turned back to Erica. "Okay, let's do this."

Sam and Erica went into the cubicle where the children sat on the same bed. Their big blue eyes warily took in the room full of strangers. Sam's heart went out to them and made her wish for a magic wand that she could wave to undo this horrible event.

Dr. Anderson handed Sam the DNA swabs wrapped for transport.

"Hi, Alden and Aubrey," Erica said gently. "My name is Erica. This is my friend Sam, and we're here to help you."

"Hi there," Sam said.

Erica sat on the edge of the mattress and talked to the children about their school, the stuffed bear that Aubrey hugged to her chest, the mermaid on her top and the football logo on Alden's shirt—anything she could think of to find a connection and hopefully a breakthrough.

She kept at it for twenty minutes until Aubrey finally giggled at something silly that Erica had said.

Alden seemed to take his lead from his sister and became more animated after her giggle gave him permission.

Sam had to give major props to Erica. She had handled them beautifully and delicately and with consummate skill.

Erica tried to bring them around to talking about what they might've seen or heard in their home the night before, but they immediately retreated from that topic, so she didn't push.

"Where's Mommy?" Aubrey asked in a tiny voice.

"She can't be here right now," Sam said.

They couldn't broach that topic until their parents were

positively identified. When the staff social worker arrived, Dr. Anderson took her outside the cubical to consult with her.

"I want Mommy," Aubrey said, her eyes shiny with tears as she plopped her thumb into her mouth.

Sam wanted to cry right along with her.

"I know, honey," Erica said, glancing at Sam.

"So, guys," Sam said, "I was wondering if maybe you could have a sleepover at my house. We can have ice cream and watch any movie you want. What do you think?"

Aubrey shook her head. "Mommy said not to talk to strangers."

"Mommy is very smart, and she's right, you shouldn't talk to strangers." Sam removed her badge from her pocket and opened it to show the children.

Alden reached for the badge.

Sam let him hold it and touch it and fully examine it.

"I'm a police officer, and my job is to keep you and everyone else in the city safe. You would be very safe with me and my family, and I promise we'd take very good care of you, right, Erica?"

"Oh yes," Erica said. "Do you know who Lieutenant Sam's husband is?"

Aubrey shook her head.

"He's the vice president of the whole United States. How much fun would it be to meet him?"

Aubrey removed her thumb. "Do you live in the White House?"

"Nope," Sam said. "That's the president's house. My husband is the vice president, but we have a nice house where you'll be very comfortable and safe."

Aubrey glanced at Alden, who only shrugged. Apparently, she was the decision-maker for the two of them.

"You're sure Mommy can't come tonight?" Aubrey asked, her chin quivering.

"Yes, honey," Sam said. "I'm sure."

After a long pause, Aubrey said, "Okay. We can go with you."

Sam released the deep breath she'd held as she waited for Aubrey to decide. "Let me talk to Dr. Anderson and see if it's okay for us to leave. I'll be right back, but Erica will be here with you." Sam stepped out of the room to consult with Anderson and the social worker, who wore a name tag identifying her as Mrs. Wallace.

Dr. Anderson introduced the two women.

"It's a pleasure to meet you." Mrs. Wallace shook Sam's hand. "I'm a big fan of yours and your husband's."

"Thank you. My husband and I are licensed foster parents, and I'd like to take the Beauclair children for the night until more permanent accommodations can be arranged. In addition to myself and my husband, we have a full-time child care provider, who is also licensed to care for the children in our absence as was required by the court when we were in the process of adopting our son."

Mrs. Wallace listened intently.

"Not to mention, we're surrounded by the finest security money can buy in the form of the Secret Service. The children will be safe with us."

"I would need to verify your licensed status, as a mere formality," Mrs. Wallace said.

"Of course. If you give me an email address, I will have my husband send it over."

Mrs. Wallace handed over her card. "I'll watch for the email from the vice president."

The way she said that had Sam wondering if the woman would frame the email. She wouldn't put it past her. People were so weird. "Let me know when I'm cleared to take the children. They've been through enough in the last twenty-four hours. They don't need to be here any longer than necessary."

"Understood," Mrs. Wallace said.

Sam walked away from them, opened her phone and called Nick.

"Hey, babe. Are you almost home?"

"Almost, but I have a slight wrinkle."

"What's that?"

Sam told him about the Beauclair children, what she'd offered to do for them and what she needed from him. "I hope it's okay. They're so little, and their parents are most likely dead and—"

"Of course it's okay. Give me the email address for the social worker, and I'll send her a copy of our license."

"Thank you." Sam closed her eyes and gave silent thanks for the best husband ever. No matter what she threw at him, he rolled with her. She tried to do the same for him, which was how she'd ended up married to the vice president of the United States. "We'll be there soon."

"I'll make beds for them."

"Just do one. I think they'd prefer to be together."

"Got it."

"Thank you for this, Nick."

"It's no problem. We certainly have plenty of room for two little ones who need a place to stay for a while."

"We'll be there soon."

"We'll be waiting for you."

When Sam returned to the cubicle, Dr. Anderson was outside, typing notes on a laptop that sat on a computer station on wheels. "All set," she told him. "He's emailing a copy of the license to Mrs. Wallace."

"She'll be delighted to get an email from him," Anderson said with a snarky grin.

"I got that feeling as well. I wondered if she might frame it."

His bark of laughter made her smile. "You surprise me, Lieutenant."

"Why's that?"

"With everything you've already got going on in your life, I wouldn't think you'd have time for foster children."

"I don't, but I'll make time."

"It's a good thing you and your husband are doing. If you're not careful, you'll get a reputation for being a softy."

"Shut your mouth. If that gets out, I'll know exactly where it came from."

"Don't worry," he said gravely even as his eyes twinkled with mirth. "Your secret is safe with me."

CHAPTER NINE

Dr. ANDERSON GLANCED at the children and lowered his voice. "What do you know about the parents?"

"Not much yet." Even though she trusted the doctor after knowing him for quite some time, she couldn't share the privileged information Avery had given them.

"I feel for them. Life as they know it is over."

"Yeah, and the sad part is, at only five, they'll remember very little about the people who loved them best," Sam said.

"Heartbreaking."

Sam's phone rang with a call from Hill. "What's up?"

"Hey, I tracked down a number for Beauclair's son Elijah."

Sam's heart fell at the thought of having to make that call. "Hang on a second." She retrieved the notebook from her back pocket and wrote down the number. "Got it."

"I can make that call if you want."

"I'd like to do it, so I can ask him a few questions."

"All right. Any word on the identity of the victims?"

"Not yet. Lindsey said some things weren't matching up with the dental records, and she needed to do further examination. It's possible they lost some teeth in whatever took place before the fire."

"Jesus," he said.

"That about sums it up."

"We should've gone into something boring like banking."

Sam laughed. "I think that every day of my life, but the boredom would've killed us."

"Probably, but we wouldn't have to call a kid in college and tell him his father and stepmother are possibly dead, and his little brother and sister orphaned."

"True. So, um, I'm taking the little brother and sister home with me tonight."

"Seriously?"

"Yeah, they needed a place, and we're licensed foster parents from when we first had Scotty."

"Wow. It's good of you to do that, Sam."

"With the Secret Service making a fortress out of our house, I figured they'd be safer with me than anywhere else we could put them tonight."

"That's certainly true, although the Secret Service should be briefed on the background with the parents."

"I was afraid you were going to say that," Sam said with a sigh, imagining what Nick's lead agent, John Brantley Junior, would have to say about her bringing the children of people who'd been tortured and burned in their home into her house. "With your permission, I'll take care of briefing them on what you told us."

"Permission granted."

"What does Elijah know about the father and his business dealings?"

"He knows everything. He had to change his name while he was in high school, so there was no hiding it from him."

"Good to know. I was thinking after your briefing earlier that if I were going to be on the run from someone who wanted me dead, I'm not sure I'd buy a mansion in Chevy Chase to 'hide' out in."

"From what I'm told, they were advised to consider living more modestly to draw less attention to themselves. However, he was still a billionaire, and apparently they have their needs."

"Did those needs get him and his wife killed?"

"That's what we have to find out."

"I'll be back on that tomorrow. For now, I need to get these kids home and settled."

"I'll check in tomorrow."

"Sounds good. Talk to you then." Sam closed the phone and returned to the exam room where Erica was continuing to entertain the children, currently with a game of tic-tac-toe that Aubrey was winning. Alden watched but didn't participate.

Mrs. Wallace returned a few minutes later, beaming. "I received the email from the vice president, and everything is in order."

Sam wondered if everyone the woman knew had already heard about her email from the vice president, which had her questioning the children's safety. "It's vitally important that you not tell *anyone* where these children are," Sam told her.

"I understand. I would never breathe a word of it."

"Thank you." To Erica, Sam said, "I need five minutes to check on Gonzo's son, who was brought in earlier. I'll be right back, okay?"

"Take your time. I'll be here."

Sam told the kids she'd be back in a minute and went to check on Alex, who was asleep in Christina's arms. "How is he?"

"They've got him on an IV and want us to stay until the fever breaks. They're trying to figure out what caused it."

"No Gonzo?"

"No," she said tightly.

Sam made a call to Dispatch. "I asked Patrol to look for Sergeant Gonzales. Any luck locating him?"

"Nothing yet, Lieutenant. We're continuing to look."

"Keep me posted." To Christina she said, "They're still looking."

"Do me a favor. When you find him, keep him far, *far* away from me."

"Christina—"

"No, Sam. I'm done. I'll do what I can to get him the help he clearly needs, but I am *done* with this nonsense. I put my life on hold for him and for Alex, and he can't even get himself to the E.R. when his son is sick? I am *done*."

Sam's heart sank at the finality of the words as she wondered if Gonzo would survive losing Christina on top of losing Arnold. "I understand," she said, sighing. "I'll check in with you in the morning to see how Alex is. If you need anything overnight, please call me."

"I will. Thank you."

Sam left them and thought about Gonzo as she followed the corridor back to where she'd left Erica and the Beauclair children. He was making such a mess of his life, and he didn't seem to care. That was so unlike who he'd been before they lost Arnold. In the last nine months, he'd become someone she barely recognized.

No way could she leave him in charge of the squad for three weeks. He wasn't up to the task in his current condition. Which meant Nick would have to go alone.

The thought of *three weeks* without Nick made her want to curl up in a ball and hide, and yes, that made her feel like the worst kind of simpering, lovesick female. But whatever. She loved him. She relied on him. She *needed* him, and three weeks without him would make her crazy.

Returning to the room where Erica waited with the children, Sam said, "We're ready to go now." She reached out to them and after a brief hesitation, Aubrey took her hand and reached back for her brother.

"Come on, Alden," Aubrey said.

Sam helped them down from the bed. To Erica, Sam said, "Give me some backup for the ride home, will you?" She was concerned about whomever had torched the parents watching what became of the kids. Sam gave the DNA swabs to Erica. "And then get these to Lindsey."

"You got it."

With Erica right behind them, Sam led the children through the emergency department waiting room to the exit, feeling the eyes of everyone they passed on her. Thankfully, no one got the big idea to stop her.

She loaded the kids into the back seat of her car and helped them with seat belts since there'd been no time to get booster seats. When she got home, she would call Shelby to let her know what was going on. Sam had no doubt that Shelby would be willing to do whatever she could for the kids. She had the softest heart of anyone Sam knew, and she loved kids.

The children were quiet on the ride home, which gave Sam time to think—and ponder why she'd felt the need to step up for two kids she didn't know. Anyone would be moved by their plight, but she hadn't hesitated to offer to take them, and that had her wondering about the deeper meaning of her gesture.

The issue of babies and children was fraught with peril for her, challenged as she was by persistent fertility problems. A few months ago, she'd decided to try fertility treatment again, but hadn't gotten around to making an appointment—probably because she knew what it entailed and the thought of it gave her the worst anxiety she'd ever had. Making the appointment was on her to-do list, something that nagged at her because it needed to be done, but she couldn't bring herself to pull the trigger.

Needles and tests and poking and prodding and hormones. The last time she'd undergone the treatment, when she was still married to Peter, had been one of the worst things she'd ever been through. Even the thought of having a baby with Nick couldn't get her over the hurdle that stood between her and the opportunity treatment offered.

A recent pregnancy "scare," if you could call it that, had resurrected a lot of emotions tied to carrying and delivering a child of her own, and she was still dealing with that disappointment.

Sam's phone rang, giving her a welcome reprieve from the direction her thoughts had taken. She took the call from Freddie. "Hey, what's up?"

"That's what I wanted to know. What'd I miss after I punched out today?"

"I'll tell you all about it if you tell me how Elin is."

"She was in a lot of pain from the wound, but she took a pain pill that knocked her out."

"And what about you? Have your nerves settled yet?"

"I'm having a big glass of the bourbon her uncle gave us for Christmas last year."

"You don't drink bourbon." It was a big deal to get a few beers into him.

"I do tonight."

"Easy, killer. Bourbon is for big boys, not novices."

"Yeah, yeah. Tell me about the case."

Sam glanced in the rearview mirror and saw big eyes looking back at her. "Hill had some info he shared with us. I'll tell you tomorrow." She couldn't say more about that with the kids in the car. "Aubrey and Alden Beauclair are coming home with me tonight. We're on our way home from GW now."

"Oh God, they were found, and you're *taking them home*?"

"Nick and I are licensed foster parents."

"Um, that's not all you are."

"Thank you, Captain Obvious, but I figured having the place crawling with Secret Service wouldn't be a bad thing in this case."

"And the Secret Service is on board with that?"

"I never got around to asking them."

Freddie laughed. "Something tells me your buddy Brant will have a few things to say about sheltering them after—"

"Don't say it." She didn't want the kids to overhear anything that could further traumatize them. "And I don't care what the Secret Service says. It's my house too, and I can bring home guests if I want to."

Freddie's low chuckle echoed through the phone. "Wish I could be a fly on the wall for that convo. I'll look forward to hearing about it in the morning. I should be able to work a regular day."

"Let's start at my house. I'm not sure what they will need, and I want to make sure they're settled before I leave."

"Got it. I'll see you at zero seven hundred?"

She glanced at the clock, which edged closer to ten o'clock. "Make it eight."

"Will do."

"And if you're not too drunk to spell, send a text to the others, letting them know to meet us at eight at my place."

"I'm not drunk, and I'll send the text."

"Tell Elin we're thinking of her when she wakes up."

"I will. Thanks for the support today. I appreciate it."

"That was some crazy sh—" she caught herself before she swore in front of the kids "—stuff."

"Yeah, I'll be having nightmares about it for years to come."

"Put down the bourbon and try to get some sleep. We've got a lot of ground to cover tomorrow, and Gonzo is… I don't know what's up with him." She paused before she said, "Do me a favor. Get me a copy of his MVA report from today and shoot a copy to my email."

"Will do. What're you thinking?"

"I don't know yet, and I shouldn't talk to you about it."

"Why not?"

"Because he outranks you, and I'm the boss and supposed to be professional."

"He's our friend, Sam. If something's going on with him, I want to help."

"Which is the only reason I said anything. Christina had Alex in the E.R. with a high fever. When she called Gonzo, he said he was coming but never showed."

"What?" Freddie asked on a long exhale.

"I've got Patrol looking for him. They can't find him."

"Sam—"

"I can't do anything more tonight. Get me that report, and we'll figure it out tomorrow."

"Yeah, all right. See you in the morning."

Sam closed the phone and held it tightly in her fist, wishing Gonzo would call her or Christina or *someone*. Where the hell was he?

CHAPTER TEN

"MR. VICE PRESIDENT." Brant followed Nick up the stairs to the room he'd set up for the children. "I need more information on who these children are and why Mrs. Cappuano is bringing them here rather than allowing social services to handle the matter."

"Mrs. Cappuano, also known as Lieutenant Holland, doesn't need a reason to bring guests to her own home."

"I understand the sensitive nature of her job—"

"Do you, Brant? Do you really?"

The agent's posture lost some of its rigidity. "She's very good at what she does. No one would ever say otherwise, but she can't bring people here to stay without clearing them through us. By now, you both know how this works. I'm just doing my job, sir, and my job is to keep you and your family safe. I can't do that if I don't have all the information I need."

"I understand what you're saying, and as soon as Sam gets home, she can brief you on what you need to know."

"In the future, that needs to be done *before* she brings home overnight guests."

"I'll mention that to her," Nick said, laughing to himself as he imagined how that conversation might go. Sam marched to the beat of her own drummer, which was one of many things he loved about her. Trying to control her was like trying to harness nuclear energy.

"Do you find this situation amusing, sir?" Brant asked, visibly annoyed.

Nick liked that the agent was comfortable enough with him to ask the somewhat cheeky question. "It's more the thought of trying to 'manage' Sam that amuses me than the situation itself."

Brant's lips moved a fraction of an inch in an upward direction, which was as far as he would go toward admitting he found that funny too.

"I know we're not always the easiest family to deal with," Nick said.

"Understatement," Brant muttered.

"But," Nick continued, pretending he hadn't heard the comment, "we do appreciate what you and the others do for us and the *challenges* presented by Sam's work." Who ever said he couldn't speak like a politician when necessary?

Standing with hands on hips, starched dress shirt taut and tie still snugly in place after a twelve-hour day, Brant seemed to make an effort not to roll his eyes. Or so it seemed to Nick as he added pillows to the bed and straightened the comforter.

Downstairs he heard the front door open and Sam's voice as she conferred with the agent working the door. What did it say about him that the sound of her voice after a long day apart made him feel elated? That he had a bad case for his wife, and he couldn't wait to see her.

"There they are," Nick said.

Brant stepped aside to allow Nick to go first out of the room and down the stairs to greet Sam and the two little blond children who hovered next to her. With one quick look, Nick could see they were adorable and traumatized, which was why Sam had offered them shelter. You'd have to be dead or unfeeling not to be moved by them.

"Remember when I told you my husband is the vice president?"

The little girl nodded, but the boy had no reaction.

"This is my husband, Nick. Nick, this is Aubrey and Alden."

Nick squatted to their level. "Hi, guys. It's nice to meet you. I'm glad you could come over tonight. This is Brant and that's Nate," he said, gesturing to the agent at the door.

"I've seen you on TV," Aubrey said shyly. "Mommy says you're cute."

As his face heated with embarrassment, Nick looked up at Sam and found her biting her lip to keep from laughing. She gave him an *I told you so* look, and he knew what she was thinking. She was forever embarrassing him by talking about his so-called hotness. *Whatever.*

"Are you guys hungry?" Nick asked. "We have some pizza. Do you like pizza?"

"We love pizza," Aubrey said, clinging to her brother's hand.

His silence worried Nick. "Right this way." He gestured for them to follow him to the kitchen, where he set them up with plates of the cheese pizza he'd ordered in anticipation of their arrival, figuring it would be easier than spaghetti at that hour. Most kids loved pizza, and he'd taken a chance they would too. "What would you like to drink? We have milk, apple juice, water and lemonade."

"Lemonade, please," Aubrey said. "Alden likes chocolate milk."

"We can do that. Our son, Scotty, is a big fan of chocolate milk."

"Where is he?" Aubrey asked.

"He's upstairs. I'll tell him to come say hello." Nick put the drinks in front of them and then sent a quick text to Scotty to let him know they had guests. He was in his room finishing his homework after dinner and a shower.

With the kids settled and eating their pizza, Nick went to Sam, put an arm around her shoulders and kissed her temple. "Hello, dear. How was your day?"

She looked up at him. "If I forget to tell you, you're the best."

"Happy to help, but Brant would like a word with you."

"Why did I know you were going to say that?"

"He's a little *unsettled* about tonight's developments."

"I wondered why he was still here long after his shift ended."

"He's waiting for you."

"He's not going to like what I have to say."

"I suspected as much."

"He won't make me…" She tipped her head toward the kids.

"I won't let him. Don't worry."

"Are you allowed to defy your detail?"

"Let me worry about them. You have enough on your plate."

Scotty came into the kitchen, stopping short at the sight of the kids eating pizza at the kitchen table. He glanced at his parents.

"Scotty, this is Aubrey and Alden. They're spending the night with us." He'd told his son in the text that the two had lost their parents in a fire.

"Hey, guys," Scotty said, approaching the table. "I'm Scotty. Mind if I join you?"

Aubrey gave him an assessing look while Alden seemed to shrink into himself even more.

While Scotty sat with them, helping himself to a piece of pizza, Nick wrapped his arm around Sam because he could and because he sensed she needed the comfort even more than usual tonight.

WITH THE KIDS OCCUPIED, Sam cozied up to Nick, letting him shoulder some of the burden that weighed her down. "Are you hungry?" he asked.

"I could eat."

"I got you that Asian chicken salad you like."

"God, I love you." She kissed his cheek and gazed up at him. "Best husband ever."

"As you would say, I do what I can for the people."

Keeping her voice down so she wouldn't be overheard, she said, "And you shall be *richly* rewarded at bedtime."

His beautiful hazel eyes were even more so when he looked at her with desire and need and love.

How would she stand to go three long weeks without him to come home to?

"How long until bedtime?" he asked in the same low tone.

"Not long at all," she said. "I'm spent from this day."

"Not *too* spent, I hope."

"When am I ever too spent for you?"

"Never, and that's what makes you the best wife I ever had." He patted her ass. "Go eat. You're going to need a second wind."

Desire was an ever-present thing whenever he was close by and often when he wasn't. She thought of him, and she wanted him. Even if "having him" meant being in the same room, talking, laughing, arguing, debating, parenting or watching TV in perfect silence. Being with him completed her in a way that nothing else and no one else ever could. And when he looked at her in that particular way, with the look that told her he wanted her every bit as much as she wanted him, it was all she could do to remember the three children in the room.

As she ate her salad, she thought of the time, before Scotty had come to live with them, when they'd had sex on the kitchen floor. Those days were long gone with a child in their midst and the place crawling with Secret Service.

While Sam ate her salad, Scotty kept up a steady stream of chatter with Aubrey.

Alden hung on Scotty's every word.

"Hey, buddy," Sam said to her son, "maybe you can show Alden one of your driving games before bed."

"Sure," Scotty said. To Alden, he added, "Do you want to play?"

Alden looked to Aubrey, who gave him a nudge. "Go ahead."

With his hand on the younger boy's shoulder, Scotty guided Alden out of the kitchen.

"My heart," Sam said to Nick, watching them go. "He's the best."

"Yes, he is."

To Aubrey, she said, "Is Alden always so quiet?"

"He's shy. That's what Mommy says. Is she coming to get us soon?"

Sam's heart broke into a million pieces. "She can't come tonight, but we should know more tomorrow."

The little girl was thoughtful as she processed what Sam had said.

"How would you like to take a bath in my big fancy bathtub? I have all different bath bombs, and you can pick whichever one you like. What do you think?" Sam had never met a girl who didn't love a bubble bath.

"That would be fun."

"Okay, let's go."

Sam offered a hand, pleased that someone would enjoy the bath bombs her niece Abby had given her last Christmas. Baths were a luxury she rarely had time for.

"Clothes," Sam said quietly to Nick before they left the kitchen. "Will you text Tracy and ask her to bring over something in the morning? Her kids must have something they've outgrown that we can use until we have time to get more."

"Yep," he said, getting busy on his phone to text Sam's older sister.

In the master bathroom, Sam turned on the water to the tub and got out the basket of bath bombs for Aubrey to consider.

She sniffed each of them before deciding on a strawberry-scented one.

Sam unwrapped it and handed it to Aubrey. "You want to put it in?"

"Okay."

She dropped it in the water, her eyes widening with delight when the water turned red.

Sam tested the temperature and got out a towel.

"Do you want me to stay and help you, or would you prefer privacy?"

"I can do it myself," she said.

"I'll be right outside the door. Call me if you need anything."

Aubrey bit her lip as she looked up at Sam. "Alden might be scared."

"I'll check on him."

"Okay."

Sam turned off the water and left Aubrey to take her bath while she went to knock on Scotty's door to check on the boys. She poked her head in the dark room that was lit only by the glow of the TV screen. Thumb in mouth, Alden was asleep on the pillow next to Scotty's.

"He conked out about five minutes after we came up."

"I can move him to the bed that Dad made for him and Aubrey."

"It's okay if he stays there. I don't mind."

"She's going to want to be with him."

"They can both sleep here. It's fine."

"You're very kind, Scott Cappuano."

He shrugged. "I've been where they are. I know how scary it can be to find yourself staying with people you don't know."

Sam went into the room and sat next to him on the bed. "I'm sorry if this brings back memories you'd rather forget."

"I don't want to forget my mom or my grandpa." He took a deep breath and looked up at her. "Sometimes I can barely remember them, and that bums me out."

Sam reached for him, and he allowed her to hug him and play with his hair.

"I hope nothing ever happens to you guys," he said. "I don't know if I could get over that."

"Nothing will happen to us. We're too ornery for that."

"*You* are," he said with a snort of laughter. "That's for sure."

Sam gave a gentle tug to a tuft of his hair. "Don't stay up too late. School night."

"Yeah, yeah. I know the drill."

"Thanks for your help tonight and for being you, which was just what Alden and Aubrey needed."

"No problem."

Sam kissed his forehead. "Love you."

"Love you too."

She returned to the master bedroom, where Nick sat on the bed, book in hand. When she started to speak, he held up a hand to stop her.

"Listen," he whispered.

Aubrey was singing—beautifully. Sam didn't recognize the song, but it had a classical sound to it—and then she realized the child was singing in another language. "Is that…"

"Italian," Nick said. "Andrea Bocelli, 'Time to Say Goodbye.'"

"How does a five-year-old know Italian?" Sam asked, riveted by what she was hearing.

The official phone that Nick was required to have with him at all times rang, startling them both. Sam always expected to hear a nuclear bomb was about to end the world when that phone rang.

He reached for the phone on the bedside table. "Yes?" After listening for a moment, he said, "I'll send her down as soon as the children are settled." He ended the call and put the phone back on the table. "Brant is waiting for you."

"Wait till he hears the rest of the story."

"What is the rest of the story?"

Because she trusted him with her life, Sam told him what they'd learned from Hill about the children's father and his business dealings.

Nick's eyes got very big. "Brant's going to shit himself when you tell him that."

"Do I have to tell him?"

"Yes, you do, because as he said, his job is to protect us, and he can't protect us unless he has all the information he needs."

"He's going to make me take them to a hotel. He'll say it's not your call."

"I'll make it clear to him that this is nonnegotiable. The kids are staying. They are far safer here than they would be in a hotel."

"That's true." Sam went to the bathroom door and knocked. "Are you ready to get out yet?"

"I'm already out," Aubrey said.

"I'll be right in with a T-shirt you can sleep in. Hold on a sec." Sam went across the hall to the bedroom she used as a closet. In one of the boxes in the far back corner she withdrew one of her prized Bon Jovi T-shirts that was far too small for her now but had once been a favorite. When she returned to the bedroom and showed Nick the shirt he laughed.

"Aubrey has no idea how lucky she is to get to wear that shirt."

"I know! It should be in a museum."

Nick rolled his eyes.

Sam knocked on the door, and when Aubrey told her to come in, Sam stepped into the bathroom. The child looked tiny and vulnerable wrapped up in the big puffy towel Sam had given her. She held up the shirt for Aubrey to see. "Bon Jovi is one of my favorite bands."

"My daddy loves Bon Jovi."

"So do I." Sam helped her into the shirt before scooping up the clothes she had removed to put them in the washer. "I'll let you in on a little secret. Jon Bon Jovi sang at my wedding."

"You *know* him?"

"Uh-huh. I've actually met him twice. He also sang at Nick's inauguration when he became vice president."

"That's so cool. My daddy wants to meet him."

Once again, Sam's heart broke for what would never be, and she wondered how they would ever find the strength to tell these precious babies that their parents were gone forever.

"How did you learn to sing in Italian?"

"Mommy loves Andrea Bocelli. We listen to him all the time."

"You have a very pretty voice."

"Thank you. Mommy says so too."

"Do you speak Italian?"

"No," she said, "I just sing what I hear."

"It's very lovely." She ran a brush through Aubrey's damp hair and set her up with a toothbrush and toothpaste. "Alden fell sleep in Scotty's room. Do you want to sleep with them or in the bed that Nick made for you?"

"With Alden. He'll be scared if he wakes up and I'm not there."

Sam showed her the way to Scotty's room and helped her into bed next to Alden. Sam turned on a Spiderman night-light that Scotty hadn't used since he first lived with them. "Nick and I are right across the hall. If you need anything during the night, come get me. Okay?"

Aubrey nodded but her big eyes filled with tears. "Are you sure Mommy can't come pick us up?" she whispered.

"Yes, honey, I'm sure."

"Does she know where we are? She'll be really scared if she doesn't know where we are."

Sam blinked back tears as she looked down at the adorable little face. "She knows where you are." Sam had to believe that was true. She leaned over to kiss Aubrey's forehead. "Try to get some sleep."

She stayed until Aubrey curled up to her brother, put her arm around him and closed her eyes. And to think she still had to call Elijah and tell him that his father and stepmother were most likely dead. She'd had more than enough of this day, and it wasn't over yet.

CHAPTER ELEVEN

NICK WENT WITH Sam to talk to Brant, who was waiting for them in the office the Secret Service had commandeered downstairs.

"I understand you wanted to see me," Sam said to Brant, who looked more stressed and tense than usual.

"I need to know more about the kids you brought home," he said. "Are they involved with one of your cases?"

"Yes."

"How so?"

"May I?" Sam gestured to the sofa that technically belonged to her, but since it was now located in their domain she asked for permission.

Brant nodded and leaned against a desk while Sam and Nick sat. Sam told him what Hill had shared earlier.

"They can't be here," Brant said bluntly when Sam finished talking.

"Well, they *are* here," Sam said. "They're traumatized, and I'm not disrupting them again tonight."

"I understand they're traumatized, and I empathize with their situation, but there's no way they can be here when their parents have been *murdered* and the case is unresolved."

"As stated," Nick said, "they're already here, so we need to put the emphasis on how we're going to best protect them rather than on how they came to be here."

"Mr. Vice President, with all due respect—"

Sam stood. "I have other work to finish before I can call it a day. I'll let you two hash out the details of how we're going to keep Alden and Aubrey safe tonight." She squeezed Nick's shoulder and left the room to go upstairs to call Shelby and then Elijah Beauclair.

Shelby answered on the first ring. "Hi, Sam."

"Sorry to call so late. Hope I didn't wake you."

"No problem. We were up. What's going on?"

"It seems that I've made your job triply difficult by bringing home two kids in need of emergency shelter." Sam went on to update their assistant on what had transpired that day.

"Avery told me a little about the case. Those poor babies."

"I was counting on your soft heart, because I'm going to need your help with this. I have no idea how long they'll be with us."

"Whatever I can do. I'm happy to help."

"Thank you, Shelby," Sam said with a deep sigh of relief. "I should've checked with you first—"

"Don't be silly. You knew I'd be fine with helping. That's what I'm here for. What can I do?"

"They need some clothing. I asked Tracy to bring over some hand-me-downs from Abby and Ethan, but they'll need more."

"I'm on it. I'll figure out their sizes tomorrow and send one of the women from the shop to the store, if that's okay."

"Of course. You have our card. Don't be afraid to use it."

"You know me—I'm an expert at spending your money."

Sam laughed. "We couldn't do what we do without

you backing us up at home. I probably don't say it often enough, but we're so appreciative of you."

"Oh stop, Sam. I get to bring my son to work where I get to love on *your* son, who's the best kid ever. I love everything about working for you guys. I should be thanking *you*. I'll come in early tomorrow and touch base with you before you leave for work. Noah is up with the chickens anyway, so it's no problem."

"That'd be great. Then I can introduce you to the kids and make sure they're comfortable before I leave. My team is coming to the house in the morning, so we'll be here for a while."

"Sounds good."

"Thanks again."

"My pleasure."

"Hey, is Avery there by any chance?"

"He's right here. Hang on."

"Hey, Sam," Avery said. "How's it going with the kids?"

"Not bad. Aubrey is adjusting, but Alden has yet to say a word to any of us."

"I really feel for them."

"I know. Me too. About their brother, I haven't had a chance to call him, and it's getting late. I wondered if you might be willing to do that for me after all?"

"Yeah, I'll do it," he said, sighing.

"I hate to ask you—"

"It's fine. I'll take care of it."

"Let me know if he has anything to say that might be of interest to me?"

"Yeah."

"We're meeting at my place at zero eight hundred if you want to join us."

"I'll be there."

"See you then—and thanks again."

"No problem."

AVERY ENDED THE CALL and handed the phone back to Shelby, dreading the call Sam had asked him to make to Elijah Beauclair, away at college and oblivious to the bomb about to go off in his life.

"What's wrong?" Shelby asked when he got out of bed and pulled on the flannel pajama pants he'd recently discarded.

Avery unplugged his cell phone from the bedside charger. "I need to call Jameson Beauclair's older son, a student at Princeton, to tell him about the fire and the possibility that his father and stepmother are dead. We were hoping for positive IDs before we notified him, but that hasn't happened yet, and we can't wait any longer."

"Ugh," Shelby said. "I don't know how you guys can stand to make those calls."

"We can't," Avery said. "But someone has to do it." He leaned over the bed to kiss her. "I'll be back."

Propped up on one elbow, she gave him a warm smile. "I'll be right here, and we can pick up where we left off when work intruded."

Things between them were better than ever, and the crisis that had nearly derailed them was now a distant memory, he thought, as he went downstairs to his office to make the dreaded call. Couples therapy had helped him put his relationship with Shelby back on track. The work he'd done on his own with the therapist had gotten him over some things from his past that had come back to haunt his present.

Avery turned on lights in his office and fired up the

laptop where he'd made notes earlier that included Elijah Beauclair's phone number. He dialed the number, which rang several times before a male voice answered, sounding rushed or maybe out of breath.

"Hello?"

"Is this Elijah Beauclair?"

"Yes. Who's this?"

Avery closed his eyes and leaned his head on his upturned hand. "This is Special Agent Avery Hill with the Federal Bureau of Investigation in Washington, DC."

"What? What's wrong?"

"I'm afraid I have some bad news. There was a fire at your father's home last night."

"Oh no!"

"He and your stepmother were most likely killed."

He gasped. "Oh my God. You don't know for sure?"

"We're awaiting positive identification from the medical examiner."

"And the kids?"

"Were found alive."

He released a deep breath. "I *knew* this would happen. My dad knew too. He said I might get a call like this one day when that son of a bitch Piedmont found them. He knew it was only a matter of time. I can't believe he's gone. And Cleo…" His deep sigh said it all. "What's being done with the kids?"

"They're with foster parents tonight. Tomorrow, the plan is to hopefully find family members who can take them."

"That's not going to happen," he said bitterly. "My dad has no family to speak of, and Cleo's family wanted her to leave my dad when the business troubles happened. She defended him, said it wasn't his fault his business partner had turned into a ruthless criminal. But they were afraid for her and the rest of us. They won't take them because they'll be afraid of the same thing happening to them."

Avery ran his fingers through his hair as he listened and absorbed what Elijah was telling him.

"I would do it, but I'm still in school and… I love them more than anything, but I don't know if I could—"

"I understand. The medical examiner will want to know about funeral arrangements. Shall I have her call you?"

"I… Yeah, I guess. There really is no one else who can do it. I'll have to come there. My semester. I… *Fuck*."

"I'm sorry, Elijah."

"Yeah, so am I. I don't mean to make it about me."

"Murder is very personal to the people left behind."

"My dad was a good guy," he said, sounding teary now. "He tried to do the right thing and look at where it got him."

"Stay focused on the good times right now. That'll help you through. If I can be of any assistance to you, call me on this number."

"Thanks."

"Could I ask you to take care of notifying any family who might need to be told?"

"I…yeah… I'll call Cleo's parents. They treated me well, like a grandson. I'm, ah… I'm going to go."

"We'll be in touch."

"Okay." The line went dead.

Avery blew out a deep breath. God, that never got any easier, no matter how many times it had to be done in the course of a career. He looked up the number for the Princeton University campus police and made a call to the department, asking for the officer in charge.

"You got him. Who's this?"

"FBI Special Agent Avery Hill calling from Washington."

"What can I do for you, Agent Hill?"

"I just had to call one of your students, Elijah Beauclair, with the upsetting news about a fire in his family's Washington-area home. His father and stepmother are presumed dead. I wanted to let someone there know that he might need some support."

"Of course. We'll take care of him. Thank you for letting us know."

"No problem. Let me give you my number if there's anything you need." After rattling off his phone number, he thanked the officer, ended the call and stood, his shoulders tense from the strain of the dreadful task. He shut off the lights and went to the kitchen to pour himself a couple shots of vodka, so he could sleep, and took the drink with him to the large sliding glass door that overlooked the dark backyard. In the spring, he wanted to get a play set for Noah to put back there.

When he heard Shelby's steps on the stairs, he finished the drink and put the glass in the sink.

She came over to him and slid her arms around his waist. "I worried when you didn't come back. Are you okay?"

"I'm better now," he said, turning to return her embrace. Everything was better when he shared it with her. He'd never been part of a relationship like theirs, and he wondered now how he'd managed to live as long as he had without her.

"Was it awful?"

"Yeah." He kissed her forehead. "Let's go to bed."

She released him and preceded him up the stairs.

Avery wasn't at all surprised when she ducked into Noah's room to check on him. She was a devoted, loving mother, and he was slavishly devoted to her and their son. That he got to be her son's father was the greatest of the many gifts she had given him, along with forgiveness and patience.

They looked down at Noah, sleeping as he always did with his arms thrown over his head and lips pursed into a kiss. More in love with their little man with every passing day, they shared a smile.

He had to give Shelby a nudge to direct her out of the room. She could stand there for hours and stare at the baby she'd waited so long to have, but she needed her rest.

Their room was right next to Noah's, and they slept with the doors open so they'd hear him even though they also had the latest in high-tech baby monitors on the bedside table. Outside of work, their lives revolved entirely around Noah, and neither of them would have it any other way.

In bed, Avery reached for Shelby and tucked her in next to him where she belonged. "We should see about giving Noah a brother or sister." They hadn't broached the subject of marriage or adding to their family in months, not since they'd started therapy.

"I wasn't sure if you wanted more kids."

"I do, but only if you do."

"I'd have ten if I could, but time is getting away from me." Already in her early forties, she'd gotten off to a late start.

"How about we try for one and go from there?"

"I don't even know if I can get pregnant the old-fashioned way. I've never tried."

"I would take great pleasure in trying to get you pregnant the old-fashioned way," he said, running his hand up and down her arm.

Shelby giggled, and the sweet sound of her laughter went straight to his heart. "I'd want to check with my doctor first to figure out the timing and everything."

"Whenever you're ready, let me know. I'll be on standby, ready to do my part."

Still smiling, she put her hand on his face to turn him toward her. "Nothing says we can't get some practice in ahead of the official effort."

"I could get on board with that." He gave a gentle tug that landed her on top of him, her lips a fraction of an inch from his.

"I love when you show me how strong you are," she said, squeezing his biceps. "So strong but so gentle with me and Noah."

"Because I love you both more than anything."

"We love you too. Noah lights up at the sight of you."

"He and his mother are the happiest part of my day."

She moved seductively on top of him, her lips warm and soft against his neck.

Avery was again overwhelmed with gratitude for her ability to forgive. He didn't deserve her, but oh how he loved her. Turning them so he was on top, he gazed down at her before kissing her.

Shelby's hands were busy pushing the pajama pants down over his hips.

He gasped when she wrapped her hand around his cock and began to stroke him. "Shelby. *Sweetheart.*" Groaning, he put his hand over hers to stop her when that was the last thing he wanted to do. "Together," he whispered, pushing up her pale pink nightgown to find her naked underneath. He loved that she was always ready for him.

He slid into her, gasping from the tight heat that gripped him. "This," he whispered, "is everything. *You* are everything."

"We are. The three of us."

Dropping his head to nuzzle her neck, he breathed in the scent of her. "Let's get married. Nothing fancy. Just us and the ones we love best. Soon."

"Avery." She raised her hips, seeking him.

He pushed back into her before pausing to gaze down at her face, which was flushed with desire. "Is that a yes, darlin'?"

"Yes! *God*, yes." With her hands on his face, she kissed him. "Tell me when and where, and I'll be there."

"Soon," he said, kissing her. "Very, very soon."

CHAPTER TWELVE

FREDDIE REFILLED ELIN'S glass of ice water and brought it and the pain pill she was due to take into the bedroom, where she was asleep and still far too pale for his liking. If he lived forever, he would never forget the sick dread or near certainty that she'd been taken from him—and on this of all weeks.

He'd learned not to expect good outcomes or reasonable explanations for things like blood all over the apartment. In his line of work, that usually meant one thing. His legs were still weak under him from the scare he'd sustained, thinking she might've been taken or dead.

He sat next to her on the bed, careful not to jostle the injured hand that rested palm up on her abdomen.

She opened her gorgeous eyes and smiled when she saw him there. "Hey."

"Time for another pill. They said it would be important to stay on top of the pain the first few days."

"I don't want any prescription stuff. Ibuprofen is fine. Can you get me some? It's in my purse."

"Be right back." He found her purse in the living room and got the ibuprofen for her. Returning to his spot next to her on the bed, he dropped the pills into her uninjured hand.

She took them and chased them with the water.

"Tomorrow, we're getting you a new phone," he said.

"Okay."

"You were supposed to get one a month ago."

"I didn't want to spend the money with the wedding and the trip and everything."

"Elin, come on. It's a safety thing. If you had any idea…"

"What?"

He dropped his forehead to lean it against hers. "If you had any idea what I went through thinking someone had harmed you, and your goddamned phone was dead."

Her eyes went wide with shock. "You said *goddamned*."

"Elin!" He drew back from her. "I'm being serious!"

After moving her sore hand out of the way, she reached for him and brought his head to rest on her chest, running her fingers through his hair. "I know you are, and I'll get a new phone tomorrow, but you said *goddamned*, Freddie. You must be really upset."

"*Upset* isn't a big enough word to describe it." He wrapped his arm around her waist. "When Sam and I walked into the building and saw your phone on the floor and blood everywhere, I almost passed out. I thought someone I'd arrested had come for you, knowing our wedding is this weekend."

"I'm so sorry to have done that to you, Freddie. It all happened so fast, and I realized it was a bad cut. I just acted. I was bleeding like crazy. It was so scary."

"I'm sure it was. And you did the right thing running for help."

"Did I really leave the apartment door open?"

"Yeah."

"I'm sorry."

"Don't apologize to me. Please don't. The only thing I care about is that you're safe. Of course, the wedding

pictures won't be quite the same as they would've been
before today."

"If I wear a flesh-colored bandage, we won't even
see it."

Raising his head, he smiled. "That's not what I meant.
I must look twenty years older than I did this morning.
That's how much I feel like I aged in the hour between
when we got here and when we tracked you down."

She caressed his face. "If this is you twenty years from
now, I'll be a lucky, *lucky* Mrs. Cruz."

"Mrs. Cruz," he said in a tone full of wonder. "It's really happening."

"In just a few more days."

"After today, I'm afraid to let you out of my sight between now and then."

"Don't be silly. What else could possibly happen that
would be worse than today?"

He furrowed his brows. "Please don't tempt fate by
asking that question."

"I think you've been working Homicide too long. You
always jump to the worst-case scenario."

"That may be true but tell me what you would've
thought if the situation had been reversed and you'd received a one-second frantic call from me, and then came
home to a dead phone *and* bloodbath."

"I'd rather not imagine that."

He released a deep, shuddering breath. "I thought I
knew how much I love you, but I realized today that it's
way more than I ever realized. I hope you know that I've
given you the power to ruin me."

"Freddie," she said, sighing, her big blue eyes bright
with unshed tears. "I'd never want to ruin you. I just
want to love you."

"If anything ever happened to you…" His throat tightened around a lump of emotion. He shook his head, unable to entertain the thought.

She continued to gently caress his face. "Maybe now you know a little bit of what I feel every day when you leave for work."

"I hate that I put you through that."

Smiling, she said, "It's worth it when you come home to me every night."

As she wrapped her arm around him, Freddie finally relaxed and let go of the debilitating tension that had gripped him from the minute he'd walked into the building to find blood on the stairs and her dead phone on the floor. "After we get back from the trip, we're moving."

"What? Why? We love it here."

"I used to love it here. Today I realized how crappy the security is. In light of what I do for a living, I want my family better protected. We're moving to a building with a doorman and better security."

"We can't afford that, Freddie."

"I can't afford to take chances with your safety or that of any children we may have. Besides, we're going to need a bigger place when Little Freddie comes along. We may as well make the move sooner rather than later."

"Little Freddie?"

Hearing the amusement in her tone, he smiled. Sam had helped to convince him that having kids wasn't something he wanted to miss out on, even if it scared the hell out of him. As she had said, they saw the worst of what could happen on the job, and he shouldn't let that keep him from experiencing one of the best things in life.

"And when is our bundle of joy due to arrive?"

"As soon as possible." He looked up at her gorgeous

face. Once upon a time, he'd taken a single glance at that face and had been well and truly hooked. In the nearly two years since he met her during the O'Connor investigation, he'd only become more enthralled by her. That he got to *marry* her *this* weekend was still unbelievable to him.

Her brows furrowed. "Why're you looking at me like that?"

"Because I still can't believe a goddess like you chose a schlub like me."

"You are hardly a schlub, Freddie Cruz, and someone had to make a man out of you. It was a terribly difficult job, but I think we finally succeeded."

"Very funny," he said, kissing her.

"Yes, you were back then." She combed her fingers through his hair. "My poor, pent-up baby."

"I was a very good student, wasn't I?"

"The best I ever had." She opened her mouth to his tongue and drove him wild with her enthusiastic response, just like always.

"And you're really going to marry me on Saturday?" he asked, breathless from the kiss.

"I can't *wait* to marry you, Freddie."

PATROL DELIVERED GONZO to the GW emergency department after midnight. His heart beat so hard and so fast, he feared he might need to be seen. He'd passed out after receiving the call from Christina about Alex. Since being roused by the Patrol officer, he'd tried to put together what happened, but his mind was blank after receiving the call. Patrol had found him half a mile from where he last remembered being. How had he gotten there?

Thank God the Patrolman had been cool about it and

had accepted his explanation that he had the same flu his son had and had been trying to get through the day. That made two encounters with the MPD in one day that had nothing to do with work. Not the best day he'd ever had.

At the desk, he asked for Alex and was shown into an exam room. Christina sat on the bed with Alex asleep in her arms. Her eyes flashed with fury when she saw him.

"Nice of you to show up."

"I'm sorry. I got sucked into a situation at work."

"Don't make it worse by lying to me. I talked to Sam. She had no idea where you were either."

He noted the IV attached to his little boy. "Is he okay?"

"He is now."

"Christina—"

"Go home, Tommy. I don't want you here."

"But—"

"Get *out*," she said in a low tone he'd never heard from her before. "And while you're at it, you should find another place to live too. I'm all done."

"You—"

"I. Am. *Done*. Any questions?"

"Christina…"

Alex stirred, his legs moving restlessly.

Gonzo took a step closer, wanting to touch his son, to hold him, to fix what had gone so terribly wrong.

"And you'll sign over custody of Alex to me, which we both know is in his best interest."

He shook his head. "No."

"Fine, then I'll take you to court. Good luck finding anyone who thinks he'd be better off with you."

"You're tired. It's been a crazy day—"

"Yes, I am tired—of *you*, of your disregard for me and your son, of a life that's gone completely to shit. I'm

tired of it all, and I am *done*. Go home, pack your bags
and get out. Be gone when we get home tomorrow. And
do yourself and everyone who cares about you a favor
and get some help. You look like a goddamned bum, and
you're probably on the verge of losing your job."

Where was all this coming from? He was too stunned
to speak. All he could do was stare at her and wonder
what'd become of the woman who'd loved him so much.
Where had she gone? "You're tired and upset about Alex."

"Yes, I am, and I'm tired of you and your shit." Her
voice caught. "I'm tired of being invisible to you."

"You are not invisible."

She held up her hand to stop him. "Please. Just go. I
don't want you here. We don't need you."

Her words sliced through what was left of his heart,
leaving him bleeding inside. He could only stare at her
as he tried to put together the pieces of what had brought
them to this point. No matter how hard he tried, though,
he couldn't reconcile it.

"*Go*, Tommy." Tears ran unchecked down her face.
She tightened her hold on Alex and rested her cheek on
his son's head, closing her eyes and shutting him out.

Tears stung his eyes, and he blinked rapidly to contain
them. Had she just broken up with him and put him on
notice that he was also going to lose his son? Had that
really just happened? His brain was still fuzzy from the
pain pill he'd taken earlier, but the pill couldn't dull the
roar of agony that surged through him when he pondered
life without Christina and Alex.

"No," he whispered. "I'm not leaving you, either of
you. I'll be in the waiting room." He stumbled from the
room, down the hallway, dodging hospital staff, who gave
him a wide berth. Maybe he did look like a bum. Rub-

bing his face, he was surprised to find the starting of a full beard. When had he last shaved? He had no idea.

In the waiting room, he took a seat next to a mother holding a baby.

She got up and moved to the other side of the room.

What the fuck? Had it really come to that? Since when was he frightening to strangers? He ran his hand over the lump the pill packet made in the inside pocket of his jacket, desperately wanting another but afraid to dull his senses when his world was crumbling around him.

Christina was leaving him.

She was leaving him and taking Alex.

She wanted him out of their home. He was losing her—and his son. Gripped by sheer panic, he could barely breathe. Pain ripped through him, sharper, fiercer, more intense than anything he'd experienced yet. He broke into a cold sweat as he tried to breathe through it. He had no idea how long he was there, fading in and out of consciousness.

"Sir."

Gonzo heard the female voice and felt the hand on his shoulder, shaking him, but the pain had him in its grip. He couldn't move or speak or breathe.

Someone called for help, and a rush of activity followed, people in his face, touching him, moving him. Then he was on his back, looking up at the ceiling rushing by as they took him somewhere. He didn't even care where they were taking him. What did it matter? He was already in hell.

An oxygen mask was put over his face, a needle jammed into his arm and his shirt pulled open. He felt like he was above the action, watching them work on him. Maybe it would be best if whatever was happen-

ing killed him. Christina would take good care of Alex.
They'd survive at work without him. His parents and sis-
ters would be sad, but they'd get over it. He'd get to see
Arnold again and tell him how sorry he was for making
him take the lead, for letting him walk into an ambush.
It would be nice to be able to tell him he was sorry. He'd
never gotten the chance. Arnold had been dead before
Gonzo had realized he'd been shot.

He heard people talking around him, heard the ur-
gency in their voices and couldn't work up the interest
to ask what was happening.

What did it matter?

What did any of it matter?

CHAPTER THIRTEEN

SAM WAS BEYOND EXHAUSTED, but she went into Nick's home office and logged into the MPD system to check her email. Hopefully, Freddie had sent over Gonzo's accident report as requested.

While she waited, she rearranged Nick's anally aligned piles of folders so he'd know she'd been there. Then she called Dispatch and asked to be connected to the Patrol commander.

"Patrol," a male voice said brusquely.

"This is Lieutenant Holland checking on the request for assistance in locating Sergeant Gonzales. Any sign of him?"

"He was found an hour ago, passed out in Volta Park."

"What?" Sam said out loud before she could think through the implications of exposing a tear in the fabric of her squad. How in the hell had he ended up there?

"He said he has the flu and apologized for the trouble."

That was possible, Sam thought after she thanked the Patrol commander and ended the call. *Maybe he has whatever Alex has.* That was a better explanation than some of the other possibilities that were running through her mind. She punched out a text to Christina:

How's Alex? Patrol said they located Gonzo. Hopefully he is there now.

Alex is better. On antibiotic. Spending the night in the
ER. Tommy was here, but I asked him to leave.

Fuck, Sam thought. The last thing he needed was to
have his relationship blow up in his face when he was still
so fragile. But she couldn't blame Christina for being fed
up. It had been a rough year for all of them, but no one
more than Gonzo—and Christina by extension.

She scrolled through her email, ignoring everything
except the message from Freddie with the accident report attached. Checking her phone, she noted that the
call from Dispatch about the fire came in at five-forty.
Gonzo would've been called one or two minutes later.
She figured he would've left the house at six. Six-ten at
the latest. His car accident occurred at eight twenty. So
where had he been for the more than two hours between
when he left his house and when the accident occurred?

And where did he go after they parted company earlier tonight? In the morning, she would need answers to
these and other questions. At times like this, the burden
of command weighed heavily on her. Something was
clearly wrong with her sergeant, but she walked a fine
line between protecting her friend and doing what was
best for the squad and the department.

"Sam?"

She turned to find Nick in the doorway. He wore only
pajama pants, and her gaze moved naturally to the chest
she never tired of looking at.

"Are you coming to bed?"

"Yeah."

"Can't help yourself, can you?" he said, laughing as he
gestured to the file folders scattered across the desktop.

"I don't know what you're talking about."

"Sure, you don't," he said, amused.

"Are you going to sneak in here after I'm asleep and fix them?" she asked as she exited the department portal and turned off the light.

"I don't know what you're talking about."

"*Sure* you don't."

In the hallway, the agent on duty nodded to them. Sam didn't recognize him, so he must be new. "Good night, Mr. Vice President, Mrs. Cappuano."

"Night, Max," Nick said.

"Is he new?" Sam asked when they were in their room with the door closed.

"He's filling in for Melinda, who's sick."

"She's probably heartsick because she can't get her hands on the sexy vice president." Sam hated the way the agent she referred to as "Secret Service Barbie" looked at her husband.

"Sam," he said, his voice dripping with disapproval. "That's beneath you."

"No, it really isn't."

Smiling, he put his arms around her. "What's wrong?"

Her heart ached when she looked up at him. "It's not looking good for me to go to Europe."

His smile faltered. "Why not?"

"Something's up with Gonzo, and I can't leave him in charge right now. He's spiraling again, and it seems worse this time, if that's possible. Cruz is going on his honeymoon, Green is too new to leave in charge, and Jeannie wouldn't want to deal with it. We've got a new case that involves the Feds, and now the kids. I'm not sure what's going to happen there, but when I saw them in that big hospital bed, I had to do something. I probably shouldn't have, but—"

He kissed her, leaving his lips on hers until she'd settled somewhat. "It's not a good time to be away. I get it."

Sam's eyes burned with tears that infuriated her. She hated when her emotions got the better of her, and they were more raw than usual after the day she'd put in.

"What's wrong?"

"I can't bear the thought of being without you for three weeks. I seriously can't handle it."

He tightened his arms around her. "Me either. Maybe I can move some things around so I don't have to be gone for three weeks. I'll see what I can do in the morning."

"Really?" Sam asked, her heart soaring with hope.

"Yes, really," he said, smiling as he kissed her. "I don't want to be away from you any more than you want me gone. I was really hoping we could have this time together, but if that's not in the cards right now, so be it."

Sam laid her head on her favorite chest and released a deep sigh. "When are you going to tell me you're sick of me, my job, the chaos, the drama?"

"Never."

"You say that now."

"I mean it forever. I knew exactly who and what I was marrying. Don't be waiting for me to start hassling you about the things that make you who you are. It's not going to happen."

"I feel extraordinarily thankful to have you."

"Right back atcha, babe."

"I feel an extraordinary need to express my gratitude in ways that will make you very, very happy."

He snorted out a laugh that made her smile. "You know I'm always available for your expressions of gratitude."

She went up on tiptoes to kiss him. "Hold that thought. I need a shower."

"Mind if I join you?"

"I wish you would."

They went into the master bathroom, and Sam turned on the shower before she began unbuttoning her top.

"Allow me," he said, taking over for her, slowly releasing each button, and then sliding the top over her shoulders and down her arms. He kissed from her neck to her collarbone to the plump tops of breasts contained by a bra that suddenly felt too tight.

Sam squirmed, wanting more but knowing better than to rush him. Whenever she rushed him, he slowed things down to remind her that faster wasn't always better. "Could I call a time-out to go make sure the kids are all asleep before we continue?"

"Make it snappy." He rubbed his erection against her belly. "You have my *full* attention."

"I'll be quick. Start without me."

"It's no fun without you."

Smiling at him over her shoulder, she shed the rest of her clothes and donned a robe, tying it at her waist as she left her bedroom and opened the door to Scotty's room, peering inside to confirm that all three kids were asleep. Aubrey and Alden slept with their arms wrapped around each other. Next to them, Scotty slept on his side, facing them, there if they needed him.

Sam was always proud of him, but never more so than tonight. He'd make an amazing big brother, a thought that made her emotional all over again. Would he ever get that chance? Sam left the door propped open and went back to her room, ignoring Max, who pretended to ignore her too.

She closed her bedroom door and locked it—for now.

She would unlock it after the shower with Nick. Walking into the bathroom, she came to a stop at the sight of him—wet, muscular, sexy, erect. Her mouth watered as she untied her robe and shrugged it off, letting it fall into a heap on the floor. She stepped into the shower and wrapped her arms around Nick from behind, pressing her body to his.

There, she thought with a sigh. *Home*. She pressed her lips to his back, while sliding a hand down to grasp his cock.

"Samantha."

"Hmm?"

"What's up?"

"Um, you are?"

His low chuckle echoed off the shower walls, becoming a groan when she stroked him. He turned and before she had a second to anticipate his next move, he had her pressed against the shower wall, his mouth devouring hers as he worked his cock into her.

Gasping, Sam broke the kiss and took a series of deep breaths. He filled her so completely that it almost hurt to accommodate him.

"*This*," he whispered, his lips brushing against her ear sending tingles down her spine, "is the best part of the day."

"Uh-huh, and you expect me to live without you and this *for three whole weeks*? I don't think I can do it."

Grasping her ass, he pushed even deeper into her, hitting the spot that only he had ever reached, making her internal muscles quiver and contract.

She looped her arms around his neck, one hand sinking into his silky dark hair.

"*Sam*." His fingers dug into her ass cheeks as he

picked up the pace, hammering into her until she came with a sharp cry that she immediately suppressed so they wouldn't be overheard.

"Ugh," he said. "I want to be with you somewhere that you can scream your head off if you want to."

"I want to," she said, breathing hard. "Every time, I want to."

He flexed his hips to show her what her confession did to him.

Sam groaned. "No more. I have to sleep."

"Okay," he said, continuing to move in slow, easy strokes that made her purr.

"Damn you," she said when she felt the telltale signs of desire begin anew.

"Sleep is for old people."

She choked on a laugh. "I'm going to look ninety to-morrow if I don't get some sleep."

"Even when you're ninety, you won't look it." He withdrew from her, put her down and waited until she was steady to reach for the body wash. Running his soapy hands over her, he said, "I can't wait to see you as a feisty ninety-year-old. That ought to be quite a spectacle."

Sam poked his belly. "Will we still be having sex in the shower when we're ninety?"

"We'll be having sex everywhere until we stop breathing."

The water started to run cold, so they moved quickly to finish rinsing off. Sam shivered as she stepped into the towel Nick held for her.

"How mad is Brant?" she asked.

"He's pretty pissed."

"We don't make it easy for him to do his job."

"We still have to live our lives while trapped in the gilded cage."

"Did I do the right thing bringing the kids home?"

"It felt like the right thing to you, and I've learned to trust that gut of yours."

"I didn't even think about it. I just acted."

"The way a mother would, no?"

She hadn't thought of it that way. "I guess so."

"You're a mom now, Sam. You did what any mom would do when you saw kids in need—you stepped up. I'm really proud of you for doing that."

"Even if it complicated things for you?"

"Eh," he said with a shrug. "What's a few more complications?"

"A major headache."

"For Brant, not me," he said, grinning as he followed her into bed. "Come here and warm me up."

Sam snuggled up to him.

"Close your eyes and get some rest, babe."

"Will you sleep?" she asked, always concerned about his insomnia.

"I hope so. I'm tired."

"Love you."

"Love you too. More than anything."

That was all she needed to hear to relax—for now anyway. She still had the specter of three weeks without him hanging heavily over her, but she could fret about that tomorrow. Tonight, he was here, and he loved her. That was enough for now.

HOT TEARS CASCADED down Christina's cheeks for an hour after Tommy walked away. She'd done it. She'd actually said the words.

We are done.

It is over.

This, *our family, is finished.*

Only a couple of years ago, she'd been working as John O'Connor's deputy chief of staff, under the misguided illusion that she stood a chance of being the one to save John from himself.

But John had been murdered before she'd ever gotten the chance to tell him how she felt about him. She'd thought she'd been heartbroken then. That had nothing on this. Losing Tommy, a little at a time over the last nine months, had been excruciating. Watching him become someone she barely recognized had been almost worse than losing John to murder, and that was saying something.

She'd still been reeling when she met Tommy shortly after John's murder. Tommy had attended the New Year's Eve party Sam and Nick had thrown to celebrate her promotion to lieutenant and his swearing in to take John's place in the Senate. So much had happened since that night.

They'd fallen madly in love, found out he had a son, he'd gotten shot in the neck and was nearly killed. There'd been a lot of strain on their new relationship, but each challenge had only brought them closer together and made them stronger as a couple. They'd been making plans to get married, to try for that new baby and move to a bigger apartment. Then Arnold was killed, and everything stopped.

Their plans and hopes and dreams gave way to grief so deep and so pervasive it'd wiped out everything that stood in its path. For the first time, Tommy had turned away from her rather than toward her. She couldn't compete with his grief. She couldn't help him—and God knows she'd tried. She'd tried everything she could think of to help him, to find him some relief, to ease his tortured mind. But nothing had worked, and now here they were at the end of their road.

Insanity was defined as continuing to do the same thing over and over and expecting different results. She couldn't keep doing this. She brushed away more tears, her chest aching and her eyes raw.

One of the nurses who'd been nice to her earlier came in, saw her crying and offered a box of tissues.

Christina gratefully took a couple and used them to mop up the flood on her face.

"Can I get you anything?" the nurse asked.

Christina shook her head.

The nurse glanced over her shoulder, and then came closer, keeping her voice down when she said, "I'm not supposed to say anything, but the man you were talking to before?"

"What about him?"

"He had some sort of episode in the waiting room. I don't know anything else, but they're admitting him."

"Can you find out what's wrong with him?"

She shook her head. "I've already said too much."

"Th-thank you." Long after the nurse left the room, Christina thought about what she should do with this new information. She pondered the possibility of calling one of Tommy's sisters or his parents to come help, but dismissed that, knowing that was the last thing he'd want her to do. She called Sam.

"Hmmm, Holland," she said.

"Sam, it's Christina. I'm sorry to wake you, but Tommy has been admitted to GW."

"How come?"

"They won't tell me, and we're… Well, we're not together anymore." She closed her eyes tight against the rush of new tears but that couldn't contain them. "I need to focus on Alex. I can't take care of Tommy too."

"I can't come there myself right now, but I'll send Carlucci and Dominguez over," she said, referring to the squad's third-shift detectives.

"Whatever. I just wanted someone to know where he is."

"Christina—"

"I'm sorry, but I just can't. Not now."

"I'll check in with you tomorrow."

"Bye, Sam." Christina had done what she could by notifying his boss. The rest was out of her hands. The only thing she cared about now was nursing Alex back to health and then figuring out the rest of her life—a life that no longer included Tommy Gonzales.

CHAPTER FOURTEEN

SAM CLOSED HER PHONE, moaning at the new wrinkle. Always something. Rarely did she get a totally uneventful day, but even by her usual standards, this has been one hell of a twenty-four hours.

"What's wrong?" Nick asked.

More than anything, Sam hated that the phone had woken him. "That was Christina. Gonzo is in the hospital."

"How come?"

"She didn't know, and it doesn't sound like she cares."

"Yes, she does."

"She told me earlier she's done with him."

Nick yawned and ran his hands through his hair as he pondered that. "Why don't we go over there and check on them?"

"Now?"

"Were you busy?"

"Yes, I was busy sleeping—and so were you."

"Now we're awake, and our friends need us."

"We can't go anywhere," she reminded him. "We've got extra kids tonight."

"Right," he said, sighing. "What do we do?"

"I'll send Carlucci and Dominguez over there to check on him." Sam opened her phone and called Carlucci, who answered on the first ring.

"Hello, Lieutenant."

"Hi there. I need a favor." She explained what'd happened and asked Carlucci and her partner to go to GW to check on Gonzo.

"We're on it."

"Give me an update by text after you see him?"

"Will do. I was composing an email to you so you'd see it first thing. We got confirmation that the remains found in the house were Jameson and Cleo Beauclair."

"Well, at least we know for sure now and can go from here."

"We're working on a few things tonight and should know more by the end of our shift."

"Brief Jeannie in the morning."

"Will do. I'll shoot you a text after we see Gonzo."

"Thank you." Sam closed the phone and tried to relax, but her mind raced with questions and concerns. "I can't believe this is happening the week of Freddie's wedding. Gonzo is one of his groomsmen."

Nick turned on his side and reached for her. "Freddie will understand. He knows what Gonzo has been through."

Sam snuggled up to him, wide-awake and spinning. "I haven't been paying close enough attention to Gonzo. He seemed better, so I backed off. But now I wonder if he hasn't been on simmer this whole time, waiting to boil over when he couldn't contain the grief any longer."

"Don't blame yourself. You have a lot of responsibility, and he's made it clear he doesn't want people hovering over him. I've been just as negligent. I can't recall the last time I talked to Christina."

"You're busy too."

"I shouldn't ever be too busy for my friends." He caressed her back in small, soothing circles. "Maybe this is just a blip for them."

"I don't think it is," Sam said. "If you could've seen her earlier, you'd agree. I've never seen her so furious, except for the day I half accused her of killing John."

"Half accused?" he asked, chuckling.

"Okay, full-on accused." Sam flattened her hand on his abdomen, which rippled under her palm. "She said she's done with Gonzo, and I believed her."

"What would that mean for Alex?"

"I don't know, but I don't see her giving him up without a fight."

"Jeez."

A noise from outside the door had her sitting up and then reaching for the robe she'd placed on the end of the bed in case she had to get up during the night.

"What?" Nick asked.

"I heard something. I'm going to check on the kids."

"I didn't hear anything."

She had definitely heard something. "I'll be right back." Sam opened the bedroom door and Max glanced at her. "Did I hear something?"

"I think one of the little ones is awake."

Sam went to look into Scotty's room, where Alden was sitting up. She went to him. "Hey, buddy, are you okay?"

He shook his head and popped his thumb into his mouth.

Sam held out her arms, inviting him to let her comfort him.

For a long moment, he only looked at her but didn't move. Then he leaned forward.

Sam picked him up, and he wrapped his arms and legs around her, clinging to her. She brought him back to her room and sat on the bed, holding him while he quivered. "It's okay, honey," she said softly. "You're okay."

Nick pulled the covers over them.

She gave him a grateful smile.

Poor baby. He mouthed the words, so Alden wouldn't hear him.

Sam rubbed his back until Alden fell back to sleep, but she was awake for a long time after she got him settled back in bed, wondering what would become of the two children who'd lost the most important people in their lives.

GONZO DIDN'T KNOW where he was when he woke out of a sound sleep. He battled the mask on his face and frantically searched for the jacket that contained his medication. Where was his jacket? He started to sit up but realized he was attached to monitors and an IV. What the fuck was going on?

"Mr. Gonzales," a woman said as she came into the room, "you need to remain still, or you'll disrupt your IV."

"I don't need an IV."

"You do need it. You were badly dehydrated among other things when you came in. Your heart rate, respiration and blood pressure bottomed out."

"They did?" Why didn't he remember any of this?

"They did, and the doctor wants you to rest and take it easy while we rehydrate you and monitor your heart rate and blood pressure for the next twelve to twenty-four hours."

"I can't be here that long. We have a new case, and I have to get back to work. And my son, he's sick. I can't do this right now."

"Mr. Gonzales, please. You need to relax."

A doctor came into the room, and Gonzo recognized him as Anderson, the E.R. doc who'd had numerous encounters with Sam. "Is there a problem, Sergeant?"

"No," Gonzo said, scowling. "No problem."

"If you could give us a minute," Anderson said to the nurse.

"Sure." She left the room, the door closing behind her.

Anderson pulled up a stool and sat, arms crossed, expression firm. "Want to tell me what's been going on?"

"What do you mean?"

He referred to the chart he'd brought in with him. "Your blood work was positive for opiates. That and other symptoms have me wondering if you're struggling with substance abuse."

"I'm on prescription painkillers for a back injury."

"What're you taking?"

Gonzo licked lips gone dry all of a sudden. "Vicodin."

"Who prescribed them?"

"I don't remember the guy's name. I saw him at one of those drop-in clinics."

"Which one?"

"I don't know. Those clinics are everywhere. I don't remember which one I went to."

"I'm going to be straight with you, Sergeant. Is that all right?"

Gonzo eyed him warily. "I guess."

"I see opioid addicts in my E.R. every day. I know what opioid addiction looks like, how it presents, and your symptoms match up with what I see on a somewhat regular basis."

Gonzo stared at him as if he had two heads. "I am *not* an *addict*. I'm on a *prescription* for a back injury sustained on the job. Since when does that make someone an addict?"

"When was the injury?"

"July."

"Were you seen here?"

"No. I told you, I went to a walk-in clinic a few weeks later when the pain didn't go away."

"And you don't remember the name of that clinic?"

"No." Gonzo maintained eye contact, refusing to blink or squirm or do anything that might make this worse than it already was. Inside, he panicked at the thought of his command somehow finding out that Anderson was accusing him of being a freaking *addict*. He was not an addict. He was in pain, and the meds helped. Wasn't that what they were for?

"What pharmacy do you use?"

Feeling cornered, Gonzo tried to think of how best to answer that question. "I don't know. My girlfriend takes care of that for me."

Anderson's eyebrows went up. "You don't know what pharmacy you use?"

"I work a lot, as you know, because you see me here quite frequently. Most days I work ten or twelve hours, so yes, my girlfriend takes care of that kind of stuff for me because I don't have time." The scene with Christina from earlier came rushing back to remind him that he no longer had a girlfriend. "Or she *did* anyway."

"Past tense?"

"She broke up with me."

"When?"

"A couple of hours ago."

"How come?"

"Is that information you need to diagnose my medical condition?"

"Possibly."

"How so?"

"It might help to explain some of your symptoms. I like that explanation a hell of a lot better than the possibility of you abusing pain medication."

Gonzo realized the breakup might be his way out of the pill inquisition. "She broke up with me because I haven't been a very good boyfriend or father since my partner was killed on the job nine months ago."

"I was really sorry about Arnold. I knew him a little. He was a good guy."

"Yes, he was." Gonzo gritted his teeth against the predictable blast of pain that seized him whenever he thought of his late partner.

"It must be hard to deal with, even now, after all this time."

To Gonzo, it felt like it'd only been minutes since that awful night. *Nine months.* How was that possible? "It is."

"I'm not here to bust your balls, Sarge. But if you need help, you'd be far better off asking for it than developing a reliance on pain meds. Take my word for it, you don't want to get hooked on that shit. Getting off it is a bitch."

At the thought of being cut off from the pills that provided the only relief he could find, Gonzo began to sweat. "I'm not hooked on anything. I just have a lot on my plate right now, and when my girlfriend dumped me… She's the only mother my kid has ever known. It's complicated. That's all this was."

Anderson stared him down for a long moment before he finally nodded, scribbled something on the chart and stood. "I want you under observation for the next twelve hours. After that, you can go."

"I need to work. I'm on duty at seven."

"I'll write you a note if you need it. I assume that dying would be inconvenient at this juncture in your life."

Despite the sarcastic delivery, the doctor's warning had his attention. "Fine."

"Good. I'll check on you later."

Carlucci and Dominguez came in as Anderson went out.

"What're you guys doing here?" Gonzo asked his colleagues.

"Heard you were here and wanted to check on you," Dominguez said.

"Heard from who?"

"The LT," Carlucci said.

Great, so Sam knows I'm in the hospital, he thought. *Fuck. Christina must've heard about what happened and called her. That's just great.* "I'm fine. Nothing to worry about."

"Are they releasing you?" Dominguez asked.

"I have to be monitored for twelve hours. Then they'll release me. You can let Sam know I'll be out tomorrow. Or I guess it's today."

"We'll tell her," Carlucci said.

"You're sure you're okay?" Dominguez asked.

"I'm fine. What's the latest with the case?"

"We got a positive ID on the fire victims, Jameson and Cleo Beauclair," Dominguez said.

"What took so long?"

"He had teeth missing."

"I heard that," Gonzo said. Some of the shit they experienced on this job would make a sane person crazy.

He'd had reason to wonder over the last nine months if he'd be able to continue doing the job indefinitely after losing Arnold. When he heard things like what'd happened to the Beauclairs, he became even more uncertain about his future. Sometimes it was just too much. It was all too fucking much. "Will you ask Sam to have someone send me an update later, so I can keep up? I'll be back to work tomorrow."

"Will do." Dominguez squeezed his shoulder. "Let us know if you need anything."

"Thanks for coming by."

For a long time after they left, Gonzo stared at the ceiling, the events of the last nine months running through his mind, taking him from the first seconds after Arnold was shot to the horrific gurgling noises that came from him in his final seconds of life to the awful task of telling Arnold's parents to the funeral to the bleak aftermath of disaster in which nothing he had done had dulled the excruciating pain he'd lived with every second since that terrible night.

Nothing, that is, except the pills. They helped. They got him through the day. They allowed him to function somewhat normally. He'd taken too many during a particularly awful day. That's all this was. He could scale it back. That was doable. But giving them up completely?

No way in hell could he do that.

CHAPTER FIFTEEN

JUST AFTER SIX O'CLOCK in the morning, a light knock on the bedroom door woke Sam from a sound sleep twenty minutes before her alarm was due to go off. Wanting Nick to sleep a while longer, she carefully got up, put on her robe, tied the belt and pushed the hair back from her face. She took her phone off the bedside charger, put it in the pocket of her robe and opened the door to Brant. Did he ever go home?

"Very sorry to disturb you, Mrs. Cappuano, but we have a Dolores Finklestein from Child and Family Services at the checkpoint demanding to see you and the vice president immediately."

"All right," Sam said, resigned to beginning a new day with a new challenge. "If you'll let her in, we'll be down in a few minutes."

"Very good."

Sam closed the door and went to wake Nick. "Hey," she said, kissing his cheek. "Wake up. CFS is here about the kids."

"What do they want?" he asked, mumbling as his eyes remained closed.

"Probably to tell us that we went about this all wrong, and now they have to get involved."

"Great." He sat up, ran his fingers through his hair and put an arm around her. "Are they going to take them?"

"Not if I can help it."

Smiling, he kissed her temple. "That's my tiger."

Sam went into the bathroom to brush her teeth and hair and then crossed the hall to her closet to change into yoga pants and a sweatshirt. As she stepped into the hall, Nick came out of their room wearing a navy sweater with faded jeans. Keeping her voice down so the agent outside Scotty's room wouldn't hear her, she said, "This would be a good time to pour on the sexy vice-presidential charm."

Nick scowled at her. "Whatever that is."

"It's you being you. Women everywhere swoon in your presence. Make her swoon."

"Are you angling for a spanking, my love?"

"Oh yes, please. Can we do that later?"

"Samantha." With his hand on her ass, he directed her toward the stairs. "Behave. I mean it. If you send me down there with a boner, she'll have the kids out of here in five minutes."

Sam smothered a giggle that was busting to get out. She managed to maintain her decorum. Just barely.

Dolores Finklestein had steel-gray hair, a stout shape and a no-nonsense expression on her face.

Sam was immediately intimidated, which didn't happen very often. "Mrs. Finklestein, I'm Samantha Cappuano." She decided to play the second lady card since it suited her purposes. "This is my husband, Nick."

"It's *Ms.* Finklestein, and it's a pleasure to meet you both." She shook both their hands and took the seat Sam offered.

She and Nick sat on a love seat, and Sam reached for his hand, hoping to demonstrate their unity. "What can we do for you, ma'am?"

Nick squeezed her hand, probably in response to her unusual deference toward authority.

Whatever. She'd do what she had to in order to protect those sweet babies.

"I understand that Aubrey and Alden Beauclair were released into your custody last night. I'm here to collect them."

"Ah, collect them?" Sam asked, her mouth suddenly dry as she glanced at Nick.

"That's correct. We have a process, Mrs. Cappuano, a process that was not followed last night. The GW social worker should not have released the children to the custody of anyone but a representative of our department."

"The children were released into the custody of licensed foster parents," Nick said. "The way I see it, they saved your department a lot of trouble by working this out for you."

"That may be the way you see it, sir, but that's not the case. I received a call at five o'clock this morning that the children had been found and placed without our involvement, which, as the social worker at GW knows, is against policy."

Nick released Sam's hand and leaned forward, elbows on knees, fiercely handsome.

Here it comes, Sam thought, wishing she could rub her hands together. *The charm offensive.*

"Let me ask you this, Ms. Finklestein… What's in the children's best interest now—removing them from a place they feel safe and subjecting them to further trauma, or allowing them to remain in our custody until other plans can be made? Is it really more important to you that we backtrack to follow procedure, or is it far more critical that we consider the needs of two children who've just lost their parents in the most tragic way imaginable?"

Sam wanted to stand up and cheer. She also wanted to kiss him. But she didn't do either of those things. Rather, she sat perfectly still and waited for the other woman to reply.

"I understand your position and agree it would be disruptive to move the children again if they're comfortable here. However, I do need to take them to be evaluated and processed."

"They're five, and they're traumatized," Nick said, beginning to sound more frustrated than charming. "What kind of evaluation and processing could you possibly need to do that couldn't be done right here where they're with people they know and have become at least slightly comfortable with?"

Her lips set in a tight expression. "I need to see the children."

"You're more than welcome to come back in a couple of hours when they're awake," Nick said.

"I need to see them now."

"I'm afraid that's not going to happen," Sam said. "They went to bed late. Alden was up during the night, and they're both still asleep, where they shall remain until they wake up on their own. At that time, you're more than welcome to speak with them."

The two women engaged in a visual standoff.

Sam refused to blink or look away.

Seeming to realize she was fighting a losing battle, Ms. Finklestein cleared her throat. "Very well, then." She put her business card on the coffee table and stood. "I'll expect a call the minute the children are awake."

"If you attempt to remove them from our custody,"

Nick said, "I'll expect you to bring a court order. Barring that, they aren't going anywhere until permanent arrangements are made for their care. Am I clear on that?"

"Crystal," she said, her tone frosty. She stormed toward the door, which was opened by the agent on duty, who then closed it behind her.

Sam jumped into Nick's arms, taking him by surprise as she kissed his entire face. "You were so *fucking amazing*. I've never wanted you more than I do right now."

"Dear God, woman," he said, as he took a step backward while trying not to topple over from the impact.

Nate, the agent at the door, cleared his throat and suppressed a laugh.

"Not in front of the agents," Nick said, his face flushed with embarrassment.

"Don't let me stop you," Nate said. "I thought you were pretty great too."

"See?" Sam said, continuing to kiss Nick's face. "It's not just me who thinks so."

The door opened to admit Shelby, who had Noah strapped to her chest. "Um, okay," she said, seeing Sam attached to Nick. "I can come back if now isn't a good time to arrive for work."

"Come in," Sam said. "Put me down."

"I don't want to," Nick said, tightening his hold on her.

"Nick!"

"To be continued later," he muttered before putting her down.

"What'd I miss?" Shelby asked Nate. "Mom and Dad don't usually PDA in front of the help."

"To recap," Nate said, "a lady from CFS came to take the kids, and Mr. Vice President let her know that isn't happening without a court order. Mrs. Cappuano *appreciated* his efforts on behalf of the kids."

"Ahh," Shelby said, laughing. "I see how it is."

"He was *amazing*," Sam said, looking up at him. "Truly amazing."

"I take it the kids are here to stay for the time being?" Shelby asked, tugging up the sleeves of her pink sweatshirt.

"Barring a court order," Nick said, "which they'll be hard-pressed to get, as we are licensed foster parents."

"If I may, sir," Brant said, joining them. "I couldn't help but overhear, and I wonder if it wouldn't be better for everyone concerned if the children were placed elsewhere until permanent arrangements can be made."

"Better for whom?" Sam asked, giving him a pointed look.

"Your husband and son, ma'am. I've been in touch with the director about the situation this morning, and he is in full agreement that the Beauclair children should not be sheltered here."

"I'm glad you're all in full agreement," Nick said. "We are not."

"With all due respect, Mr. Vice President," Brant said, "the person who set the fire at the Beauclairs' home did so knowing there were four people in the house. They were willing to incinerate those children."

His blunt words made Shelby whimper.

"What's to stop them from trying again?" Brant asked.

"*You*," Nick said. "You and the rest of our security make it impossible for anyone to get anywhere near us or them."

"You and I both know that's not one hundred percent true. We do everything we can to protect you, but no security is completely infallible as much as we'd like to believe otherwise."

"Let me ask you this," Nick said. "Where are those children safer? With us or with another foster family that doesn't have world-class security?"

Brant shifted his weight from one foot to the other. "I hear what you're saying, but—"

"They're staying, Brant," Nick said. "For as long as they need emergency shelter, they are *staying*. Make it work."

"Yes, sir." Brant turned and left the room.

Sam looked up at Nick, fanning her face. *"Hot."*

He rolled his eyes.

"See what I'm saying, Shelby?" Sam asked.

"Oh, I see it. I *definitely* see it."

"Be quiet," Nick said, scowling. "Both of you."

"I need to clean up before my team arrives for our eight o'clock meeting," Sam said.

"I'll start some coffee for y'all," Shelby said.

"Bless you," Sam said. To Nick she added, "Could I have a word upstairs, please?"

He gestured toward the stairs. "After you." Following her up, he cupped her ass and gave a squeeze.

Ignoring the agent who watched them, Sam grabbed a handful of his sweater and pulled him into her closet, closing the door behind them.

"What's—"

Sam dragged him into a tongue-tangling kiss.

"—up?" he asked when they resurfaced for air minutes later.

"Thank you so much for what you did down there."

Smiling, he shook his head at her. "I did what anyone would've done."

"No, babe, you went above and beyond for two kids you don't even know when it would've been much easier to cede to Brant's wishes and relocate them."

"Easier for whom?" he asked, echoing her question from earlier.

"I love you. I love you all the time, but today I love you more than I ever have before."

"I need to step up for kids I don't know more often if this is how you're going to react," he said with a teasing grin.

"You did this for me, because it's important to me, and don't think I don't know that."

"Whatever you want, whenever you want it, my love."

"Including two extra kids who may have targets on their backs?"

"Whatever you want." He kissed her and gazed down at her. "I'm thinking we probably ought to stay close to home today to make sure our little friends aren't relocated without our permission."

"Can you do that?"

"I'll have Terry move some things around. I can take a couple of meetings here, rather than at the White House."

"I've got my team coming at eight. I can give them their assignments and then work from here. Although, I'm down to a skeleton crew of three with Gonzo out for who knows how long and me stuck here."

"Maybe you can get the captain involved? Doesn't he like an excuse to pound the pavement every now and then?"

"He does. I'll ask him."

"Maybe your dad can help too."

"Another good thought. You must've slept well last night. You're firing on all cylinders this morning."

He rubbed his erection against her belly. "I'm always firing on all cylinders when my beautiful wife is nearby."

She snorted with laughter. "While I'm in here," she said, whipping off her sweatshirt, "I ought to put on real clothes."

"Or not," he said, caressing her breasts.

Sam wished they had time for a quickie, but they didn't. Not with so many other things going on this morning and Scotty needing to get up for school. "Hands off, love. We've got shit to do."

He took another squeeze before he dropped his hands and leaned against the door to watch her put on jeans, a sweater and running shoes. "We need another vacation away from this madhouse."

"That'd be awesome. Let me close this case and get the Beauclair kids settled, and we'll get away for a night or two to the cabin. After your trip, of course." Her heart sank at the reminder that he'd be gone for three interminable weeks.

"Shortening that trip is at the top of my to-do list today."

"Don't get my hopes up. Let's go wake the boy and check on our other babies."

"An unexpected day at home with my wife. This makes me very happy."

"Your wife, her team, your team, Shelby, the Secret Service…"

"I'll take what I can get."

Sam smiled at him. "Me too."

"You go ahead and wake up Scotty. I need a minute…"

Sam glanced down at the hard ridge of flesh behind his zipper and licked her lips. "I sure wish we had time."

"Go," he said, frowning. "That's not helping anything."

She was still laughing when she stepped into the hallway, closing the door behind her, aware of the watchful eyes of the agent on her. He probably knew exactly why she'd come out ahead of Nick. They often joked that the agents on their detail would have *one hell* of a book to write after he left office.

In Scotty's room, Aubrey and Alden were still asleep but Scotty was awake.

"I was wondering if you guys had forgotten to get me up," he whispered.

"No such luck. Time to get moving."

"Maybe I should stay home today to help with Aubrey and Alden."

"Dad and I are staying home with them."

"No fair. How come I can't stay home too?"

"Because." Sam had hated answers like that from her mother and had sworn she'd never say such things to her own children. The thought made her smile.

"What?" he asked.

"I used to hate when my mom said 'because' to me when I asked that kind of question."

He smiled. "*Because* it's not really an answer."

"Exactly. Now get moving, buster. Your detail is leaving in thirty minutes."

Scotty groaned but he got up.

His groan woke Aubrey, who looked at Sam with big, haunted eyes that immediately filled with tears.

"Mommy," she said. "I want Mommy."

"I know, sweetheart." Sam extended her arms to her and after a moment of hesitation, Aubrey reached for her.

Sam picked her up and snuggled her. Next to them, Alden was still asleep. "We should let him sleep for a while longer," Sam whispered.

"Okay."

Sam carried her downstairs where Nick was conferring with Brant. "Brant, this is Miss Aubrey. Aubrey,
this is our friend Brant. He helps us out around here."

"Nice to meet you, Aubrey," Brant said with a warm
smile that Sam appreciated.

Aubrey burrowed into Sam's embrace.

"She's a little shy at first but once she gets comfortable she's a regular chatterbox," Sam said, rubbing the
little girl's back. "How about some breakfast?"

Aubrey nodded.

Sam walked her into the kitchen and introduced her
to Shelby and Noah. Aubrey's eyes lit up at the sight of
the baby. "Aubrey is ready for some breakfast, Shelby."

"Great timing," Shelby said. "Noah and I made pancakes. Do you like pancakes, honey?"

Aubrey nodded again.

"Perfect," Shelby said. "Maybe you could hold Noah
for me while I get you some?"

"Can I?" Aubrey asked Sam.

"It's up to Shelby. He's her little guy."

"It would be such a big help to me if you held him for
me," Shelby said. "Have a seat at the table."

Sam sent Shelby a grateful smile.

Aubrey lit up with delight when Shelby carefully
transferred Noah to her arms. "He's so cute!"

"I think so too," Shelby said, keeping a close eye on
Aubrey and Noah while she put a pancake on a plate for
Aubrey. "I've got one of the women from the shop going
to the store this morning for basics. She'll be by shortly."

"That's great," Sam said. "Thank you for that. I need
to speak to Nick." To Aubrey, she said, "I'll be right out
there, okay?"

"Okay," Aubrey said, captivated by baby Noah, who was, in fact, completely adorable.

Sam went into the living room, where Nick was having another tense conversation with Brant.

"That little girl has an X on her back, Brant," Nick said, pointing to the kitchen. "That innocent baby. That's who we're protecting here."

"I get it, and I empathize with what the children are going through, but my job is to protect *you* and your son. My bosses are on me like white on rice about this situation, and they may contact you directly."

"They're more than welcome to."

Sam curled her hand around Nick's arm in a show of support.

"I'll let them know that," Brant said, walking away.

CHAPTER SIXTEEN

AFTER SHARING A grimace with Nick, Sam called her dad's house to let him know her team would be gathering at her house shortly if he wanted to join them.

"We're just getting him up and dressed," her step-mother, Celia, said. "I'll send him over as soon as he's ready."

"Great, thanks." She ended that call just as her phone rang with a call from her sister Tracy. "What's up, Trace?"

"I went through Abby's and Ethan's clothes, and I found a few things that might work. I asked Ang to check Jack's stuff too," she said of their sister and nephew.

"Thank you. I appreciate it. I don't know when we'll be able to get into their house to get their stuff."

"I just saw something about the fire on the news. It's so sad."

"It really is. I gotta run. I'll see you when you get here, and thanks again."

"Sam."

"Yeah?"

"I'm worried and Ang is too."

"About?"

"You getting attached to the kids and then having to hand them over to someone else."

Sam sighed. "Thank you for the concern, but I'm okay. I know what this is—and what it isn't." But even as she said the words, she acknowledged that her sisters' concern wasn't misplaced. It wouldn't take much for her to become extremely attached to the two little ones who'd been entrusted to her care.

"Just be careful okay? It's a great thing you guys are doing, but it's dangerous for you in more ways than one."

"Believe me, we've gotten an earful from the Secret Service, who are none too pleased about it."

"I'm sure they aren't."

"I'll see you when you get here."

Sam finally had a second to read the text Carlucci had sent the night before about Gonzo.

He seems okay and said they are monitoring him for twelve hours, so he'll be out today.

Sam wanted more info about what'd happened to him last night, but that would have to wait until later.

Scotty came down the stairs carrying Alden, who had his thumb in his mouth.

She closed the phone and stashed it in her pocket.

"He was crying," Scotty said. "So I got him up."

"Thank you," Sam said, caressing Alden's messy blond hair.

He reached for her, and she took him from Scotty. "Aubrey is having pancakes with Shelby. You guys want to join her?"

Alden nodded.

"Shelby's pancakes are the best." Scotty led the way to the kitchen, where they found Aubrey still holding Noah, who was all smiles for her.

"Alden, come see Noah," she said.

While the two children were occupied with the baby,

Scotty whispered, "Will they still be here when I get home?"

"I don't know for sure."

"I hope they are. They're cute."

"Yes, they are." Realizing she wasn't the only one getting attached, Sam gave him a one-armed hug and kissed the top of his head. "Hurry up and eat." She released him, so he could take the plate Shelby handed him.

"Morning, handsome," she said.

"Morning, Shelby," he said in a long-suffering tone. Like his father, hearing he was handsome embarrassed him. He'd better get used to it, because her handsome boy was going to grow into a very handsome man, like his dad.

Shelby nodded to the living room, letting Sam know she had things under control in the kitchen if she needed to be elsewhere.

"I'll be right out there," she said. "Come get me if you need me."

"We're good," Shelby said. "Right, guys?"

"Right," Aubrey said.

Sam went into the living room just as the agent at the door admitted Green, McBride and Hill. She appreciated that they'd come early, knowing how much needed to be done that day.

"Morning, everyone. Shelby has coffee in the kitchen but go in one at a time. The Beauclair kids are in there, and I don't want them overwhelmed by strangers."

"How're they doing?" Jeannie asked, her warm brown eyes brimming with compassion.

"Okay, all things considered. They both got some sleep, and Scotty has been a huge help."

"He's the best," Jeannie said.

"I might be biased, but I agree."

"You're his mom," Jeannie said. "You're allowed to be biased. I've got a few updates for you from Carlucci and Dominguez. Lindsey and her team have confirmed that our victims were the Beauclairs."

Sam nodded as she sighed. It'd been a long shot to hope otherwise. "What else?"

"Carlucci said she told you Gonzo will be out today."

"Yes." Sam would have to find time today to talk to him—and Malone. With Cruz out for the next two weeks on his honeymoon trip to Italy and now Gonzo's status questionable, there was no way she could leave town.

Hopefully, Nick could work something out so he wouldn't have to be gone for three weeks. If he couldn't, she'd have to figure out what she would do without him for all that time. She sighed and pushed those thoughts aside to focus on work. The case had taken a back seat to the drama circulating within the squad and the situation with the children. They had to get back on track with the investigation, beginning right now.

The front door opened, and Freddie came in, looking tired and spent. *Great.* Her team was hardly firing on all cylinders at the moment.

"How's Elin?" Sam asked him.

"She had a rough night. She's in a lot of pain."

"The poor thing," Sam said. "The last thing she needs this week."

"Yeah, I hope she feels better by Saturday. I don't want anything to ruin her big day."

"She'll be fine. She's got a few days to get past it."

"Hope so. What's up with the case?"

"We're about to start." Sam sat next to Jeannie while

Freddie took the chair next to Green. "What's the latest, people?"

"Per your request yesterday," Jeannie said, "I've put together a report on APG, the falling-out between Armstrong and Piedmont and the aftermath of the company's meltdown." She distributed printed copies to everyone. "The bottom line is they went from best friends and business partners to mortal enemies seemingly overnight when Armstrong delivered the dossier on Piedmont's activities to the Feds."

"Armstrong had a fiduciary and legal responsibility to report the irregular activity," Hill said. "He did the only thing he could to keep himself out of jail, but it came at an awful cost. From all reports, he'd resurrected the business from the ashes of APG, since he still owned the patent on the software he developed, but he'd been plagued by depression and anxiety issues."

"Apparently, with good reason," Green said, producing photos from the crime scene that were passed around the group. The entire left side of the ten-thousand-square-foot home was in ruins while the right side appeared virtually untouched, which explained how the children were able to survive the inferno.

Thank God they'd survived, Sam thought. After having the chance to get to know them a little, the thought of them dying in such a horrible way was more than she could bear to consider.

When Scotty came downstairs, dressed for school, backpack on his shoulder and Secret Service detail in tow, Sam got up to kiss him goodbye. "Have a good day."

"You, too," he said, waving to her team. "I'm just going to say goodbye to them." He gestured toward the kitchen.

"Don't make it sound like you won't see them again."

"Got it."

"Hey," she said, straightening his hair. "Thanks for all your help. Love you."

"Love you too."

Sam rejoined the meeting, waving as Scotty left a minute later with his agents.

"I spoke with the Beauclairs' older son last night," Hill said, glancing at Sam. "Needless to say, he took the news about his father and stepmother very hard. I asked about potential guardians for the children, and he said he'd be surprised if anyone in the family would take them, especially after what'd happened to his father and Cleo. Apparently, her family in California had been afraid of something just like what happened."

"They'd let two children who've lost their parents go to strangers?" Sam asked, incredulous.

"They're afraid," Hill responded.

"Unreal." If anything happened to either of her sisters, God forbid, she'd do whatever it took to protect their children, regardless of the circumstances. That's what family did.

The front door opened and her dad, Skip, came rolling in, controlling his wheelchair with the one finger that retained motion after the devastating gunshot injury almost four years ago that had ended his career three months before he'd been due to retire. His blue eyes were sharp and focused as he joined the gathering. "What'd I miss?" he asked.

Sam quickly summarized the case and held up the crime scene photographs for him.

"Did I hear you've got custody of the kids?" he asked, raising an eyebrow. He got a lot done with that eyebrow.

"You heard correctly." She knew what he was thinking,

so he didn't have to verbalize whether she'd crossed the line by taking in the kids of her murder victims. Maybe she had, but she'd do it again in a hot second. To the others, she said, "While the Feds focus on finding Piedmont, I want to look at the possibility that this had nothing to do with APG or Piedmont."

"You don't think that would be a waste of time?" Hill asked.

"These people lived complicated lives. Are you going to tell me that Piedmont was the *only* issue they had? I refuse to believe that. I want to go back to the neighbors and friends, the kids' school, associates of Jameson's from his business dealings, Cleo's friends, etc. Let's take a closer look at their lives from the time they landed here and find out who else might've had a motive for murder."

"I agree with the lieutenant," Green said. "Sometimes the obvious is too simple. When you're sitting on a billion-dollar fortune, life is complicated, even when you aren't on the run from your former business partner. I'll follow the money, if that's okay."

"Please do," Sam said.

"I'll go back to the school and the neighbors," Cruz said.

"Take Jeannie with you. Find out who else they associated with, any clubs or organizations they belonged to, that kind of thing. I also want to know if there was any hint of marital trouble, infidelity, etc."

"We're on it," Cruz said, as Jeannie nodded in agreement.

"I also want to talk to the older son," Sam said. "I'll follow up with him today and find out what he wants us to do with the bodies when Lindsey releases them."

"What about other employees of APG?" Cruz asked.

"Maybe someone who lost their job after the meltdown or had a stake in something the company was doing that would've been adversely impacted by Armstrong going after Piedmont?"

"Definitely worth considering," Sam said.

"We'll take that angle," Hill said. "And I'll be having a conversation with Gorton, the third APG partner today. He's been thoroughly interviewed in the past, but it never hurts to backtrack."

"Very true. Nick and I are staying here today, fending off CFS from taking the kids out of our custody. If everyone could be back by four or report in by then, I'd appreciate it. I'll update the brass on where we are."

She'd no sooner said the words when the front door opened to admit Ms. Finklestein. Sam rolled her eyes at her team and got up. "That'll be CFS," she said. "Keep me posted, people."

As the other officers filed out to see to their assignments, Sam walked over to greet Ms. Finklestein, who wore the same stony expression she'd sported earlier.

"Mrs. Cappuano, since I haven't yet received a phone call from you, I trust the children are up and available for my visit?"

"Yes, ma'am. I was going to call you after they finished eating. Right this way." She led the woman into the kitchen, where Shelby had cheerful music playing on her phone, probably so there was no chance the meeting in the next room could be overheard. She was seated at the table with Noah and the kids, who were coloring. Sam would have to ask her later where she'd gotten the crayons and coloring books. But for now, she gave silent thanks for the angel who was Shelby.

"Hey, guys," Sam said, "this is Ms. Finklestein. She wanted to come by and see how you're doing."

Neither Aubrey nor Alden stopped what they were doing to greet her.

"May I?" Ms. Finklestein said of the fourth chair at the kitchen table.

"Please," Sam said. The sooner she completed her "inspection" or whatever this was, the sooner they could be rid of her.

She sat and pulled out a notebook and pen. "What're you coloring, Aubrey?"

"It's a bird," Aubrey said, too polite to add the word "duh" to the statement the way some kids would have. "And Alden is coloring a house."

"I can see that. You're both doing a very good job."

"Coloring is easy."

"How did you sleep last night?" Ms. Finklestein asked.

"Fine," Aubrey said.

"How about you, Alden?"

Sam shook her head at the woman, hoping she'd get the message that he wouldn't reply. "Alden was up during the night, but we were able to comfort him until he fell back to sleep."

"I was hoping to hear from him," Ms. Finklestein said pointedly.

"Alden has been very *quiet* since he came to stay with us," Sam said, returning the pointed look. "We aren't pushing him to do anything that makes him uncomfortable."

Alden put down his crayon and turned toward Sam, who lifted him into her arms before taking his seat at the table. Moved by the trust he'd placed in her, she wrapped her arms around him and kissed the top of his head.

The kitchen door opened, and Tracy came in, bearing a bag of clothes. "Sorry that took so long." Tracy stopped when she collided with Finklestein's stony expression. "Oh, sorry to interrupt. I'll be out there with Dad." She backed out of the kitchen.

"There're a lot of people in this household," Finklestein said.

"Yes," Sam said, "it's the home of the vice president of the United States, which is protected by the United States Secret Service. My husband and I are conducting business here today so we could be available when you returned. That was my sister. She gathered some clothing for the children at my request and was bringing it to us. Shelby is our assistant. She helps out with our son as needed, among many other things. Any questions?"

"I'm simply stating it's a lot of activity for two children who've—"

Sam sent her the filthiest look she could muster. If the woman said it out loud, Sam would have her job.

Fortunately, Ms. Finklestein took the hint and kept her yap shut about what'd happened to the children. "What did you have for breakfast?" she asked Aubrey.

Did she think they hadn't fed them? Sam seethed silently, which was *so* not her style. She far preferred to seethe out loud.

"Shelby made pancakes." Aubrey concentrated on the bird's wing, which she colored blue. Looking up at Shelby, Aubrey said, "Can I hold Noah again?"

"After his nap," Shelby said, patting the sleeping baby's back. "He'd love that."

"Okay," Aubrey said, returning to her work.

"If there's nothing else," Sam said, eager to move this along.

"I'd like to see the room where the children will be sleeping," Finklestein said.

Sam wondered if she really wanted a closer look at the vice president's home. "Alden, would you like to finish your picture while I take Ms. Finklestein upstairs?"

Alden nodded, and Sam returned him to his seat, though he eyed Finklestein with thinly veiled distrust. He understood the threat she posed to whatever security he'd allowed himself to feel in their home, and that irked Sam greatly.

She glanced at Shelby, who nodded, indicating she'd be there with the kids.

"Mrs. Cappuano," Nate said when Sam stepped into the living room with Ms. Finklestein. "Your sister and father said they were going to his home. Your sister left the bag she brought." He pointed to the bag next to the front door.

"Thank you, Nate." Wondering where Nick was, Sam led Ms. Finklestein upstairs to the guest room Nick had prepared for the children, which had gone unused the night before, not that she needed to know that. There were probably reams of manuals that prevented children placed in emergency shelter from sharing beds with anyone, which made sense, until a child was alone and terrified and in need of comfort. Then all bets were off. "We figured they'd prefer to be together, so we have them in here," Sam said.

"And where are you in proximity to them?"

"Right there." Sam pointed to their closed door. "And our son's room is there. Whenever Scotty is in residence, a Secret Service agent is positioned outside his bedroom door. It would be good if someone could get into the Beauclairs' house today to retrieve some of the children's things. I'm sure there are stuffed animals and other items that would bring them comfort at this difficult time." They had only the one stuffed animal that Aubrey had brought with her to the hospital.

"I'll see what can be done about that."

"And you'll ask them what they'd like to have?"

"Of course." After a pause, she said, "I'm not the enemy here, Mrs. Cappuano. I'm concerned only with what's best for the children, and despite the trauma they've endured, they seem comfortable here."

"We've done our best to make them comfortable. They're asking for their mother. We haven't told them anything yet. In the meantime, we're answering their questions with vague responses. We only just got confirmation this morning that the fire victims were their parents. I was hoping to consult with their older brother to get a feel for how best to handle telling them what's happened to their parents."

"I'm going to recommend the children remain in your custody until permanent arrangements can be made for their long-term care."

"Thank you." Relief rippled through her, releasing tension in her neck, chest and shoulders. Even her jaw ached. Later, when she had time to fully unpack the emotions swirling through her, she'd be able to better understand why it mattered so much that they got to keep—for now—two children she'd never met before yesterday. At least she hoped she'd be able to make sense of it, because none of the emotions made sense to her in the moment.

She led Ms. Finklestein out of the room just as Nick emerged from the room they used as a home gym. Wearing only gym shorts, he was the sexiest thing she'd ever seen, even dripping with sweat.

Ms. Finklestein, the poor thing, could only stare.

"Is everything all right?" he asked.

"Ms. Finklestein was just saying that the kids can stay with us until something more permanent can be worked out. Right, Ms. Finklestein?"

"Oh, um, yes," she said, seeming to make an effort to look anywhere but at the sexiest vice president in history.

Nick hooked a towel around his neck. "That's great news. We'll make sure they're very well cared for."

"Excellent," Finklestein said.

"We'll let you grab a shower while we go downstairs to work out any logistics." Sam gestured for the other woman to go ahead of her, then she waggled her brows at Nick, who rolled his eyes in response.

Sam led the other woman to the living room, which was now devoid of cops and FBI agents. They sat across from each other.

"He's as nice as he seems on TV," Ms. Finklestein said.

"Yes, he is, and he's not hard to look at either."

The other woman giggled. She actually *giggled*. "No, he isn't." She shook her head, probably trying to stop thinking of her thirty seconds in the presence of the half-naked, sweaty, sexy vice president. That would very likely be the image in her mind as she took her last breath in this life. Sam had no doubt similar images of him would be among her final thoughts. "Anyway, about the children..."

"Yes, back to business."

"I think it's a good idea to speak to their brother about how he'd like things handled."

"I agree. I'd like to ask him about next of kin."

Sam relayed what the brother had told Avery the night before about Cleo's family being afraid to take the kids in light of the way his father and stepmother had died and the threat still posed by a former business associate.

"Well, there has to be someone."

"We've only begun to scratch the surface of this case, so I'll tell you what I know, and you can dig in further with the extended family."

"That sounds like a plan."

CHAPTER SEVENTEEN

AFTER THEY CONFERRED with the children—or Aubrey, who'd spoken for both of them—about what they'd like to have from home, Sam ushered Ms. Finklestein out the door just as Nick's chief of staff, Terry O'Connor, came up the ramp. "Hey, Terry."

"Hi, Sam. Heard you've caught another homicide."

"Look at you, speaking the lingo."

"That's what happens when you live with the medical examiner."

"She's raised you right. Come in. Nick is in the shower. He'll be down shortly."

"I talked to him briefly this morning, and he indicated there might be a complication with the trip?"

Shelby emerged from the kitchen with Noah asleep on her chest and Aubrey and Alden holding her hands.

"Meet the complications," she said in a low tone only Terry could hear. "Terry, this is Alden and Aubrey. They're staying with us for a while." To Shelby, Sam said, "My sister left a bag of clothes for the kids."

"Great," Shelby said. "We were going to go upstairs and take showers and get dressed." She gestured for the kids to go ahead of her and took the bag from Sam.

"Thank you, Shelby."

"It's no problem at all. They're adorable."

"Yes, they are." Add Shelby to the list of people becoming invested in the children. It would hurt like hell when they had to turn them over to someone else, even if that someone else was their family member.

"The dining room is probably the only place you'll get some quiet today, Terry," Sam said, gesturing for him to go ahead and make himself comfortable there. "I'll send Nick in as soon as he comes down."

"Thanks, Sam."

Left alone in the living room, she decided to call Gonzo to check on him before she moved on to Elijah Beauclair. Gonzo's phone rang several times before he took the call.

"Hey, Sam. I hope you got the message I gave Carlucci and Dominguez."

"I did. I'm calling to see how you're feeling."

"I'm okay."

"What happened?"

"Things got a little intense last night with Christina, and I don't know... I guess my heart rate and blood pressure bottomed out. I don't remember much of it."

"It's a good thing you were already there when it happened."

"Yeah."

"What's up with Christina?" Sam asked, even though she already knew. She wanted to hear his take on it.

"She says we're done. I don't know anything more than that. The nurses told me they released Alex this morning, and they went home. I haven't heard from her."

He sounded so broken. Sam couldn't think of a better way to describe the vibe coming from him. Closing her eyes, she searched for the right words. "I'm sorry." That was all she could think of to say. "Maybe this is just a bump in the road, and she'll feel differently after she gets some rest."

"I don't think so. She seemed pretty sure last night."

Sam had gotten the same impression. "How long are you going to be there?"

"Until later today. They wanted to monitor me for at least twelve hours before they release me."

"If you need somewhere to stay, we can squeeze you in here."

"Thanks, but I'll figure something out. I heard you took in the Beauclair kids."

"Yeah, much to the Secret Service's dismay."

He grunted out a laugh. "I'll bet." After a pause, he said, "I'm sorry about the shit I said last night. It was uncalled-for."

Yes, it had been, but Sam decided to let it go in light of the bigger things he was currently dealing with. "Gonzo... I want you to do something for me."

"Um, okay."

"Will you talk to Trulo?" she asked.

"Aw, come on, Sam," he said on a groan. "Been there, done that. Don't make me go there again."

"You're not yourself, Tommy. Anyone who knows you can see it. I want you to feel better and get back on track."

"Are you saying I'm not doing the job?"

"Did those words ever come out of my mouth? I'm worried about *you*, my *friend*, not my colleague. But I won't lie to you. I'm worried about your personal issues eventually leaking into the job. If that happens, I can't promise I'll be able to protect you."

He had no response to that.

"I'm going to ask Trulo to stop by today. It's up to you

if you talk to him or not, but I'd really encourage you to try. He helped a lot after Stahl attacked me."

His deep sigh came through loud and clear. "I don't know what you want me to say."

"Tell him how you *feel*, Tommy. Tell someone, before it ruins your life."

"Hasn't it already?"

"Not yet it hasn't. You can still put things back together, but you have to want to. Let us help you, please?"

After another long pause, he said, "I'll talk to him."

"Thank you."

"Not sure what good it'll do."

"Give him a chance to help you. That's all I ask."

"Yeah, all right."

"I'll call him now."

"What's happening on the case?"

"Don't worry about that. We've got it covered. Just focus on you right now and take care of yourself. Please? A lot of people care very much about you."

"Thanks."

"I'll check in later."

"Okay."

Sam ended the call and put through another to Trulo, who answered on the first ring.

"Lieutenant," he said. "To what do I owe the honor?"

Sam smiled. "Good morning, Doc. I need a favor."

"Whatever I can do."

"My sergeant, Tommy Gonzales, is in the hospital after suffering some sort of attack that resulted in his heart rate and blood pressure bottoming out."

"Hmm."

"What does that mean?"

"I'm just wondering if he's on anything. Like opiates, for example."

The words struck fear in Sam's heart. Of course, she and her team were well aware of the epidemic raging all around them and regularly saw signs of it on the job. But Gonzo wouldn't… Oh God, *would he*?

"Sam?"

"I'm just processing this possibility. I honestly don't know. The thought never occurred to me. He's been in bad shape since he lost his partner, but we thought he was doing better. Now I don't know. I just don't know. And his girlfriend, who has been a mother to his child, broke up with him last night."

"Ouch. Sounds like things are piling up on the guy."

"Indeed. They're monitoring him for the day at GW. If there's any chance you can go over there and talk to him, I'd appreciate it."

"I'm on it. Thanks for letting me know."

"If there's anything I can do to support him, say the word. I'll do whatever he needs."

"Will do. Try not to worry. Grief is a process, and it's never pretty."

"Thanks, Doc. I appreciate your help."

"You got it."

Sam closed her phone, hoping Trulo could get through to Gonzo, that *someone* could get through to him before whatever was going on got any worse.

Nick came down the stairs, fresh from the shower and dressed for the day in the jeans and sweater he'd had on earlier. He came over to sit next to her on the sofa.

"Terry is waiting for you in the dining room."

"First things first. How'd it go with Ms. Picklestein?"

"Stop!" Sam said, laughing. "Don't put that in my head, or I'll end up calling her that!"

"You gotta admit, the name fits."

"You should've seen her after she caught sight of you, shirtless and sweaty. She was positively *giddy*."

He grimaced. "Stop it. She was not."

"Oh yes she was. Even Picklesteins know a smoking hot man when they see one."

Rolling his eyes, he said, "Anyway, about the kids…"

Sam smiled at his predictable deflection and studied his handsome, freshly shaven face.

"What?" He rubbed his cheek. "Did I miss some shaving cream?"

"Nope."

"Then what're you looking at?"

"My wonderful, sexy, amazing husband, who let me bring two kids home, even if it caused him headaches, and is doing everything he can to protect them while they're with us. I just appreciate it—and you—very much."

"My headaches are nothing compared to their heartache."

"Isn't that the truth?"

"Have they been told anything yet?"

Sam shook her head. "I'm going to call their older brother now and discuss the best way to broach that topic."

"You ought to make that call somewhere they can't overhear it."

"I will."

"And when the time comes to tell them, we'll do it together."

"Okay."

Nick leaned in to kiss her. "What if they can't find anyone who will take them?"

The question landed like a punch to her gut. "They will. They have family."

"What if?" he asked again, looking madly vulnerable.

She shook her head. "I can't go there. I'm already worried about how attached to them everyone is getting—you, me, Scotty, Shelby…"

"Think about it anyway. Just in case."

"In case of what?" she asked, feeling more undone by the second.

"Sam. Take a breath. I'm simply asking you to consider what we'll do if Picklestein can't find anyone to take them."

"We… We can't, Nick. It's too much. They'll need everything, and we…"

"Could give them anything and everything they need."

She shook her head. "Please. Don't do this to me. It's already going to be hard enough to hand them over to their family members."

"Fair enough." He kissed her forehead and then her lips. "I'm sorry."

"No need to apologize. I appreciate what you're saying, but I just can't go there."

"I understand, babe." He kissed her again. "Maybe the little ones will take a nap this afternoon and we can score some time alone on this unexpected day at home."

"That'd be nice."

"Let's try to make it happen." After stealing one more kiss, he got up. "I'd better go see what I can do about this trip I'm supposed to take, in light of the fact that we now have two extra kids living with us. I probably shouldn't be out of the country while that's happening at home."

"Definitely not," she said, smiling. "Keep me posted."

"Will do."

She enjoyed the fine sight of him walking into the dining room to find Terry before she took her phone and went upstairs. Outside the bathroom in the hallway, she could hear Aubrey chattering and Shelby talking, but still nothing from Alden. She wished there was something she could do or say that would make everything better for him, but there was nothing anyone could do to reduce the impact of what he and his sister would have to be told—soon.

With that in mind, Sam went into her bedroom to place the call to Elijah.

"Hello?" he said, tentatively. He was probably afraid to answer his phone after the dreadful call he'd received last night.

"This is Lieutenant Sam Holland, Metro PD in Washington, DC."

"You're the one who's married to the VP."

"Yes, I am. I'm also the one who's taken temporary custody of your brother and sister."

"How are they? They're all I can think about."

"They're doing okay, but they're going to need to be told what's happened. I wondered if there's any chance you might be able to come here. It would help, I think, if you were here when we tell them."

"I've got tickets on the train at noon. I'll be there by midafternoon."

"That works." Sam gave him their address. "I'll let the Secret Service know you're coming. They'll need ID at the checkpoint."

"No problem."

"Could we talk for a minute about your father and stepmother? I know you've been away at school, but did either of them mention any problems they were having with other people, any issue that might've led to something like this?"

"I've been trying to think of anything since Agent Hill called me last night, but there's nothing that I knew of, except the madness with his former business partner, which I'm sure you already know about."

"Yes, we've been briefed by the FBI. What was your dad doing for work since relocating to DC?"

"He'd been consulting with high-tech companies who wanted his expertise on the software he developed. I don't really know the specifics, but he was in demand."

"Do you know if he continued to work under his real name or if he used the alias?"

"His real name."

"I'm wondering why he did that if he'd gone to the trouble to relocate his family under new names."

"That was the name his professional reputation was tied to—or what was left of it after that son of a bitch Piedmont ruined everything for him—and the rest of us. It's been a fucking nightmare." He paused before he said, "I'm sorry."

"You don't need to apologize to me. I can't imagine what you and your family have been through."

"I wouldn't believe it if I hadn't lived through it. My poor dad. Everything he worked for his whole life, gone because of someone else's greed. And then we had to change our names and go into hiding. Because of *him*. Because they were afraid he would do something just like this."

"Can you think of anyone else, besides Piedmont, who might've had a beef with your father and stepmother?"

"It was him. It had to be him."

"I understand why you would be so certain, but I've

learned to look beyond the obvious when investigating homicides."

"Agent Hill said they were tortured, bound and set on fire. No one else in this world would have reason to do something like that to them other than Piedmont, who blamed my father for everything when he was the one who ruined their lives. Not my dad."

Sam could tell she wasn't going to get anything else from the son, who firmly believed there could've only been one person responsible. "Are you in touch with your mother?"

"Yes," he said tentatively. "What about her?"

"Can you tell me her name and where I might find her?"

"Why do you need her? She's been out of my father's life for fifteen years."

"Just being thorough."

"Her name is Margaret Armstrong. She never changed her last name after they divorced."

"And she lives where?"

"Ojai, California."

"When did you last see her or talk to her?"

"I saw her over the summer and talked to her last week. I still don't understand why you'd ask about her."

"I'm covering all the bases, Elijah. That's how this works. Was your parents' divorce amicable or hostile?"

"Sorta hostile. They fought over me for two years. My mom said my dad squashed her with his money. But that was a long time ago now."

"What precipitated their breakup?"

"He met Cleo."

And there we have it, Sam thought. "Can you tell me more about how that transpired?"

He sighed deeply. "Cleo was hired as a marketing expert to help promote the software developed by APG. My dad swore to me that nothing happened between them until after he and my mom had split, but my mom never believed that."

"What do you believe?"

"My dad never lied to me. If he said nothing happened, nothing happened. Things between my parents were messed up long before he ever met Cleo."

"How so?"

"My mom is a good person, a really good person, but she's had a lot of challenges."

"What kind of challenges?"

"This won't be in the paper or anything, will it?"

"It's for my information, unless our investigation leads in your mother's direction."

"It won't," he said emphatically. "She had nothing to do with this."

"Tell me about her challenges."

"She's suffered from schizophrenia in the past. She's on good meds now and doing really well. It's been years since she's had any kind of incidents."

Sam took frantic notes. "In the past, when she would have incidents, what did they involve?"

"There were voices, in her mind, that directed her to do things that were wildly out of character for her."

"Was she ever violent?"

"Sometimes," he said hesitantly before quickly adding, "but not because she wanted to be. It was the disease."

"Was she ever violent with you?"

"I don't get why this matters. She had nothing to do with my dad's murder. If she were going to murder him, she would've done it years ago."

"Do you think she'd be capable of murdering him?"

"I gotta go. I've got class and then a train to catch."

"I understand that this is extremely difficult for you, but you and I are on the same side. We both want justice for your dad and Cleo, and for you and your siblings."

"My mom didn't do it. Duke Piedmont killed them. That's all I can tell you."

"One more thing before I let you go. When was the last time you saw your dad and Cleo?"

"I was home for the weekend two weeks ago."

"Did you pick up on any unusual tension or anything out of the ordinary?"

After a pause, he said, "No, I didn't. I need to go, or I'll be late for class."

"No problem. We'll see you when you get here."

When the line went dead, Sam closed her phone and drew a big circle around the name of Margaret Armstrong. There was definitely more to the story there, and Sam would be looking hard in her direction.

CHAPTER EIGHTEEN

GONZO REPEATEDLY TRIED to call Christina, but she didn't pick up. When he tried a fourth time, the call went straight to voice mail, which made him wonder if she'd turned off the phone. He decided to text her.

I'd like to know how my son is doing.

It took half an hour for a reply to come through, and when it did, he was sorry he'd asked.

NOW you want to know how OUR son is doing?!? That's awesome. Haha! Where were you last night when I had to sign legal documents as if I'm his LEGAL parent, which I am NOT?!?! Go to hell, Tommy. I packed up your clothes, and Freddie is picking them up after work. Have a nice life.

"*Fuuuuck*," he said as he fell back against the pillows, closing his eyes. Pain ripped through him, starting in his chest and working its way to the rest of him. She'd had time to pack his shit, which must mean Alex was better. He ran his fingers through his hair, trying to make sense of what she'd said and what it meant.

They were really over. He expected a burst of predictable pain that didn't materialize. He'd gone numb where she was concerned. She'd become one more thing he couldn't handle in the aftermath of Arnold's death, one more person who wanted something he no longer had to give.

Despite the pain that had him craving the relief he could only get from Vicodin, the thought of losing Christina had no impact on him whatsoever. But his son was another story altogether, and he had no intention of losing him. As soon as he got out of here, he'd call Andy, Nick's lawyer friend who'd helped him in the past, and ask for advice on how best to proceed. He had no desire for any kind of legal hassle with Christina. It was in Alex's best interest to have them both in his life, and that's what he would have. But there was no way Gonzo would allow her to cut him out of his own son's life. That was not going to happen.

A knock on the door had him turning to see who was there. *Oh fucking hell.* Goddamned Trulo. They hadn't wasted any time getting the department shrink over there. He'd probably come running when Sam called him. Of course he had. It wasn't every day Trulo got to work with a head case like he'd become lately.

Trulo, a wiry guy with thinning hair, looked at Gonzo with kind gray eyes and empathy Gonzo didn't want. Why couldn't everyone just leave him the fuck alone? "May I come in?"

"Can I stop you?" Gonzo asked, not caring in the least that he was being rude to someone who'd been kind to him since that awful night last January. Not to mention that Trulo could take him off the job, if he deemed it necessary. And wouldn't that cap off a spectacular twenty-four hours?

"Actually, you can stop me," Trulo said. "If you don't want me here, just say the word."

I don't want you here, he thought. But rather than say that, he only shrugged. "I promised Sam I'd see you, so I'll see you."

Trulo gestured to the chair next to Gonzo's bed. "May I?"

"Go ahead." Gonzo resigned himself to getting through this so he could go back to figuring out what to do about Christina and Alex, not to mention where he was going to live now that she'd kicked him out of the home *he* paid for. Not that she didn't do her share to support their family, but how was he supposed to swing the rent on *two* places in DC on a detective's salary?

He was well and truly fucked in more ways than one. When would that nurse be by with his meds? Checking his watch, he saw that it'd been four hours since she'd been in, and the dose she'd given him then was beginning to wear off. He could always tell when the meds were wearing off. Edginess set in, his anxiety spiked and the pain... Jesus, it could take down a horse. He'd never experienced anything quite like it.

"Sergeant?" Trulo's voice interrupted the increasingly desperate thoughts running through his mind.

Gonzo glanced at him, noted his brows were furrowed. "Yeah?"

"I was asking about what happened last night that landed you in the hospital. You didn't hear me?"

"Sorry, I was just thinking." He shifted to find a more comfortable position, and pain reverberated through his body. Where was that fucking nurse? Or, better yet, where was his coat with the pills he'd stashed in the inside pocket? Remembering he had them was like finding water in the desert. If he could just get rid of Trulo, he could have a pill. The thought of the relief that would follow calmed him ever so slightly.

"Tommy?"

"I, um, my girlfriend broke up with me. I hadn't eaten all day, and I guess my blood sugar was low, so my blood pressure and heart rate dropped. That's all it was. No big deal."

"You said your girlfriend broke up with you? As I re-call, the two of you have been together awhile."

"Almost two years," he said through gritted teeth.

"Why did she break up with you?"

"You'd have to ask her that."

"You mind if I do?"

Startled, Gonzo looked at him. "For real?"

"I'd like to know what's going on with you. I figure she's probably got some insight."

"I, ah, I don't know how I'd feel about that. She's pissed, and you have the power to control my job. That combination doesn't sit well with me."

"No one's after your job, Sergeant. That's not what this is about."

"Then what's it about?"

"It's a check-in to see how you are. You've been through a lot. There'll be steps forward and steps back-ward as you work to get past what happened last January."

"Get past it?" Gonzo asked, instantly infuriated. "You expect me to *get past* watching my partner be slaughtered right in front of me? You expect me to get over the fact that he was killed because I was annoyed by him and told him he could take the lead with the suspect if he would only *shut the fuck up* about how cold and hungry and

tired he was? What's the timeline for getting over that? I'd sure like to know."

"I apologize for my poor choice of words. Obviously, the impact of Detective Arnold's death is still very present for you."

"You mean Detective Arnold's *murder*, don't you?"

"Yes, of course."

"I have to testify soon at the probable cause hearing for the scumbag who killed him. It's taken this long because they gave him a full psych eval to make sure the poor baby is up for enduring the trial. Did you know that?"

"I hadn't heard that, but I'm not surprised you have to testify as you were the only witness."

"Yeah, lucky me."

"Is the probable cause hearing stressing you out?"

"What do you think?"

"Is the stress perhaps making you do things that you wouldn't ordinarily do?"

"Like what?"

"I don't know. You tell me."

Gonzo rolled his eyes to high heaven. "Do they make you guys take a class in shrink school on how to ask vague questions?"

Trulo laughed. "Nah, we figure out how to do that on our own. We find that when we let the patient figure out their own crap, it tends to be more effective than when we lead them to it."

"If you say so."

"Back to whether you've been doing things out of the ordinary. Perhaps it's because you're feeling stressed about having to testify against the man who murdered your partner. I mean, that would make anyone stressed.

For instance, I imagine the lieutenant is stressed about having to testify against Stahl."

Gonzo shrugged. "I don't know. I guess she is. She hasn't said anything about it to us."

"Doesn't mean she isn't feeling it, the same way you have to be feeling this next stage in getting justice for Arnold and what that'll require of you."

The words "getting justice for Arnold" resonated with him. He'd do whatever he could to make sure the man who killed his partner would spend the rest of his life rotting in jail. That would be a small price to pay for what he'd done to a young man who'd had his whole life in front of him.

For fuck's sake. Gonzo realized tears were rolling down his face. He angrily brushed them away. The last thing he needed was to break down in front of the department shrink.

Trulo handed him a tissue from a box on the bedside table. "You're dealing with a lot. What can we do to help you through it?"

You can take me back to that night in January. I would've done it all differently. I would've taken the lead the way I always did. It should've been me. I wish it had been me. "Nothing."

"Can I offer one piece of advice?"

"If you must."

"Keeping it all inside is a recipe for disaster. You're surrounded by people who want to help—at home and at work. People care, Tommy."

"What can they do? No one can change what happened nine months ago, so what exactly do you want me to say to them?"

"Tell them how you feel. Tell me how you feel. Tell *someone*."

"I feel like fucking shit! All the time! What do you want to me to say? That I can't get a minute's relief from the images that torture me, of the gurgling sound he made when he was trying to breathe or the way he was dead before I even realized what'd happened? Do you want me to say I don't give a shit about anything or anyone—not the woman I supposedly love or my job or anything other than my son? Is that what you want to hear?"

"It's a good place to start."

Exhausted by the outburst, Gonzo fell back against the pillows.

"Does it give you any relief to say those things out loud?"

"No. Nothing brings relief." Except the Vicodin, but he couldn't say that, or Trulo would lock him up, and he'd be unable to get it. The thought of being without it was enough to spark a full-on panic.

"Before I came over, I took a quick look at your jacket to refresh my memory on a few things," he said, referring to Gonzo's employment file.

Panic overtook him. Where was he going with this?

"Not that long before you lost your partner, you were shot in the neck in a near-fatal incident."

Gonzo pointed to the three-inch scar on his neck that served as a reminder of another day he'd much rather forget. "My war wound. Ironic that Arnold was the one who saved my life by applying pressure to the wound, huh? I couldn't do a fucking thing for him, but he saved me."

"In addition to that, your lieutenant was kidnapped and tortured by the man who used to command your squad. Detective McBride was kidnapped and raped. The mother of a son you didn't know you had until he was several months old was murdered, and you were briefly considered a suspect."

"What's your point, Doc?"

"You've been through a lot, Tommy. Any one of those things would be enough to rattle the strongest person. Taken together, and I wonder how you're still soldiering through on the job."

A twinge of discomfort rose above the numbness. Gonzo didn't like where this was leading. "What would you have me do, Doc? I have a family to support—or I did until last night anyway. I don't have the luxury of walking away like Will did."

"Let's talk about Will, shall we?"

"What about him?" What the hell did his former co-worker have to do with anything?

"Were you close to him?"

"Not particularly. We were work colleagues. He was a good detective. I was sorry to see him go. He was Arnold's closest friend. I didn't even know that until after Arnold died." Gonzo let out a huff of laughter. "Some sergeant I turned out to be, huh? I don't even know that my partner's closest friend was someone who sits right next to us every day."

"Why did Will leave?"

"You know why he left. He couldn't deal with the way Arnold died and what happened to Sam and Jeannie and me getting shot. Police work lost its luster for him. He's a single guy with no responsibilities to anyone but himself. He can do what he wants."

"What would you do if you could do anything you want?"

"What does it matter? I can't do anything I want."

"Roll with me. What if you could?"

"I'd go to the Florida Keys and spend a month fishing."

"Why don't you do it? You have forty days of sick leave on the books. What're you saving it for?"

"I don't take sick leave when I don't need it, Doc."

"I think maybe you might need it, Tommy. It might do you good to get away from it all for a little while. Your girlfriend takes good care of your little boy, right?"

"Yeah," he said softly. "She adores him."

"Maybe if you told her you need a little time to get yourself sorted, she might actually understand."

Gonzo shrugged. "I've already asked too much of her."

"What's one more thing? I assume she loved you at one time, and she's proven that she loves your son. You ought to take a break from the pressure cooker for a while and see if you can't find a productive way to cope with what's happened."

Gonzo took note of the way he said that. A productive way. Did that mean Trulo knew about the decidedly unproductive ways he'd been coping? "I'll think about it."

"Do I have your permission to speak with Christina?"

He took a deep breath. "Yeah, I guess. Knock yourself out. She's fucking furious with me right now. Good luck."

"She's not furious with me. I'll be fine." Trulo stood and handed Gonzo his card. "Call me if I can help. Day or night. If you need me, call me. Nothing that happens between us will ever affect the status of your job, unless I feel you're a danger to yourself or others. Okay?"

Gonzo nodded and took the card. "Thanks for coming by."

"Go easy on yourself, Tommy. As crappy as it might seem to you, what you're feeling is perfectly normal in light of what you've been through. I really want you to consider some time away. I think it might help." He extended his hand.

Gonzo returned the handshake.

"I'll check in on you later."

He was almost out the door when Gonzo said, "Hey, Doc?"

Trulo turned back, eyebrow raised.

"Thanks again."

"Anytime, Sarge."

For a long time after he left, Gonzo stared down at the business card in his hand, thinking about what the doctor had said. The idea of getting away appealed to him but going away without Alex and Christina didn't. Maybe it was time for all of them to take a break—together—and see if they could somehow put their family back on track.

First, though, he had to get Christina to talk to him. That would take some doing.

WITH NICK SEQUESTERED with his team in the dining room and the kids upstairs watching a movie with Shelby and Noah, Sam dug into the Beauclair case reports her squad had put together yesterday, thoroughly reviewing the principal players in the case—Jameson Beauclair/Armstrong, Cleo Beauclair/Armstrong, Duke Piedmont, Margaret Armstrong and others associated with the now-defunct APG. Sam was thankful for the break in the action that gave her time to read early in the day rather than later when she was tired, and her dyslexia tended to kick in.

More than one thousand employees had been let go when APG shut down, and Sam wrote down the name of the human resources director in case they needed to look into who, if anyone, might've been out for vengeance on the guy who'd done the right thing and cost a lot of people their jobs. It was a stretch, but Sam had learned to pull every thread and stretch in every direction when investigating a homicide.

Jameson had been a rock star. There simply was no better way to describe his meteoric rise in the high-tech industry, which began with work on what would turn out to be APG's signature product while he was still living in a Stanford dorm room. With the help of his friends, Piedmont and Gorton, he'd built APG into a *Fortune* 500 powerhouse and made himself and his partners billionaires with software that had revolutionized the way products were moved around the country. Anyone with a warehouse and shipping function had adapted APG's software, and it had become state-of-the-art within three dizzying years of its initial launch.

The company had been among the darlings of Silicon Valley, with their employees housed within a one-million-square-foot campus that teamed with innovative hipsters in hoodies and Chuck Taylors. The APG principals had been on the covers of *Forbes* and *Wired* and had been featured no fewer than six different times in the *Wall Street Journal*, once in a story about self-made billionaires.

They'd had the world by the balls. Until one of them got greedy. She read the reports in the *Los Angeles Times*, *Wall Street Journal* and many other publications that chronicled the company's downfall. They'd gone from Silicon Valley darling to pariahs, with the SEC, FBI and other regulators swooping in and shutting them down so fast that employees hadn't even been able to retrieve their personal belongings before being locked out of the office.

One high-tech publication had called it "A Dizzying Fall from Grace," noting how the company had gone from one of the top ten most buzzed about companies to ruin, literally overnight after Armstrong reported what he'd uncovered about his partner, Piedmont, to the SEC. The downfall had been swift and merciless, with Piedmont charged with insider trading days after the company was shut down.

Again, she was struck by the obvious decline that played out in Jameson Armstrong's appearance. He went from a handsome, dark-haired, smiling, youthful man to a gray-haired shell of his former self in the span of six months. The change in him was startling and told the true story of the strain he'd been under as he put together the case against his former partner, friend and Stanford roommate.

Piedmont, on the other hand, had remained larger than life through it all, smiling and deflecting and generally claiming it had all been a big mistake, and the truth would come out when he got his day in court. Except, long before that day arrived, he took off, and no one had seen or heard from him in more than three years. He'd since been connected to criminal enterprises that ran the gamut from drugs to prostitutes to gambling to murder. Before it all went bad, he could've been the star of a reality TV show called *Rich Guy Gone Wild*. His playboy lifestyle had been a source of tremendous interest. Pictures of him with women hanging from him had appeared in newspapers, on entertainment shows and gossip websites.

Sam couldn't help but sympathize with Armstrong,

who'd remained faithfully devoted to the company while Piedmont went wild, his behavior eventually leading to their downfall.

Her phone chimed with a text from Avery.

Sent you an email. You didn't get this from me.

CHAPTER NINETEEN

SAM OPENED HER email and noted Avery had sent the message from a personal account, rather than his official FBI address. *Interesting.* She clicked on the attached PDF and opened what she quickly realized was the dossier he had told them about yesterday, in which Armstrong had laid out the case against Piedmont. He'd basically done the job of the SEC and FBI investigators for them, with every offense neatly documented. She skimmed the twenty-page document that had served as a summary of the case against Piedmont.

Armstrong's meticulous work, done while knowing it would spell professional ruination and the loss of the company he'd poured his heart and soul into, was admirable, to say the least.

Sam tried to put herself in his shoes, having learned something about his partner and friend that could ruin them all, and still doing the right thing. That said a lot about what kind of man Jameson Armstrong/Beauclair had been.

Since the kids were still settled with Shelby, Sam kept moving forward, looking next at Cleo Dennis Armstrong/ Beauclair, who came from a prominent Northern California family known for its connections to the wine industry. Her parents owned a company that lobbied on behalf of the wine industry. They worked between Napa,

Sacramento and Washington. Sam made a note of the parents' names with the intention of speaking to them at some point today.

Prior to her tenure at APG, Cleo had worked on the staff of a hip blog in San Francisco that tracked fashion trends. Sam went back to one of the earlier articles about APG from the good times. She read Jameson's account of meeting Cleo at a dinner party and being immediately attracted to her crackling intelligence and sparkling wit.

"I was in the process of beginning divorce proceedings from my first wife and in no position whatsoever to begin something new, but the minute I met Cleo, I knew she would change my life," he'd said in a *Forbes* article. "Selfishly, I wanted to keep her close until I was ready for her, so I hired her to work in APG's corporate communications department."

In a *Los Angeles Times* article that had followed the company's implosion, ten inches was given to Armstrong's ugly divorce from his first wife, Margaret, and the ensuing custody battle over Elijah, who'd been six at the time. Margaret's mental health challenges had become public during the case, which Jameson claimed to be horrified about. "That never came from me or my attorneys," he'd said adamantly.

The case had dragged on for two years, during which time Jameson was never seen in public with Cleo. In the end, he'd been awarded primary custody of Elijah during the school year, with Margaret awarded liberal visitation, all holidays and school vacations, provided she underwent mental health evaluations four times a year. That the terms had been made public at all said much about the level of interest in Armstrong and his family at the pinnacle of APG's impressive run.

"My ex-husband is a powerful and influential man," Margaret had said in a local TV interview after the case had been resolved. "Powerful and influential people can get away with things the rest of us can't, and this case is certainly proof of that." She'd paused before adding, "Having my personal medical condition made public has been a huge violation of my privacy, but that's what happens when you're David up against Goliath."

The woman's heartbreak and outrage had come through loud and clear. She was someone they needed to look at very closely. Not only had Jameson fallen for Cleo while he was technically still married to Margaret, but her mental health challenges had been used against her in the custody battle. Even though all of that had happened years ago, sometimes resentments festered for years before they boiled over.

Out of the corner of her eye, she saw the French doors to the dining room open. "I can *feel* you watching me," she said, smiling but not looking up from what she was doing.

"You're my favorite thing to watch. The story never gets old."

"Someday, the story will get old and wrinkly."

"And it'll still be my favorite story ever. The story of my life." He pushed off the door frame he'd been leaning against and came over to her, sitting next to her and putting his arm around her. "How's it going?"

"Slow and steady wins the race—or so I hope. I want justice for those babies upstairs so damned badly."

"So do I. If anyone can get it for them, you can. Are you leaning in any particular direction?"

"The ex-partner is the obvious choice. The guy has motive up the wazoo because he blames Armstrong for ratting him out to the Feds, although Armstrong had no choice. If he hadn't, he could've been prosecuted himself. What a catch-22. Report your ex–best friend and business partner, destroy the business you've spent your entire adult life building in the process, or run the risk of your own criminal trouble."

"He did the only thing he could."

"Yeah. Then there's his ex-wife, the schizophrenic, who he battled for custody of the older son. Her mental health challenges were made public during the custody case, and she blamed him for that, even though he adamantly denied it. The first wife, Margaret, was also convinced that he was fooling around with Cleo while he was still married to her, even though he adamantly denied that too."

"If she were going to come after him, wouldn't it have happened a long time ago?"

"Sometimes these things simmer for years until one small thing causes an explosion. Their son, Elijah, is coming from New Jersey and will arrive later in the day. I hope to get the chance to speak with him some more about the dynamic between his parents."

Nick rubbed her back, and she closed her eyes to enjoy the stolen moment with him. Even in a houseful of people, he made her feel like they were the only two people in the world.

"I have good news," he said.

Sam opened her eyes and glanced at him. "What kind of good news?"

"The kind where I only have to go to Europe for one week instead of three."

Sam let out a happy shout and hugged him. "That is the best news *ever*. How'd you pull that off?"

"I said I was willing to go for one week only, and they could decide how best to use the time. The secretary of state is stepping up to do some of the other stuff they had me doing. I told Terry I won't travel for more than a week at a time. *Ever.*"

"God, I love you. Have I told you that lately?"

His low chuckle rumbled through his chest. "I hope it's obvious that I love you too, so much that I caused headaches for an entire administration, all so I don't have to be away from my beautiful wife any longer than necessary."

Sam breathed in the fresh clean scent of him, the scent of home. Even a week without him would be torture, but that was better than *three* weeks. "Did you create an international incident?"

"Quite possibly. Terry said some of the foreign dignitaries we were due to meet with will be crushed that I'm not coming."

"You're as popular over there as you are here."

"I only care about being popular right here in this house."

"You get the award for most popular man in the house *and* most likely to get laid tonight."

His laughter made her smile. Everything about him made her smile.

"Um, Mr. Vice President?" Terry said from the dining room. "We need you in here."

"Duty calls," Nick said. "Kiss me—and make it a good one to hold me over until later."

Sam didn't care that there was a Secret Service agent minding the front door or Nick's team in the dining room. All she cared about was the chance to kiss her sexy husband in the middle of a workday. She placed her hand on his face and went for broke, slipping him a hint of tongue as a preview of things to come later. When she pulled back, he looked rather stunned and undone. "Get back to work, Mr. Vice President."

He stole another kiss. "Mmmm. To be continued. I'm still hoping for a late-afternoon snuggle if you can get everyone out of here and the littles take a nap."

"You'll get my ultradeluxe service for cutting that trip by two weeks."

"What does ultradeluxe service include, just so I can look forward to it all day?"

She leaned in and whispered in his ear, pulling back in time to see his gorgeous eyes go wide with surprise.

"I thought I only got that on my birthday and anniversaries?"

Sam laughed and bumped him with her shoulder. "Go away. I have work to do and so do you." She stood when he did. "And I need to go check on my babies."

"Sam."

"Figure of speech. I know they're not mine." *But I wish they were.* The thought came over her so suddenly, she staggered slightly under the weight of the realization.

"Babe? Are you okay?"

"I'm fine. Stood up too fast, and I'm hungry."

"Take it easy, will you? We don't need you getting sick on top of everything else."

"It's all good," she said on her way up the stairs. "Don't worry about me."

"May as well tell me not to breathe."

Working from home had many perks, not the least of which was time with Nick in the middle of the day. She found Shelby and the kids in Scotty's room. They were on his bed, with Shelby in the middle, Noah asleep in her arms and one little blond child on either side of her, resting their heads on her as they watched *Minions*.

Aubrey perked up when Sam appeared in the doorway. "Is Mommy here?"

"No, honey."

"Where is she? She never leaves us this long. Is she worried about us?"

Though Alden didn't say anything, he watched Sam with wise, knowing eyes. She wondered if he already understood something his sister had yet to fathom.

"I'm not sure." Sam felt like shit for lying to them. But she would wait for Elijah to get there before they shared the dreadful news with the children. "How about some lunch? Is anyone hungry?"

Aubrey shrugged as if nothing would interest her except her mother.

Sam's heart broke for them both. After lunch, she would call Trulo for some advice on how best to go about telling the children. The thought of having to shatter their little world made Sam ache.

She glanced at Shelby, who blinked back tears.

"How about grilled cheese?" Shelby asked cheerfully. "Scotty says mine are the best ever. You want to see if he's right?"

Aubrey nodded. "Okay."

Thank God for Shelby, Sam thought again as they trooped downstairs. Her sweet sincerity was just what they needed.

"Let me settle Noah, and then we'll see about some grilled cheese," Shelby said. She kept a small portable crib in the laundry room off the kitchen.

Sam had poured apple juice for the kids and gotten them settled at the table when her phone rang.

"Go ahead," Shelby said. "I've got this."

"Thanks," Sam said, taking the call from Freddie. "What's up?"

"Might be nothing, but I found a report in the system that warrants further investigation. A traffic altercation Cleo had on Friday. Apparently, a fender bender escalated into a screaming match."

"Send it to my email. Anything else?"

"Jeannie and I are working the neighborhood again today, and Green is taking a closer look at the kids' school."

"What about the school?"

"I'm not sure yet. He said he's following a hunch."

"Tell him to call me and clue me in on this so-called hunch."

"Will do. We'll be there at four or we'll check in."

"Sounds good. Thanks." She ended the call with him and took a call from Green five minutes later.

"Afternoon, Detective."

"Hey, Lieutenant. Cruz told me to give you a call to fill you in. In addition to following the money trail, I'm taking a high-level look at the school. I've heard a few things from friends who've had kids go there that makes me think it's worth a deeper look."

"What kinds of things?"

"Mostly about the parents being crazy, for lack of a better word."

"How so?"

"Competitive, malicious, vindictive. Too much money, too much time on their hands. That kind of thing."

"Sounds like a lovely place," Sam said.

"It sounds like private school."

"And you have some experience with private school?"

"Far too much. Thirteen years of that nonsense. My mother could tell you a few stories about the parents."

"I'd be interested to speak to someone who has kids there now. Preferably someone normal."

"I have someone you can talk to. I'll have her call you. Her name is Marlene Peters. I play football with her husband, Dave."

"You play football?"

He laughed. "Flag football. We're all too old and too busy to risk injury."

"This I need to see."

"You're more than welcome to come by the field any Sunday, but only if you cheer for my team."

"I'd love to. We'll make a plan for that."

"Sounds good. I'll have Marlene call you. She actually reached out to me when she heard about the Beauclairs."

"How come?"

"First to ask me if it was true they were killed and then to express disbelief."

"Did she know them?"

"She knew Cleo but not Jameson. Apparently, Cleo was known as a supermom. She was the mom who volunteered for everything, had the elaborate birthday parties, organized playdates and crafts and generally made everyone else look like a slouch in the mom department."

The description alone was enough to make Sam feel inadequate. Should she be organizing playdates and crafts for Scotty? Would he suffer someday for not having had a mother like that? The thoughts overwhelmed and saddened her. She would never be that kind of mother, but no one would ever love him as much as she did.

"Sam?" Green said. "Are you still there?"

"I'm here. Just trying to process everything these poor kids have lost."

"How are they?"

"Confused and quiet. The boy, Alden, hasn't said a word to any of us. I'm particularly concerned about him. Their older brother, Elijah, will be here later today. I'm hoping he can help us break through to poor Alden."

"I hope so. It's such a sad thing."

"Yes, it is. I'll let you go to keep pursuing the school angle, and I'll look forward to talking to Marlene."

"I'll have her call you right away."

"Thanks, Cameron."

"No problem."

Sam closed her phone and went into the kitchen to join the kids for lunch. She had downed half a grilled cheese when her phone rang again. She left the kitchen and took the call from a number she didn't recognize. "Lieutenant Holland."

"This is Marlene Peters. Cam asked me to call you?"

"Yes, thank you. I appreciate you taking the time."

"You're kidding, right?" she asked with a laugh. "I'll dine out for weeks on the fact that I got to talk to you. My friends will be green with envy."

Sam was never certain how to reply to comments like that. "Oh, um, thank you?"

She laughed again. "I don't mean to make you uncomfortable. I know you want to talk about Cleo and her family. I'm just so heartsick over what's happened."

"It's very tragic, indeed."

"The children… I just can't stop thinking about them."

"They're okay, all things considered. We're waiting for their brother to arrive from college, so we can tell them what's happened."

"Those poor babies. Cleo was such a wonderful mother."

"That's what I've heard. Can you tell me more about her?"

"She was amazing, the kind of woman you'd love to hate if she hadn't been so damned sweet and kind and caring. At first, people at the school weren't sure what to make of her. We knew her husband was loaded, but we weren't sure what he did, so of course there was speculation that he was into something illegal. And then there was the fact that she never once left the school while the kids were there, which was weird. Most moms live for that little break from their kids, but not Cleo. She stayed and filled in wherever she was needed. We joked that she made the rest of us look like slackers. But I sensed that she stayed because she was afraid of something happening to the kids when she wasn't there."

"What made you think that?"

"There was a wariness to her. As sweet and kind as she was, she didn't get close to any of the other moms. Her kids started in the summer program, and we were both room moms. I didn't know her any better months later than I did at the beginning, even though I talked to her just about every day."

"Did she ever mention her husband or their marriage or anything like that?"

"No, never. I never heard her speak of him at all. Their neighbor, Lauren, she knew him a little because her husband played golf with him a couple of times. She said he seemed like a nice guy, but like his wife, he kept his cards close to the vest. He never talked about his work or anything overly personal except when it came to the kids. They both obviously adored their kids and were extremely devoted to them. I just can't help but wonder what they had to hide that made them private to the point of being secretive, you know?"

"Yes, I do, and I know what they were hiding from. You will too before much longer. Suffice it to say they had good reason to keep a low profile."

"Hmm. Interesting. I like that explanation better than what some people have said about them."

"And what's that?"

"That they were standoffish and arrogant. I never picked up that vibe from her, and that's not how Lauren's husband described Cleo's husband. He said he was a friendly guy who was an extremely good golfer."

"So, they were the subject of a lot of speculation at the school?"

"How can I say this without sounding like part of the problem?" After a pause, she said, "Usually when people move into our part of town or enroll their kids at Northwest Academy, they come with a bit of a pedigree, if you will. They're CEOs, ambassadors, former senators, prominent lobbyists, grandchildren of presidents, even. We know who they are. The Beauclairs were the exception to that rule. No one knew anything about them, which made people rabidly curious."

To Sam, it sounded like they needed to get lives of their own, but then again, she never had understood the frantic need to know every detail of other people's lives. "Was anyone particularly hateful toward Cleo or her family?"

"Enough to murder them? No, but there was one woman, Emma Knoff, the president of the PTO at the school, who was annoyed by Cleo."

"In what way?"

"She felt Cleo was stepping on toes with all her volunteering and helping out. She was particularly vocal about the fact that Cleo never left the building when the kids were at school. *Weird* was the word she used to describe it, but Emma is the kind of person who wants to be in charge of everything. Cleo made her feel threatened in her little fiefdom."

Sam shook her head in disbelief. Who *were* these people? "Can you tell me where I might find Emma?"

"You won't tell her I sent you, will you?"

"No, I won't mention your name. I'll just say some of the parents we spoke to recalled her being upset about Cleo's presence at the school. Something like that."

"Well, that's the truth. She was upset about it." Marlene gave her Emma's address and phone number.

"I really appreciate your help," Sam said. "If you think of anything else that might be relevant, feel free to call me back. Just don't give my number to your friends."

Marlene laughed. "I'll do my best to refrain from handing it out."

"I'd appreciate that."

"Before you go, if I could just say that my husband and I... We admire and respect you and your husband so much. Thank you both for your service."

Touched, Sam said, "Thank you. That means a lot. And thanks again for your time."

"Happy to help. I hope you're able to get justice for those poor children."

"Oh, we will. You can bet on that."

CHAPTER TWENTY

SAM THOUGHT ABOUT the insight Marlene had provided. For someone who'd always wanted to be a mother, she didn't understand the mob mentality that often came with motherhood or the parents who pushed their kids almost to their breaking point in search of elusive athletic or academic scholarships.

Thankfully, her mother had never been that way. She'd had other faults that had come out when her marriage imploded, but at least she hadn't been overly pushy. Sam desperately wanted to get out there and interview Emma Knoff herself, but since she couldn't, she called Freddie and passed it along to him and Jeannie to investigate further.

"Got it," Freddie said. "Will do."

"Anything popping?"

"Not yet," he said, sounding tired and frustrated.

"We need a thread to pull, and we need it soon."

"We're on it, LT. Lot of ground to cover."

"I'll let you get back to it."

Sam decided to take the chance to reach out to Cleo's parents and Margaret Armstrong while she could. Using online white pages, she found the phone numbers she needed, and called Cleo's parents.

The phone rang several times before it was answered by a woman.

"This is Lieutenant Sam Holland, Metro PD in Washington, DC, calling to speak with the parents of Cleo Beauclair."

"You mean Cleo Armstrong, right?" the woman asked with thinly veiled hostility. "That's who she really was, and that's why she's dead."

"And you are?"

"Her sister Keely. We're living our worst nightmare, Lieutenant. We told her this was going to happen if she stayed with Jameson. He had an X on his back, and he took her down with him."

"It's possible their deaths had nothing to do with their problems with Duke Piedmont."

"Right," she said with a harsh laugh. "Now let me sell you some valuable swampland in Florida. He said he was going to kill my brother-in-law for turning him in to the Feds, and he finally made good on it, taking my beautiful sister too. If you're looking at anyone other than Duke Piedmont, you're wasting taxpayer dollars."

"May I speak with your parents, please?" Sam asked, finding it interesting that Keely hadn't asked about the children. That would've been her first question if Cleo had been her sister.

"They're not doing well, as you can imagine."

"I won't take but a few minutes of their time."

"Hold on a minute."

Sam heard low murmurs and rustling in the background before another woman came on the line.

"This is Leslie Dennis. You wanted to talk to me about my Cleo?"

"Yes, ma'am," Sam said. "This is Lieutenant Sam Holland with the Metro PD in Washington, and I'm very sorry for your loss."

"Thank you," she said, sounding tearful. "For years now, I've feared that this day would come, but I always hoped it wouldn't."

"Was your daughter fearful too?"

"Very much so. She never let her babies out of her sight, except for an occasional outing with her husband. But they never went far. Cleo couldn't relax if she wasn't with her kids. That's what Duke Piedmont did to her and to Jameson. They were always afraid."

"In the course of our investigation, we learned that your family urged her to leave Jameson after what happened with Piedmont and the company. Is that true?"

"*Yes*, we urged her to leave him! We wanted her and the children to be safe. Piedmont wanted him dead—and we had no doubt he'd make him suffer first, perhaps by killing Cleo and the children in front of him. Her father and I have had nightmares for *years* about what might happen to them. Do you have *any idea* what it's like to live with that kind of fear? I'll be honest with you, Lieutenant. Dreading this outcome was almost worse than the reality."

"You're going to hear from social services about the children."

"Tell them not to call us. We can't live like this anymore."

"Your daughter's children—"

"She made her choices when she decided to stay with him. We can't subject anyone else in our family to that kind of danger. Whoever has those children will be in danger for as long as Duke Piedmont is still alive and on the run. He has enormous resources, thanks to my son-in-law. Those children will be in danger no matter

where they are, and that's not going to be here. I have to
go tend to my family."

"Thank you for your time," Sam said, sickened by the
fact neither their aunt nor their grandmother had asked
about the children.

Though shaken by the disturbing conversation with
Cleo's mother, Sam placed the call to Margaret Armstrong, taking advantage of the current quiet to get as
much done as she could. Sam had begun to prepare her
voice mail message when a woman took the call.

"Is this Margaret Armstrong, formerly Mrs. Jameson
Armstrong?"

"Who's this?"

"Lieutenant Sam Holland, Metro PD in Washington,
DC."

"You're married to the vice president."

"Yes. Are you Jameson's ex-wife?"

"I am. Is my son all right?"

"He is, but your ex-husband and his wife have been
murdered."

She gasped. "Oh God. Does Elijah know?"

"Yes, ma'am." Sam made a note of the fact that he
had known since last night and hadn't told his mother
himself. She found that interesting. "When was the last
time you saw your ex-husband or had contact with him?"

"At my son's high school graduation, several years
ago. Why?"

"When someone is murdered, it's common practice to
thoroughly examine their past as we search for motive."

"And of course, that search led you directly to the ex-
wife he cheated on and then sued for custody of their
child while making sure the whole world knew about
her medical challenges. Am I right?"

Sam felt oddly ashamed of herself. "Yes, ma'am."

"Let me assure you that I had nothing to do with his death, but I can't help but note the karma. What goes around comes around."

"Where were you the day before yesterday?"

"Right here at home."

"Can anyone attest to that?"

"My partner, Richard. Let me put him on the phone."

"This is Richard French. How can I help you?"

Sam introduced herself and asked if he could confirm that Margaret was at home in California the day before yesterday.

"I can indeed. In fact, after five years together, this lovely lady agreed to marry me last weekend. We've been together without interruption ever since."

"Thank you for the confirmation."

"I'll put Margaret back on the phone."

"Satisfied?" she said.

"Yes, thank you and congratulations."

"I didn't kill Jameson," Margaret said, "and it breaks my heart to know what my son will have to go through because he loved his father. But people who ask for too much out of life often get what's coming to them. Jameson treated me badly. That's all I've got to say. Now, I need to go so I can call my son."

"Thank you for your time."

The line went dead, and as she closed her phone, the front door opened to admit her father and Dr. Harry Flynn, a close friend of hers and Nick's.

"Hey, boys," Sam said. "What're you two doing running around together?"

"We met up on the sidewalk," Harry said. "I'm here for a meeting with the esteemed vice president."

"I came for an update on the case," Skip said.

To Harry, Sam pointed to the dining room and tipped her face to accept a kiss on the cheek from the charming doctor. "How's my Lilia doing?" Her chief of staff at the White House had been seeing Harry for some time now.

"She's delightful and spectacular and *sexy*."

Sam put her hands over her ears. "That's way too much information."

"What can I say? I'm thoroughly besotted."

"Are you really?"

"Yes," he said, laughing. "I finally get why my buddy Nick is such a doofus since he met you. Now I'm just like him."

"Who you calling a doofus?" Nick asked from the dining room doorway.

"You, Mr. Vice President," Harry said, winking at Sam.

"My gorgeous wife is entirely worth being labeled a doofus," Nick said, smiling. "Now get in here. I don't have all day."

"Apparently, I have official business with the vice president," Harry said in a conspiratorial whisper. "What'd you make of that?"

"I haven't a clue. No one tells me anything."

"I'll tell you about it after," he shot over his shoulder as he went to shake hands with Nick, who closed the door behind them.

"What'd you suppose that's all about?" Sam asked her dad.

"If I had to guess, it would be that the president and vice president are required to travel with personal physicians, and Nick may be asking Harry to accompany him on his upcoming trip to Europe."

"Huh," Sam said. "I didn't know they were required to travel with doctors. Isn't that kinda paranoid?"

"Say he was poisoned. Wouldn't you want someone there who knew what to do and cared enough to do it as quickly as possible?"

"Gee, thanks. Like I didn't have enough things to worry about where he's concerned. Thanks for adding that to my list."

Skip laughed. "It's never happened, so you don't need to worry about it. I was tossing out a hypothetical."

"Keep your hypotheticals to yourself. I'm already terrified someone is going to take a shot at him or something." Sam shuddered. "I can't bear to think about it."

"It's far more likely to happen to you than him," he said, all hints of amusement gone.

"I know, but I wouldn't be around to have to deal with me after something happens to him."

His eyes boggled. "I'm almost afraid to admit that I actually followed that logic."

"You speak me."

"Yes, I do, baby girl. How's the case?"

"Painstaking and slow," Sam said, glancing at the kitchen door. "The kids are having lunch with Shelby. Their older brother is on his way here from Princeton, where he goes to school. We're going to tell them about the parents when he gets here." Sam glanced at her dad. "I'm worried about Alden, in particular. He hasn't said a word to any of us since he's been here. He follows Aubrey's lead."

"The little guy is traumatized. Do you think maybe he saw something?"

"I don't know. Possibly. I have to call Trulo and get his advice on how best to handle telling them."

"That's a good idea. Don't let me hold you up. I just came to see how you're doing and if I could help at all."

"Stick around. I want to bounce a few things off you if you have time."

"I got nothing but time, and I'm happy to bounce with you."

Sam smiled at his predictable reply as she put through the call to Trulo.

"Lieutenant," Trulo said. "What can I do for you?"

Eyeing the kitchen door and keeping her voice down, she said, "I have to tell two five-year-olds the worst possible news about their parents. I'm looking for a little guidance if you have a minute."

"Ah, that's a tough one."

"For sure. Their older brother is coming, and he'll be here when we tell them, but I have to admit, I'm a little out of my league here, Doc."

"Totally understand, and I'm glad you asked. One of the most important pieces of advice I can give you is to make sure they are told their parents are dead. Use that word, because they will understand it. Often, we're tempted to use gentler-sounding terms such as passed away, but that doesn't help the child to understand the finality of what they're being told. You also want them to know they're allowed to ask questions at any time. They may not react the way you or I expect them to. Sometimes they can seem almost nonchalant about life-changing news, but it could be that they're still processing what you've told them and don't fully understand yet."

Sam sat on the sofa and took notes.

"If they have comfort toys like stuffed animals or blankets, it's good to have them close by when you tell them and do it in a place where you're not likely to be disturbed in any way. They need a safe, peaceful, quiet place. I think that's the important stuff. If you'd like me to be there when you tell them, I'm more than willing to come by."

"I think we'll be okay, but I really appreciate the offer." Sam feared too many additional strangers underfoot when they were already surrounded by strangers.

"No problem. If there's anything else I can do, please feel free to reach out. While I have you, I saw Sergeant Gonzales earlier. Without giving anything away, I want you to know I encouraged him to take some time off. I think it would do him good."

"Is he okay?"

"I can't really answer that."

"I understand. Thanks again, Doc."

"Anytime."

Sam closed the phone and said to her dad, "One more call and I'm all yours."

"Take your time."

Sam called Ms. Finklestein—and yes, the word *Picklestein* ran through her mind. Damn Nick for putting that in her head! When she picked up, Sam said, "This is Sam Holland. I'm wondering if you were able to get into the Beauclairs' home to get the items the children requested. We're going to share the difficult news with them when their older brother arrives this afternoon, and it would be good to have their comfort items here by then."

"I just heard from the fire marshal, and someone from their office is going to take me in shortly. I'll come straight to your home from there."

"Very good, thank you."

"I would like to be present when they're told."

"As long as you allow us and their brother to be the ones to tell them."

"That's fine."

"We'll see you soon, then." Sam ended the call before the woman could comment further. She never had gotten along well with authority and having a social worker up in her grill made her nuts. While she knew it was entirely necessary, it still rankled and reminded her of the days when they'd had regular visits from social workers while they were in the process of adopting Scotty. Thank God that was all in the past now. "Social workers are right up there with receptionists," she said to her father, who grunted out a chuckle.

"My baby girl never did like being told what to do."

"It's a character flaw." Sam put her feet up on the coffee table, taking a break while she could. Who knew that working from home could be as ass-kicking as a day on the streets?

Skip rolled his chair closer to her and lowered his voice. "What're you thinking on this one?"

"My thoughts are all over the place, darting from the obvious ex-business partner with an ax to grind to the ex-wife who blamed the husband for outing her mental health issues during their divorce. I just ruled her out, so now I'm wondering about the moms at the kids' school who disliked Cleo for her sweetness and dedication."

Skip's brows furrowed. "They disliked her for being sweet and dedicated?"

"Apparently, those traits aren't welcome in someone new when there's already a squad of alpha bitches running the joint."

"Ahhh. I see. Your mom used to refer to it as the Mommy Brigade. She used to come home from meetings at school ready to murder someone. She'd go right for the liquor cabinet."

Sam laughed. "Maybe I'm more like her than I thought."

"You have a lot of her qualities. You're loyal and loving and a great mom."

Sam couldn't recall the last time she'd heard her father pay such a glowing compliment to the ex-wife who'd cheated on him.

"Don't look at me that way. I loved her. We were good for a long time. Until we weren't. With hindsight, I don't blame her for what she did. I was a shitty husband for the last ten years we were together."

"Wow. You're all evolved and stuff."

"Having nothing to do but sit still all day gives a guy lots of time to think and reflect."

"If you wanted to come into HQ a couple hours a day, everyone would be thrilled to have you and your brain at their disposal. You know that."

"I appreciate it, but there's nothing worse than retirees hanging around pining for the glory days."

"That's not what you'd be doing. You'd be contributing. I've got Cruz out on his freaking honeymoon for the next two weeks and Gonzo possibly taking some 'personal' time. I could use your help if you're willing to give it."

"Always willing to help you. You know that."

"Good, then you're hired starting Monday. Don't be late or I'll bust you down to Patrol."

"Nice try, Lieutenant, but I still outrank you every day and twice on Sunday."

"Are you already being insubordinate, proby? That'll be noted in your jacket." She let out a giddy laugh. "This is fun!"

Skip rolled his blue eyes, one of the only parts of him that still worked exactly the way it had before his devastating injury. "What's the next step in the investigation, Your Highness?"

"Everyone's due to report to me in person or on the phone by four. I'll know more then."

"How are the little ones doing?"

"Okay. Thank God for Shelby."

"How many times in a day do you say or think that?"

"Too many to count."

"You're not getting too attached to those kids, are you?"

"Probably. They're awfully cute."

"Sam."

"I know," she said, sighing. "Tracy said the same thing. It's hard not to get attached when they're so sweet and going through such an awful thing."

"I'll confess to being surprised to hear you'd brought them home with you. It's not like you to bring the job home."

"I know, but they needed to go somewhere, and I acted before I thought it through. Not that I regret offering, because I don't."

"Still."

"Trust me. I get it. If I've heard you say it once, I've heard it a million times. Leave the job at the office."

"Sometimes it's almost impossible to follow that advice."

"This was one of those times."

"Try not to make a habit out of it."

"Don't get too big for your britches, proby," Sam said with a small smile.

"Wouldn't dream of it."

"Right," she said, laughing. "Sure you wouldn't."

"Have you heard from Joe about the kids?" Skip asked, referring to his close friend, Joe Farnsworth, the chief of police.

"Not yet. Will I?"

"I'd pretty much count on it."

"He's going to freak, right?"

"Probably."

She took a deep breath. She'd deal with that when she had to. One thing at a time. "I'd better go check on my charges and see if I can convince them to take a little rest before their brother gets here."

"I don't envy you having to tell them this news. They'll always remember it."

Sam's chest and stomach felt heavy with the weight of what she needed to tell them and the knowledge that they would forever tie her and Nick to the worst moment of their lives. Maybe it was just as well that they wouldn't get to keep them.

"Come give your old man a smooch."

She got up and went to him, rested her hands on shoulders that were now bony rather than brawny the way they once had been, and kissed his forehead. "Love you, Skippy."

"Love you too, baby girl. Feel free to come cry on my shoulder later if you need to."

"I will, thanks."

CHAPTER TWENTY-ONE

SAM SAW HER dad out and then went to check on the kids, who were playing a game of Candy Land with Shelby at the table. "Where'd that come from?"

"Tracy brought it with the clothes."

"Who's winning?"

"Alden," Aubrey said. "He just sent Shelby all the way back to the beginning."

Shelby pretended to glower at him, and Alden laughed. The joyful noise was the best thing Sam had heard all day. Then she remembered what was ahead for Alden and his sister, and her heart began to ache for them again.

"Hey, guys, I was thinking you might want to take a little rest since you were up so late last night."

"That's a really good idea," Shelby said. "There's been some yawning during the game."

"Can we finish the game later?" Aubrey asked.

"I'll make sure no one touches it," Shelby said.

"Okay."

Sam and Shelby took them upstairs and got them settled in the room Nick had made up for them the night before.

"Can we go in Scotty's room?" Aubrey asked.

"Not this time," Sam said. "He'll be home from school soon, and he needs to do his homework, but I'm sure he'll want you to come see him when you wake up."

They tucked in the kids and drew the blinds to darken the room.

"We'll be right downstairs if you need us," Sam said, leaving the door partly open so they could hear the kids if need be.

Their little faces looked particularly tiny in the big bed, and Sam's eyes welled with tears as she left the room and leaned against a wall to gather herself.

"I feel the same way," Shelby whispered. "It's unbearable."

Sam took a step toward Shelby, who had moved to hug Sam.

They pulled back from each other a minute later, wiping their faces and laughing at themselves.

"We're a hot mess," Shelby said.

"This is why my dad is always telling me not to bring my work home."

"You did the right thing. Those babies needed us, even if it's only temporary."

"Keep telling me that when I have to let them go."

"I will if you do the same for me."

"It's a deal."

The portable baby monitor attached to Shelby's pocket came to life with a little cry from baby Noah. "One nap ends as the other begins." They walked downstairs together. "What's the plan for telling the kids about the parents?"

"We'll do it after their brother gets here from New Jersey."

"I'll stay if you think it would help. I can have Avery pick up Noah."

"You don't have to do that."

"I'd like to be there, if you don't mind."

"I'd actually appreciate it, but I didn't want to ask."

"I'll do whatever I can to make this easier on them. Please feel free to ask for whatever you need."

"Thanks, Shelby. I really appreciate it."

"No problem. My colleague from the shop got waylaid by a bridezilla, but she said she'll be here soon with the clothes I asked her to pick up for the kids. Just to make sure they have what they need wherever they end up."

"The mother's family doesn't want them. What do you suppose will become of them?"

"How could their family not want them?"

"They were living under a threat from a former associate. Cleo's family believes he's responsible for their deaths. Hell, everyone thinks so. Cleo's mom said they can't live like that anymore. Neither she nor the aunt I talked to even asked about the kids."

"Unreal. They're *family*. How do you turn your back on two innocent five-year-old kids? There is nothing— and I do mean *nothing*—that would keep me from taking my sisters' kids if the need ever arose, God forbid."

"Same. I don't get it, but we aren't the kind of people to let fear drive us."

"Well, you're not," Shelby said. "I'm afraid of my own shadow."

Sam laughed at that. "I worry all the time about something happening to him." She nodded toward the dining room where Nick was still sequestered with his team and Harry. "Especially when he's far away."

"He's surrounded by the best security in the world."

"I still worry. So many people love him, but those who don't, really don't."

"He wouldn't want you to worry about him."

Sam smiled. No, he wouldn't, but she did anyway, the same way he worried about her.

The front door opened to admit Scotty with his Secret Service detail in tow.

"Are they still here?" he asked when he spotted Sam and Shelby.

Sam knew exactly what he was asking. "They are. They're taking a little nap right now, and their older brother is due to arrive later."

"Will you have to tell them then? About their parents?"

Sam nodded, slipped an arm around him and kissed the top of his head. He'd brought the scent of fresh air in with him. "Yeah, buddy."

"I should be there when you tell them. I've been through it myself. I understand better than anyone what it's like to lose the most important people in your life when you're way too young to understand it."

Struck by his maturity and insight, she hugged him tighter as Shelby dabbed subtly at her eyes. "You're absolutely right. We'd appreciate your help when we tell them."

"How about a snack?" Shelby asked.

"Do we still have the brownies you made yesterday or did Mom eat them all while she worked from home?" he asked with a cheeky grin for Sam, who play-punched him.

"I didn't touch them!"

"I hid them for you," Shelby said, hearing Noah begin to chatter in earnest through the monitor. "Let's go get Noah up and find the brownies."

"I want to get Noah." Scotty dropped his backpack and took off toward the kitchen with Shelby right behind him.

Smiling, Sam picked up his backpack and marveled at

the weight of it. "What the hell is in here? Rocks?" She put it by the stairs just as the dining room doors opened and Nick came out with Harry.

"Did I hear Scotty?" Nick asked.

"Yep." Sam gestured to the kitchen. "He went after Noah and brownies—in that order. How was your meeting?"

"Very good," Nick said. "Meet the vice president's new personal physician."

"I thought you already *were* his personal physician?" Sam asked Harry.

"I was, or I should say I *am*. Now, however, I get to travel with him." Harry waggled his brows. "It's all *official* and stuff."

"That's cool," Sam said, strangely comforted to know that Harry would be with Nick whenever he traveled on official business. "So you'll make sure he doesn't get poisoned or anything?"

Nick's eyes bugged. "What're you talking about? I'm not going to be poisoned."

"Harry? If something like that happened, you'd know what to do?"

"I'd know what to do."

"And you'd do *anything* to keep him safe?"

"Anything and everything possible."

"Then I approve of you being his official physician."

"I'm still in the room, you know," Nick said dryly.

"I'm not talking to you," Sam said. "I'm conferring with your personal physician."

"Why do I feel like I've made a huge mistake here?" Nick muttered.

Harry laughed and kissed her cheek. "Don't worry

about a thing. I'll take good care of him. I've got to run, but I'll see you at the wedding."

"I'll be the one standing next to the groom," Sam said. "What the hell was he thinking?"

"I've made sure he's asked himself that every day since he was stupid enough to ask me."

Harry was still laughing when the Secret Service let him out.

"You're worried I'm going to be *poisoned*?" Nick asked when they were alone—or as alone as they ever were in the public spaces of their home these days. "This is new."

"It was just a thought that occurred to me when I was talking to my dad earlier."

"Your imagination has run away with you, babe."

"You're saying it can't happen?"

"I'm saying it *won't* happen. I don't want you worrying about stuff like that when I'm away."

"I worry about a staggering array of things while you're away."

"Samantha," he said, sliding his arms around her and nuzzling her neck. "Don't. I promise you have nothing to worry about."

"You can't promise that, and you shouldn't promise things that're out of your control."

"I have to go back in there and finish up with Terry. But we're going to talk about this later, you hear me?"

"Yes, dear."

He kissed her. "Let me go say hi to my boy real quick."

"You have to hear what he said about Aubrey and Alden." Sam filled him in and watched the emotion of Scotty's statement register in the way Nick's face softened.

"That's really amazing," he said. "I hate that he lost his mother and grandfather so young."

"I know."

He kissed her again and went into the kitchen to see Scotty.

Sam watched him go, her stomach twisting with anxiety. Even though he'd shortened the duration, she wished he didn't have to take the trip at all.

WITH AN HOUR until they had to report in at Sam's, Freddie and Jeannie hunted down Emma Knoff, head of the PTO at Northwest Academy. After checking to see if she was at the school, they were told they could find her at her home in The Palisades neighborhood on the city's far western border. The neighborhood was tucked between the Potomac River and Georgetown University.

"Of course, it had to be way the hell out here," Freddie grumbled. They'd have to battle traffic across the city to get to Sam's and then he'd have to come back this way to go home.

"This is where the one percent live," Jeannie said, taking in the massive house that had to be at least five thousand square feet. "What do people do with all that space?"

"I'd imagine they spread out," Freddie said, ringing the doorbell that chimed through the house like bells in a cathedral. "Sam always says that rich people have the craziest doorbells."

"That noise would scare the crap out of me."

A middle-aged woman came to the door, wearing yoga pants and a sweatshirt. "Yes?"

Freddie showed his badge while Jeannie did the same. "Detectives Cruz and McBride for Mrs. Knoff, please."

She glanced between their badges. "Wait," she said, closing the door.

"Friendly," Freddie said.

"People are always so happy to see us," Jeannie said, her tone tinged with sarcasm.

"We're nice people."

"Try telling them that," she said, nodding toward the door.

Freddie rang the bell again. "Sam would give them a lecture about wasting our time."

"You should do it. She'd be so proud."

He rang the bell again.

A blonde woman came rushing from the back of the house and opened the door, seeming out of breath. "I'm so sorry. I was on a call, and Frieda just told me you were here. I'm Emma Knoff. What can I do for you?"

Freddie wanted to ask if she was deaf, because she'd have to be not to hear that doorbell. He produced his badge and introduced himself and Jeannie. "May we have a few minutes of your time?"

"Is this about Cleo? It's such a tragedy! And the children. Are they all right? No one seems to know where they are."

"Mrs. Knoff," Freddie said, running out of patience. "May we come in?"

"Oh yes, of course. Please come in. I'm so sorry. This day has just been… It's been awful. We're organizing a fund-raiser for the children and trying to do what we can to help. I'm just heartbroken."

Behind her back, Jeannie rolled her eyes at Freddie.

They were led into a formal living room. "May I get you something? Coffee or other refreshments?"

"No, thank you," Freddie said. "This isn't a social call, unfortunately."

"I'm sure you're very busy at a time like this. I heard the vice president's wife was investigating the case. Do you work with her?"

"We do," Freddie said. In the back of his mind, he could hear Sam's voice telling him to *take control of this interview—and do it now.* "Mrs. Knoff, our investigation has found there was no love lost, for lack of a better way to put it, between you and Cleo Beauclair."

Emma's mouth fell open and then snapped shut, her eyes flashing with what could only be called rage. "*Who* said that?"

"We've heard it from multiple sources. Can you please describe your relationship with Mrs. Beauclair?"

"I'm just…" She shook her head. "I'm so sorry. I'm stunned to hear that anyone would describe my relationship with Cleo as less than cordial."

Freddie wanted to groan with frustration. "I understand, but that is in fact how it was described to us. If you're unable or unwilling to answer our questions here, we'd be happy to take you downtown for a formal interview."

"Are you saying I'm a *suspect*?"

"I'm saying we have questions, and either you're willing to answer them, or we'll make you our guest at the city jail," Freddie said. "Is that clear?"

"Y-yes," she said, the slight stammer a welcome hint of humility. "What do you want to know?"

"How would *you* describe your relationship with Cleo Beauclair?" he asked. "And I'd advise you to be honest with us. There's nothing we dislike more than people who waste our time."

"If I'm being honest," she said, haltingly, "I'd have to say I didn't like her very much."

Now we're getting somewhere, Freddie thought, as he took notes. "And why was that?"

"Who did she think she was coming into *my* school and trying to turn herself into volunteer of the year? *I'm* the PTO president. I decide who does what and when, not *her*. And what's with her never leaving the building while her children were there? *Who does that?*"

"She did," Jeannie said. "And I guess I wonder why it would matter to you if she wasn't asking you to do the same."

"It's just not *done*," Emma said, her glare frosty. "New mothers don't come into the school and take over the volunteer positions. That's not how it works."

"Most people would be thrilled to have the extra help," Jeannie said.

"I wasn't," she snapped back.

"Were you angry enough to kill her?" Freddie asked.

Emma's face went completely white before it turned bright red, the entire cycle occurring within seconds. "*Absolutely not!* Ask anyone who knows me! I wouldn't harm a fly!"

"What the hell is going on here?" A good-looking man came into the room wearing a three-thousand-dollar suit and a frown on his face. He was the picture of success and good fortune, from his styled hair to his Italian shoes.

"Oh, Cal," she said, jumping up to hug him. "Thank goodness you're here. These detectives had the *gall* to ask if I *killed* Cleo Beauclair. Can you *imagine* such a thing?"

"Are you accusing my wife of a crime?" he asked.

"Not at this time."

"Then I'll need you to leave my house. If you wish

to speak to her again, you'll do so only with an attorney present."

Without another word, Freddie and Jeannie stood and headed for the front door.

Behind him, Freddie heard Emma say, "That's it? They're just going to leave after accusing me of murder?"

"Shut up, Emma," the husband said. "Just shut your mouth."

Freddie closed the door and took a deep breath of the fresh air.

"Holy shit," Jeannie muttered. "That was intense."

"I don't know about you, but I'd like to request an interview with her downtown just to give those people a dose of humility."

"Right there with you."

"It sure would be fun to make her twist in the wind."

"Yes," Jeannie said, laughing. "It will be. And PS, Sam would've been proud of you back there. You were awesome."

"Oh thanks. She's always in my head, for better or worse."

"I'd say it's for better—most of the time anyway."

"Except until I want to unleash a string of profanity. Then it's not so good."

"Such as shit, fuck, damn, hell?" Jeannie asked, referring to one of Sam's favorite sayings.

"Yes, that. Exactly that." They got in Freddie's car and started battling their way through late-day traffic on the way to Sam's house.

"Ugh, this traffic," Jeannie said. "This is why people say things like shit, fuck, damn, hell."

Freddie laughed. "Seriously."

"Could I ask you something?"

"Sure."

"What's going on with Gonzo?"

"I wish I knew. Whatever it is, it's not good."

"Not good at all," Jeannie said with a sigh.

"Christina called me this morning and asked me to come by after work and pick up the bags she'd packed for him."

"Ahh, crap."

"That's what I said too. I tried to talk to her, but she wasn't having it."

"What do you suppose this means for Alex?" Jeannie asked.

"I don't know, but I really hope they aren't going to end up fighting over him, because that would truly suck."

"Yeah, for sure."

WHEN DR. ANDERSON came through on afternoon rounds, Gonzo demanded to be released from the room they'd taken him to after they'd admitted him. "I'm totally fine, and while I'm sitting on my ass in here, my life is falling apart." When he'd had the room to himself, he'd gotten up to find his jacket in the closet and had taken a pill that had gone a long way toward calming his nerves and settling the relentless pain.

He'd overdone it with the meds yesterday. That's all it was. He wouldn't do that again. He'd take just enough to keep the pain manageable but not so much that he blacked out or half killed himself looking for relief. As bad as he felt—and he felt pretty damned bad most of the time—he didn't actually want to die. He wanted to watch Alex grow up and become a man. His son needed a father, and Gonzo was determined to be there for him.

So he only took one pill when he really, really wanted two.

Anderson checked Gonzo's chart, listened to his heart

and sat on the stool next to the bed to type notes into the computer. "I'm not going to lie to you, Sarge. I'm worried about you, and for the record, I don't believe one word you said to me yesterday." When Gonzo started to object, the doctor held up his hand to stop him. "As you well know, the opioid epidemic is out of control. We see it every day in here. I know what it looks like, and it looks just like this."

He gestured to Gonzo. "A professional guy who has his shit together until he suffers some sort of injury that requires pain meds. Suddenly, the pain meds are essential, and the perfectly healthy person can't do without them. Couple that with the tragedy you suffered earlier this year, and you've got a recipe for disaster."

"I'm not hooked on anything, Doc. You've got it all wrong."

"Maybe I do. But if you don't mind giving me five more minutes of your time, let me tell you where it goes from here. Soon enough, whatever you're taking isn't going to be strong enough to feed the beast. That's when you'll turn to heroin."

Gonzo recoiled. "I would *never* touch that shit. Come on, Doc. I'm a *cop*, for Christ's sake. I know what happens to people who get hooked on that crap. That's not going to be me."

As if Gonzo hadn't spoken, the doctor continued. "When heroin doesn't do it for you anymore, that's when you'll go looking for fentanyl. And that shit… That shit makes heroin look like aspirin, and it *will* kill you. We're losing people just like you to fentanyl every single day. If you think it can't happen to you, think again. If you stay on the current path, it *will* happen to you. The best thing you can do for yourself is ask for whatever help you need. *Get help.* If you don't want to end up dead, *get help.* I promise you this isn't going to end well if you don't stop it *right now*."

"I know all this," Gonzo said, his teeth gritted. "I've had the training at work."

"And I haven't even *mentioned* the career you've worked so hard for," Anderson said, again as if Gonzo hadn't spoken. "If you're scoring heroin or fentanyl or anything else that's not prescribed for you by a doctor, you're risking your badge, and you damned well know that. You've had the training. You know better than most people that this is a path that ends in the morgue. Is that what you want for your kid? A father who OD'd and left him to fend for himself in this world? What about that really pretty girlfriend of yours? You think she's going to be sitting on her ass at home waiting for you to get your shit together? A woman who looks like her, who takes care of your son the way she does—she's not going to be on the market for long. You want some other guy raising your kid and loving your girl? *That's* where this is heading, Tommy. That's the only place this is heading—you dead and the two people you love best going on without you. But hey, if that's what you want, far be it from me to get in your way."

Anderson scrawled his signature across the bottom of a piece of paper, took it off the clipboard and handed it to Gonzo. "Your walking papers."

Gonzo stared at the stark white paper as an image of Christina and Alex with another man—a nameless, faceless guy walking between the two of them, holding hands with them—appeared in vivid detail. The man wasn't him. He'd been replaced. Someone else was raising Alex in the scenario he could see so clearly it made his heart ache

with agony. They were in a park, and Alex was laughing
and talking. To someone else. A stranger. A stranger who
Alex would love because he'd be the only father the child
would ever know. He wouldn't remember his real father.

In all the words that had been thrown his way in the
last twenty-four hours, those were the ones that finally
got his attention. The thought of Alex growing up without him, calling another man Dad. *That* was truly unbearable to him.

"Tommy? You're free to go."

"I..." His heart raced, and the pain lanced through
him like a live wire, stealing the breath from his lungs.
"I think I need help."

CHAPTER TWENTY-TWO

SHORTLY BEFORE FOUR, Hill, Green, Cruz and McBride arrived at Sam's, bringing with them new reports from the ME and fire marshal. Hill remained outside on a call while Sam read through Lindsey's report first, skimming through the gruesome details of torture and possible sexual assault of Cleo. In addition to Jameson's missing teeth, he'd had broken fingers on both hands.

"The fire marshal determined the fire was set in the living room and aided by an accelerant that was detected throughout the room," Jeannie said. "As the victims were found in the middle of the room, the fire marshal concluded the accelerant— most likely gasoline—was placed in a wide circle around them."

"Whoever did this wanted them to know they were going to burn to death."

"That's the fire marshal's conclusion as well," Jeannie said, her expression grim.

"I don't know about you guys," Sam said fiercely, "but I want the motherfucker who did this to *pay*."

"Totally with you," Cruz said, briefing Sam on the conversation with Emma Knoff. "I gotta say… These people were unreal. If it's all right with you, I'd like to bring her in for a more formal interview downtown, if for no other reason than to instill some humility."

"Proceed," Sam said. "Set it up for first thing in the morning."

Hill came in from outside. "We might have a significant break."

"Speak to me."

"We nabbed Duke Piedmont at Dulles," he said of the airport located twenty-six miles west of Washington in Northern Virginia. "Our investigators can put him in the city the night of the murders."

"Holy shit," Sam said, having to concede that sometimes the obvious suspect was actually guilty. "What's the plan?"

"We're taking him to headquarters. I'm meeting our agents there in an hour. I assume you want to be there when we talk to him?"

Sam felt torn in a thousand directions. "I do, but I can't leave the kids. Not tonight. We're going to tell them…"

"I understand."

"Will you update me as soon as you can?"

"Absolutely."

"What do we do until we know for sure it was him?" Freddie asked.

"We keep doing our thing and keep pulling the threads," Sam said. "It's not over until we're one hundred percent sure." After hearing about how the Beauclairs had died, Sam wanted vengeance as much as she wanted justice for their precious children. "What else have we got?"

"I followed the money," Green said, "and found that Jameson Beauclair continued to make plenty of it from his patented software long after APG shut down."

"How's that possible if the company was defunct?" Freddie asked.

"He still held the license for the software, which

means other companies could produce it while he continued to profit."

"All this corporate shit gives me a headache," Sam said. "So even though APG is defunct, the software isn't?"

"Right," Green said. "The licensing agreements were very profitable." He produced documentation that showed Beauclair's earnings from the year before had topped three-hundred-million dollars.

"Damn," Sam said. "Where was this info when I was picking a career?"

The others laughed. The much-needed moment of levity broke some of the tension that had hung over the group after they'd discussed how their victims had perished.

"At least the kids will be set for money," Sam said, perusing the staggering balance sheet Green had unearthed.

"Small comfort," Freddie said.

"True." To Green she said, "Where'd you get this anyway?"

"He incorporated a new business in Delaware as Jameson Armstrong called JAE for Jameson Armstrong Enterprises, and the balance sheet was part of a required public filing with the Delaware secretary of state."

"He did a piss-poor job of hiding," Sam said. "If Piedmont wanted to find him, it wouldn't have taken much effort on his part."

"No, it really wouldn't have," Green said, "which leads me to wonder—why now? Why after all this time would Piedmont pick this week to make his move? JAE was incorporated more than eighteen months ago with Armstrong listed as the CEO and sole proprietor."

"You didn't pick up anything new from a business standpoint?" Sam asked.

"Three months ago, *Forbes* had a story about Armstrong rising from the ashes of APG to forge a new path for his revolutionary software. But again, that was months ago. If Piedmont was going to react to the news that Armstrong was continuing to profit from the software, why would he wait?"

"Is it possible he hadn't seen it before now?"

"Possible but not probable," Hill said. "The guy was a fugitive from federal law enforcement. I'd bet he stayed on top of anything and everything having to do with Armstrong, APG and the software."

"The thing I don't understand at all," Sam said, "is why they bothered to change their names and relocate if Jameson was going to continue to do business like nothing had happened?"

"Our supposition," Hill said, "is that they panicked when everything first went down with APG. Piedmont took off, threatening Armstrong and his family on the way out of town. Armstrong and his wife were offered protection and they took it out of fear for their safety and that of their children. They didn't think it all the way through to include the implications for his ability to continue to profit from his invention."

"*Why* did he need to continue to profit?" Sam asked. "Didn't he make billions the first time around?"

"The software was going to continue to exist in the market with or without his involvement," Hill said. "He chose for it to be *with* his involvement."

"Even if that put him and his family in danger?" Sam asked.

"Even if," Hill said.

"One more thing about the money," Green said, handing Sam another printout. "This just popped up half an hour ago. Cleo withdrew one hundred thousand in cash from her bank the afternoon before the fire. I've put in a request for security footage from the branch where she made the transaction, and I'm waiting to hear back. Apparently, the request has to go through the bank's corporate offices in New York."

Sam glanced at Hill and handed the printout to him. "Can you see what you can do to speed that up?" Sometimes things happened quicker when the FBI asked, not that Sam would ever admit to such a thing out loud.

"Yep." He was typing a text before she finished asking the question.

"Let's get over there and interview the people at the bank," Sam said.

"I'll do that as soon as they open in the morning," Green said.

Shelby came out of the kitchen with Noah attached to her chest.

Hill lit up at the sight of them. After he sent the text, he got up and went over to see them both.

The baby let out a squeal of excitement when he spotted his daddy.

"I'm going to check on Alden and Aubrey," Shelby said. "Sorry to interrupt."

"We're glad you did," Hill said, kissing Noah's forehead before he rejoined the meeting.

"Thank you, Shelby," Sam said.

"This is the report from Patrol about the accident Cleo was in on Friday." Freddie handed over a printout of the report that had been sitting in her email for most of the day waiting for her to have a chance to review it.

Sam read the report, filed by Patrolman O'Brien, who she'd worked with in the past, detailing the altercation between Cleo and a man named Victor Klein. She'd been driving her white Audi SUV westbound on Connecticut Avenue when she was allegedly sideswiped by Mr. Klein, who'd been driving an older silver BMW.

She skimmed O'Brien's account of the accident, including the fact that Cleo Beauclair was nearly arrested for the way she acted in the aftermath. "Mrs. Beauclair was screaming at Mr. Klein that he'd endangered her children's lives with his reckless driving. He was screaming back at her, telling her to shut her fucking mouth. It was discovered that Mr. Klein was wanted on a warrant for failing to appear in court, and he was taken into custody. It's worth noting that both parties were unusually agitated after what we would call a routine MVA. Mr. Klein was furious about being arrested and was also charged with resisting arrest."

"Who is he?" Sam asked.

Freddie handed her a printout of Klein's rap sheet, and as she studied it, a tingle of sensation traveled the length of her backbone. In a career of crime that covered everything from petty larceny to B&E, he was what they often referred to as an escalator—his crimes started simple and graduated to more serious offenses. The warrant had stemmed from a failure to appear in court on a child support matter.

He was on parole for the B&E charge. Other than the child support issue, he hadn't been in any trouble since being released from prison a year ago.

"I want to look at this guy," Sam said. "Did he get a load of Cleo and her fancy car and see dollar signs?"

"I pulled his financials," Freddie said, "and he's up to his eyeballs in debt. The outstanding child support alone is over six figures."

"I want to know every step he made from the second he was released from custody—and *why* was he released if he still owes that much in back child support?" Sam asked.

"Probably because we were full to overflowing in the city jail last weekend, and they arraigned and released anyone charged with nonviolent crimes," Freddie said.

"Cruz, Green and McBride—brief Carlucci and Dominguez on where we are and get them on Klein tonight. I want anything and everything we can get on this guy. What else does anyone have?"

"McBride and I talked to the neighbors and again to the women we talked to yesterday who knew Cleo, but we didn't get anything new there," Cruz said. "We didn't pick up on any hint of marital trouble or infidelity or anything like that, but we also didn't get the sense that the people we talked to would know if there was trouble in paradise."

"I'm going to see if I can explore that line of questioning more thoroughly with the older son when he gets here," Sam said.

"I've got my people checking into disgruntled APG employees," Hill said, "but that's slow going. They're scattered all over the place, so we're tracking them down one by one. I'll let you know if anything pops there."

"Good work today, everyone," Sam said. "Let's reconvene at HQ tomorrow at zero seven hundred and see where we are." She had to go into the office tomorrow, so she'd need to ask Ms. Finklestein whether she could leave the children with Shelby. Until they figured out who had killed Jameson and Cleo, Sam didn't think the children should return to school.

After the others left, Sam went upstairs to check on

the kids, who were still sleeping. She hadn't seen Shelby upstairs, so she must be back in the kitchen. Then she looked in on Scotty, who was doing his homework with headphones on. When he saw her come in, he took off the headphones.

"What's up?" he asked.

"Just checking on all my kids."

"Are they still asleep?"

Sam nodded. "We'll have to get them up in about half an hour or so. Their older brother is due here soon."

"Do you think we'll get to keep them?" Scotty asked.

Sam went to sit on the edge of his bed. "Probably not. We offered them temporary shelter until something more permanent could be arranged."

"I know."

"I'm sorry if you're disappointed that they can't stay. If it makes you feel any better, I'm disappointed too."

"You are?"

"Yeah. It didn't take long to get attached to them."

"They're cute."

"Yes, they are."

"Where will they go when they leave here?"

"We don't know that yet. The social worker is trying to find family members who'd be willing to take them. It's all very complicated and compounded by the tragic loss the family has already suffered."

He looked up at her with big eyes. "Will you make sure that wherever they go, they'll be safe and well cared for? Before you let them leave here?"

"Yes, buddy," Sam said, hugging him. "I'll make sure."

"Not all foster homes are as good as this one."

A feeling of acute unease had her sitting up straighter. "Scotty—"

"I need to finish this stupid math homework, okay?" He gave her a pleading look, all but begging her not to pursue it further.

But how could she hear that and *not* want to know what he'd meant? "Okay." She got up to leave the room and encountered Nick coming up the stairs. "Did Terry and the others leave?"

"Just now. How are the littles?"

"Still sleeping. We'll have to get them up soon." She glanced at Darcy, the Secret Service agent sitting outside Scotty's door, and took Nick by the hand, tugging him into their room and closing the door. "Scotty just said something."

"What did he say?"

"We were talking about the kids and where they might end up. He wanted me to promise I'd make sure they end up in a good place. He said not all foster homes are as good as this one."

Nick's jaw tightened. "What do you suppose that means?"

"He cut me off before I could say anything. It was obvious he didn't want me to ask."

Nick stood with his hands on his hips, his posture unusually rigid. "The thought of anyone being unkind to him makes me murderous."

"I know. Me too."

"We've never really talked to him about the time between when his mother and grandfather died and when he ended up with Mrs. Littlefield in Richmond."

"Do you think we should?"

"Part of me is afraid to ask."

Sam sighed. "Me too. But now I need to know. There was definitely something to the way he said it that has me freaking out a little about what we *don't* know."

After a long pause, Nick said, "Let's table this for now. We'll talk to him when the time is right, and while we're in the middle of the situation with Aubrey and Alden is not the time. Do you agree?"

"Yes, that works for me. But we do need to talk to him."

He put his arms around her. "We will."

"I wish there was a way to go back and erase everything that hurt him."

"That'd be nice," Nick said, "but all we can do is let him know we're here and he can tell us anything."

"This parenting gig is hard sometimes."

"True, but most of the time he makes it easy on us."

"Yes, he does, because he's the best kid ever."

"You won't hear me arguing." Nick drew back and put his hands on her face before he kissed her. "There's no one else I'd rather be navigating the parenthood maze with than you."

"Even if I'm a hot mess of a mother most of the time?"

"You are not. Why would you say that?"

"You ought to hear the stuff Cleo did for her kids. Volunteering at their school, craft parties and playdates—"

Nick kissed her until she forgot what she was going to say. "You're a wonderful mother, and your son adores you."

"For now. How will he feel when he finds out I was supposed to have craft parties?"

"He'll be damned thankful you never put him through that nonsense. Now if you wanted to have his friends over for a video game tournament, he'd be all for that."

"Let's do it. When you get back, we'll tell him to invite as many friends as he wants for a sleepover with video games and movies and pizza and up-all-night fun."

"And who will be the one to supervise this up-all-night fun?"

"*Duh*. You. You're the one with insomnia. It may as well be useful for once."

Nick laughed and then kissed her again. "You're a wonderful mother, Sam. Don't ever think otherwise. You'd lay down your own life for that boy."

"I really would."

"That's all that matters."

CHAPTER TWENTY-THREE

CHRISTINA'S EYES ACHED from crying. Every part of her mourned the loss of a relationship she'd expected to go the distance. She and Tommy had been the real thing from the very beginning. She'd never had a connection to a man like the one she'd shared with him, and to lose that… It was like what she imagined losing a limb would feel like.

Thankfully, Alex had slept much of the day after his fever finally broke. She hoped that wouldn't mean he'd be up all night. Not that she expected to sleep much. Her mind was too full of unsettling thoughts—such as whether she'd be able to get another job after being out of the political game for most of the last year or how she would manage single motherhood or whether Tommy would fight her for custody when he knew he didn't deserve it.

The idea of a contentious battle with him made her feel hopeless and despondent. She'd wanted a life with him, not an ugly battle that she probably wouldn't win because she wasn't Alex's biological mother. But she was the only mother the child had ever known, and that ought to count for something.

She needed a lawyer and a drink. And not necessarily in that order. She was about to get up to see what she had in the way of alcohol in the house when her phone rang. The caller ID showed a number she didn't recognize, making her almost afraid to take the call. What fresh hell would this bring?

"Hello?" she said tentatively.

"Is this Christina Billings?"

In the second that followed the inquiry from a male voice she had one thought: *Please, God, please don't let Tommy be dead.* New tears filled eyes already raw and aching.

"Ms. Billings? Are you there?"

"Yes. Who is this?"

"Dr. Anderson from GW. I'm calling about Thomas Gonzales."

Her heart contracted in her chest, which was so tight she could barely breathe. "What about him?"

"He's made a significant decision, and he'd like very much to speak to you about it even though he knows you're angry with him—and with good reason, which are his words, not mine."

He wasn't dead. He wasn't dead, and he thought she had good reason to be angry with him. These were the most positive developments in weeks.

"Ms. Billings? Are you able to speak to Sergeant Gonzales?"

"Um, yes. I'll speak to him."

"Very good. Here he is."

Christina braced herself for whatever it was he had to tell her and how it would affect her—and Alex.

"Babe," he said.

Was he *crying*? Oh my God.

He spoke quickly, as if he was afraid she might hang up before he could get in everything he needed to say. "I'm so sorry about last night, about everything. I've totally fucked up, and I wouldn't blame you if you took Alex and left me. But please don't do that. Please don't. I'm going to fix it. I don't want to lose you. I don't want to lose my son, my family. *Please*."

"Tommy," she said as tears spilled down her face.

"I know I've already asked so much of you, but I need one more chance. Please give me one more chance. Everything has been so bad since I lost A.J. It's all my fault. None of it is your fault. It's me."

He was saying everything she'd longed to hear for so long, but how could she know that this time would be different than the previous instances when he'd proclaimed to be "on the other side" of the terrible grief that had all but ruined them?

"I'm going to check myself into rehab."

Wait. *What?* Rehab? "Wh-why do you need rehab?"

"I… I've been… I've been taking pain meds to numb myself. It's… It's gotten a little out of hand. Lately."

Oh dear God. Was he saying he was *addicted* to pain meds? When the hell had that happened?

"Christina. Babe. Please, I know I've asked so much of you with Alex—"

"Do *not* bring him into this. I take care of him because I love him. He's my son as much as he's yours."

"Yes, he is."

"I want something in writing that says that. I want protection from the possibility of being frozen out of his life."

"That's not going to happen. You have my word on that."

"You'll have to forgive me, but your word isn't good enough for me. Not when it comes to Alex. I want legal guardianship of him."

"I'll make that happen. Today, before I go."

Hearing that, the tight knot of stress that'd been constricting her chest eased somewhat.

"I should've done that a long time ago, and I'm sorry I didn't. You never should've been in the spot you were in last night when he needed care and I wasn't there. You should have the legal authority to act on his behalf."

He was saying everything she'd wanted to hear for so long, but the foundation they'd built their relationship on had been rocked by the events of the last nine months. Whether or not it could be rebuilt would remain to be seen. "I pretended I had the legal authority, but it would be nice to not have to fake it."

"Babe," he said softly, so softly she could barely hear him. "I love you so much. I love you and Alex and our little family. I'm going to work really hard to get back to you."

She wiped away tears as his words of love went straight to her broken heart. "Where will you be?"

"I don't know yet. Dr. Anderson and Dr. Trulo are figuring that out now."

"Trulo's involved?" She had a call and voice mail from him that she hadn't gotten around to dealing with yet. "What will this mean for your job?"

"He swears it'll have no impact on my job. I'll be out on medical leave. No one except Sam and Freddie will know where I really am or why."

"You honestly think you can keep a lid on this in light of the attention your squad gets these days?"

"We're going to do everything we can to keep it private."

Her stomach hurt at the thought of it getting out. If

the press found out that Sam's sergeant was in rehab, that would be big news.

"I know I have no right to ask this, but I'm going to need you to help me through this. I can't do it without you."

"That's not true. You have to do it for yourself."

"I just want to know that you'll be there on the other side. I can't bear to think about how much I've hurt you and Alex. I don't want to be this guy anymore." His words were choked by sobs. "I don't even know who I am anymore."

Her eyes filled, and she closed them against the new flood of tears. "It's not your fault, Tommy. You went through something awful, and I tried to help you. We all tried, but—"

"There was nothing you or anyone could've done that you didn't do. Dr. Trulo is looking for a place that can deal with the pills and the PTSD from Arnold's death. He said I have to do both or it won't work."

"I hope the department is footing the bill. This happened to you on the job."

"Insurance should cover most of it. They're working on all that."

After another long pause, she said, "I'm glad you're doing this, Tommy. I hope it helps you to find a way to live with what happened without having to resort to drugs."

"I hope so too. I'm just sorry it got to this point. I tried really hard to power through it. Look at where that got me."

"Let's keep the blame where it belongs—on the guy who killed A.J. This is his fault, not yours."

"It's generous of you to say that, but a big chunk of it is on me and how I chose to handle it."

"That's not fair, Tommy," she said with more feeling than she'd had toward him in longer than she could remember. "It's not like there's a handbook out there to tell you how to cope with something like this."

"Yeah, I guess there isn't."

"Could I... Could Alex and I see you before you go?"

"I'd really like that. They're keeping me at GW until they can set something up. They didn't say so, but I don't think they trust me to be out on my own."

"I'll come by in the morning with Alex." Another thought occurred to her. "What about the wedding?"

"Oh *shit*," he said, groaning. "I never even thought of it. That's how self-absorbed I've become."

"Don't worry about it. I'll let Freddie know. He can ask Will to stand in for you."

"Will you please tell him how sorry I am?"

"I will, but I know he'll be glad you're getting the help you need. Everyone knows how much you've suffered."

"I just want to know...," A sob choked him.

"What do you want to know, Tommy?"

"Do you still love me, Chris? After everything I've put you through, do I still have any chance of putting things back together with you?"

"I do still love you. If I didn't love you, I wouldn't have spent the entire day crying over what I thought I'd lost forever. As long as we still love each other, there's always a chance."

"That's all I need to hear, babe. Those words will get me through whatever the next few weeks have in store for me."

After that, both were quiet for a time, except for the occasional sniffle on both sides of the call.

"How's Alex doing?" he asked.

"He's much better. The fever broke, and he's been sleeping a lot. He had a rough night."

"You did too. I'm sorry I wasn't there."

"You will be next time, right?"

"Yeah, I will." After another long pause, he said, "I'm gonna go call Andy about the guardianship paperwork, but I'll see you in the morning?"

"We'll be there, Tommy. In the morning and for whatever comes next."

"Thank you," he whispered. "I love you."

"I love you too."

Christina ended the call and used a tissue to mop up her tears as she processed everything he'd said. She'd had no idea he was hooked on anything, but that certainly explained a lot.

She sent a text to Freddie.

Change of plans. No need to come here for Tommy's stuff, but I need to talk to you when you get a minute. Please call me when you can.

Then she got up and went into the kitchen. She no longer needed a lawyer, but she still needed a very big drink.

ELIJAH BEAUCLAIR ARRIVED at five twenty, walking into a houseful of people who had gathered to help him break the terrible news to his younger brother and sister. Ms. Finklestein had returned after an earlier trip to drop off the stuffed animals and blankets the kids had requested. The faintest hint of smoke had clung to the items, but

Sam had turned them right over to the kids, who'd been thrilled to have them.

Sam and Nick greeted Elijah at the door. "I'm Sam Holland, and this is my husband, Nick Cappuano."

Tall, dark-haired and handsome, Elijah shook hands with both of them. "It's nice to meet you both, although I wish it was under different circumstances."

"We're very sorry for your loss," Nick said.

"Thank you. How are Aubrey and Alden? I can't stop thinking about them. Cleo was such an amazing mom. And my dad, he adored them."

"They're doing okay," Sam said. "They're confused and asking for their parents. We've held them off until you could get here. Before we let them know you're here, I wanted to tell you that I consulted with a therapist about how best to tell them, and he said being very clear is the best way to go. Using words like *died* and *dead* help them to better understand, even if they're words that might be hard for them to hear."

Elijah's expression was grim, but he nodded in agreement. "I hate this," he said softly. "I hate that we have to do this to them."

"I know," Nick said. "We do too."

Elijah looked down at the floor. "I don't know if I can say it."

"I'll do it," Sam said, squeezing his arm. "There's one thing. Alden hasn't said a word since he's been with us. I suspect he saw something, and if there's an opportunity to get him to share what he saw, that would help tremendously. He might be more forthcoming with you than he would be with us."

"I'll see what I can do."

"This is Ms. Finklestein from Child and Family Services," Sam said. "She's been helping out with the kids."

Elijah shook her hand and accepted her condolences.

"Shall I let them know you're here?"

Elijah took a deep breath and then nodded. "If you wouldn't mind."

While Sam went to the kitchen where the kids were having dinner under Shelby's supervision, Nick said to Elijah, "Can I get you anything?"

"No, sir," Sam heard him say. "Thank you." She went into the kitchen where the kids and Scotty were just finishing Scotty's favorite dinner—spaghetti and meatballs. Shelby was wiping their hands and faces while Noah sat in a high chair taking it all in.

"Hey, guys," Sam said to Aubrey and Alden. "I have a surprise for you. Can you come with me?"

"Is it Mommy?" Aubrey asked, her little face bright with hope.

Sam ached for her and hated herself for not choosing better words. "No, honey, but I think this surprise will make you happy." She took Aubrey and Alden by the hands and led them into the living room where Elijah stood waiting for them.

Both kids let out happy cries when they saw him, and his face crumpled at the sight of them. He scooped them up and held them tight for a long time while Sam, Nick and Shelby, with Noah now in her arms, dabbed at their eyes.

Alden clung to Elijah, crying his little heart out.

"It's okay, buddy," Elijah said, rubbing his brother's back while Aubrey leaned into them. "I'm here now."

Alden cried for a long time, and Elijah held him through the storm as tears rolled down his own face.

"Where's Mommy and Daddy?" Aubrey asked her older brother.

"Come sit over here with me, and we'll talk about that," Elijah said.

He'd been a typical college student until Hill called him, and Sam felt like she was watching him become a man before her eyes as he sat on the sofa with his siblings. With Alden on his lap and his arm wrapped around his sister, Elijah said, "You know there was a fire at home, right?"

Aubrey nodded while Alden whimpered.

Elijah looked to Sam, who sat on the coffee table between Nick and Shelby, who held Noah.

Scotty went around the sofa and sat next to Aubrey.

"I'm so sorry to have to tell you that your mom and dad died in the fire," Sam said, her heart breaking into a million pieces as she watched her words register with the children, who knew what the word "died" meant.

She'd done this before. Too many times to count, but it had never hurt as much as it did this time.

Aubrey broke down while Alden buried his face in Elijah's shoulder

"We're so, so sorry," Sam said. "Everyone has told us how much they loved you and how proud of you they were. And they'd be so proud of how strong you've been."

"I want to go home," Aubrey said, her chin wobbling.

"I know, honey," Sam said. "But that's not possible right now."

"Wh-where will we live, Lijah?" she asked.

"We're still figuring that out, sweetheart," he said. "But you will *always* be safe and loved. I promise you that."

"My mom and grandpa died when I was about your

age," Scotty said. "It was really hard at first, but you get used to it. You never forget them, but it does get a little easier. Eventually."

Sam sent him a grateful smile. "We'll give you guys a little time alone," she said, standing as Nick did the same.

Aubrey climbed into Scotty's lap, and he put his arms around her.

Sam followed Nick into the kitchen and stepped straight into his outstretched arms. He held on as tightly to her as she did to him. Everyone had warned her about getting overly attached to two children who weren't theirs, but Sam would dare anyone not to fall hard for those two angels.

"That was brutal," he said after a long period of silence.

"Totally."

Nick took a deep breath and released it in stages. "Tell me you're going to get whoever did this to them."

"We'll get them. I haven't wanted justice for anyone this badly since my dad was shot."

"We weren't supposed to get attached."

"I was just thinking the same thing."

"Knock, knock," Shelby said as she stuck her head into the kitchen. "Is it safe to come in."

"Yeah, come join our group hug," Nick said.

With Noah in her arms, Shelby came in and walked right over to them. "That was the worst thing I've ever been a part of," she said with tears in her eyes as they hugged her and Noah into their circle. "I don't know how you do that as often as you do."

"That's as bad as it gets. I just wish I knew what's going to become of them."

"Ms. Finklestein wants to speak to you."

Sam had nearly forgotten about the social worker, who'd done as Sam asked and stayed off to the sidelines while they talked to the kids. "Why do I have a feeling I'm not going to like this?" Sam said as she drew back from Nick, wiped her eyes and ran her fingers through her hair in an attempt to straighten it. On the inside, she felt like she'd been kicked by a horse. "Will you ask her to come in here, Shelby?"

"Sure thing."

"Then come join us. Whatever she has to say involves you too."

While Shelby went to get Ms. Finklestein, Sam glanced at Nick, noted his grimace and reached for his hand, holding on tight to him for whatever came next.

Ms. Finklestein came into the kitchen. "I'm sorry to disturb you. I know how difficult that had to be."

"Have a seat," Nick said, always the gracious host. "Can I get you anything?"

"Some water would be excellent."

"Coming right up."

Nick poured tall glasses of ice water for Sam, Shelby and their guest, and then joined them at the table.

"I've been in touch with Mrs. Beauclair's sister Monique. While she has concerns about the safety of the children and her own family in light of the threat posed by someone in Mr. Beauclair's past, she can't bear the thought of her niece and nephew being raised by strangers. She and her husband are discussing whether they might be able to take them in."

The feeling of being kicked only intensified when Sam heard that news. In her heart of hearts, she'd hoped that no one would come forward and they'd get to keep the kids. Foolish, maybe, but the hope had taken root anyway.

"The man who threatened them has been taken into custody by the FBI," Sam said, feeling dead inside. That information would make it possible for Aubrey and Alden to go home to Cleo's family.

"I'll pass that on to their aunt. I'm sure it'll be a great relief to her and expedite their decision-making process."

"That'd be for the best, I suppose," Sam said, despite the ache that overtook her when she thought of saying goodbye to Alden and Aubrey.

"Would it be possible for them to remain here with you while I wait to hear back from Mrs. Beauclair's sister?" Ms. Finklestein asked.

"Yes, of course," Sam said. "However, my husband and I need to return to work tomorrow, and I don't feel comfortable sending the children back to school while their parents' killer may still be on the loose."

"Agreed," Ms. Finklestein said.

"Their brother and Shelby will be here with them," Sam said. "Shelby is licensed, which was required when we first had custody of Scotty."

"Then that's fine."

"I'll take very good care of them," Shelby said. "And having their brother here will help."

"Yes, it will." Ms. Finklestein gathered her belongings and stood. "I appreciate you opening your home to the children. I hope we can resolve their situation sooner rather than later so you all can get back to normal and they can be settled in their new home."

Normal, Sam thought, was such a relative state. What would the new normal look like for Aubrey and Alden? Would they be with a family who truly loved and wanted them, or would they end up with people who were taking them out of obligation and would make them feel like a burden? She shook off those unpleasant thoughts to focus on the present, resolving to double down on the case tomorrow.

If she couldn't do anything else for them, she could find the person or persons who'd murdered their parents.

CHAPTER TWENTY-FOUR

WITH ELIJAH'S HELP, they got the kids settled, but the children were reluctant to let him out of their sight. He crawled in between them and held one of them in each arm, the three of them like survivors of their own personal apocalypse.

"I'll stay with them until I'm sure they're really asleep, if that's okay," he whispered to Sam when she checked on them an hour after they went to bed.

"You can stay right there all night if you want to. You've had a long day, and there's no need for you to leave. I can set you up with a bed of your own if you'd like."

"I'm fine right here with them," he said. "Thank you. For everything. I really appreciate it."

"I wish we could do more."

"I hate this for them," he said, his eyes filling. "They're so little."

"I hate it for all of you," she said, a lump forming in her own throat. "I'll let you get some sleep. We're right across the hall if you need anything."

"Thanks again."

"No problem." Sam closed the door to give them some privacy from the Secret Service agent in the hallway. She looked in on Scotty, shut off the television as well as the bedside lamp that were still on after he'd fallen asleep.

Pulling his comforter up and over him, she kissed his forehead, lingering for a moment to breathe in the fresh clean scent of his hair, which smelled a lot like Nick's.

At some point, he'd started using the same shampoo as the dad he worshipped, and for some reason, that simple detail brought tears to her eyes. She was a freaking emotional disaster area the last few days. Tomorrow she would get back on track, even if she was quite certain she'd remember this time with Aubrey and Alden for the rest of her life.

Sam left Scotty's room, avoiding the gaze of the agent on duty. She didn't have it in her to make small talk tonight, so she skipped the usual end-of-the-day pleasantries.

Stepping into her own room to the sound of the shower running, she closed the door, leaned her head back against it and closed her eyes, fighting the emotions that threatened to take her under. This day… Scotty's inference that his foster life before the state home had been less than great, having to tell Alden and Aubrey the awful news about their parents, learning more about the details of Jameson and Cleo Beauclairs' lives and how they'd died, her worries about Gonzo.

Bending at the waist, she propped her hands on her knees and breathed through the tidal wave of emotion. She was known for her ability to soldier through the worst of times, but sometimes it was just too much for even her to handle. What would become of Aubrey and Alden now that their lives had been shattered by violence? How would she know if they were being well cared for by the aunt and uncle who had to *think about* whether or not they wanted to take them in?

And Scotty, Gonzo, Christina, Nick's trip…

Sam shook her head and stood upright, swiping at tears and taking a series of deep breaths. She was still propped against the door when Nick emerged from the shower, a towel slung around his hips, wet hair pushed back from his face, splendid chest on full display. All he had to do to make her feel better was walk into the room.

He stopped short at the sight of her propped against the door. "Babe? Are you okay?"

"I'm better now." She forced a small smile for his benefit, pushed herself off the door and went to him, sighing with relief when he wrapped his arms around her.

"Did something happen?"

"Only what you predicted would happen. I let myself get invested and now…"

"It's not just you. We're all invested in them."

"I'm probably going to hear about it at work tomorrow. Farnsworth wants to see me at eight. I assume it's not a social call."

"You did what you thought was right. You can't be faulted for that."

"Maybe so, but taking them in was technically a conflict of interest, and he's going to remind me of that."

"Your heart was in the right place."

"My heart is broken at the thought of them leaving, possibly as soon as tomorrow."

He tightened his hold on her.

"It's okay if you want to say I told you so."

"Not going to say that. Asking you not to feel for those babies would be like asking you not to breathe."

"Thank you for always understanding. I'm not sure what I ever did to deserve that from you, but whatever it was, I'm incredibly thankful."

He drew back to look down at her, his heart in his eyes. "You love me. That's all you ever have to do."

"I love you so much."

"I love you just as much. Nice how that works out, huh?"

She smiled when she wouldn't have thought she could.

"You want to go upstairs for a little getaway?"

"I don't feel like trooping past the agent."

"I'll take care of that." He kissed her forehead. "Give me five minutes."

"I need a quick shower."

"Come up when you're ready."

She'd had a long, exhausting day and another loomed on tomorrow's horizon, but she needed the comfort only he could provide before she could sleep.

Nick put on pajama pants and a T-shirt before leaving the room, closing the door behind him.

Sam rushed through a quick shower and smoothed on the lavender-and-vanilla-scented lotion that Nick loved before donning the robe that hung on the back of the bathroom door. Sticking her head out the bedroom door, she found the coast clear of prying Secret Service eyes and darted through the hallway and up the stairs to the loft where Nick waited for her.

He'd lit the coconut-scented candles and was reclined on the double lounger he'd bought as part of his effort to re-create the scene of their memorable trips to Bora Bora for their honeymoon and first anniversary.

He held out his hand to her.

She dropped the robe on the floor and joined her hand to his, holding on to the one thing that always made sense to her.

Nick drew her into his embrace and pulled a blanket over them.

Safe in his arms, Sam felt the tight knot in her chest begin to ease ever so slightly. No matter how awful life could be outside this room, they could always find their way back to each other within these four walls. Usually they had the hottest sex of their lives up here, but that wasn't what she needed tonight.

She pulled back to look up at him.

"What're you thinking?" he asked, pushing the hair back from her face.

"That we usually jump each other the second we're alone up here."

Smiling, he said, "Actually, *you* usually jump *me*, but I don't complain. I like to think I'm an accommodating husband."

She lost it laughing, another thing she wouldn't have thought herself capable of tonight. But leave it to Nick. "*Whatever.* We all know you're the one who does most of the jumping."

"All? Who all knows that?"

"Me and all my people."

His brows lifted with disbelief. "Are you kissing and telling, Samantha?"

"Of course not. By all my people, I mean Sam Holland, Samantha Cappuano, Lieutenant Holland and Second Lady Samantha Cappuano. That's a lot of people to deal with."

"Believe me, I know."

She poked his belly, and he laughed. "Did you come up here hoping to get lucky?"

"I get lucky every time I get to hold you, no matter what we do or don't do."

Placing her hand on his face, she held him still for a fairly platonic kiss by their standards. With her lips pressed to his, they simply existed together, breathing the same air, suspended on an extended break from the rest of their lives for that one moment in time.

"I want to keep them," she whispered many minutes later.

"I do too."

"I'm sorry I did this to us."

"Please don't be sorry. They needed us, even if it was only for a short time."

"This proves that we can never again foster a child unless we know we get to keep them."

"That's probably true. Look how fast we got attached to Aubrey and Alden."

"We suck at it."

"We suck at remaining detached from sweet kids in need of a loving home. I can live with sucking at that."

A sob erupted from her chest, taking them both by surprise as tears slid down her cheeks. "I want to make everything all better for them."

"No one can do that."

"I want to try."

"I know, sweetheart." His hand made small soothing circles on her back.

She hated the tears, but they did make her feel a tiny bit better as the storm subsided. Suddenly, she was very, very tired. "We need to go downstairs so they can find us if they need us."

"I need five more minutes of this first."

"I can do that." After a long period of silence, she said, "You really have to go away for a whole week?"

"It's not three weeks."

"Even one week. Too long."

"I know, babe. For me too. I keep thinking that maybe we might eventually get over this madness between us, but it only seems to get worse—and I mean that in the best possible way—the longer we're together."

"I know. We're hopeless. I used to make fun of couples like us."

"Did you?"

"Oh yeah." She made gagging, retching sounds that made him laugh. "It was so disgusting to me. Like Angela and Spence when they were first married. Ugh. So happy and in love and always touching and other gross stuff. And now look at me. Look what you've done to me."

"I've made a complete mess of you."

"At least you're aware of it."

"Oh yes," he said suggestively, "I'm very much aware of you and everything about you." He moved ever so slightly, but it was enough to put him on top of her as he gazed down at her.

As naturally as she breathed, she raised her knees and spread her legs to make room for him as she wrapped her arms around him. She hadn't thought she needed more than sweet comfort tonight, but with him hard and pressing against her suggestively, she suddenly needed *him* in every possible way.

"Nick."

He kissed her neck and rolled her earlobe between his teeth. "What, honey?"

She raised her hips in blatant invitation.

His lips skimmed her jaw on the way to her lips. "I thought we needed to go downstairs."

"We do," she said, feeling and sounding breathless.

He was the only man who'd ever made her breathless. "Soon."

"So what you're saying is we need to be quick?" As he spoke, he continued to move against her, making her crazier with each thrust of his hard cock against her sensitive flesh.

"That's exactly what I'm saying."

"I can do quick." He slid into her, giving her all of him in one deep thrust that made her cry out from the shock and the thrill.

One thrust was nearly enough to make her come, and *that* had certainly never happened with anyone but him.

Nick moved slowly, reverently. This was still more about comfort than it was about sex, and it was just what she needed.

Sam clung to him, the way she so often did when the life she had chosen got to be too much for her.

He held her tight against him and made slow, sweet love to her, giving her everything he had the way he always did. "Samantha," he said on a gasp that told her he was waiting for her.

Her emotions were such a jumbled mess tonight that she wasn't sure she could let go enough to come, but of course he knew that and used every trick he had to ensure a satisfying conclusion for them both.

Sam's head spun, and her body quaked in the aftermath. *How* did he do that so easily? He played her like a maestro every single time. Completely spent, she had nothing left for the walk downstairs.

"Wake up, babe. We need to go down."

"I know."

"Now, Samantha," he said, kissing her until her eyes popped open. "There you are. One minute until sleep.

Come on." After withdrawing from her, he helped her up and into her robe, tying the belt around her waist before he got dressed and blew out the candles. "I'll go down first and ask the agent to take a break. Don't lie down again."

"Yes, Dad."

His playful scowl was the last thing she saw before he disappeared down the stairs in full vice president mode to get rid of the agent in the hallway. A minute later, he called up to her. "Coast is clear, my love. Let's go."

Yawning her head off, Sam got up and half walked, half staggered to the stairs where he waited at the bottom for her.

"Should I be prepared to catch you?" he asked as she descended with the finesse of a drunken sailor.

"Quite possibly."

He kept an arm around her until they were in their bedroom with the door closed.

Sam went directly to the bed and landed at an angle across the mattress.

"Samantha."

His voice was the last thing she heard before sleep claimed her.

FOR A LONG time after Nick got Sam into bed, head on pillow and under the covers, he was awake staring at the ceiling, thinking about Alden and Aubrey and wondering what would become of them—and what had become of him and Sam and their family since the children had entered their lives just over twenty-four hours ago.

One day.

So much could happen in a day.

In his life, some of the biggest events had happened

in a single day. When he met John O'Connor at Harvard and made a friend for life in the course of an hour. When he met John's father, Senator Graham O'Connor, and found his life's work. When he met Sam and fell irrevocably in love with her—and stayed that way for six long years until he saw her again and discovered that nothing had changed after all that time. When John was murdered, which ironically had launched him into the political spotlight—albeit reluctantly. When he met Scotty and knew, almost instantly, that the boy was going to change his life. When President Nelson asked him to be his new vice president.

Single days that changed his life.

Strangely enough, he'd experienced a similar tilting of the axis beneath him when he met Aubrey and Alden. Maybe they were intended to be a short-term lesson, to remind him of his many blessings. But he couldn't shake the feeling that they were intended for more than the short-term, despite how things seemed to be turning out.

He'd meant what he told Sam that it was in the children's best interest to be taken in by family members, or at least it seemed like it would be. But he also meant it when he said he wished they could've kept the children with them. They could give them a nice life, surrounded by people who would love and care for them as if they were their own.

Would the aunt and uncle do that? How well did Alden and Aubrey even know them?

A sound from the hallway had him up and out of bed, heading for the door to see what was going on. He found Elijah carrying Alden, who was sobbing uncontrollably.

"So sorry to bother you," Elijah said. "I was hoping I could get him downstairs before he wakes Aubrey."

"No bother," Nick said. "Let me get the lights for you." He went ahead of them and turned on lights.

They went into the kitchen where Elijah sat at the table with his brother still clinging to him as he cried his little heart out.

Uncertain of what he should do, Nick poured glasses of water for them and put them on the table.

Elijah sent him a grateful look before returning his attention to Alden. "Did you have a bad dream?"

Alden shook his head.

"You want to talk about it?" Elijah wiped the tears from his brother's face with the paper napkin Nick handed him.

Alden nodded.

Nick wondered if he should leave the room, but something kept him there, afraid to move out of fear that even the slightest distraction might prevent Alden from speaking.

"What's wrong, Alden?" Elijah asked gently. "Are you sad about Mommy and Daddy."

"Uh-huh," Alden said.

That was the first word Nick had heard from him since he arrived. To his knowledge, Alden hadn't actually spoken to any of them.

"I... I saw them."

Nick's heart rate slowed to a crawl as he waited to hear what else the child would say.

"Who did you see?" Elijah asked.

"The bad men." He buried his face in his brother's T-shirt and began to cry again.

Electrified, Nick met Elijah's panicked gaze.

"Let me get Sam." Nick left the kitchen and quickly went up the stairs. He sat on Sam's side of the bed, hating to disturb her, but who knew if Alden would be able to speak about this twice. "Sam." He gave her a gentle shake. "Samantha."

"Mmm, what?"

"It's Alden. He saw something that night, and he's talking to Elijah about it."

Her eyes popped open. "Now?"

"Right now. In the kitchen."

She sat up, and he moved so she could get out of bed.

"Sorry to wake you, but I thought you'd want to know."

"Definitely." She tightened the knot of the robe around her waist. "I need to use the bathroom, and then I'll be down. See if you can hold him off until I get there."

"Will do."

CHAPTER TWENTY-FIVE

NICK WENT BACK down to the kitchen where Elijah held the glass of water for Alden. "Sam will be down in a minute."

Elijah nodded and cuddled his brother, rocking him gently as Alden's little body echoed with leftover sobs.

Sam came into the kitchen, her blue eyes sharp as she took in the scene before taking a seat at the table.

"Hey, Alden," Elijah said, his gaze fixed on Sam. "What you said about seeing the bad guys, can you tell me what you saw?"

"They...they made us go in the car to the bank and... They were hurting Mommy. She was screaming, but when Daddy saw me, he shook his head."

Under the table, Sam reached for Nick's hand and held on tight.

"What did you do?"

"I went back upstairs, but I could still hear." Alden sniffed and wiped his nose with his sleeve.

"What did they say?"

"They wanted Daddy to give them money. He said..."

"What did Daddy say, Alden?" Elijah asked, his own eyes bright with unshed tears.

"That he would give them money, but they had to stop hurting Mommy."

Sam held up one finger, then two, then three, hoping Elijah would ask how many guys.

He nodded "How many strangers were there?"

"Two."

"You're sure?"

"Uh-huh."

"What did they look like?"

"One of them was big with brown hair and the other one was skinny. He had yellow hair like mine. The big guy was on top of Mommy, and she was screaming." His voice caught on another sob. "He was hurting her. I wanted to help her, but Daddy shook his head. Should I have helped her, Lijah?"

"No, buddy," Elijah said, tears running down his face. "You did the right thing. You did what Daddy told you to. He would be so proud of you for that."

"I wanted to help Mommy. She always helps me."

"I know, but Daddy didn't want you to get hurt too."

"When I smelled the smoke, that's when I went to get Aubrey. We hid in the closet."

"That was really smart. You kept her safe."

Alden put his thumb in his mouth, his eyes heavy. The poor guy was probably exhausted from holding all that in.

"I'm going to take him back to bed," Elijah said.

"We'll be right here when he's settled," Nick said.

After Elijah left the room, carrying his brother, Sam and Nick sat for a full minute in complete silence.

"He saw the whole thing," Sam said, dabbing at her eyes. "He saw them rape his mother in front of his father, who was bound and helpless."

Nick sucked in a deep breath and released it slowly, aching for the child who had witnessed such horror and the man who'd had to watch the woman he loved be assaulted. The senselessness of it all overwhelmed him.

Sam withdrew the cell phone she kept on her at all

times since the night Arnold was killed in the line of duty while she slept through it. She placed a call to Captain Malone. "It's Sam. We've had a break in the Beauclair case."

"I HAVE TO go in to work," she said ten minutes after Elijah and Alden left the room.

"You need to sleep, Sam."

"I told Malone I'd meet him at HQ."

"Call him back and tell him you'll be there at six." When she started to protest, he placed his hand on hers. "You can't function on an hour of sleep. Tell him you'll meet him at six."

"Fine," she said with a huff of aggravation. "But you're not the boss of me."

"Sweetheart," he said, laughing, "ain't nobody the boss of you."

Sam smiled, even though she ached on the inside for poor, sweet Alden. "That's kinda true, isn't it?"

Nick raised that eyebrow that made him look extra sexy. *"Kinda?"*

Sam called Malone again. "My bossy pain-in-the-ass husband says I have to sleep for more than an hour before I can come out to play."

Malone snorted with laughter. "Meet me at six?"

"See you then. I'll give Carlucci and Dominguez some marching orders in the meantime."

"Sounds good."

"Happy now?" Sam asked Nick when she'd closed her phone.

"I'll be happy when you're back in bed."

"One minute." She called Detective Carlucci and asked her to get photos of anyone else related to the case, so they would have them if they were forced to show them to Alden for an ID. Sam hoped it wouldn't come to that. If they were able to get the perpetrators another way, it would be her preference not to involve him at all.

"A five-year-old eyewitness to murder," Carlucci said. "How does he get past that?"

"I have no idea," Sam said. "But one step at a time. Let's catch the bastards who killed his parents."

"We're on it. We'll get the photos together."

"Thank you." She put down her phone, propped her chin on her hand and looked at Nick. "How will I ever sleep with the things he said in my mind?"

"You might not sleep, but at least you can rest. Come on."

Sam took his hand and let him lead her upstairs to bed. In the hallway, she paused outside the bedroom where the children were staying with their brother, wishing there was something more she could do for them.

Nick's hand on her back kept her moving toward bed. He tucked her in and then cuddled up to her, putting his arm around her.

Sam tried to relax her racing mind and rigid muscles as she went through the various pieces of the puzzle one by one.

"Stop," Nick said softly. "It'll still be what it is in the morning. Close your eyes and rest, Samantha."

She wouldn't have thought she could sleep, but the next thing she knew, the alarm was going off, making her groan. Five hours was about four less than she needed, but that was all she was going to get.

"I'll make you some coffee," Nick muttered.

"Don't get up on my account. Get another hour."

"I'd rather spend that time with you."

"You're insane. If I didn't have to work, not even you could get me out of this bed."

"Good to know," he said with a low chuckle as he squeezed her ass.

"I'll be in the shower. If I'm not out in ten minutes, come after me."

"I may come after you anyway."

"After you start the coffee."

"Of course."

Sam dozed off under the hot water, coming to when Nick's arms slid around her, his lips skimming her shoulder. "In case I forget to tell you, you're the best husband I ever had."

"It was a low bar," he said as he always did. Since her ex-husband, Peter, was murdered in a plot that involved President Nelson's son, it wasn't as much fun as it used to be to talk about what a lousy husband he'd been.

Sam turned in Nick's arms and took five more minutes she didn't have to marshal the strength she would need to get through another difficult day on the job. "Will you be able to stick around until Shelby gets here to take over?"

"Yeah, I'll stay. I told Terry I'd need some flexibility this week."

Sam curled her hand around his neck and brought him down for a kiss. "Thank you. For everything. Every single thing you do for me. Especially the coffee."

His smile stretched slowly across his sinfully handsome face.

"I'm going to talk to Malone about finding a way to go with you next week."

"Really?"

"With Gonzo and Freddie both off, it's a huge long shot, so don't get excited yet."

"Too late. I'm already excited."

"Can you hold that thought for the next twelve to fourteen hours?"

"That's apt to cause injury. The commercials say you ought to seek medical help after four hours."

Sam laughed, kissed him and stepped out of the shower. By the time she made her way downstairs fifteen minutes later, Nick had coffee and toast waiting for her.

"Do you think other vice presidents make their own coffee and toast?" she asked after taking the all-important first sip of hot coffee. She still craved diet soda for her morning jolt of caffeine but didn't miss the brutal stomach pain it used to cause.

"I have no idea. I think the Naval Observatory comes with a chef."

"So, we could have a chef if we wanted one?"

"I suppose. Do we want one?"

Sam took a bite of peanut butter toast. "I don't, but if it's a perk of the job, it might be fun to see what it's like."

"I'd hate to get used to that perk and then have to give it up when I leave office."

"True." She glanced at the clock on the stove and saw that she had twenty minutes until she was due to meet Malone. "What's the deal with Harry traveling with you?"

"I had inherited Gooding's doctor," he said of the former vice president who had recently passed away after a battle with brain cancer. "But he's retiring, and they told me I could pick whoever I wanted."

"Well, just so you know, I'll be giving the various scenarios significant thought now that I know you're required to travel with a personal physician."

"Don't let your imagination run away with you."

"Too late." Sam downed the last of her coffee and put the mug in the sink. "And on that bright note, I'm off to figure out who tortured and murdered the parents of those sweet kids sleeping upstairs." She bent to kiss him as he sat at the table with the morning paper, which had a feature story on the fire at the Beauclair home. She skimmed the story and saw much less than she already knew, which pleased her.

"Have a good day," he said, looking up at her. "Call me if you need me."

"You do the same."

She was about to walk away when he took hold of her hand and brought it to his lips. "Take good care of my wife out there. She's my whole world."

"I will. Don't worry."

"Ha. Now tell me not to breathe."

Sam gave her hand a gentle tug to get him to let go, when that was the last thing she wanted. But duty called, as it always did. The idea of a full week away from the grind with him became more appealing all the time. Not to mention the chance to meet the queen! As she went down the ramp that led to the sidewalk, Brant was on his way up, wearing a sharp gray suit with a red-and-blue-striped tie.

"Good morning, Mrs. Cappuano."

"Morning, Brant." She was almost past him when she stopped and turned. "Brant…"

"Ma'am?"

"Why is the vice president required to travel with a personal physician?"

"So medical assistance is immediately available, should he require it."

"He's perfectly healthy. Why would he require immediate medical assistance?"

"As you well know, anything can happen."

"Anything as in what?"

"You want specific scenarios?"

"Yes, that's what I want."

"There could be an accident, or he could catch the flu, for example. Having a doctor on standby who is loyal to the vice president is in his best interest."

"Would it be possible for someone to poison his food?" Brant's eyes went wide.

"Roll with me. I'm told I have a vivid imagination."

"Our advance team works with the hotels and other establishments, so that would be highly unlikely."

"But it *could* happen."

He rubbed the back of his neck. "Anything is possible. Our jobs are to reduce the likelihood of anything happening, and I promise you we take that very seriously. Which is why I had no choice but to object to the children being brought here. Ma'am."

"I understand, and I apologize for making your job more difficult than it already is."

"Never forget that you and I have the same goals."

"Yes, we do. Thank you for your time. You have a good day."

"You do the same, ma'am."

CHAPTER TWENTY-SIX

As SAM DROVE to HQ, she thought about what Brant had said about the two of them having the same goals. That was certainly true. Nothing mattered to her more than the safety of her loved ones.

Her phone rang, and she took the call from Gonzo. "How're you feeling?"

"I'm okay, but I wanted to let you know that I'm going to be out for a while."

"Trulo told me he suggested you take some time off."

"That's not what this is." He paused before he said, "I'm going to rehab, Sam."

Stunned, she said, "For *what*?"

"I, um, I'm apparently addicted to pain meds. I've been relying on them to get by, and it, well, it's gotten out of hand."

Unable to process what he'd said while driving, she pulled over and came to a stop. "You're hooked on *pills*?"

"Yes."

"Please tell me you haven't done anything illegal to get them."

"I wish I could," he said with a deep sigh.

"Oh, my fucking *God*, Gonzo." Her mind raced with the implications.

"I'm so sorry, Sam," he said tearfully. "I've been a disaster since Arnold died, and I fucked up. But I'm going to fix it. I swear to God, I'm going to fix it. The place I'm going treats PTSD too."

"I don't even know what to say."

"Just tell me I still have a job to come back to."

"You know you have my full support, but if it gets out—"

"It won't."

Sam wished she shared his certainty. "Are you still at GW?"

"Yeah."

"I'll be by to see you this morning."

"Okay."

"I hope you know how much we all care about you, Tommy."

"I do," he said softly. "It means the world."

"I'll see you soon."

Reeling, she ended the call, pulled back into traffic and tried to make sense of what he'd told her. At least he was taking the steps necessary to get it under control, but he was *addicted* to pain meds. And she'd never noticed. What did that say about her as a friend and commander?

At HQ, the first person she encountered upon entering the lobby was the chief. *Great. She'd expected to have* two more hours to prepare for this meeting.

"A word, Lieutenant," he said, his expression stern. Or possibly annoyed. She took a closer look. Definitely annoyed.

She began to tell him that she had a meeting to get to with Captain Malone, but the chief trumped the captain every day and twice on Sundays.

Farnsworth, the man she'd called Uncle Joe growing up, led her from the lobby to his suite of offices where his faithful assistant, Helen, was already on duty, looking far more perky than anyone should at six in the morning.

"Close the door," the chief said as Sam followed him into his office.

He went around the desk and sat, gesturing for her to take one of his visitor chairs. "Just when I think I have you figured out, Lieutenant, you throw me a curveball. I spend *one day* in meetings at City Hall and come back to the news that you have *custody* of the Beauclair children. I think to myself, that can't be possible because she's the *lead investigator of their parents' murders.*" He folded his hands on the desk and directed his steely glare at her. "Would you care to tell me how you *ended up with custody* of the Beauclair children *while investigating their parents' murders*?"

"It just sort of happened," Sam said, trying not to squirm. "It was very late, and they needed a place to go. Nick and I are licensed foster parents. It was really that simple."

"As you and I both know, there's nothing simple about it, and it's a conflict of interest for you to be *caring for the children of your murder victims.*"

"I understand."

"The children will be immediately removed from your custody—"

"But—"

He held up a hand to silence her. "Or you will be removed from the case. One or the other, Lieutenant. You can't have it both ways."

"I pick the kids," she said without hesitation.

His brows went up, and his mouth opened before snapping closed. "Very well. You're off the case."

"Before you decide anything, I found out in the middle of the night that one of the children currently in my custody witnessed his parents being tortured and possibly murdered. My plan today was to figure out how best to use this witness account to help us nail the people who committed these murders. In light of this development, I shall be taking an unplanned personal day to tend to my foster children, who need me very much right now." Sam stood, preparing to make a grand exit. "I'm sorry to leave you in the lurch with Sergeant Gonzales in the hospital, but I'm sure Captain Malone can oversee the investigation in my absence."

"You think I don't know what you're doing, but I'm wise to you, Lieutenant."

"I'm following your orders. Sir."

"Sit down."

She sat.

"What did the child tell you?"

"Just to be clear—are you asking me that as your lieutenant in charge of the Homicide division or as the foster parent to the child in question?"

"Sam," he said through gritted teeth, "*I swear to God*..."

She told him what Alden had revealed in the middle of the night.

For a long moment after she finished speaking, he stared at the far wall. He was so still that she wondered if he was breathing. Then he shifted his gaze toward her and said, "What's your plan for using him as a witness?"

"My goal is to do everything I can to *not* have to use him as a witness. If we can sew up the case using other means, then that's what we'll do. I'm due to meet with Malone about our next steps." She glanced at her watch. "Ten minutes ago." Clearing her throat, she added, "Sir."

"I assume you'll be consulting with Dr. Trulo about counseling and care for the child?"

"He's second on my list for the day."

After another extended silence, the chief said, "Carry on."

"Sir?"

"Work the case."

"I'm not relocating the kids at this point, because it wouldn't be in their best interest. Their older brother is with them, and an aunt and uncle may be stepping up to take custody. I won't have them for much longer." Everything inside her rejected that realization, but with so many other things to deal with, she refused to get sucked into that rabbit hole. Not now anyway. There would be plenty of time after they were gone to fall apart. Right now, they needed her to find the people who'd murdered their parents and ruined their charmed lives. Hopefully, someday it would matter to them that she'd gotten justice for their family.

The chief returned her mulish stare with one of his own. "I'd like your assurances that this sort of conflict won't happen again."

"I'd like to promise you that, but I'm not sure I can guarantee I wouldn't do the same thing again if I saw other children in distress."

"Perhaps you need to spend some time thinking about your priorities, Lieutenant."

Sam nearly recoiled from the shock of that statement. "Wow. *Really?*"

"Yes, really! You can't go around taking in the children of murder victims *when you're the lead investigator on the case!*"

"Why not?" Even knowing she was stepping way out of line couldn't stop her from doing it anyway. "The kids had nothing to do with it. They're innocent victims. And if I hadn't taken in the Beauclair children, we might never have known that Alden witnessed the murders. Think about that."

He rubbed his face with his hands, and when he looked up at her, she saw exhaustion in his eyes. "You know why I haven't retired when I could've quite some time ago?"

Stunned by the unexpected segue, she shook her head.

"One word: *You.* Y-o-u. *You* are the reason I can't retire."

Sam had no idea what to say to that.

"Anyone else in this job would have your badge and your ass in a sling before the first week was out. What people say about you in the department? That you get away with murder even as you investigate murders?" Leaning forward, he said, "It's *true.* You do. After you close this case, I want you to take an unpaid week off and think about whether you and this job are going to be able to coexist in the future. I'm putting you on notice, Lieutenant. I won't always be here to run interference for you."

Though his words shocked her, she didn't hear much after "unpaid week off." If she could close the Beauclair case before the weekend, she would be free to accompany Nick to Europe where she could do some "thinking" about whether she had a future as a member of the MPD. The timing would be convenient, but she couldn't let the chief know that.

She gave him a defiant look. "I'm sorry if you feel my performance is less than satisfactory, sir."

"*No one* thinks your performance is unsatisfactory, Lieutenant. It's your methodology that could use some fine-tuning."

They engaged in a staring contest that ended when the chief looked away. "Get to work, Lieutenant, and keep a lid on the fact that the kids are with you. We don't need that all over the news. Am I clear?"

"Yes, sir." Sam got the hell out of there before he changed his mind about taking her off the case, but as she made her way to the detectives' pit, his words echoed through her mind. *You are the reason I can't retire.* Well, damn. That kinda hurt. And he really thought she got away with murder while catching murderers? That was also news to her. In her mind, she did what she had to in order to get the job done, and if he thought someone could do it better, they were welcome to try.

Okay, well, not really, but she did an ugly job the best way she knew how. Later, when she had time to breathe, she would talk to her father about the things the chief had said and get his take on it. What if he felt the same way Farnsworth did but had never said so? Wouldn't that beat all?

Shaking off those unpleasant thoughts, Sam found Malone in his office. "Sorry I'm late. I got waylaid by the chief."

"Who wasn't *at all* happy to hear you're fostering the Beauclair kids."

"I know. My ears are still ringing."

"He wants you off the case."

"So he said—until he heard that my foster child might actually be able to help us. Then he didn't seem quite so determined to take me off the case."

"You're walking a very fine line here, Sam. He's absolutely right that it's a clear-cut conflict of interest, and you know that."

"I do. But in the moment, all I saw were two little kids who needed something I could give them. You'll have to pardon me if my first thoughts weren't about my job."

"You know as well as I do that our first thoughts *always* need to be about the job."

"I'll take the hit if you all feel I deserve one." She'd already made her peace with the fact that she might never advance beyond the rank of lieutenant. "No problem. Do what you've got to do, but I wouldn't have done anything different if I had it to do over again."

"No one is questioning whether your heart was in the right place. That's not the issue here."

"I'm well aware of what the issue is, and like I said, I'm willing to take whatever hit you all feel is appropriate to get me back in line. In the meantime, I have a homicide investigation, two foster children, a sergeant in the hospital and a wedding to contend with. You'll have to excuse me if I don't have the time to fully explore my many transgressions."

Malone rolled his eyes. "Save the drama and tell me what's up with Gonza."

"You heard me. He's out on medical leave indefinitely."

"What's he got?"

"I'm not at liberty to discuss that, and I believe you're technically not at liberty to ask me."

"I'm not asking you as the captain. I'm asking you as his friend and colleague."

"Who also happens to be his big boss."

"Fair enough. How long will he be out?"

"I'm planning to see him this morning, and I'll get the particulars."

"Wish him well for me and let him know that we've got him covered here."

"I'll tell him. I'm sure that'll mean a lot to him." She looked down at the floor and then back at him. "The chief indicated that after we close Beauclair, I'm to take an unpaid week to think about the alignment of my personal and professional goals, as well as my impertinence."

His brows lifted. "Is that right?"

"Uh-huh. If we're able to close this in the next couple of days, that means you'll be down three people in Homicide next week, in case you want to make some contingency plans."

"Good to know," he said drolly.

"I need to check with Hill to find out the latest on Piedmont, the former business partner who's been in the wind the last three years. They caught him at Dulles trying to leave the area and can put him in the District the night of the murders."

"That sounds like a slam dunk close to the case," Malone said.

"Maybe so, but the description Alden gave us doesn't match Piedmont."

"A guy that rich could hire it done."

"No doubt, but we still need to grab the guys who actually did the crime."

"Agreed."

"I have to figure out how to handle the info Alden gave us. I had Carlucci and Dominguez pull photos of everyone involved in the case, so we have them if we have to involve Alden, but my goal is to do it without him if at all possible. I'm going to talk to Trulo about how best to handle this process with a traumatized five-year-old."

"I was going to ask what the plan was there."

"I've got to talk to Carlucci and Dominguez before they leave, and then I want to catch Trulo before his appointments begin. After that, I'm going to see Gonzo."

"Keep me posted. On all of it."

"Will do."

Sam left his office and went to her own, where her first order of business was a call to Avery Hill.

"Morning," he said.

"How's it going with Piedmont?"

"You won't believe it if I tell you."

"You've got my attention."

"He and Jameson Armstrong were back in touch."

Sam dropped into her desk chair. "You wanna run that by me one more time?"

"I know. It made my head spin too, but Piedmont told us he'd reached out to Armstrong about three months ago to say that if he was willing to help Piedmont make some money, he would take back the threats he'd made against Armstrong's family. Apparently, Piedmont was dead broke and out of options."

"Can you confirm any of this?"

"Actually, we already have. He produced his financials that show every account down to less than a thousand dollars."

"And we know those are *all* his accounts?"

"We're still confirming that, but he turned over everything, including offshore accounts to our investigators, and they're all tapped out. In addition, Armstrong's assistant in his DC office has confirmed that he'd been in touch with Piedmont and met with him the day of the murders."

"This is too coincidental. How could he *not* have been involved?"

"I thought the same thing until we told him Jameson and Cleo Armstrong had been murdered. He was inconsolable for hours after receiving that news."

"Was he putting on a show?"

"It didn't seem that way to us. His grief seemed genuine."

"I'm extremely confused right now. This guy who *threatened Armstrong's family* to the point that they felt the need to relocate and live under different names, comes out from under his rock years later, and *Jameson takes the call and agrees to do business with him*?"

"It wasn't that simple. Jameson made him come to DC to get the money, so he could look him in the eye and tell him this was it, the only money he was ever going to get in exchange for Piedmont swearing to leave him and his family alone. Piedmont had a cashier's check for twenty million dollars on him when he was apprehended. The check was drawn on the accounts of JAE in Delaware."

"This happens on the same day Armstrong and his wife are tortured and brutally murdered? How can it be unrelated?"

"We're asking ourselves the same thing, but Piedmont's profound shock and grief over the news of their deaths was legitimate. Everyone who witnessed it had the same impression."

Sam released a deep breath. "Are you willing to rule him out as complicit in the murders?"

"I believe so."

"Let me ask you this. If he cared so much about them, why did he make their lives a living hell for years after the company imploded?"

"He says much of that was 'heat-of-the-moment' and shock when he found out his longtime friend and partner had basically handed the government their case against him. He admits to being enraged and saying things he came to regret, but he never had any intention of harming Jameson or his family. Or so he says."

"The head spins."

"I know. I feel the same way, but like you said at the outset, sometimes the obvious answer isn't the correct one."

Sam blew out a deep breath. "We had a break overnight." She updated him on what Alden had told them.

"Ah, God. How do you go about using him as a witness?"

"We don't, unless we absolutely have to."

"Let me know what we can do to help. Whatever you need."

"I will. Thanks for the update and let me know if you get anything else from Piedmont that might help."

"You'll be the first to know."

Sam ended the call and sat for a long moment attempting to make sense of what she'd learned from Avery and trying to figure out their next move. She went through the folder of photos she'd requested from Carlucci and Dominguez. Attached to the folder was a note from Dominguez that they'd been called by Detective Lucas to assist with an SVU investigation.

The photos included Jameson Beauclair's former partners, Piedmont and Dave Gorton, several of his current business associates that Green and McBride had interviewed and Victor Klein, the man who'd been in the traffic altercation with Cleo Beauclair last Friday.

According to DOB on his sheet, he was twenty-nine. She studied the mug shot of Klein, a big guy with dark hair and hard brown eyes, which dovetailed with Alden's description of one of the men who'd attacked his parents. Klein's face was devoid of expression, which made it impossible to get a read on him.

Sam picked up the phone and called one of her favorite government employees ever—Brendan Sullivan, who'd been such a huge help to Sam in the case involving her ex-husband. Brendan had been Peter's parole officer. He answered her call on the second ring.

"Brendan Sullivan," he said, sounding rushed.

"It's Sam Holland."

"Oh, hey. What's up?"

"Got a question for you. Does the name Victor Klein mean anything to you?"

"He's one of mine. Why? What's he done?"

"Maybe something. Maybe nothing. What can you tell me?"

"He's an arrogant punk who thinks the world owes him something, and when it doesn't deliver, he has no problem taking it."

"You think he'd be capable of rape, torture and homicide by fire?"

"Are we talking about that home invasion in Chevy Chase?"

"I can neither confirm nor deny."

"Is this an official or unofficial inquiry?"

"Unofficial at this point."

"I can tell you he's someone who had every advantage—a nice family, good schools, college, etc. But he's always working an angle, a get-rich-quick scheme. He ended up in the can for his role in a robbery ring that landed several victims in the hospital with serious injuries."

"What kind of injuries?"

"Broken bones, lacerations, concussions. If he sees a chance to make easy money, he stops at nothing to get it."

"If we were talking about the home invasion in Chevy Chase, you think he'd be capable, hypothetically speaking, of course, of raping a man's wife while the husband is bound and helpless, and then binding them both before setting them on fire after knocking some teeth out so they can't be easily identified?"

After a long silence, Brendan said, "I assume they were rich?"

"Filthy."

"Then yeah, I can see him doing that or helping someone else to do it."

Sam felt a tingle in the area of her backbone, which was almost always a good sign. "Do we know his associates?"

"I could make a few calls and see what I can find out if that would help."

"It would."

"What put him on your radar?"

"He was in a traffic altercation with the wife a couple of days before the home invasion."

"I'll get on it and call you when I have something."

"Appreciate the help."

"Not a problem."

Sam called Carlucci. "Are you guys still with Lucas?"

"No, we're on our way back to HQ."

"Can you pick up Victor Klein on the way?" She passed

along the address Sullivan had given her, which matched the address on the accident report.

"We're on it," Carlucci said.

"Call for backup before you go in."

"Will do."

CHAPTER TWENTY-SEVEN

SAM STASHED HER phone in her pocket as she headed for Trulo's office upstairs. As she was leaving the pit, Freddie came in escorting a well-dressed, frightened-looking couple and another man who looked like a lawyer. Realizing he had the bitchy PTO president in for an interview, Sam gave him a thumbs-up that they couldn't see. Their eyes bugged at the sight of her, which gave her a dose of satisfaction.

Freddie smiled and winked at her as he pointed the people toward the interrogation room where he'd dole out a much-needed dose of humility.

She continued on to Trulo's office, and wasn't it just her luck to come face-to-face with Sergeant Ramsey. Sam hoped he'd stay on his own side of the staircase, so she wouldn't be tempted to push him down the stairs—again. Since she'd barely escaped an assault charge the first time, she kept moving and didn't make eye contact.

"If it isn't Mary Poppins, taking in the poor, helpless children and compromising her investigation? Such a do-gooder. Do the people who license foster parents know you're guilty of assault?"

Sam never stopped moving. "Does your family know you're guilty of being a dick? Oh wait, of course they do. Silly of me to ask." She pressed on, resisting the urge to look back, and didn't stop walking until she was outside Trulo's office. Her heart beat fast, as if she'd been chased. She had no idea if Ramsey had followed her, and she wasn't about to look to find out.

Trulo's office door opened. "Lieutenant. What can I do for you?"

"You got a minute?"

He stepped back to admit her and closed the door behind her.

She breathed a sigh of relief.

"Everything all right?" Trulo asked.

"Yep."

"You seem unusually rattled."

"That's what happens when you resist your baser urges to punch a fellow officer and send him flying down the stairs—again."

Trulo's lips quirked from the effort it took not to laugh. "Congratulations on the successful effort."

"It wasn't easy. I fear I may be growing up."

He effected an expression of mock horror. "Say it isn't so!"

"I know. Revolting development."

"As amusing as this development is, something tells me that's not what brought you to me this morning."

Sam dropped into the chair where she'd been forced to spend many an hour after Stahl took her hostage. Though she'd resisted Trulo's efforts at first, she credited him with putting her back together and making it possible for her to return to the job. "I need some advice about possibly guiding a five-year-old witness to murder through the process of identifying his parents' killers."

"Ah," he said, taking the seat across from her and crossing his legs. "So, one of the kids saw something?"

Sam nodded. "The boy, Alden. He hadn't said a word

since he'd been with us, but when his older brother arrived, he let it all out." Sam told him what Alden had conveyed to them in his middle-of-the-night outburst.

When she had finished, Trulo released a deep sigh. "Someday, many years from now, Alden will realize that the very last thing his father did in his own life was to save his son's life."

The profound statement stirred Sam's already-raw emotions. "Very true." She cleared her throat. "So, if it comes to it, how do we do this?"

"Carefully," Trulo said, stroking his chin. "First of all, we go to him. He doesn't come here."

Sam nodded in agreement. "We'd have to show him the photos."

"Yes."

"And at some point, he'd have to testify."

"Also true. If you're forced to use him, I'd spend some time with him afterward to get a feel for what he's going to need long-term. I can make some recommendations to his new guardians."

"Will he always remember?" Sam asked.

"Possibly, but the memories may fade in time, or they may remain very vivid for the rest of his life. It's hard to say for certain."

"Thanks for the insight," Sam said, gripping the arms of the chair for support as she stood. "On to my next thing—visiting Gonzo in the hospital."

"He's going to be all right, Sam. Eventually."

"The thing that nags at me is that I didn't notice he was in such a bad place, and I'm with him every day. How did I not see it?"

"Because he didn't want you to. He didn't want anyone to see it. Emotional devastation is a tough thing to manage in this macho environment in which we work. We're often seen as weak if we allow people to see our inner turmoil. You know what that's like. You've been there yourself."

"Yes, I have."

"He's going to get through this. It's just going to take some time."

"I hope you're right."

"When have you ever known me not to be?"

Sam laughed as she moved to the door. "That sounds like something I would say."

"Would you like me to check the hallway for you?"

"If you wouldn't mind."

She stood back so he could stick his head out the door. "Coast is clear, but just to be safe, put your hands in your pockets and keep them there until you're back in friendly territory."

"Will do, Doc," she said, amused by his commentary. "I'll let you know if we have to involve Alden."

"I'm free all afternoon."

"Appreciate the help." While keeping her hands planted firmly in her pants pockets, Sam moved quickly down the stairs, releasing a deep breath when she arrived in the safety of her pit, her home away from home. Carlucci and Dominguez had returned, so Sam went to find out how it had gone with Klein.

"No sign of him at his place," Dominguez said. While Carlucci was tall and blonde, Dominguez was petite with olive-toned skin and dark hair. "Neighbors said they haven't seen him in a few days."

"Let's put out an APB for him," Sam said.

"I'll do it," Dominguez said.

"You got the photos we left, LT?" Carlucci asked.

"Yes, thank you. What's up with the SVU case?"

"Nothing to do with us. They just needed a couple of extra hands."

"Good answer." They had enough on their plate. "Let's get everyone in the conference room for a quick meeting before you two take off. I'll be there in a minute." She went into her office, gathered the photos, her notes and summoned her legendary mojo. Today could make or break this case. She was determined to make it as quickly as possible for the sake of Alden, Aubrey and Elijah. She'd also love to have it done before Freddie's wedding overtook them this weekend.

Freddie came into her office, smiling widely. "Damn, that was fun."

Sam laughed. "Now that you've had your fun for the day, let's figure out what's next."

They went into the conference room, where the others waited for her along with Malone and Farnsworth, who stood against the back wall observing. "First things first, the FBI has ruled out Duke Piedmont as a suspect in the home invasion and murders." She went over what had transpired since Piedmont was apprehended at Dulles the previous day.

"I find it really, *really* hard to believe that he was in the city but had nothing to do with this," Freddie said.

"I did too, but Hill said he and the other agents involved found Piedmont's shock and grief over the deaths of Armstrong and his wife to be sincere and legitimate. He'd also gotten what he'd come for—twenty million that would set him up for the rest of his life."

"Where do we go from here?" Green asked.

"We're looking for this guy," she said, holding up the photo of Victor Klein, sharing what Brendan Sullivan had told her about him. She pinned the photo of Klein to the center of the murder board. "Here's what I think happened. Klein sideswiped Cleo in traffic three days before the murders. She made a BFD out of how he could've killed her and her children. He took a look at her Audi SUV, possibly noticed the rock on her finger and smelled money. He was locked up on an outstanding warrant until his arraignment Monday morning. When he got out, he got her address off the accident report. Then he recruited another scumbag to help him with the promise of a windfall and paid the Beauclairs a visit."

"Where were the kids while this was going on?"

"We know they were in the car when he took her to the bank to withdraw a hundred grand."

"You really think it was Klein when Piedmont had made actual threats against their family and was in the city the day of the murders?" Farnsworth asked, incredulous.

"Agent Hill and his team are convinced that Piedmont had nothing to do with it. Piedmont had been back in touch with Armstrong for months. They were living in plain sight while Armstrong continued to promote the software he'd founded. If Piedmont wanted to take him out, he'd had ample opportunity. It's time to shift our focus. Let's find Klein."

"Might be a stretch, Sam," Freddie said. "This is pure speculation on our part."

"Understood, but I spoke with Klein's parole officer, who believes Klein is capable of something like this. He's been escalating, moving from petty shit to assault and did time for B&E. According to the reports, Cleo took a piece of his ass after the accident, so that might've pissed him off enough to hunt her down to teach her a lesson about how to speak to him. Perhaps he took one look at that crib in Chevy Chase and dollar signs started dancing in his eyes."

"We know she withdrew a hundred grand from the bank the same afternoon as the home invasion," Green said. "My first stop after this is the bank where she made the withdrawal."

"A hundred K wasn't enough for Klein," Sam said, feeling the buzz of certainty that she was onto something with this theory. That buzz never disappointed her. "He owed that much in back child support. I want to know who Jameson called to get more money. The kind of cash they had isn't just sitting at the local branch. It would be in brokerage accounts that aren't as easily accessible. Get me a call to a broker, a financial adviser, someone who can confirm they made the request."

"I can give it a few more hours," Carlucci said. "If that would help."

"I'll take all the help I can get."

"I'll stay too," Dominguez added.

"Thank you both. I've got an errand to do outside the building, but I'll be back shortly. Get to it. Cruz, you're with me."

Sam went into her office to grab her jacket, keys and portable radio.

"Where're we going?" Cruz asked.

She kept her voice low when she said, "To see Gonzo before he leaves for rehab."

Freddie's eyes went wide with shock. He released a deep breath. "Oh."

"Needless to say, he probably won't be at your wedding. I know that's a huge disappointment to you, but this is truly in his best interest."

"I know."

"Could you ask Will to stand in for him in the wedding party?"

"I suppose so. He'd do it."

"Yes, he would, and he'd be honored to be asked. I'm really sorry this is happening, this of all weeks, Freddie."

"So am I, but if it means he's getting what he needs, then it's worth it."

"You're a good friend. It'll mean a lot to him to hear you say that. That's why I wanted you to come with me."

They headed for the morgue exit where they were waylaid by Lindsey McNamara. "I was going to call you. I need to know who to contact within the Beauclair family about arrangements for the bodies."

"I'll speak to Mr. Beauclair's son Elijah later today about what he wants to do." She told Lindsey how their younger son had witnessed the crime.

"Oh dear God."

"I'll have Elijah get in touch with you."

"There's no rush. Whenever he's ready."

"I'll let him know that. Thanks, Lindsey."

"Heard the trip was pared down to a week. Did you have anything to do with that?"

"Maybe," Sam said, with a sly smile. "Maybe not."

"Either way, you won't hear me complaining."

"Me either. See you later."

Sam and Freddie drove to GW in unusual silence, both of them tense about what they would hear from Gonzo. She pulled into a parking space outside the emergency department and shut off the car. "What're you thinking?"

"I'm wondering how I didn't notice he was so messed up. I'm with him every day. He's one of my best friends."

"I asked Trulo that same question this morning—

about myself. What kind of boss or friend am I if he was in such bad shape and I didn't notice. He said Gonzo didn't want us to know. It's not going to do either of us any good to blame ourselves. All we can do now is support him—and Christina—going forward."

Freddie nodded in agreement, but Sam could tell he was still troubled by what he'd missed.

Hell, she was too.

They showed their badges at the info desk and were given Gonzo's room number. In the elevator, several people did double takes when they recognized Sam, but she ignored them. She wasn't in the mood to play gracious second lady. Not when she had far bigger things to contend with.

Outside Gonzo's room, Sam glanced at Freddie before she knocked.

"Come in."

They stepped into the room, and Sam's eyes had to adjust to the darkness after the brightly lit hallway. The blinds were drawn, and only a small light over the bed was on.

Gonzo looked like hell. His eyes were swollen and rimmed with red, his jaw covered in stubble and his dark hair stood on end. "Hey," he said, averting his gaze as if ashamed.

Sam hated that for him. "How're you doing?"

"Never been better," he said with a tight little smile. "They're weaning me off the pain meds. Good times all around."

Sam noticed a puke bucket sitting close at hand.

Gonzo glanced at Freddie. "I'm really sorry about the timing."

"Don't be. Your health is more important than anything."

"I'll be really sad to miss it."

"We'll take a lot of pictures for you."

"That'd be nice."

"What can we do for you, Tommy?" Sam asked.

"Check in with Christina while I'm gone?"

"We will. Definitely."

"I'm sorry about work. I know this leaves you in a lurch with the honcymooner here out the next two weeks."

"Don't worry about us," Sam said. "Malone said to tell you we've got you covered." She didn't mention her unplanned week off, because that would only add to his stress. Under normal circumstances, he'd be in charge while she was away. Now Malone would have to do it.

"What's going on with the case?"

Sam told him about the breakthrough with Alden.

"Christ, and I think I've got problems," he said. "That poor kid."

"We're taking good care of him."

The door opened, and Christina came in, carrying Alex, who gave a happy squeal at the sight of his daddy.

"We'll go and give you guys some time alone," Sam said, squeezing his arm. "Call if you need anything at all and let us know when you're ready for visitors."

"Will do. Thank you." Gonzo reached out a hand to Freddie, who took it and leaned in to give his friend a hug. "Have the best day ever on Saturday. I'll be thinking of you and Elin."

"Take care of yourself, bud. We're here if you need us."

"That means a lot."

"I'll check in with you," Sam said to Christina, who nodded.

Freddie turned to the door, his jaw tight with tension.

As they walked toward the elevator, Sam put her hand on Freddie's back, more determined than ever to make sure he had a perfect day on Saturday, even if the life swirling around them would never be perfect or simple. For one day, he and Elin deserved nothing less than perfection.

CHRISTINA APPROACHED THE bed tentatively, shocked by Tommy's disheveled appearance.

He held out his arms, and she handed Alex to him.

"Hey, buddy," Tommy said, kissing the little guy's cheek and neck until he squealed with laughter.

A sight she'd seen a million times before brought tears to her eyes, knowing it would be at least a month before they saw him again. That felt like a lifetime.

She'd told Alex that Daddy wasn't feeling good and that he had to be gentle, so Alex snuggled into his father's embrace rather than trying to wrestle with him as usual.

Tommy held out a hand to her.

Christina took it, because she still loved him, even after the hell he'd put her through.

"I'm sorry," he said, his eyes brimming with tears. "I know I've asked so much of you, but if I could just have a little more time to get my shit together, I promise things will be better."

"I'm not going anywhere, Tommy," she said, wiping tears.

"I owe you so much, babe. What you've done for me—and for Alex."

"Is because I love you both. I want you back. I want my Tommy back."

"I'm going to do my best to find him."

"Are you sick, Daddy?" Alex asked.

"Yeah, buddy. I'm not feeling good at all. But I'm going to get better. I promise."

Alex patted Tommy's face, making her throat tighten with emotion.

"Daddy sad. Don't want Daddy sad."

"I don't want that either," Tommy said, hugging his son as tears streamed down his face.

Christina wept for both of them. For *all* of them. For A.J. and the life that had been stolen from him, his parents, sisters, colleagues and the devoted partner who blamed himself.

Dr. Anderson came into the room, stopping short at the sight of Christina and Alex. "I can come back."

"No, it's fine," Tommy said. "This is my fiancée, Christina Billings, and our son, Alex."

Hearing him call Alex *their* son went a long way toward consoling Christina.

"I've made arrangements with the rehab in Baltimore," Anderson said. "They said you can get there anytime today. I want you to go right from here to there with no stops in between. I'll take you myself if need be."

"That's not necessary," Christina said. "I'll take him. I brought his bag with me. I just need to drop Alex at the sitter, and then we can go."

"If you want to go do that," Anderson said, "I'll make sure he's ready when you return."

"My lawyer is going to stop by," Tommy said. "I need to see him before I go so I can make Christina Alex's legal guardian. He should be here anytime."

"Great," Anderson said, heading for the door. "I'll

start the discharge paperwork, so you're ready when Christina returns."

"He seems really nice," Christina said.

"He's been great. He's the one who talked me into going."

"Then I guess we owe him a debt of gratitude."

"Hey, buddy," Tommy said to Alex. "Daddy has to go away on a trip for a little while, so I can feel better. Will you do me a huge favor while I'm gone?"

Alex nodded solemnly, his eyes big as he looked back at the father he resembled so closely, right down to the dimple in his chin.

"I need you to be a really, really good boy for Mommy, okay?"

"Okay, Daddy."

"Do whatever she asks you to, and if you're a really, really good boy, I'll have a surprise for you when I get home."

"I'll be good, Daddy. I promise."

Tommy sobbed quietly as he hugged his son.

Alex never squirmed or tried to get free the way he normally would. Rather, he let Tommy hold him for as long as he needed to. And when Tommy finally released him, Alex wiped the tears from his father's face and kissed him. "Love you, Daddy."

"Love you too, little man."

Mopping up more tears, Christina reached for the child, who held on tight to her. "I'll be back," she said.

"I'll be here."

CHAPTER TWENTY-EIGHT

CAMERON AND JEANNIE were waiting outside the door to the local branch of the National Deposit Bank & Trust when it opened at nine o'clock. He had calls into financial advisers who'd worked with Jameson Beauclair, hoping one of them would've gotten a call from him during the home invasion.

They showed their badges to the manager, who held up his hands to keep them from advancing into the bank. "I'm not authorized to speak to you. You'll need to contact our corporate office in New York."

"What we need to speak to you about happened *here*," Cameron said firmly. "So you *will* talk to us, or we'll arrest you for interfering in a homicide investigation."

"We don't know anything about any homicides," the manager said, his face red with agitation.

"I want to talk to the teller who assisted Cleo Beauclair with the withdrawal of one hundred thousand dollars on Monday afternoon." To the tellers watching anxiously from behind the counter, Cameron said, "Which one of you assisted her with that withdrawal?"

A dark-haired young woman raised her hand. "I did."

Cameron and Jeannie pushed past the protesting manager and went to talk to her.

"Your name?" Cameron asked.

"Sarah Braxton," she said, handing him her business card.

"Sarah, shut your mouth," the manager said. "We're not allowed to talk to anyone without corporate's approval."

"If she doesn't talk to us, we'll arrest you both," Jeannie said. "We can talk here or downtown. Your choice."

"I'll do it right here," Sarah said with a defiant look for the manager. "I told him there was something strange about that transaction, but he said I'm not paid to psychoanalyze our customers and that I was to shut up and do my job."

"He didn't want to deal with it because he'd have to get corporate involved, and that's a hassle," one of the other tellers said.

"I'll have your jobs," the manager said, sputtering with outrage.

Cameron glanced at Jeannie, who walked over to the manager. "You're under arrest for interfering with a homicide investigation." Jeannie had his hands cuffed behind his back before he realized what was happening. "You have the right to remain silent. Anything you say can and will be used against you in a court of law."

The tellers appeared stunned and possibly gleeful as their manager was hauled out of the building.

"Couldn't happen to a better guy," Sarah said. "I knew something was wrong about that transaction, but he wouldn't let me call the police. I almost called on my own, but I was afraid of losing my job." Her eyes filled. "I'm a single mom, and I need this job."

"Take me through it from the minute she approached your window and tell me what happened."

"She was really nervous. Her hands were shaking, and it took two tries to punch in her code on the keypad."

"Had you seen her before?"

"No, never."

"Can you describe the man who was with her?"

"He was tall with dark hair. He had on a black coat and reflective sunglasses that made it impossible to see his eyes. He never said a word, but I could tell she was afraid of him. And she kept looking outside. It was all very weird, which is what I told Lenny, but he said I should shut up and mind my own business, that she and her husband were excellent customers and didn't need us nosing into their business." Her eyes filled. "Then I saw on the news that their house had burned, and they were dead. I knew something was off. I should've called 9-1-1."

Cameron felt for her. She would carry the guilt of her inaction with her for the rest of her life. "This is very helpful. Thank you."

Sarah handed over another business card with an 800-number written on it. "That's our corporate office in New York. You have to go through them to get the video."

"I believe the FBI has already been in touch with them, but I'll follow up."

"I'm really sorry I didn't make that call," she said, wiping tears. "I'll regret that forever."

Cameron handed her his business card. "If you think of anything else that might be relevant, please call me. My cell number is on there."

"I will." She looked out the front door to where Jeannie had the bank manager in handcuffs and was leading him to Cameron's car. "What'll happen to him?"

"We'll take him downtown, process him and charge him with a misdemeanor count of interfering with an investigation. He'll probably be released before dinnertime. Unless we can't get a judge to arraign him. In that case, he'll spend the night as a guest of the city."

"I sure would like to see that happen. He's such an

asshole. If he'd let me make that phone call, maybe those people would still be alive."

"Perhaps the judges will be extra busy today."

She smiled tearfully at him. "We can only hope."

BRENDAN SULLIVAN CALLED as Sam and Freddie were on their way back to HQ. "You're on speaker so my partner can take notes," Sam said.

"No problem. I've got a call into Klein, who'd better call me back ASAP if he doesn't want to get picked up, and I've got names and addresses of some of his associates."

"Go," Sam said, navigating morning traffic as Freddie took notes.

None of the names Sullivan gave them rang a bell with Sam. "Any of them have records?" Sam asked.

"All of them."

Sam felt the nuts-on-the-block buzz that made this job so fucking exciting, usually when they were on the verge of nailing a murdering monster or two. "This is very helpful, thank you so much."

"Happy to help. Let me know if you need anything else."

"Will do, and if I haven't told you before, you're my most favorite bureaucrat ever."

"That is *high* praise," Freddie said. "Trust me on that."

Sullivan laughed. "In light of who your husband is, it's very high praise indeed."

"Okay, make that *second* favorite," Sam said.

The two men laughed.

"Have a good day," Sullivan said.

"You do the same." She slapped her phone closed. "I *love* that guy."

"You all but told him that just now."

"How often do we get that kind of help from *anyone*?"

"Hardly ever."

Sam's phone rang again, this time with a call from Darren Tabor of the *Washington Star*. "You're catching me in a rare good mood, Darren. What can I do for you?"

Her comment was met with total silence.

"Darren?"

"I'm here. Just processing the fact that you're in a good mood."

Freddie snorted with laughter.

"What'd you want?"

"A statement on the Beauclair case. The fire marshal won't give me anything other than they suspect arson. Judging by the fact that you and the FBI are involved, that tells me they suspect murder. Can you confirm or deny?"

"Confirm. Jameson and Cleo Beauclair were definitely murdered."

"Wow, that was unusually easy."

"Like I said, I'm in a generous kind of mood."

"Can you tell me how they were murdered or where you are in the investigation?"

"I can't tell you how, but I can tell you we're making good progress."

"And is there any truth to the rumor that you have their two youngest kids staying with you?"

"I'm going to tell you the truth, Darren, but I'm going to do it off the record, okay?"

His groan echoed through the speakerphone. "Fine," he said.

"My husband and I are acting as their foster parents at the moment, but they have family members arriving from out of state. It was a temporary arrangement." Her heart hurt as she said the words. She did not look forward to saying goodbye to those precious kids.

"Why does that have to be off the record?"

"Because I crossed a number of lines by taking them in, and it's an issue with the department. There's also the possibility that they're still in danger from whoever did this to their parents. My job is to keep them safe, and that's what I'm going to do."

"I get it. I don't like it, but I get it. It was good of you to step up for them."

"Try telling that to my brass. They don't see it quite the same way."

"Because it's a conflict of interest."

"So they say."

"Heard a rumor that Gonzo's in the hospital. Any truth to that?"

"Stomach flu," Sam said. "They're treating him for dehydration, but I'm sure he'd rather not see that in the paper."

"He won't."

"Thank you, Darren."

"Always a pleasure to speak with you, Sam."

"Now that's just a flat-out lie," Freddie said, making them both laugh.

"My little Freddie is all grown-up and about to get *married*," Sam said, dabbing at a fake tear.

"And no longer afraid of you, apparently."

"That's a problem," Sam said.

"Congrats, Freddie," Darren said. "Hope it's a great day for you."

"Thank you."

"Over and out," Sam said, closing the phone. To Freddie, she said, "Look at you with your wiseass comments."

"Learned from the expert."

"God, I've really made a mess of you, haven't I?"

"Nah, you've helped to make a man out of me."

"Jesus," Sam muttered. "Don't say *that* anywhere near HQ, or we'll be the talk of the place."

"No chance of that, and what have I asked you about using the lord's name in vain?"

"When did I do that?"

"Like five seconds ago!"

"Sorry," she said.

"Sure you are."

"You really think I made a man out of you?"

"You helped. I had a lot to learn when we first partnered up. You've taught me everything that matters about the job and how to have this job and a life too."

"Hmm, well, I do what I can for the people."

He rolled his eyes at her predictable response.

"Let's visit a few of Victor's scumbag friends before we head back to the house. Maybe they can tell us what he's been up to the last few days."

Their first stop was at an apartment building off Massachusetts Avenue in a rough neighborhood full of run-down row houses, convenience stores and pawnshops.

"Should we have backup going in here?" Freddie asked, eyeing the building warily.

"Probably. Call it in."

A Patrol car responded, appearing at the address about three minutes later.

"Look at this day," she said, glancing in the mirror as the Patrol car pulled in behind her car, "cooperating with me in every possible way."

"My partner taught me not to say stuff like that. It'll jinx us."

"Your partner is a wise, wise woman," Sam said as they got out of the car to meet the two Patrol officers.

"So she likes to tell me. Frequently."

Anthony Jenkins lived on the third floor, and as they trudged up the stairs, Sam strapped on her bulletproof vest while Freddie did the same. Behind them, the Patrolmen would provide additional cover. When everyone was in position outside the door to 3D with weapons drawn, Sam used a closed fist to pound on the door. "Metro PD. Open up."

They heard scurrying sounds from inside the apartment.

Sam nodded to one of the Patrolmen, who took off down the stairs, in case their guy got a big idea about heading out the window. She pounded again. "Police. Open up."

More scurrying, which only served to aggravate her.

"We're going to take down this door if you don't open up."

Through the cheap thin door, she heard the distinctive sound of a gun engaging and acted before she thought, shoving Freddie out of the way as the door exploded in a blast of splinters. Her ears rang, and her left shoulder burned, but she reacted quickly to return fire, aiming low so as to incapacitate rather than kill.

"Lieutenant!" the Patrol officer behind her cried. "You're hit."

Inside the apartment, the shooter howled with pain and outrage. Through the shattered door, Sam could see him holding his bloody knee as he screamed.

"What the hell, Sam?" Freddie asked as he helped her up. "Why'd you do that?"

"Because you're getting married in two days, and you're *not* getting shot. Not this week."

"I hate to be the one to tell you, but it looks like you did."

She glanced down at the hot spot radiating from her shoulder, her vision swimming at the sight of the large patch of red that greeted her. "Crap. That's gonna show in the pictures."

Freddie shook his head, grabbed the radio attached to her hip and called for a bus.

"I don't need a goddamned bus."

"Yes, you do, and so does he." Nodding toward the apartment where the Patrolman had cuffed the suspect, Freddie placed a hand over her wound and applied pressure that made her scream.

"*What the fuck?* Knock it off!"

"Shut up, Sam. And if you feel like you're going to faint, lean into me."

"I don't have time for this shit today."

"Then you shouldn't have pushed me out of the way."

"Don't have time for you to get shot either. Got to keep you pretty for the wedding." She wrestled free of his tight hold. "Wanna talk to this guy while I can."

"Sam."

She ignored him and marched into the apartment where a man with dark hair and tan skin lay on his side on the floor, hands cuffed behind him, writhing in pain. At one point, he might've been handsome, but now there was a hard, bitter edge to him. "Quit your whining," Sam said. "If you hadn't shot at us, none of this would've happened."

"You shattered my knee, *you fucking twat*!"

"Awww, sticks and stones will break your bones, and apparently bullets will too. Who knew? Oh wait, everyone knows that." Was it hot in there? It seemed really hot, and the ground was kind of shimmery. Sam shook off the weird feeling. "Where's Victor Klein, Anthony?"

"I don't know nobody named Victor."

Sam glanced at the Patrolman, nodded to the bloody knee, and he pretended he was going to touch it.

Anthony let out a shriek. *"Stop!"*

Sam squatted so she'd be closer to him —and to the floor if she actually fell over. *"Where is he?"* She reached out her hand in a menacing claw aimed for his bloody knee.

"Don't fucking touch it!"

"Then tell me where he is *and don't say you don't know him.* We know you do. If you hold out on us, we'll add interfering with a murder investigation to the charges you're already facing."

Paramedics appeared in the doorway, but Sam held them back with a raised hand.

Seething with outrage, which was funny under the circumstances, Anthony said, "I don't know where he is, and I don't know nothing about no murder. He said he had to get outta here for a while, but he'd be back."

"Who would know where he is?"

"How am I supposed to know?"

"I bet you'd like to have some pain meds right about now, wouldn't you?" Sam asked as her shoulder began to ache like a bitch. "I can stay here all day while you bleed out on the floor." She eased out of the crouch into a seated position and rested her injured left arm on her leg, which brought relief. "I got nothing better to do."

Freddie glared at her from the doorway.

She began to whistle a catchy tune to entertain herself and hopefully aggravate Jenkins. To the paramedic standing in the doorway, Sam said, "How long does it take to bleed out from a leg injury?"

"If the bullet nicked the femoral," one of them said, "not long at all. Minutes."

"Talk to Danny Baker," Anthony said through gritted teeth. "He's Victor's best friend."

"See how easy that was?" When the paramedics would've advanced into the apartment, Sam held them off. "Where will we find Baker?"

"He works at a pizza place called Rolling in Dough in Southeast. I don't know where he lives."

She waved in the paramedics. "I can't thank you enough for your help and cooperation." To the Patrol officer, she said, "Stay with him and get him processed as soon as he's medically able."

"Yes, ma'am."

One of the paramedics homed in on her. "You're bleeding profusely, Lieutenant." Before she could tell him to leave her alone, he pressed on the wound and she passed out.

CHAPTER TWENTY-NINE

FREDDIE CALLED NICK as he followed the ambulance through midday traffic, bobbing and weaving around cars that wouldn't get the hell out of the way.

"Hey, Freddie. What's up?"

"She's fine, but Sam got grazed by a bullet to the shoulder. At least I think she was only grazed. There was a lot of blood."

"Grazed by a bullet? Isn't that the same as shot?"

"She was totally fine afterward, busting the balls of the guy we were after, but she passed out and is in an ambulance on the way to GW."

"I'll head over there right away. Thanks for calling."

"No problem. See you there." After he ended the call with Nick, he called Elin, who'd wisely taken this week off from work and had encouraged him to do the same. Next time, he would listen to her.

"Hey, babe," she said when she answered, sounding breathless.

"What're you doing?"

"Working out."

Freddie loved to watch her work out—and he loved to have sex with her afterward, when she was still sweaty. But he couldn't think about that. Not now anyway.

"Freddie? Are you there? What's wrong?"

"Sam got shot. She's okay, but they're taking her to GW."

"Oh jeez. This is turning out to be quite a week."

"That's not all. Gonzo is out of the wedding party."

"*What?* Why?"

"He's going to rehab."

"For what?"

"Apparently, he's been numbing the loss of Arnold with painkillers."

"Oh God, Freddie."

"I know this is far bigger than the wedding, but we're left with an opening. Sam suggested I ask Will."

"He would do it."

"I know he would, but I actually have someone else in mind."

"Who?"

"Nick."

"As in *Nick, the vice president*?"

"As in Nick, who was my friend long before he was the vice president."

"Still. You think he'd do it?"

"Yeah, I think he would."

"So, you're going to ask him?"

"If I get the chance. He's got a lot going on right now."

"You want me to come to the hospital? I will if you want me to."

"Nah, no need. I won't be there long with the case heating up."

"Okay, let me know how she is."

"I will, and babe, you were right. I should've taken this week off."

"Oh, Freddie. Don't you know by now that I'm *always* right?"

"Jeez, I walked right into that, didn't I?"

Her laughter made him smile. "How's the hand?"

"Still really sore, but not as bad as it was yesterday."

"Glad to hear it's better. I'll let you know what time I'll be home."

"I'll be waiting for you while I wrestle with the seating chart."

"That sounds like fun."

"Not so much but our wedding will be. That's for sure."

"I can't wait."

"Neither can I. Love you, Freddie."

"Love you too." As he ended the call with her, he took one from Captain Malone. "Hey, Cap."

"What the hell happened?"

Freddie told him what'd gone down in Jenkins's apartment building.

"Ugh, she could've been killed."

Freddie tightened his grip on the wheel of Sam's car while trying not to think about what *could've* happened. "She got him to roll on another of Klein's associates. As soon as I confirm she's okay, I'm going back out to track down Klein."

"Green and McBride are on their way to GW to check on the lieutenant and meet up with you. The three of you stay together. Crime scene got DNA off dishes in the sink that differs from what was taken from the victims and their children. That might help us put this one away."

"I sure hope so." Freddie agreed with Sam—whatever it took to not have to use Alden as a witness.

"Keep me posted on the lieutenant and what you guys are doing."

"I will."

At the GW E.R., the same nurse who'd been on duty the day before waved at him to follow her to the cubicle where Sam was being treated.

"Fucking hell," Sam said, "that burns like a *mother-fucker.*"

Yep, he thought. *She's fine—and thank God for that.* Freddie stepped into the crowded room where Anderson and a nurse were tending to the wound on Sam's left arm.

Sam's gaze locked on him. "*Get out of here and go find Klein!* Right now!"

"That's the plan as soon as I confirmed you're okay."

"I'm fine. Go. I'll meet you in thirty minutes. Let me know where you are."

"You need stitches, Lieutenant," Anderson said in a long-suffering tone. "That's going to take more than thirty minutes."

"No stitches," Sam said. "Butterfly it. I got shit to do, and I'm in his wedding this weekend. I don't need a big ugly wound on my arm."

"I'm glad to see that as always your priorities are straight, Lieutenant," Anderson said dryly.

"I'm getting sick of people discussing my priorities today," Sam said.

"I, uh, I called Nick," Freddie said, wincing. "He's on his way."

Sam groaned and tipped her head back on the pillow.

"I figured you'd rather he hear it from me than on the news."

"Yeah, I guess. Thanks for calling him and making sure I'll get a full lecture before I can go back to work."

"Sorry."

"Go. Get me Klein, and all is forgiven."

"I'm on it." Freddie turned to leave the room, and as he was exiting the emergency department, Nick's motorcade pulled up. Freddie waited to have a word with the vice president.

Nick got out before his agent Brant, who gave him a foul look behind his back. "How is she?"

"Totally fine, pissed off and barking out orders to the doctor."

Nick smiled as he sagged with relief. "Sounds like business as usual."

"Yep. She ordered me back on the case."

"Thanks for the call, Freddie. I appreciate it even if she doesn't."

"Gee, how'd you guess?"

Nick laughed. "I know my wife."

"She pushed me out of the way," Freddie said.

"What do you mean?"

"The bullet would've hit me, but she pushed me so it hit her instead of me. She said she couldn't let me get shot the week of my wedding."

Nick stared at him, incredulous. "So, she got shot."

"Thankfully, it only grazed her arm."

"Thankfully indeed."

"I know you want to get in and see her, but could I ask you something real quick?"

"Sure."

"I find myself in need of a last-minute groomsman, and since you probably own your own tux, I thought I might ask if you'd mind…"

Nick's smile stretched across his face. "I'd be honored, Freddie. Truly."

"Really? Thanks so much. I really appreciate this and the use of the Naval Observatory, which is just the coolest thing ever."

"Happy to do it. You know that Sam and I consider you one of our closest friends."

"The sentiment is entirely mutual," Freddie said, feeling strangely emotional as he extended his hand to Nick, who shook it. "Thanks again."

"See you Saturday, if not before."

NICK WALKED INTO the emergency waiting room, and every head in the place swiveled to get a better look at him. By now, one would think he'd be used to feeling like a goldfish inside a bowl everywhere he went. One would be wrong.

"Mr. Vice President," the nurse at the triage desk said breathlessly. "Right this way, sir."

Nick followed her, stopping three doors from Sam's cubicle to listen to her bitching at the doctor to "*hurry the fuck up*" because she had a murderer to catch and shit to do. Nick smiled, shook his head and proceeded to her room.

She was so engrossed in her raging that she didn't notice him at first, which gave him the opportunity to just look—and looking at her was one of his favorite things to do. Perhaps his *most* favorite thing to do, even when she was in a rage.

"Samantha."

The single word from him silenced her.

"Are you giving these nice people a hard time?" he asked, moving to the side of her bed that was free of medical personnel.

"Would she give us a hard time?" Dr. Anderson asked with a grin for Nick.

"Not our Sam," Nick said. "She's the picture of decorum at all times."

Anderson cleared his throat and coughed from the effort not to laugh.

"I'm in the room, you know," Sam said.

"Babe, there's never a time when people don't know you're in the room." Taking hold of her hand, he leaned over to kiss her forehead and get a better look at the wound that Anderson was currently cleaning. Located on her triceps, it measured about two inches in length and maybe another inch deep. The tank top she'd worn under her sweater was covered in blood that made him feel queasy.

"Just a scratch," Sam said, looking up at him with eyes that looked bigger than usual due to shock.

Nick sat gently on the edge of the bed, careful not to jostle her. "Heard you pushed Freddie out of the way and took one for the team."

"He's getting married in two days. My goal is to keep him alive until then, but if he keeps ratting me out, I might have to strangle him."

"My goal is to keep you alive until you're ninety. Your goals and mine don't seem to be lining up."

She gave him a murderous look that would've cowed a lesser man. Thankfully, he wasn't a lesser man, and her murderous looks only made him love her more than he already did. However, in deference to her badassery, he dropped the subject until Anderson finished stitching her up and left the room to complete her discharge paperwork.

"I know what you're going to say, and before you lecture me on taking unreasonable chances, I'd do it again if I had it to do over. He's getting married. *In two days*. He and Elin have already had enough nonsense this week. They don't need more."

Nick brought her hand to his lips. "You forgot the part where you love him like a little brother, and you'd rather die yourself than have anything ever happen to him."

"That too," she said in a more conciliatory tone.

"I get it. I don't like it, but I do get it."

"Go ahead and get the lecture out of the way so we can move on." She rolled her hand in encouragement.

"No lecture. I'll just say I'm glad you're okay and that he is too. And I'll add that he asked me to take Gonzo's place in the wedding party, which I assume is okay with you."

"He did? That's awesome."

"I think so too."

"See, our goals aren't out of alignment, and you shouldn't say that stuff in public unless you want to read about our marital problems in the paper."

He quirked an eyebrow, endlessly amused by her. "Do we have marital problems?"

"We will if you're going to make me go home after getting *scratched* by a bullet. We're *this close* to getting our guys. I'm feeling the nuts-on-the-block buzz that comes from closing in. No way am I going to miss that."

Nick winced. He went out of his way to make sure his nuts were never anywhere near her so-called block. "I wouldn't want you to miss it. I'll only ask if you're sure you're up to it. Looks like you lost a lot of blood."

"I'm fine. I swear."

"Then I guess I'll have to let you go do what you do."

"How're the kids?"

"They're quiet. Elijah and Shelby are with them."

"We may be able to get this done without involving Alden."

"That'd be good."

Sam leaned around him. "Where's Anderson? I want out of here. Can you give me a lift to HQ on the way home?"

"Yeah. I can do that."

"Are you going into the office today?"

He shook his head. "I did a bunch of meetings from home this morning. I wanted to be around if anything came up with the kids."

"That's good of you. Thank you."

"It's no problem. I've forgotten how nice it is to work from home. I used to do it once in a while when I needed to write for John. Seems like a lifetime ago."

Dr. Anderson returned with Sam's discharge paperwork. "I had this made for you," he said, handing her a card that had a hole punched in it.

Nick busted up laughing when he saw what it said. GW E.R. Frequent Flier.

"Hardy har har," Sam said. "Have your laughs, Doc. I help keep you in business."

"That you do, my friend. That you do."

Nick escorted Sam through the waiting room, where he again felt everyone looking at them. Outside, his motorcade waited. He ushered Sam in ahead of him and told Brant they were dropping her at HQ on the way home.

"Yes, sir," his faithful shadow said.

He liked Brant as much as it was possible to like the man charged with overseeing his every move.

Nick raised his arm, and Sam snuggled into his embrace, whimpering when her injured arm made contact with his side. "How close are you really to getting these guys?"

"Close. We've had some significant breakthroughs today. I'm hoping for a win before the end of the day." As always, their "wins" came with the hollow realization that, while they might've gotten justice for the survivors, their loved ones were still gone forever, and their lives permanently altered. She updated him about the latest with Piedmont.

"It's hard to believe he wasn't involved."

"I agree, but Hill and his people really believe he wasn't."

"It would be nice to get this sewed up before the wedding."

"That's the goal," she said.

"You really pushed Freddie out of the way?"

"I really did, and I'd do it again."

"That's going to be a problem going forward, Sam."

"How do you figure?"

"You've lost all perspective where he's concerned. You forget that he's a decorated police officer in his own right, trained to be the best by the best. He wouldn't want you to sacrifice yourself for him."

"This week, I think he can live with it. But I do hear what you're saying, and I'll add it to the many things I'll think about during the unpaid week off the chief is making me take to reexamine my priorities."

"For real?"

"Yep. He's pissed that I took in the Beauclair kids while investigating their parents' murder. And he's right. It's a total conflict of interest, but something I'd do again if I had it to do over. I saw kids in need, and I stepped up. I refuse to apologize for that."

"While I'm totally on your side in this, I do see his point."

"So do I, but I can't be anyone other than who I am. I wouldn't know how to be anyone else."

"Luckily for both of us, I love you exactly the way you are, and I'm thrilled that you'll have a week off to reexamine your priorities. I look forward to helping you with that while we're away."

"The trip depends on closing the case."

"My money is on you, babe. You'll get it done so you can spend a whole week getting me done."

"You're a mighty appealing incentive package," she said, cupping his package with her right hand as she kissed his neck.

All too soon, the motorcade pulled into the HQ parking lot. "Back to reality." She gave him a lingering kiss. "Thanks for coming to the hospital."

"I'd say it was a pleasure, but you know how I hate when you find yourself on the business end of a gun."

"Everything's okay," she said, kissing him again. "Keep me posted on how things are going at home."

"I will. Hurry up and nail these guys so we can enjoy the weekend and your unexpected week off."

"I'm on it. Love you."

"Love you too."

CHAPTER THIRTY

SAM GOT OUT of the SUV and was met by a scrum of reporters wanting an update on the Beauclair case. They
also shouted questions about Nick's trip and whether she
was going with him. She took one minute she didn't have
to give them a brief update on the case.

"We're making headway in the Beauclair case, and I
expect to have more for you later today."

"Are you going on the vice president's trip to Europe?"
one of the TV reporters asked.

"Info about his trip is available from his office, and
you may as well stop wasting your breath asking me
about him, his job, his travels. I'm never going to answer
those questions. Have a good day."

"Lieutenant! Wait!"

Sam ignored their cries for more info and darted inside HQ, breathing a sigh of relief when she reached the
relative safety of the lobby. Her relief was short-lived,
however, when she encountered Malone engaged in a
screaming match with Ramsey, who had his back to her.
This day got more interesting by the minute. Sam wished
she had some popcorn to enjoy while she listened to
Malone rip Ramsey a new one.

"Get over it, Sergeant. The USA declined to press charges."

"Because she's married to the fucking vice president,
not because she didn't do it!"

"I'm going to tell you this one more time—if you can't keep your grievances out of this building, you won't work in this building. Do I make myself clear?"

"Yeah, you do, and it's no surprise to me that she's probably sucking your dick too."

"That's it. Get out."

"I have rights. You can't just kick me out."

"*Get out*," Malone said in a tone Sam had never heard before, "or I'll have you arrested. Your choice."

"You'll be hearing from my union rep."

"I'll look forward to it."

Ramsey spun around to leave and came face-to-face with Sam, watching the show.

She smiled and waggled her fingers.

Like a bull seeing red, he charged her.

She darted out of the way in time to avoid him barging into her, but the forward momentum took him right through the window next to the door, which shattered on impact. Glass rained down upon the red-faced sergeant, who quickly became the subject of interest to the reporters and photographers stationed outside the door.

"That'll be the lead story on the six o'clock news," Sam said to Malone.

"Walk away, Lieutenant," he said through gritted teeth. "Just walk away."

For once, Sam did as she was told, whistling a jaunty tune as she made her way to the detectives' pit. Her day had already been made, and she had a good feeling it was about to get even better.

FREDDIE, CAMERON AND JEANNIE arrived at the pizza shop, Rolling in Dough, which had a lunchtime line out the door.

"What's the plan?" Cameron asked.

"Let's call for backup," Freddie said, eyeing the layout of the restaurant. "I want someone minding the back door before we go in."

Jeannie made the call, and while they waited for Patrol, they kept a watchful eye on the restaurant. "This is our guy," she said, calling up a photo of a skinny white man with blond hair on her phone. "Danny Baker. He's got a long list of priors, mostly petty stuff, but he's been working his way up the criminal food chain."

"He has that in common with his buddy Klein," Freddie said.

When the Patrol officers arrived, Freddie asked them to cover the restaurant's back door in case Baker was stupid enough to run. Freddie hoped he would, so they could take him into custody and get him into interrogation. Being arrested, processed and interrogated at HQ tended to loosen even the tightest of lips.

With everyone in position, Freddie gave the go-ahead. He walked in first, excusing himself as he worked around the line of people who grumbled about line cutters. Flashing his badge, he shut them up as he went up to the counter. "Detectives Cruz, Green and McBride, Metro PD. Looking for Danny Baker."

The wide-eyed woman working the register spun around and focused on a lanky guy in the back who was spinning dough. "Danny!"

He looked her way, saw cops with badges, dropped the dough to the floor and bolted for the back door.

Freddie jumped the counter, crashed into a woman carrying a tray of large sodas and took down Baker, in the span of about ten seconds.

Hearing the commotion inside, the Patrol officers opened the back door and looked in to find Freddie, knee in Baker's back, cuffing him as he recited his rights. All in a day's work.

"Nice takedown," Cameron said when he and Jeannie caught up.

"What'd he do?" an older man with a beer belly and a comb-over asked. He wore a flour-stained red apron with the restaurant's logo on it.

"I didn't do nothing!" Baker said as Freddie hauled him to his feet and turned him over to the Patrol officers.

"Get him downtown and let me know when he's in interrogation."

"Is he in big trouble?" the man asked.

"Remains to be seen but running from cops is never a good idea." Freddie's stomach let out a loud grumble. "You got a large pie I could buy?"

The man boxed a pizza right out of the oven and handed it to Freddie. "On the house, if you wouldn't mind getting outta my kitchen."

"Don't mind at all. Thanks."

They left out the back door and returned to Cameron's sedan, which he kept immaculate. Freddie hoped he'd be allowed to scarf down some pizza in the car, because he wasn't inclined to wait until they got back to the house. He needed food, and he needed it now.

"That was a hell of a leap," Jeannie said when they were back in the car.

"I'm motivated to close this case before the wedding." Freddie dived into the pie as he realized he'd forgotten to grab napkins. Oh well, that's what T-shirts were for. "You want a slice?"

"I'd love one."

Freddie handed over a slice to her in the front seat. "Cam?"

"I'll wait until we get back." He looked in the rearview mirror. "Don't get it all over my car."

"I'll try not to." Freddie ate three slices in the time it took to drive across the city. They were two blocks from HQ when he took a call from his mother. "Hey, what's up?"

"The news is reporting that Sam was grazed by a bullet. Is she okay? Are you?"

"We're both fine."

"Oh thank goodness. I tell you—sometimes I'm afraid to look at the news, knowing you're out there in the middle of the madness."

"Right now, I'm eating pizza in the back of my colleague's car after a very satisfying arrest. All is well."

"Two more days, Freddie. I can't wait to dance at your wedding."

"Neither can I. Hey, Mom, can you do me a favor and grab my tux? I haven't had a chance to do it yet, and Elin is going to kill me if I don't get it soon."

"I'll take care of it, honey. Let me know if there's anything else I can do to help."

"I will, thanks."

"Love you."

"You too."

"Is Mama Cruz feeling anxious?" Jeannie asked.

"Just a little." Out of the corner of his eye, he noticed something happening outside the main doors. "What's up over there?"

"Let's go find out," Green said, taking the first available parking space.

"Holy crap," Freddie said when he saw Ramsey lying

in a sea of shattered glass. "I really hope Sam had nothing to do with this." Still carrying the pizza box, he made his way around the building to the morgue entrance with Jeannie and Cameron in pursuit. They found the LT in her office, cheerfully attending to administrative tasks. Her cheerfulness put Freddie on alert. "What'd you do now?"

"What're you talking about?"

"Ramsey and the shattered glass. Don't tell me you had nothing to do with that."

"You're *so* suspicious." Sam told them what'd happened.

Freddie hooted with laughter. "I *knew* it had something to do with you!"

"I didn't do anything. I just happened to be standing there."

Freddie laughed so hard tears filled his eyes.

"Quit your laughing and tell me you got Baker."

"We got him, and he should be in interrogation any minute."

"Excellent. Let's get this wrapped up. But first, give me a piece of that pizza."

SAM MADE SURE Hope Miller, one of the identical triplets that served the District as assistant U.S. attorneys, observed the interrogation along with Captain Malone.

Baker was so nervous his hands shook and his pale cheek twitched.

Good, she thought. *That'll make this a hell of a lot easier than it is with the arrogant ones who aren't afraid of anything.* She could work Baker's fear to her advantage.

"Danny Baker," she said upon entering the room with Cruz right behind her.

Baker nearly jumped out of his pants.

The Patrolman who'd been watching over him stepped out.

While Freddie engaged the recording device, Sam said, "I'm Lieutenant Holland, and I believe you've met Detective Cruz."

Baker's brows narrowed with displeasure at the sight of Freddie.

After she recited the details of who was present for the record, she said, "You've been apprised of your rights in this matter?"

"Yeah."

"I heard you tried to run from my officers. Why'd you do that?"

Baker crossed his arms and returned her steely stare with one of his own. "I want my lawyer."

Sam and Freddie stood. "We'll go talk to Victor, then, and see what he has to say about what went down at the Beauclairs' house," Sam said. "But then again, we already know he had a traffic altercation with Cleo Beauclair and decided to pay the rich lady a visit. We'll see what he has to say about how he got you involved. Of course, if he cooperates with us, that'll leave you out in the cold, but that doesn't matter to us. As long as we find out what happened that night in Chevy Chase."

"Wait."

Sam had her hand on the doorknob. Suppressing a smile, she turned back to note that what little color Baker had in his cheeks was gone now. Raising a brow, she waited for him to speak.

"What do you want to know?"

"You've requested an attorney. We're not able to speak further with you."

"I don't want a lawyer. I'll tell you what you want to know."

Sam and Freddie returned to the table.

"Detective Cruz, please note for the record that Mr. Baker has rescinded his earlier request for an attorney."

"So noted."

"Will you again apprise Mr. Baker of his rights in this matter?"

While Freddie recited the modified Miranda warning, Sam turned her most potent stare on the man, who squirmed under the heat of that glare.

"Start with how you got involved," she said.

"Victor. He called me. He said he had a line on some easy money and could use some help. I wasn't doing anything, so I went with him." Baker swallowed hard, his Adam's apple bobbing in his skinny neck.

"Did you know he planned to rob, rape and murder these people?"

"No! He never said nothing about any of that. He said easy money."

"Tell me how it went down, from the second you got there until the second you left, and don't leave anything out."

"We got there around four thirty, and Victor, he pulled a gun on the rich lady. He asked who was in the house, and she said her kids and the maid was there. He saw she was wearing one of those panic buttons and took that from her. He told her to get rid of the woman or he'd kill them both. She told the maid she was fired for stealing and told her to get out. The lady was upset, but the rich lady told her to get out before she called the cops."

"Where were you when this was happening?"

"Outside the kitchen door listening. The maid left, and

the rich lady told us she was gone. Victor said he wanted money. She said she didn't have any, but she could ask her husband to get some on the way home. Victor told her he didn't want to wait for the husband. That's when she said she had kids upstairs and couldn't leave them. Victor told her to go get them. We'd bring them with us. She said she didn't want to get them, that she didn't want to involve them. He told her to get them, or he'd kill her and her kids. She went and got them."

"How did you get to the bank?" Sam asked.

"We took her car, and Victor sat in the front with her. She didn't want to go in the bank without the kids, who were crying, but Victor told her she didn't have a choice and she was wasting time. The two of them went in the bank while I stayed with the kids. They were in there a long time, and the kids were driving me crazy asking for their mother. They finally came out, and Victor was pissed because she'd only been able to get a hundred grand. We went back to the house to wait for the husband. Victor said he was the fat cat. She sent the kids upstairs and told them not to come down for any reason."

Sam's stomach ached imagining the ordeal the children had been through with two strange men with guns telling their mother what to do in their home. "What happened then?"

"Victor said we should have some fun with her while we waited for the husband." Baker rubbed at the sweat that beaded on his upper lip. "He made me do her first."

"He *made* you?" Sam asked, incredulous.

"He held a gun on me, so yeah, he made me."

"Did he make you get a boner too?" Sam asked, thoroughly disgusted.

"The rich lady was hot," he said with a shrug.

MARIE FORCE 357

"What happened after that?" Sam asked through gritted teeth.

"Victor did her too. He was still doing her when the husband came home and freaked out. She was screaming and crying." Baker shook his head, as if trying to rid himself of images that she hoped would haunt him for the rest of his life. "Victor told me to tie him up. He said he'd give us anything we wanted, but we had to leave his wife alone. Victor hit him in the face with the gun and said he wasn't the one with the power now, and he needed to shut the fuck up."

Sam's stomach turned as she listened to what Cleo and Jameson had endured at the hands of two half-wits who'd targeted them because they were rich.

"The guy begged him not to hurt her. He said he'd give us a million dollars if Victor would stop. Victor stopped and told him he had four hours to get the money. The guy said he'd need more time. Four hours, Victor said. The guy made calls, and we waited. The money didn't get there, so Victor started beating the guy up, broke his fingers, had another go with the wife. It kinda went like that until Victor got sick of waiting and said we should take the money we already had and burn the place so there wouldn't be any evidence left behind."

Sam laughed at that. "You forgot to burn the dishes you used when you ate their food. I guess Victor isn't as smart as you thought. So where is he?"

Baker's mouth fell open. "You said you had him."

"I lied. Where is he?" When he didn't reply, Sam stood and slapped her hand on the table. *"Where the fuck is he?"*

Baker jumped a foot, his Adam's apple bobbing in his skinny neck. "He's hiding out at my place."

"Is he armed?"

Baker nodded.

Sam pushed a notebook and pen across the table. "Write down the address, draw me a picture of the place, tell me where he's apt to be and don't even think about fucking with us. You're already looking at murder one, arson, kidnapping, sexual assault, to start with."

"I didn't do none of that stuff! Victor made me."

"Tell it to the judge." She got up to leave the room.

"Wait! You said you'd help me if I told you what happened!"

"I lied about that too." After leaving the room and letting the door slam shut behind her, she took deep breaths of the fresh air in the hallway.

Hope and Malone came out of observation.

"That was brutal," Hope said bluntly. "Go pick up Victor so we can lock them both up for the rest of their lives."

"I want SWAT on this," Malone said fiercely. "So there's no chance this son of a bitch can escape."

"I'll make the call," Freddie said.

CHAPTER THIRTY-ONE

THINGS MOVED SLOWER when SWAT was involved, and it took almost two hours to get all the players in place surrounding Baker's Marshall Heights townhouse. They cordoned off the block so no one could come in, evacuated the houses closest to their target and told the other nearby neighbors to shelter in place. They worked in almost-total silence so as not to alert their target that they were coming for him.

Since Klein was hiding out, they weren't afraid of him trying to leave. They took their time to get it right and to ensure the safety of everyone in the area.

Captain Nickleson, the SWAT commander, came over to Sam. "We're ready when you are."

"Do it."

Because they knew Klein was in there, it'd been decided that SWAT would breach the house through every available door and window at the same time to take him completely by surprise and lessen the possibility of him firing on them. Hopefully, they'd have him neutralized before he could reach for his gun. That was the goal anyway. There were a million ways things like this could go sideways.

Nickleson gave the order, and Sam held her breath watching the synchronized way in which the SWAT team moved in. The sound of glass breaking shattered the silence.

One by one, team members reported in with areas of the house that had been cleared until the one report they'd wanted most was delivered: "Target located and neutralized."

"Got him," Nickleson said euphorically, moving toward the front door to be there when his team brought Klein out in shackles.

Klein's dark hair stood on end, his face was unshaven, and he wore only boxer shorts. He kept his head down.

"Got him out of bed, sir," one of the officers said, handing over a large cooler with a shoulder strap. "He had this on the bed with him."

Donning gloves, Sam opened the cooler to find stacks of cash that would probably add up to a hundred thousand dollars.

"Well done," Nickleson said.

"We'll take it from here," Sam said, nodding to Cruz and Green to take their prisoner. "Thanks for the assist, Cap."

"Always happy to help take another scumbag off the streets," Nickleson said.

"This one is particularly scummy," Sam said, watching as Cruz and Green loaded him into the back of a Patrol car for the ride to HQ.

They'd gotten him. That's all that mattered to her, but along with the arrest came the realization that she no longer had a reason to keep Aubrey and Alden in her custody. They could safely be released to family members, which tempered the elation she normally experienced at closing a difficult case.

She trudged back to her car, where she sat in silence

for a long time before she opened her phone to call Ms. Finklestein. When the woman answered, Sam said, "I wanted to let you know that we've closed the case, and we're confident we have the men who killed the Beau-clairs in custody. The family members will also want to know that Mr. Beauclair's former business partner, Duke Piedmont, has been apprehended and is in federal custody on insider trading and other charges. He's been cleared of any involvement in the deaths of Mr. and Mrs. Beauclair."

"Congratulations, Lieutenant. The entire city will breathe easier knowing the men who carried out this heinous crime have been caught."

"Thank you," Sam said, feeling hollow in her victory.

"Mrs. Beauclair's sister and brother-in-law are due to arrive early this evening. As you can imagine, they will be eager to see the children."

Sam had nothing to say to that. They hadn't been eager to see the children when their parents were first killed, but now that there was no threat of danger, they'd be right there for them, not to mention the billions of dollars that would come with them. Sam was prepared to hate these people on sight. "That's fine," she said. "What're their full names? I'll alert the Secret Service that you'll be bringing them by.

"Monique and Robert Lawson."

Sam wrote down the names.

"I know it'll be difficult for you to say goodbye to the children," Ms. Finklestein said, "but we find that chil-dren in these circumstances do better when they're placed with family members."

Sam wanted to demand that she produce the evidence to back up that statement. What did "do better" mean?

Better than what? But she didn't ask the questions that
burned the tip of her tongue. Instead she said, "We'll
make sure they're ready."

AN HOUR LATER, she stood outside the main entrance to
HQ briefing the media on what had transpired Monday
afternoon and evening at the Beauclairs' Chevy Chase
home, and the steps taken to apprehend the two men responsible for the murders of Jameson and Cleo Armstrong. For the first time, Sam made the couple's true
identity public, running through a condensed version of
why the couple had relocated and changed their names.

"In addition to the arrests of Mr. Baker and Mr. Klein,
the FBI has apprehended the former business partner of
Mr. Armstrong. Duke Piedmont had been a fugitive from
justice for more than three years after being charged with
insider trading and other crimes associated with APG,
the former company owned by the two men."

After she had run through a summary of the details
of the case, the reporters began peppering her with questions about the investigation, the men they had charged
with murder, arson, aggravated assault, sexual assault,
kidnapping and other charges. She answered each question that came her way, giving as much information as
she could without compromising the case.

"What will happen to the Armstrongs' two minor children?" Darren Tabor asked.

"Social Services is working with Mrs. Armstrong's
extended family to place them with family members."
Sam felt detached as she said the words, as if she didn't
have a personal stake in what became of the children. It
was time to start taking a step back from the "littles," as
Nick had called them.

After she'd dealt with the media, she went back inside to oversee the completion of the paperwork. As she reviewed the reports that her team had generated, the words began to swim the way they did when she was tired or stressed. Sam closed her eyes and rubbed her temples, as exhaustion swooped in.

What a week, and it was still only Thursday.

She took a deep breath and let it out before picking up the phone to call Nick.

"Hey, babe," he said. "I saw your press conference."

"Sorry you had to hear about us closing the case on TV. Everything happened fast."

"No worries. I'm just glad it's done for the sake of everyone involved."

"Yeah."

"You okay?"

"Never better. Ms. Finklestein will be bringing the aunt and uncle to get the kids at some point this evening. Can you ask the Secret Service to put their names on the list? Monique and Robert Lawson."

"I'll take care of it."

"This blows," she said, sighing.

"Yeah, it really does, but we're going to be okay, Samantha. Maybe the aunt and uncle will allow us to keep in touch with the kids."

"That'd be nice," she said, feeling sadder by the minute. "I'll be home soon. Just tying up a few loose ends here."

"We'll be waiting for you."

"That's the only thing getting me through this day. See you soon." As she ended the call with Nick, Lindsey appeared in her doorway.

"Good news from the lab," Lindsey said. "Baker was a match for DNA found on a glass and fork at the scene."

"That's very good news."

"I took a sample from Klein and have sent it to the lab with orders to expedite."

"Thanks, Lindsey."

"Knowing what he'd done to those poor people, it was all I could do not to stab him in the eye while I had him."

"I know that feeling."

"Lieutenant!"

The shout from the pit had Sam standing and rushing toward Cameron Green's cubical, with Lindsey right behind her. Over Green's shoulder, she watched the long-awaited security video from the bank where Klein had taken Cleo to get the money. She watched as he stood by her side while the teller counted stacks of money, turning them over one at a time to Cleo, who put them in the tote bags she had brought with her. Seeing her lovely and alive and terribly afraid touched Sam deeply.

Klein stood close enough to her that Sam deduced he had a gun on her the entire time.

Every thirty or so seconds, Cleo stretched her neck to look out to the parking lot, no doubt trying to check on her children, who were in the car with Baker.

"How could the teller not know something was wrong?" Sam asked, shaking her head.

"She did know," Green said. "The manager refused to allow her to call it in because he didn't want to deal with the hassle from their corporate office. She's a single mom who needs the job, so she did what she was told, but she feels awful about it."

"I want the manager charged with failing to report a crime in progress," Sam said.

"I'd be happy to file those charges," Green said.

Sam glanced at Jeannie, who was wiping away tears

as she watched the video. As a sexual assault survivor, the case had no doubt brought up a lot of difficult memories for Jeannie.

Sam hugged her.

"Sorry."

"Don't apologize. Don't ever apologize." To the others, she said, "This was a tough one, people. If you need help, please ask for it. You all did great work, as usual. Detective Cruz, you're done for the week. Go on home and enjoy every minute of your wedding weekend. We're looking forward to helping you and Elin celebrate."

"Thank you, Lieutenant," he said with a warm smile.

"The rest of you can go as soon as the reports are filed. Let's get this wrapped up."

SAM WAS ALMOST home when she received a call from Ms. Finklestein.

"There's been a development," the other woman said, sounding stressed.

"What kind of development?" Sam asked, immediately on edge.

"I received a call from Mr. and Mrs. Armstrong's personal attorney, who provided the couple's custody provisions for the children in the event of their deaths."

Sam waited breathlessly to hear what she would say.

"They left all decisions concerning custody and guardianship of the minor children in the hands of Mr. Armstrong's elder son, Elijah."

Sam felt like Alice must've as she fell into the rabbit hole of hope and despair and uncertainty.

"I don't think he knows that," Sam said. "He hasn't said anything about it."

"The attorney, who is in California and only heard

the news about the murders from your press conference today, confirmed that Elijah doesn't know. Apparently, his father and stepmother didn't want him burdened by the weight of that potential responsibility while he was in college. They wanted him to be free to live his own life, but according to the attorney, they were very clear that they wanted him—and *only* him—to decide what should be done with the children. He is sending me a copy of their instructions now."

"I'm almost home and will let him know about this." Sam was waved through the Secret Service checkpoint at the end of Ninth Street and pulled into her assigned parking spot, her mind racing with possible outcomes and implications.

"The Lawsons have arranged for hotel rooms for themselves and the children for the coming week, so they have time to pack up the children's possessions and attend the memorial service that's being planned for next Friday."

"I'll pass that on to Elijah."

"I'll be there shortly with the Lawsons, who think they're coming to pick up the children."

Not so quick, Sam wanted to say, but she refused to think beyond the next ten to fifteen minutes. One step at a time, as she would say when investigating a case.

As she walked up the ramp, she left Lieutenant Holland behind and stepped into her favorite role as Mrs. Cappuano, Nick's wife and Scotty's mom. "Evening, Nate," she said to the agent at the door.

"Evening, Mrs. Cappuano."

She walked through the door he held for her and into bedlam. Nick, Scotty and Elijah were on the floor, under attack from Aubrey and Alden, whose joyful laughter was all she could hear.

Shelby stood on the sidelines with Noah, laughing at their antics.

Sam could only stand there and watch, as a profound feeling of completeness came over her.

"Uh-oh," Scotty said, as Alden pinned him down. "Mom's home! Mom! Rescue me from the little monster!"

"I'm coming, son! Hold on!" She leaned over Scotty to pry Alden off him. "Got him," Sam said, kissing Alden's cute face.

He giggled and squirmed until she put him down. The second his feet hit the floor, he was in the air again, this time aiming for Elijah, who responded with an "ooph" as his brother landed on him.

"Nice to see them laughing," Shelby said when Sam joined her and Noah on the sidelines. The baby kicked his feet wildly, clearly wanting in on the action on the floor.

"It sure is." Sam gave them a few more minutes to play before she asked Elijah if she could have a word with him. She gestured for Nick to come too.

"Scotty, they're all yours," Nick said when he got up off the floor.

"They don't scare me," Scotty said as both kids jumped on top of him.

Nick and Elijah followed Sam into the kitchen.

"They wore me out," Nick said.

"You're getting to see them the way they usually are," Elijah said with a small smile. "First thing we usually do when I come home is have a big wrestling match. They love it."

"They obviously love you very much," Sam said.

"And I love them. I was an only child who'd always wished for siblings until I was fifteen and got two on the same day. Best day of my life." He combed the hair back from his face, which was red from exertion.

"There've been a few developments," Sam said.

"Nick told me you got the guys that killed my dad and Cleo."

"We did."

"Did they say why they did it?"

"We believe it was motivated by money."

Elijah sighed and looked down at the floor. "My dad would've given them everything he had if it meant keeping Cleo and the kids safe."

"From what we were told, he offered them a substantial amount of money, but it took too long to get it."

Tears filled his eyes as he shook his head in disbelief. "Do people think it's just sitting in vaults inside the house?"

"There's something else," Sam said tentatively. "Two things, actually. The FBI has Duke Piedmont in custody." She filled him in on why Piedmont had come to the area.

"I'd like to say I'm surprised to hear my dad was back in touch with Piedmont, but I'm not as shocked as I should be. They were so close back in the day. Even after everything that happened and the threats Piedmont made, my dad still mourned the loss of their friendship. They went through so much together, and my dad never got over what he had to do to Duke in order to save himself from prosecution. He would've welcomed the chance to make things right with Duke—and to eliminate the threat that'd hung over all our lives these last few years."

"For what it's worth, the FBI agents involved in his case said his grief over learning of the deaths of your father and Cleo was genuine," Sam said.

"In my mind, he's been a monster. It's good to know

that maybe he had some humanity left after all." Elijah glanced at Sam. "You said there were two other things."

"The second thing involves custody of your siblings."

"What about it?" he asked, instantly on full alert.

"Apparently, your dad and Cleo designated you as their legal guardian in the event that anything should happen to them."

"*Me?*" he asked softly as his brown eyes went wide with shock.

Sam nodded.

Elijah sat in a chair someone had left pulled out from the table. "Why would they choose *me* when I can barely take care of myself?"

Sam sat next to him. "Probably because they knew you love them as much as they did."

Propping his elbows on his knees, Elijah dropped his head into his hands. "I don't know if I can do it. I'm only twenty and not even through college. They need so much."

Nick rested a hand on the young man's shoulder. "I don't think anyone expects you to step up personally for them if you're not prepared to do so. There're other options."

"Such as?" Elijah asked, glancing at Nick.

"Appoint guardians to stand in for you until you're ready to assume responsibility for them."

"Cleo's sister and brother-in-law are on their way here now," Sam said. "Ms. Finklestein is bringing them by shortly."

Elijah contemplated that for a quiet minute before he looked up at Sam. "When I called Cleo's parents to tell them what'd happened, no one asked about the kids. They didn't ask where they were or if they were all right or

what would become of them. They said they'd told Cleo
this was going to happen, and she should've left my dad
when they told her to." He wiped away tears. "She loved
my dad. She never would've left him. How do I let my
brother and sister go to live with people who were more
concerned about being right than they were about two
kids who were suddenly orphaned?"

"They're more than welcome to stay with us as long
as they need to," Nick said.

Sam could barely breathe while she waited to hear
what Elijah would say.

"You've both been so generous toward the kids and
me, but we've already put you out enough. I can't ask
that of you. It's not your problem."

"We'd like it to be," Nick said, glancing at Sam, who
took his hand and held on tightly. "We've talked about
how much we all love them and would do anything we
could to get them through this difficult time."

"I don't know what to say. I'm so overwhelmed right
now."

"You don't have to say anything," Sam said. "Do whatever you think is right, knowing you have our full support. Nick and I will be there for you and for the kids,
no matter where they end up. I'm sorry to say you're
stuck with us."

Elijah gave her a weak grin. "You've been so incredibly nice. All of you. I don't know how we would've gotten
through this week without both of you, Shelby and Scotty.
Even the Secret Service agents have been amazing."

"You should talk to Cleo's sister and her husband,"
Nick said. "Spend some time with them and see how it
feels. You don't have to decide anything today or even
tomorrow."

Sam wanted to say, *No, no, no! Don't spend time with uncaring people. Leave those babies right here with us, where they're safe and loved and protected from anything that could harm them!* But she couldn't say any of those things. She had to bite her tongue and let this play out the way it was meant to.

"I suppose that would only be fair since they came all this way," Elijah said.

"I'll give you a piece of advice that I often refer back to when investigating a case," Sam said. "One step at a time. Take each thing as it comes and give yourself the time to process it before you move on to the next. The aunt and uncle have hotel reservations for the coming week, so they have time to pack up the children's belongings and to attend a memorial service that's being held next Friday. Are you aware of that?"

He nodded. "Some of my dad's business associates offered to arrange the service for us. I said that was fine, because I have no idea how to go about handling that. I gave them Cleo's parents' phone number, so they could include her family."

"That buys you some time to make sure you're making the best possible decision for the kids," Nick said.

"You don't know us at all, and you've all been so amazing. I can never thank you enough."

"We're here if you need us." Nick squeezed Elijah's shoulder. "There's no expiration date on that offer."

"Thank you," Elijah said softly.

CHAPTER THIRTY-TWO

Ms. Finklestein arrived a short time later with the Lawsons, an attractive couple in their mid- to late-thirties, by Sam's estimation. Monique, who was tall and blonde, resembled her late sister. Her eyes were red and swollen from days of crying. Her dark-haired husband, Robert, had a no-nonsense way about him that immediately put Sam on alert. The last thing Aubrey and Alden needed was a stern guardian.

"It's a pleasure to meet you," Robert said, clearly dazzled to be in the home of the vice president and to be shaking his hand. "I'm a big fan and supporter."

"Thank you," Nick said.

Sam could tell Nick was unimpressed with a guy whose first thought wasn't for his grief-stricken niece and nephew.

"Aubrey and Alden," Elijah said, "you remember Aunt Monique and Uncle Robert, right?"

The children huddled into their brother's embrace.

"You guys have gotten so big!" Monique said as she sat next to the three of them on the sofa. "Your mom sent me pictures, but they didn't do you justice."

Sam wondered if five-year-olds knew what that meant.

"They're a little overwhelmed," Elijah said as he rubbed their backs.

"Totally understandable," Monique said. "Shall we head to the hotel?"

Alden whimpered and clung to Elijah, while Aubrey began to cry.

Sam's eyes filled with tears, but after the advice she had given Elijah, she decided she needed to help him, not make everything worse than it already was. "Hey, guys," she said. "Your aunt and uncle have come so far to see you. They want to help you. We packed up all your toys and new clothes and Alden's blanket."

"I don't want to go," Aubrey said between pitiful sobs that broke Sam's heart.

The little girl threw herself into Sam's arms, holding on to her for dear life. "It's going to be okay, sweetheart," Sam said, hating herself for lying to the child. Nothing would ever be okay for her again. "Your aunt and uncle want to help you and your brother."

"I want to stay with you," Aubrey said, choking on sobs. Her little arms were tight around Sam's neck. "Please don't make us go."

Elijah looked stricken as the scene played out.

"Who's in charge here?" Robert asked, hands on his hips. "The kids or the adults?"

Sam wanted to punch him in the face, but since she couldn't do that, she rubbed soothing circles on Aubrey's back and breathed in the fresh, clean scent of her soft hair.

"I'm sorry you came all this way," Elijah said softly, so softly that no one but Sam heard him over the heart-broken sobs of the children.

"You take Aubrey, Monique," Robert said. "I'll take Alden."

"No," Elijah said, his roar silencing his weeping siblings. *"No."*

"Excuse me?" Robert said, eyebrow raised in annoyance.

"I'm sorry you came all this way, but they're not going with you."

Hearing that, Sam wanted to stand up and cheer.

Shock registered on Robert's face. "Now wait just a minute—"

Sam rocked Aubrey while Elijah tended to Alden.

"It's okay," Elijah said. "You don't have to go with them. We'll figure out something."

"I can't believe this," Monique said. "We were told they needed a home. We're willing to take them."

"No," Elijah said, his jaw set as he met her furious gaze. In his eyes, Sam saw resolve and determination. "My dad and Cleo made me their legal guardian, and they are *not* going with you."

"God, you're just like your father, aren't you?" Monique said, her tone shrill. "It was always his way or the highway."

"If you think you're insulting me by comparing me to my father, you'd be mistaken," Elijah said. "He was the finest man I ever knew."

"That fine man got my sister murdered!"

"Actually," Sam said, "the reason they were murdered was because of a traffic accident that *she* was in."

"You're actually *blaming* her?" Monique asked, seeming astounded that Sam would have the audacity.

"Nope," Sam said. "I blame the people who carried out the crime. But her traffic accident was what put them on the radar of the men who've been arrested—not your brother-in-law. And I don't think we need to be having this conversation in front of the children, do you?"

"Let's go, Monique. Clearly we aren't needed here."

His wife cast desperate eyes on the backs of her niece and nephew. "But—"

"Let's go!"

Aubrey startled at the angry tone of his voice.

"Shhh," Sam said, softly. "It's okay. He's leaving."

"We'll be at the W if you change your mind," Monique said to Elijah.

"Thank you, but I won't."

"You're not in any way equipped to raise these children," she said with a nasty snarl.

"I'm certainly better equipped than you are. Now please go. You're not needed here, and you're making everything worse."

Monique grabbed the purse she'd placed on the coffee table and followed her husband out the door.

For a good two minutes after the door closed behind them, no one said anything.

Aubrey finally broke the silence. "Thank you for making them go away, Lijah. I don't like them."

"I don't either, honey. Don't worry. You won't have to see them again." He had just made the first of what would be countless decisions on their behalf, but when his gaze met Sam's, all she saw was despair.

HOURS LATER, after the kids were in bed, Sam and Nick sat with Elijah in the kitchen.

"I'll leave school and buy a house for the three of us. I'll have Milagros come back to help me take care of the kids. She loves them as much as I do. I can make this work. My dad left us with the funds to do whatever needs to be done. I can't leave them. They need me too much."

"You could transfer to a school in DC," Nick said.

"Maybe Georgetown? I could make some calls and see what I can do."

"Maybe. I'll think about that."

"I'd like to toss out one more option," Sam said tentatively.

"What's that?" Elijah asked.

Sam's heart beat so hard and so fast she felt breathless, but she knew if she didn't make the suggestion, she would always regret it. "Leave them here with us while you finish school. You could come here for every long weekend, vacation, holiday. We would take care of them for you until you finish school. At that point, we can reevaluate and decide next steps."

"That's too much to ask of you guys."

"You're not asking." Sam glanced at Nick, who nodded in support. "We're offering. Our lives are crazy and unpredictable, but we're surrounded by an incredible support system, and the children would have a large and loving family around them every day—and they could remain in their school, which would bring some normalcy back to their lives."

"If we were to have legal custody of the children," Nick added, "they would receive Secret Service protection as well. We could set it up so you make all the big decisions, but we handle the day-to-day for you until you're able to do it yourself."

"Why would you want do this for three people you didn't even know a few days ago?"

"I don't know if you've noticed," Sam said, smiling, "but everyone associated with this household has fallen in love with them."

Elijah offered a weak smile. "They're easy to love."

"Indeed," Sam said. "One thing that needs to happen

sooner rather than later is counseling for both of them. If you'd like, I can get you some names of people who specialize in grief and trauma for children."

"That'd be very helpful."

"You don't need to decide anything right now," Nick said. "We have Sam's partner's wedding on Saturday, and on Sunday, we're due to leave for a week in Europe. You and the children are welcome to stay here while we're gone, and Shelby would be happy to help you with the kids. Take the time you need to make the best possible decision for all of you. We'll respect whatever you decide, and you'll have our support no matter what you do."

"I wish my dad was here to tell me what to do. He always knew what to do."

"He and Cleo put tremendous faith in you by making you the children's guardian," Sam said. "You'll do the right thing, Elijah."

"I hope you're right."

THE NEXT DAY passed in a blur of details, paperwork and press briefings as the full story of the murders made the national news, thrusting Sam and her team into the spotlight she detested. She went through the motions, dotting the *i*s and crossing the *t*s to make sure there was no way Klein and Baker wouldn't be convicted and sent away for life. All the while, she tried not to think about what might happen next with the kids.

For now, Elijah was following their advice to take his time to make the best possible decisions for the kids. The three of them attended the memorial service for Jameson and Cleo Armstrong, going out of their way to avoid the aunt and uncle who had upset them.

On Friday night, Sam was awake for hours after she

went to bed, which didn't bode well for the pictures at Freddie's wedding the next afternoon.

"What're you thinking about?" Nick asked.

"I thought you were asleep."

"Not going to happen tonight. Too much on my mind. I can't stop thinking about that horrible couple who had no idea how to deal with traumatized kids. Not that we know much better, but anything would be better than them."

Sam shuddered. "They were horrible."

"I'm glad Elijah spoke up, and I didn't have to beg him not to give the kids to them."

"I know. Me too."

Sam turned over and curled up to him. "We have no business offering to take them in."

He put his arm around her. "Maybe not, but if they need us, we'll make it work. Somehow. I just want you to remember—our family was perfect before them, and we'll be perfect after them, no matter what Elijah decides."

"I know, but we'd be much more perfect *with* them."

"Samantha."

"Don't worry. I'm keeping it real."

"Promise?"

"Yeah." She said what he needed to hear but didn't want to think about Aubrey and Alden—or even Elijah—exiting their lives.

Though she hadn't expected to sleep, she awoke from a deep, dreamless sleep at nine o'clock. She looked over to find Nick's side of the bed empty and forced herself to relax while she could. Hair and makeup people were due at two to beautify her for the four o'clock ceremony. She sent a text to Freddie.

How you holding up?

Fine.

You need me over there?

Absolutely not.

    Sam chuckled at his reply.

I'm hurt.

No, you're not. You want to be home with your family today.

You're right. But I'm here if you need me.

I need you at three thirty at the observatory.

I'll be there with bells on. The midget strippers are coming too.

    Before his bachelor party, she'd tortured him with hints of what she had planned, which was in fact an elegant dinner party for him and Elin.

Shut up, Sam.

Make me.

I'm getting married today. Leave me alone.

She laughed at the predictable reply and responded with one of her own.

Why should today be different from any other day?

Her beloved Freddie was getting *married*. The thought brought tears to her eyes, probably the first of many on what promised to be another emotional day.

Sam heard whispers outside the door and wondered what was going on. A soft knock on the door had her sitting up in bed and pushing her hair back from her face.

Nick poked his head in the door. "We made breakfast. Are you interested, and more important, are you decent?"

"As decent as I ever am." She'd slept in one of his T-shirts, but she pulled the covers up around her waist anyway.

"Go ahead," Nick said.

Scotty carried the tray while Aubrey and Alden "helped" him.

"What'd you guys make?" Sam asked.

"Pancakes, bacon and eggs," Aubrey said.

Alden was, as always, quieter than his sister, but he took in the goings-on with interest. "This looks yummy," Sam said, smiling up at Scotty when he placed the tray on her lap. "Did you cook?"

"I helped," Scotty said, "but Dad did most of it."

"We helped too," Aubrey said.

"I'm sure you did," Sam said, ruffling her hair. "You want some of my bacon?"

"Scotty and Lijah are going to take us to the park," Aubrey said. "We just hafta wait until…" She looked to Scotty. "Who has to go with us?"

"My Secret Service detail," Scotty said.

"Oh yeah," Aubrey said. "They have to come. What's Secret Service again, Scotty?"

"My dad is the vice president, so they keep us safe."

"I wish my dad had been vice president," Aubrey said solemnly.

Before they could react to that heartbreaking statement, Debra Nixon, the lead agent on Scotty's detail came to the door. "Pardon the interruption, but we're set to go, Scotty. If you're ready."

"We're ready," Scotty said. "Come on, guys. Let's go."

Aubrey and Alden bounded off the bed and followed Scotty out the door.

"It'll be good for them to get outside after being cooped up the last few days," Nick said as he closed the bedroom door and then stretched out next to Sam on the bed.

"Definitely." She took a bite of bacon and fed some to him. "Thanks for breakfast in bed."

"Glad you got to sleep in."

"Did you sleep at all?"

"A little."

"It's going to be a long, emotional day and I'm already emotionally drained." Waiting for Elijah to decide what to do with the kids had taken a toll on them both over the last few days, but they were giving him space and breathing room to think.

"I know, babe. So am I. But we'll rally for Freddie and Elin."

She linked her fingers with his. "Yes, we will."

CHAPTER THIRTY-THREE

THE BRIDE AND GROOM had given Sam carte blanche to wear whatever she wanted as Freddie's best man-woman. As always, Sam blazed her own trail with a halter-style black cocktail-length dress, which matched the color and length of Elin's bridesmaids' dresses. In deference to her status as a groomsman, Sam added a black wraparound bow tie to her outfit.

Her hair had been done in long spiral curls and her makeup was subtle but effective enough that she wouldn't ruin the pictures. Over the wound on her left arm, she wore a flesh-colored bandage. Standing before the mirror, she decided she looked as good as she ever did.

Nick came into the bedroom, decked out in a tux, and Sam's mouth went dry at the sight of him. He was always gorgeous, but the tuxedo took him to a whole other level of dashing.

"You look beautiful, babe."

"Funny, I was just thinking the same about you."

Smiling, he said, "Are you ready?"

"Just a minute." She put on the engagement ring she only wore for special occasions and gazed lovingly at the diamond key necklace Nick had given her as a wedding gift. Normally she would wear it on a day like this, but today she wore the bow tie instead. Then she stepped into the black Louboutin heels Nick had given her for Christmas and declared herself ready.

She took the arm he extended to her and walked with him down the stairs where Scotty waited for them wearing the new blazer and khaki pants they'd bought him for the wedding. He'd grown so much in the last few months that he would soon be taller than his mother but had more growing to do before he would catch up to his six-foot-four-inch father.

"You guys look really nice," Scotty said.

"So do you," Sam said, smoothing the hair back from his forehead. "Where are Elijah and the kids?"

"In the kitchen."

Sam and Nick went into the kitchen to check on their guests before they left.

Elijah sat with the kids at the table, watching over them as they played Candy Land.

"We're off to the wedding," Sam said. "If you need us for anything, text Scotty and he'll let us know." They'd given him all their phone numbers, so he could reach them at any time.

As Elijah nodded, Sam noticed the dark circles under his eyes. "Have a good time and don't worry about us. We'll be fine. We're going to meet Milagros for dinner, so she can see the kids."

"That'll be fun."

"You look pretty," Aubrey said with a shy smile.

"Thank you," Sam said, returning her smile and bending to kiss her and Alden. "We'll see you in the morning."

Sam, Nick and Scotty went outside to where the motorcade awaited them.

Down the street, Sam noticed Celia helping her dad

into the specially outfitted van the police union had bought for him after his injury. Sam waved to them.

"See you there," Celia called to her.

The motorcade left Ninth Street, headed northwest toward Number One Observatory Circle and the Naval Observatory, the traditional home of the vice president.

"Did you know the Naval Observatory houses one of the nation's oldest scientific agencies and is the keeper of the Master Clock?" Nick asked when they were underway.

"History lessons by Vice President Nick Cappuano," Scotty said in a deep voice as he grinned.

"Well, did you know?" Nick asked, amused by his son.

"No, Dad, I didn't know." Scotty rolled his eyes at Sam. "What does this Master Clock do, exactly?"

"I'm so glad you asked." Nick referred to his phone. "According to Wikipedia, it 'provides precise time to the GPS satellite constellation run by the United States Air Force.'" He read more about time interval, earth orientation, astronomy and celestial observation duties performed at the observatory and mentioned the world's largest astrophysical periodicals collection.

"Well, there're a few things I didn't know when I woke up this morning," Sam said dryly.

"I do what I can for the people," Nick said.

"That's her line," Scotty said, using his thumb to point at Sam.

"And it's copyrighted," Sam added.

"What you're basically telling us," Scotty said to his father, "is that we could be living in the coolest place in the world and instead we're stuck in a boring double townhouse in Capitol Hill."

"Basically, yes," Nick said, grinning.

"Good to know."

Sam didn't bother to mention that they lived where they did so they could remain close to her dad, because Scotty already knew that and was a frequent visitor to Skip's home.

"What's the deal with there being no traffic today?" Sam asked. "Have aliens landed or something no one told me about?"

"It's a rare Saturday with no home games for any of our teams and no huge rallies of any kind," Nick said.

"Freddie and Elin picked a good day to get married," Scotty said.

In addition to the less than average traffic, the weather was also cooperating with a day well into the seventies, with bright sunshine and a cloudless sky. "I *love* this time of year," Sam said.

"I hate it," Scotty said, scowling. "Summer is the best."

"Aw, come on! Autumn is so beautiful with the leaves changing and the weather warm but not scorching."

"Blah, blah, blah," Scotty said in a teasing tone. "Autumn means *school*. Summer means *freedom*. I pick summer any day."

Nick smiled at Sam, who shook her head in amusement. She couldn't really argue with her son. She'd felt the same way at his age when school had been such an awful struggle for her, with undiagnosed dyslexia plaguing her.

"Hey, buddy," Sam said, tentatively, "the other night you said something that's had me thinking ever since."

"What did I say?"

"That not all foster homes are the same—"

"You knew that already."

"Yes, but it made me wonder if you were in bad places

before you ended up with Mrs. Littlefield." Sam had struggled for days to find the opportunity to discuss it further with him. In the motorcade, he was a captive audience.

He shrugged. "They were mostly fine. Sometimes the people care more about the money they get from the state than the kids."

Nick squeezed Sam's hand. "Here's what's been making me crazy since Mom told me you said that—the fear that someone was unkind or cruel to you."

"I was really young, so I don't remember much about the people, but they weren't mean. More like indifferent. Not like you guys at all." Grinning, he added, "Sometimes I wish you were a little *more* indifferent. I could do without all the homework nonsense that goes on in our house."

Nick laughed. "Too bad. You're stuck with me and my determination to get you into Harvard."

Scotty rolled his eyes. "We need to aim a little lower."

"Not happening. I have no doubt that you're fully capable."

"It'd be far more likely if you were to succeed in outlawing all forms of math."

Nick laughed. "I don't think even I have the power to make that happen."

"If there's ever anything you want to talk to us about," Sam said, "I hope you know you can."

"I know. Don't worry. I'm fine."

"That's all that matters to us."

"You guys are awesome parents, even when you're making me do my math homework and kissing all the time." He glanced at Sam. "Could I ask *you* something?"

"Anything."

"Are we going to get to keep Aubrey and Alden?"

"We don't know yet." He knew they'd offered to keep the children, but that it was up to Elijah. "We might not know for a while. Elijah has some decisions to make, and we've told him to take the time he needs."

"It would be cool to have siblings."

"I know," Sam said, moved by his statement, "but let's take a wait-and-see approach to them for now. I don't want any of us to end up heartbroken if they have to leave us."

"I think we'll all be a little heartbroken if they leave," Scotty said.

"Yeah," Sam said. "You're probably right about that."

They arrived a short time later at the observatory, and Nick pointed out the digital Master Clock outside the gates.

"How many times have I driven by that and paid no attention to it?" Sam asked.

"You should know this stuff, Mom. You grew up here."

"Chastised by my thirteen-year-old."

Scotty laughed. "We should have a contest to see who knows more about this city—me or you."

"You'd probably win," Sam said.

"Um, I'd *definitely* win," Scotty said.

Nick nodded in agreement.

But when Sam sent him a challenging look, he shook his head. She laughed at the way he played both sides, like the nimble politician he was.

They pulled up to the front entrance a minute later. The first person they encountered inside was Shelby Faircloth, dressed to the nines in a sexy pink suit and sky-high pink heels. She wore a headset and carried a walkie-talkie.

"The vice president, second lady and Scotty Cappuano have arrived," she said into the radio.

"Shelby," Scotty said, his eyes wide with surprise. "You look so pretty!"

"This is how I used to look every day, sport," she said. "You want to give me a hand?"

"Definitely."

"Come back in a few so I can show you around," Nick said.

"We've got all day to look around," Scotty said, hooking his arm through Shelby's.

Over her shoulder, Shelby said, "Freddie's upstairs. Go on up."

Sam started up the stairs with Nick following, taking the opportunity to slide his hand up her leg.

"Stop!" she said, laughing.

"Don't wanna stop."

They found Freddie with his parents in one of the smaller bedrooms. Judging by the noise coming from down the hallway, Elin and her bridesmaids had taken over the master suite.

At the sight of her partner in a tuxedo, Sam rested a hand over her heart, overcome by what was sure to be the first of many emotional moments during the course of this day. She walked over to him and hugged him while Nick shook his hand.

"Thank you, guys, for being part of this," Freddie said.

"We wouldn't want to be anywhere else today," Sam said.

Juliette Cruz hugged them both. "It's such an honor to have you both here and as such special friends to our Freddie."

"We love him," Sam said bluntly. Today was not the

day to pretend otherwise. Today was a day to celebrate her best friend, her partner, the brother of her heart.

A FEW MINUTES after they arrived, Nick was called into duty to help escort the guests to their seats for the ceremony that would take place in the backyard. A huge tent stood ready to host the reception. Each of the one hundred and fifty guests had been vetted by the Secret Service. The details assigned to Nick and Scotty had promised to be discreet during the day, but they were always watching. After closing the Beauclair case, Sam was more grateful than ever for their presence, even if it was intrusive at times. Nothing like the horror perpetrated on the Beauclairs would ever happen to her family on the Secret Service's watch.

"Try not to make any of the ladies swoon," Sam said, flattening her hands on Nick's chest before he went downstairs.

"Give me a break."

"You have no idea of the *impact* you have on the female population. I want you to take your duties seriously and smile for all the selfies, you hear me?"

Rolling his eyes, he kissed her and left the room.

"People are gonna freak when they realize who their usher is," Freddie said with a laugh.

"That's what I was trying to tell him." She turned her full attention on Freddie, giving him a critical once-over.

"What?" he asked.

"Just making sure you're perfect." She brushed at some imaginary lint on his sleeve and straightened his perfectly straight bow tie.

"Quit fussing over me. My mom has been on me all day."

His parents were seated on the other side of the room, visiting with Juliette's sister and her husband.

"While it's just us, I wanted to say that even though I've made you sorry you asked me every day, I'm really happy and honored to be your best man-woman."

"And I want to say that while you did, in fact, make me sorry every day since I asked you, there's no one else I'd rather have standing next to me than you."

Sam looked up at him. "Nick said something the other day that has me thinking."

"What did he say?"

"After Jenkins shot at us, he said we probably shouldn't be partners anymore, because I've lost perspective where you're concerned."

His stricken expression was just what she'd hoped for. "We're not gonna be partners anymore?"

"Hell, yes, we are. Who else could put up with my shit the way you do?"

"No one," he said, breathing a visible sigh of relief. "There is no one on God's green earth who could tolerate you the way I do."

"Exactly. As I always say, if it ain't broke, don't fix it. Although, there is some truth to what Nick said."

"Yes, there is. You can't push me out of the way at your own expense, Sam. I don't expect you to do that."

"I know you don't. It's not like I had a long chat with myself in which I consciously decided to do that. I just did it."

"And that's the problem Nick is talking about."

"I'll add that to my long list of things to think about during my unpaid week off to reexamine my priorities."

"There's nothing wrong with your priorities. Don't spend too much time reordering them. We get justice for people who need it most. We do a job most people could never do, and we do it the best way we know how. Don't forget that."

"I won't, my wise little grasshopper."

"Not so little anymore."

"He may be growing up and getting married, but he will *always* be my little grasshopper." Sam hugged him as tightly as she could, careful not to get any makeup on his pristine black tuxedo coat.

"Your grasshopper can live with that."

CHAPTER THIRTY-FOUR

RIGHT AT FOUR O'CLOCK, Freddie escorted his mother while Sam took his father's arm to walk down the stairs and out to the back veranda. Shelby stood with them, waiting for the right moment to send them on their way to the floral arbor that had been erected at the end of the aisle. When everyone had taken their seats, the string quartet providing music shifted into something Sam actually recognized from her own wedding: "Jesu, Joy of Man's Desiring."

"Go," Shelby said.

Shelby had thought of everything, even the flooring that had been laid under the white runner that kept Sam's heels from sinking into the grass. She held on tight to the arm Miguel Cruz provided and was thankful for his presence here today. He'd spent twenty years absent from his son's life while he battled bipolar disorder.

Juliette was a new woman since her husband had come back to her healthy and determined to put his family back together. The two of them beamed with pride as they watched their handsome son shake hands with the minister from the church he'd grown up in and take his place on the right side of the aisle with Sam at his side. Because Elin wasn't religious, they'd compromised, having the ceremony outside with Freddie's childhood minister presiding.

Next to her, Nick stood where Gonzo was supposed

to have been. He subtly linked his fingers with hers as they stood with Freddie to watch Elin's two sisters come toward them, one of them holding hands with her daughter, Elin's six-year-old niece, who was the flower girl.

While they waited for the bride to appear with her father, Sam scanned the assembled group and saw her dad and Celia in the back next to her sisters, Tracy and Angela and their husbands, Mike and Spencer. Cameron Green was there with a woman Sam hadn't met. She saw Jeannie and her husband, Michael, Captain Malone and his wife, Avery Hill, Will Tyrone and his girlfriend, Lindsey McNamara and Terry O'Connor, Lieutenant Archelotta from the IT division, Dominguez and Carlucci, and Harry and Lilia.

Christina Billings stood off to the side, waiting for the bride to make her entrance before she took her seat. Sam was so happy to see her and was glad she'd come despite Gonzo not being there. She belonged there as much as anyone, and Sam looked forward to the opportunity to speak to her at the reception.

When Elin and her dad appeared on the back porch, the music shifted to "Ode to Joy."

Sam liked the emphasis on the word *joy*. At first, she hadn't thought Elin worthy of Freddie, but over time, Elin had proven her devotion to him, and Sam couldn't be happier for both of them.

Freddie gasped at the sight of his stunningly beautiful bride, who had worn a classy, sexy gown that showed off a body honed from years of working as a personal trainer.

Sam looked up at him and saw tears in his eyes as he waited for Elin to join him. Sam hooked her hand through Freddie's arm and held on tight.

He never took his eyes off his love as she completed the journey with her father, who hugged her, kissed her and shook hands with Freddie before joining Elin's mother in the front row.

Nick handed Sam a handkerchief, so she could dab at her tears.

As Freddie and Elin exchanged vows, Sam was thankful she'd worn waterproof mascara.

"Now that Freddie and Elin have exchanged traditional vows, they would like to share a few thoughts they prepared on their own," the minister said. "Elin, if you're ready."

"I'm so ready," Elin said to laughter. "I feel like I've been ready for this day since we first met. One of the saddest things in my life became one of the happiest when I met you," she said, referring to John O'Connor's murder. "I remember that first day so vividly, as well as when you came back to find me. Every day since then has been like something right out of a dream. Well, except for the day when you got shot because of me, but we're not talking about that today."

Freddie laughed and used the sleeve of his coat to wipe away tears.

From inside his coat pocket, Nick produced a packet of tissues. He handed one to Sam, who passed it on to Freddie. Leave it to Nick to do her best man-woman duties better than she ever could.

"I used to picture my future husband and figured he'd probably be one of the muscle heads from the gym where I spend most of my time. I never pictured that a sweet, gentle man with a heart of gold would turn out to be the man of my dreams. I love you so much, Freddie, and I can't wait to spend the rest of my life with you."

Freddie leaned in for a kiss that had their guests whistling and clapping.

"Your turn, Freddie," the minister said, smiling.

"I was," he said, "quite simply besotted from the first second I ever saw your amazing blue eyes. I'd never seen eyes that shade of blue before, and even though I was painfully aware that you were way, way, *way* out of my league, I had to go back and find you. I fully expected you to laugh in my face and tell me to get lost, but that's not what you did, and no one was more surprised by that than me."

"I was," Sam said, raising her hand to laughter.

Chuckling, Freddie continued. "Sam told me I didn't stand a chance with you, but I had to find out for myself. I'm glad that for once I didn't listen to her. We've already been through so much, and each thing that's happened has only made us stronger and more determined to be together and to stay together. I love you with everything I am, and I can't wait to have forever with you."

After they exchanged another kiss, the minister walked them through the exchange of rings before declaring them husband and wife.

"Mr. Cruz, you may now kiss Mrs. Cruz."

"Mrs. Cruz," Freddie said, grinning like a loon. "How awesome is that?"

"Finally," Elin said, drawing him into a barn burner of a kiss while their loved ones applauded.

They posed for photos on the lawn, ate a delicious meal and shared in the joy of two people who'd found each other and decided to make a life together.

Sam couldn't recall the last time she'd had so much fun, and having Nick sitting right next to her at dinner made it even better. "I'm sad that Gonzo had to miss this, but I'm glad I get to sit with my date."

He took her hand and brought it to his lips, a move the photographer captured.

Sam would have to ask for a copy of that photo.

Freddie and Elin were called to the dance floor for their first dance as husband and wife. They'd chosen Ed Sheeran's "Perfect," and once again, Sam battled tears watching them and thinking about so many memories with Freddie over the last few years.

"The bride and groom would like to invite Lieutenant Holland and Vice President Cappuano to join them on the dance floor."

Thunderous applause rocked the tent.

Appreciating the use of her police title, Sam held Nick's hand on the way to the dance floor, where they joined the bride and groom as well as Elin's sisters and their husbands.

"I think it's safe to say these people support you," Sam said to Nick.

"They support *us*. They're our people."

Sam slid an arm under his coat and held on tight to him, already preparing for his departure in the morning. She hadn't said anything to him yet, but with things still up in the air with their "littles," she couldn't leave. As much as she wanted to go with him, now wasn't the time. They would have other opportunities to travel, but she wouldn't have a minute's peace worrying about the kids—and Elijah, who'd also become theirs over the last few days.

Funny how that happened. She'd yearned to be pregnant, to have a baby, to have the family Nick hadn't had growing up. They seemed to be stumbling into their own perfectly imperfect little family, made up of kids who needed them. Off to the side, she noticed Scotty sitting between her dad and Celia, conversing with Tracy, Mike, Angela and Spencer. Scotty was now so much a part of them, it was hard to remember a time when he hadn't been.

"What're you thinking about, babe?" Nick asked.

"So many things."

"Things I'm going to like?"

"Some of them."

"Uh-oh."

She held on tighter to him. "Let's have the best time ever today, okay?"

"Any time I get to spend with you is the best time ever."

AFTER DINNER, Shelby came over to Sam, microphone in hand, and Sam was instantly nervous, realizing it was time to give the toast traditionally offered by the best man. She took the microphone from Shelby and stood, clearing her throat until the tent fell silent.

"I'm Sam Holland Cappuano, Freddie's *other* partner."

"I think they know that, babe," Nick said to laughter and applause.

Sam scowled playfully at him. "As I was saying before being rudely interrupted, I'm Freddie's partner at work, and I've had the pleasure of a front row seat as he fell madly in love with Elin. There are a lot of things I could say if I truly wanted to embarrass Freddie."

"Please don't," Freddie said as everyone laughed.

"But all I will say is that I was blessed the day you became my partner, Freddie Cruz, and you were blessed the day you met Elin. I wish you a lifetime of love and joy and happiness and many, *many* children." This last part she added with a pointed look for her partner, who'd recently told her he didn't think he should have kids after the crap they witnessed on the job.

Sam had told him he would have children, and that was that.

He stood to hug her. "Thank you for the restraint."

"It was painful, but when the midget strippers get here, all bets are off."

Freddie groaned. "You aren't allowed to call them that," he said, resurrecting their old argument.

"They call *themselves* that!"

After the formalities were seen to, Sam and Nick went to sit with her dad and the rest of her family. While Nick chatted with his brothers-in-law, Sam took the first opportunity she'd had to debrief the case with her dad.

"I can't believe it all stemmed from a traffic altercation," Skip said.

"Sort of like what happened to you."

"True."

"I've been given a week of unpaid leave, during which I've been directed to rethink my priorities."

"Ouch. Who said that? Joe?"

"Yeah. He's really pissed that I took in the kids during the investigation. And before you say it, I know it was a conflict of interest, but I'd do it again in a hot second."

"That says a lot about where your priorities are."

"I know, and they're not compatible with the job."

"Most of the time they are, and I would hope Joe can see that."

"He said I'm the reason he can't retire, because anyone else in his job would have my ass in a sling and my badge inside of a week."

"He's full of shit," Skip said, scoffing. "He has no desire to retire. Marti has been after him for years to retire, but he always says he'd go crazy without something to do. Don't let him put that on you."

"I think he meant it, though. He said it's true what people say—that I get away with murder while investigating murder."

"You do a hellacious job better than just about anyone else ever has. And he knows that as well as you and I do. Take your rap and your week off but keep doing what you do. Maybe avoid taking in the children of your murder victims in the future."

"Nick and I might keep them." It was the first time she'd said the words out loud.

His brow went up. "Seriously?"

Nodding, she filled him in on where things stood with Elijah and the kids. She and Nick hadn't breathed a word of it to anyone but Scotty and Shelby, fearful that it wouldn't happen, and they'd have to backtrack.

"Wow. The aunt and uncle didn't pan out?"

"They were *awful*. Elijah said thanks but no thanks to them. But we could tell he was panicking about what to do, so we offered." She shrugged, trying to pretend that offer wasn't one of the biggest things they'd ever done. It was certainly bigger than Nick becoming vice president. That was for sure.

"You want these kids, baby girl?" he asked softly.

"I think I do, but I'm trying not to get my hopes up."

"It's a hell of a thing you did even offering to help their brother. I'm sure he appreciates it."

"He does. He's a really nice kid too. Either way," Sam said, forcing a cheerful tone, "we told him they're stuck with us. We're invested now."

"They're lucky to have you guys and Scotty invested in them."

"They have more money than they can spend in a lifetime, but at the end of the day, they're really alone in the world. Elijah has his mom, but he doesn't seem particularly close to her, and besides, she's not going to take in the kids her ex-husband had with his second wife, you know?"

"Yeah, it's messy, and you're right that money can't buy a family."

"No, but it can give them security they wouldn't have without it."

"I still think about a kid I met during one of my cases. I always wondered what became of him after his parents were killed. It's good that you won't have to regret not taking the next step with them, because you would've regretted it and always wondered what became of them."

"Yeah, I would've."

Christina approached them. "Sorry to interrupt, but could I have a word, Sam? I've got to get home to Alex. One of my neighbors is watching him so I could come."

"Of course," Sam said, kissing her dad's forehead as she stood.

She and Christina stepped outside the tent, which was surrounded by Secret Service agents trying to be subtle and failing miserably.

"How're you doing?" Sam asked.

"A little better than I was actually. It's a huge relief to know that Tommy is getting the help he needs, even if Alex and I miss him."

"When can you see him?"

"Not for a couple of weeks. They're going to let me know."

"If there's anything we can do for you, please ask. We can take Alex. Whatever you need."

"Thanks, Sam."

"You and I got off to a rough start at first, but I hope you know that you and Tommy and Alex... You're family to me and Nick."

"I know that and so does he. It means a lot to both of us."

Sam hugged her. "We're going to get him through this and figure out what's next."

Christina hugged her back and nodded as she glanced wistfully at the tent. "Maybe someday we'll be dancing at my wedding."

"I'll be first in line for that dance. Keep me posted on what's going on?"

"I will. Take care, Sam."

"You too."

As Sam walked back to the tent thinking of Gonzo and what he might be going through at rehab, Harry and Lilia came out of the tent, arm in arm, caught up in each other. Sam delighted in seeing them together. For so long, she'd wanted Harry to find someone. That he'd met Lilia through her gave her a kick—and the ability to take full credit for their relationship.

"Cutting out early, lovebirds?" she asked, startling them.

"I've got to pack," Harry said. "Air Force Two is wheels up at eight in the morning."

Sam's spirits plummeted at the reminder of Nick's looming departure. "Nick has been packed for a week."

"We all know he's not normal," Harry said.

"That's our vice president you're slandering," Lilia said.

"He *isn't* normal," Sam said, making them both laugh. "He's an anal-retentive freakazoid."

"I hadn't gotten official word that you're going too until yesterday," Lilia said. "I'm woefully unprepared to support you."

Sam glanced at the tent where Nick was dancing with Celia before returning her attention to Harry and Lilia.

"I haven't told Nick yet, but I'm not going. We have a situation at home."

"Not Scotty?" Harry asked.

"No, not Scotty. Some other children have recently come into our lives, and they need one of us to be home right now." Being a mother, she was finding, meant making sacrifices that would've been unheard of before children. She wasn't Aubrey or Alden's mother, but she would care for them the way a mother would for as long as they needed that from her.

"Is this a story that's going to make headlines?" Lilia asked with a kind smile.

"Possibly," Sam said. With so many other things to contend with, she hadn't given the potential for headlines much thought.

Lilia reached out to squeeze her arm. "We'll help you navigate that when the time is right."

"It may not happen, but if it does, you'll be among the first to know."

"As always, I am at your service," Lilia said with the devotion that had endeared her to Sam since she first met her. Recalling that she'd been prepared to dislike the woman seemed silly now.

Sam hugged Harry. "Take good care of my husband while you're gone."

"You know I will."

"I'll rest easier knowing you're with him."

"We'll be back before you ladies miss us," Harry said.

Sam glanced at Lilia, and together they said, "No, you won't."

CHAPTER THIRTY-FIVE

THEY DANCED, they drank a lot of champagne, they ate cake, and then devoured the burgers and fries that appeared sometime after ten.

"Shelby has this wedding thing down to a science," Scotty said, his mouth full of cheeseburger.

"She sure does," Sam said, dipping a salty fry in ketchup, hoping the late-night snack would soak up the vast quantities of champagne she'd consumed. "You know what the best thing is about having a Secret Service detail?"

"There's a best thing?" Nick asked, brows furrowed.

"Two words—designated drivers."

"I think it might be time to get you home, Samantha."

"Is she going to fall over or pass out or anything embarrassing?" Scotty asked.

"Not yet, but she's about to turn into a pumpkin."

"I am not!" Sam protested even as her eyes wanted to close and stay closed for no less than eight hours.

"Let's say our goodbyes," Nick said.

They found Freddie and Elin at a table full of her friends from the gym, all of whom went silent at the approach of the second family.

"We're going to call it a night," Nick said, hugging Elin and then Freddie. "Congratulations and thank you for letting us be part of it."

"Thank you for making it so we're the only people we know who had the vice president in their wedding party," Elin said.

"Speaking of that," Nick said, appearing uncomfortable. "Would you mind if Terry released one photo to the media of the four of us together from earlier?"

"Not at all," Freddie said. "Go for it."

"Thanks. Apparently, there's interest in the second couple being in a wedding."

"I can't imagine why," Sam said, making the others laugh. She hugged Elin. "Make him happy."

"That's my goal."

And then she hugged Freddie and found she had no words.

"Thanks for being my best man-woman."

"An honor and a privilege."

"Try not to get into any trouble while I'm gone."

"That might be a tall order," Nick said.

"Have the best time ever!" Sam said as Nick led her away. Okay, she might be a teensy bit drunk. "Send pictures!"

"Get a smartphone and I will."

Sam stuck her tongue out at him before she remembered the photographer who'd been a little too interested in her and Nick during the wedding. Hopefully the photo of the second lady with her tongue out wouldn't end up on the front page of the paper in the morning.

SAM FELL ASLEEP on the way home and roused when Nick kissed her awake.

"We're home, sweetheart. Come on." He took her hands, helped her out of the SUV and steered her up the ramp with Scotty following behind them.

"What time is it?"

"After midnight," Scotty said.

"Straight to bed with you, mister," Sam said.

"Why did I know you were going to say that? Will you guys be gone when I get up?"

Sam glanced at Nick and then looked away.

"I will be, buddy," Nick said. "Mom is staying home with you and the littles."

Scotty visibly brightened, "She is? Really?"

Sam nodded, "I'm afraid you're stuck with me."

"Hurry back," Scotty told his dad. "She's a bear when you're not here."

Nick laughed and cuffed his son's chin. "I'll be back as soon as I possibly can. In the meantime, you're in charge around here."

"Hey!" Sam barely had the energy to protest.

"Don't worry about a thing," Scotty said to his father. "I got you covered."

"Give your old man a hug."

Scotty went to Nick and hugged him fiercely.

Nick kissed the top of his head and let go reluctantly. "Love you, buddy."

"Love you too, old man," he said, grinning. "Tell the queen we said hello."

"I will. Next time, I'll take you guys with me."

"That'll be good, preferably at a time when I can miss as much school as possible."

"I'll keep that in mind. Go on up to bed and try to be quiet. Elijah and the kids are asleep."

"I will. I'm so glad they're still here." Scotty scooted off to bed.

As he went up the stairs, Elijah came down wearing

a Princeton T-shirt and pajama pants. He gave Scotty a fist-bump as they passed on the stairs.

"Good wedding?" Elijah asked Sam and Nick.

"A fantastic wedding, complete with far too much champagne," Sam said, riding the buzz for as long as she could.

Elijah ran his fingers through his hair, seeming nervous. "I know it's late and you've got an early flight..."

"Let's go in the kitchen," Nick said, realizing before Sam did that something was up.

He steered her ahead of him into the kitchen and into a chair with a minimum of fuss.

Sam, who'd been half-asleep a few minutes ago was now wide-awake and on alert for whatever Elijah wanted to tell them.

"I've been thinking a lot about what you offered," Elijah said haltingly. "The kids... They... This has been so hard on them, but you guys, all of you, have made it so much easier for them than it would've been otherwise."

Under the table, Nick gripped her hand as they held their breath.

"What you said about them staying with you while I'm at school... Are you sure—"

"We're sure," Nick said. "One hundred percent positive."

Elijah dropped his head into his hands. "I have no idea what the right thing to do is, but this... With you guys... It feels right to me."

Sam put her hand on his arm. "It feels right to us too. We'll do everything we can for them and for you for as long as you need us."

"That's apt to be awhile."

"That'd be fine with us," Nick said. "You and your

brother and sister are family to us now. We'll do this together."

"I'll never have the words to properly thank you for everything you've done and are going to do."

"I mean it from the bottom of my heart," Nick said, "when I tell you it's our pleasure."

AFTER ELIJAH WENT up to bed, Sam removed her heels and went upstairs with Nick, nodding to Darcy, the agent on duty in the hallway.

Nick ushered her into their room and closed the door.

Sam turned to him. "Did that really just happen?"

"It really did," he said, his smile filled with the same joy that she felt. "I feel terrible leaving you to handle everything."

"Don't worry. I've got an unplanned week off I'll use to get them on a schedule, back to school and set up with therapists."

"After we've worked out the legalities, I'll talk to Brant about getting them Secret Service protection. And I'll get with Terry about how we handle letting the media know that we've taken in two more children."

"When did you figure out I wasn't going on the trip?" she asked.

"Around the time that Elijah sent the Lawsons packing. I knew you wouldn't go if the littles were still here."

"You knew before I did."

"I kept trying to tell myself it's none of our concern. And yet."

"And yet," she said with a wry grin. "Here we are, fully concerned and involved."

"And we wouldn't have it any other way."

Sam rested her head on his chest. "I really, *really* wanted to go with you."

"I really, really, *really* wanted you to come."

"Next time. I promise."

"Ah, babe, don't make promises you can't keep. If there's one thing we ought to know by now, it's that there's nothing predictable or guaranteed about this life of ours."

"That's not entirely true," she said, rubbing against him shamelessly. Blame the champagne, which always lowered her inhibitions. "Some things are entirely predictable *and* guaranteed."

Chuckling, he said, "You know what the best part of being an anal-retentive freakazoid who packs a week before a trip is?"

"There is a best part?"

"Yep," he said, nuzzling her neck. "I have nothing to do until seven o'clock tomorrow morning but make love to my beautiful wife."

"Your wife might be asleep, but feel free to knock yourself out, big guy."

He laughed. "You won't be asleep."

"You're really only going to be gone for a week, right?"

"Not one minute longer."

She looped her arms around his neck. "I should be able to survive that long without you. But not one minute longer."

* * * * *

ACKNOWLEDGMENTS

THANK YOU SO MUCH to all the Fatal Series fans who are so passionately invested in this series and show up for each new book with so much enthusiasm for Sam, Nick and the rest of the Fatal cast. *Fatal Invasion* took me on a wild ride, and I hope you enjoy reading it as much as I enjoyed writing it. I've always hoped that Sam and Nick would "acquire" more children, and I'm excited to see what's ahead for them as Aubrey, Alden and Elijah join their family.

Special thanks to my friend, retired Captain Russ Hayes of the Newport, RI, Police Department, who reads every Fatal book to check me for accuracy and authenticity. I so appreciate his involvement and enthusiasm for the series. Thank you to Sarah Spate Morrison, Family Nurse Practitioner, for answering my medical questions.

Thank you to my team at Harlequin and HQN, especially Dianne Moggy, Allison Carroll and Alissa Davis. And to the team that supports me every day: Julie Cupp, CMP, Lisa Cafferty, CPA, Holly Sullivan and Isabel Sullivan, as well as my husband, Dan, and our kids, Emily and Jake, who aren't really "kids" anymore, but don't tell them that!

Thirteen books into this series, I see no end in sight. Thank you for coming with me, Sam and Nick on this amazing journey!

This book is dedicated to the memory of Sergeant Sean Gannon, who was murdered on the job April 12, 2018, in a town close to where I live. Sergeant Gannon's death is a reminder of the sacrifices made by the men and women in blue who serve our communities. I encourage anyone who wishes to donate in his memory to consider the fund established by the Yarmouth Police Department for Sergeant Gannon's widow at: yarmouthpolicefoundation.org/donate/. Make sure to designate your donation to the Sean Gannon Memorial Fund. Thank you to all who serve.

XOXO
Marie

Knowing what a private person Wyatt could be, Bailey
waited until they were alone before saying anything.

"Okay, tell me what you want me to do," she repeated,
waiting.

"What I want," Wyatt told her, slowly measuring his
words, "is for you to leave the ranch."

That was not what she'd expected to hear. It took Bailey
a moment to recover. And then her face clouded over as she
geared up for a fight. "Look—"

Wyatt raised his hand as if to physically stop anything
she was about to say.

"Hear me out," he said. "It's not safe for you here with
all this potential bad press and even worse feelings milling
around. I won't have you putting up with all that," he told
her fiercely, talking fast so she didn't have an opportunity
to protest. "Once the killer is found and all this blows over,
you can come back and we'll pick up where we left off. You
know," he added in case she thought he was talking about
them having a future together, "making a baby."

"You finished?" Bailey's eyes pinned Wyatt in place.

Feeling he had made his point, he answered, "Yeah."

"Good," she replied crisply. "Because I'm not leaving."

Taking her by the arm, Wyatt drew her even farther aside, closer to the house and away from the others. "Bailey, it's not that I don't appreciate what you—"

She pulled her arm away, her eyes darkening. "I don't want your appreciation, Wyatt. I'm not leaving because I know you would never hurt anyone, let alone kill them. If I leave, it'll look as if I'm afraid that you are the killer." Seeing him open his mouth, she shook her head. She wasn't finished yet and he needed to hear her out. "I know people better than you think, Wyatt. They'll read into that. And it doesn't take much to agitate a mob. I'm not about to be the one to incite that," she informed him in no uncertain terms.

"Bailey—" Wyatt began wearily.

"Listen, you can talk until you're blue in the face, but you're not going to get me to change my mind. Besides, we all know that you're not much of a talker and I am, so I can outlast you—hands down," she informed him. Taking a breath, she continued, "Now, if you're through trying to lecture me, I have a sick calf I need to tend to. I'm assuming that Fox put her in the main barn." She looked toward that building now.

Wyatt shook his head at her, surrendering. "For the life of me, Bailey, I don't know whether to chew you out or hug you."

"Well, if I get a vote in this, I vote for the latter," she retorted.

Don't miss
Colton Cowboy Standoff *by Marie Ferrarella,*
available January 2019 wherever
Harlequin® Romantic Suspense books
and ebooks are sold.

www.Harlequin.com

HRSEXP6181

Get 4 FREE REWARDS!

We'll send you 2 FREE Books plus 2 FREE Mystery Gifts.